The Gambler's Fortune

By Juliet E. McKenna

The Tales of Einarinn
THE THIEF'S GAMBLE
THE SWORDSMAN'S OATH
THE GAMBLER'S FORTUNE

THE THIRD TALE OF EINARINN

JULIET E. McKENNA

The Gambler's fortune

An Imprint of HarperCollins*Publishers*

This is a work of fiction. Names, characters, places, and incidents are products of the author's imagination or are used fictitiously and are not to be construed as real. Any resemblance to actual events, locales, organizations, or persons, living or dead, is entirely coincidental.

EOS
An Imprint of HarperCollins*Publishers*
10 East 53rd Street
New York, New York 10022-5299

Published by arrangement with Little, Brown and Company (UK)

Eos Trademark Reg. U.S. Pat. Off. and in Other Countries, Marca Registrada, Hecho en U.S.A.
HarperCollins® is a trademark of HarperCollins Publishers Inc.

Printed in the U.S.A.

For Michael, Rachel and Philip,
who contribute so much without even realizing.

Acknowledgments

First and foremost, I must thank my brother Philip Hucknall for his inspired suggestion for the title, with a grateful nod to all who contributed to the great "singular or plural" debate.

Once more, Steve, Sue and Mike have ploughed nobly through drafts, revisions and rewrites, for which they have my sincere thanks. I cannot continue to put down ideas on the page without constantly seeking new inspiration, so I am most grateful to those friends who have allowed me to plunder their knowledge, recollections and bookshelves, most notably Liz, Alan, Helen and Jo. For the peace needed to turn ideas into narrative, I thank Sharon and Newland Pre-School.

Tim and Lisa, Cassie and Adrian continue to be all that an author could wish for in editors, publicity and sales support. As I spend ever more time about the business of being a writer, I would also like to thank those booksellers, university and local SF/Fantasy groups who have invited me to visit, listened with interest and encouraged me with their zeal. For enabling me to make such trips, I am indebted to Ernie and Betty.

People around the world are taking the time and trouble to share their enthusiasm for these stories through the Internet, something I find both rewarding and challenging. My thanks to you all.

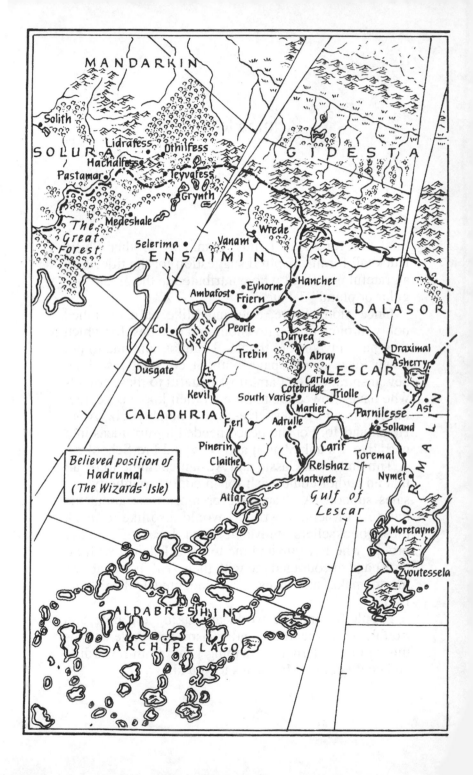

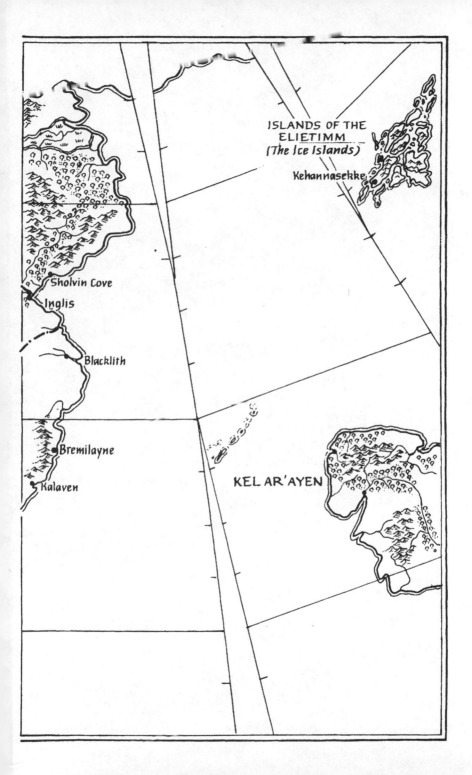

One

Songs of the Common People
Being gathered on travels throughout
the Tormalin Empire in the reigns of
Castan the Gracious and Nemith the Wily,
by Maitresse Dyesse Den Parisot

The House of Den Parisot has dwelt in the Nyme Valley since the days of the earliest Emperors. As the wisdom of Tormalin advances to embrace ever wider lands, the men of the House work ceaselessly in the service of their Name and Den Parisot responsibilities now run from farthest east to the very fringes of the Great Forest. The bonds of affection between my husband and myself were so sorely tested when these obligations drew him from home that I resolved to go on the road in his company. While fulfilling my wifely duties on our travels, I made a study of the tales and music we heard and present them here for a wider audience. Music is always a proper occupation for women, from the lullaby that soothes the fractious babe, to the genteel airs we teach our daughters, to the round songs we share in good fellowship. In these songs gleaned from the commonalty of the Empire, I have found beguiling melody, tales to provoke tears and laughter and no little wisdom. Much of value and beauty has been found across the Empire to ornament the great Houses of Tormalin and music is but a less tangible wealth to enrich us.

1

I present these songs as an entertainment, and too, as evident proof of all that unites the Empire, however many leagues might divide its peoples. While we beseech Drianon's blessing on our fields of wheat, so the people of the boundless plains commit their mares and foals to her care. I have been welcomed in Ostrin's name to the leathern tents of cattleherds, just as devoutly as on the threshold of the Imperial palace. Divine authority pays no heed to bounds of time or distance and the same is true of music. A song of woodland birds sung to a babe beneath the leaves of the wildwood will beguile a silk-swathed princeling just as happily. Stirring adventures from northern mountains will warm the blood of youths in the cohorts and teach them much of courage and duty besides.

Harmony delights the ear more than the solitary voice. A threefold cord is not so easily broken as a single strand. Brothers united in common purpose fare better than those divided by rivalry or suspicion. Such truths are acknowledged the length and breadth of the Empire. You will find these and more besides in this collection.

Selerima, Western Ensaimin,
First Day of the Spring Fair, Morning

There's a certain kind of man whose common sense shrinks almost exactly as fast as his self-conceit swells. Perhaps it's an inevitable law of nature, one of those things Rationalists will bore on about, given half a chance. Whatever, there are enough of them about, especially at festivals, to let me turn a rune—or in this case, a nutshell—for profit any time I choose.

I leaned forward and smiled confidingly. "You've been watching close now, haven't you, friend? Care to risk another penny on it?"

The stout man's eyes flickered upward to my face, halting for a breath at the tempting ruffle of my loose-laced shirt. As his gaze left the crumb-strewn tabletop, my fingers moved unseen beneath my other hand to make sure I'd be taking his coin once again.

"I'd say I've got it this time," he chuckled, confidence gleaming in his eyes like the fancy braid on his cuffs. Still smiling, I held his eyes with mine although a whisper of cold air on the nape of my neck stirred the hairs like those of a wary cat. A door behind me was being held open for some reason pressing enough to let the tavern waste its heat on the chilly spring day outside.

The merchant made up his mind and reached for the middle of the three nutshells. I laid a soft hand on his hairy fingers. "Copper to choose, silver to see," I dimpled, all innocent charm.

"Fair enough, girlie. I've got you this time." He tossed a copper onto the table and snatched boldly at his chosen shell. As he gaped at the bare wood beneath, I managed a look of wide-eyed startlement to match his own surprise. Several onlookers laughed, but I never do that, not since my early days on the road. A disgruntled cowherd once backhanded me across the face, losing his sense of humor along with his meager hoard of pennies.

"Saedrin's stones, I could have sworn I had it that time!" The merchant rubbed a fat hand over sweaty jowls and reached again. As I spread a warning hand over the shells, I heard the scrape of nailed boots coming down on flagstones with a measured tread.

"Silver to see, you know the game," I braced myself in my chair, unnoticed but ready to rise.

Frustration never lets them not know. The merchant tossed an ill-tempered and tarnished penny at me, which I swept briskly into my pocket. As he picked up one shell then the other to reveal the errant kernel, I let the eager bystanders close in to the table.

"But how, by all that's holy—" the luckless mark looked

up, exasperated, but the townsfolk in their holiday best had
me effectively concealed from view. I edged away. A tug at
the laces drew my shirt to a more respectable neatness and I
paused for a moment in the shadow of the stairwell to reverse my jerkin unseen. Unhurried, I pulled the far door
closed behind me as I shrugged into dun homespun, pulling
the gaudy scarf from my head and stuffing it in a breeches
pocket. There was no mistaking the bellow of a Watch ser-
geant behind me, asking who had been running the game.
Various gullible fairgoers whose coin jingled in my purse
would doubtless be eager enough to give him a description.
A woman unremarkable of height or build, they'd say, but
with a bright red jerkin and a headscarf patterned in yellow
and crimson imperfectly concealing her straight black
locks. With that scent to follow, the Watch were welcome to
try and find me to demand a cut of the coin. Using my fingers, I combed through the soft auburn waves of my hair
and plucked out a few errant wisps of dyed horsehair. I let
these fall inconspicuously onto a brazier burning incense in
the doorway of a little shrine to Halcarion. The smoke
could carry my thanks to the Moon Maiden, for keeping my
luck bright for another day.

Five chimes rang from the nearby Wool Audit Hall and a
hurrying peddler bumped into my back as I halted. I
scowled at him, suspicious hands checking purse and belt-
pouch, but a second glance showed he was no pickpocket.

"Your pardon, fair festival," he muttered, trying unsuc-
cessfully to keep to the flagway; the gutters were already
choked with dung and garbage. The holiday was barely
started but the city's population was doubling or trebling
for the Equinox fair. Still, by the end of five days' celebrations there would be drunks and paupers enough buying
their way out the Watch's lock-up by clearing the streets.

Tall wooden houses loomed over the cobbled street, three
and four stories high; each stepped a little farther out. The
newly limewashed plaster of the walls shone bright against

the dark oak beams in the spring sunshine. Shutters swung open above my head as some busy housewife hung featherbeds out to air. Dust billowed from open doorways as floors were swept clean for the festivities. Memories ten years or more past teased me. I could almost have been back in Vanam, Selerima's nearest rival among the great trading cities dotted among the patchwork of fiefdoms that make up Ensaimin. But I had taken myself off from my so-called home and fallen by Halcarion's grace into the far more rewarding, if more risky, life of chance and gaming. I was no harried housemaid, roused before dawn to scrub and fettle. Looking down at my well-kept hands, remembering them red with toil and a winter's chilblains, I rebuked myself and slipped off the gaudy ring I'd been wearing as I separated the local clods from their coin. Some Watchman more alert than most might just be looking for such a bauble.

A more distant tower struck its own brazen version of noon with a handful of rising notes. I gathered my wits; the diverse opportunities of the fair were distracting me. This was no time to be yearning for a high-stakes game of runes or raven. The game I was setting the board for promised to set me up for life, if I made the play successfully. I just needed the final pair of pieces. Walking briskly past the tuppenny liquor houses where I'd spent that morning turning a pretty profit, I took a narrow alley to the off-hand and came out onto the broad, sunlit sweep of the high road. There it was, the lofty tower of the guilds' Conclave Hall, decked out with flags and pennants to proclaim Selerima's wealth and power to all and sundry flocking to the fair from ten days' travel in any direction. All the adornments couldn't disguise the ramparts, the watchtowers and the high narrow embrasures for the crossbow men, though. It might be a handful of generations since Selerima last had to fight for its rights but the city fathers still make sure young men do their militia drills in the exercise halls maintained by each guild. I wondered about trying my luck in a few of them. No, no one would be shooting bales of old hay full of arrows with all the fun of the fair to be had.

If the Conclave Tower was to my sword-hand, I needed to go uphill. I wove through excited crowds with practiced ease to the luxuriously appointed, stone-built inn where I was currently sleeping. Sleeping very well too, on soft goose feathers and crisp linen, a meek lass hurrying to light my fire and bring hot water for my washstand first thing every morning. High spirits put a spring in my step as I sauntered toward the gentlefolk's parlor.

"Livak, at last! I was wondering where you had got to." My current traveling companion hurried down the stairs. The dour expression on his thin face did nothing to dampen my sunny mood. "You could have left a note or message," complained Usara mildly, raising a hand to summon wine. We seated ourselves at an expensively polished table.

"It's only just past noon." I nodded to the boy, who filled my goblet and earned himself a copper to ensure a discreet withdrawal. "The streets are busy, hadn't you noticed? Sorry, you're not used to big cities or festival crowds, are you?" I blinked mock contrition over the rim of the elegant crystal.

Usara answered me with a half-smile. "Have you managed to find these friends of yours?"

"Not just yet." I shook my head, unconcerned. "I've left messages at the likely taverns, the more adventurous brothels. They're bound to arrive sometime today or tomorrow."

Usara frowned. "This is all very vague and uncertain. How can you be sure they're even coming to Selerima?"

"I know because Charoleia told me they were coming here. They wouldn't lie to her and she has no reason to lie to me; we're friends and that means we trust each other." I took a sip of excellent Tormalin wine. Selerima might have shaken off the honor of being the Old Empire's most westerly city long since but merchants have always maintained links with the East and for more than the convenience of a common language. This vintage had been carried clear across the civilized world to delight discerning patrons at this elegant hostelry. The flagons had probably traveled nearly as many leagues as me.

Usara ran a hand over his thinning sandy hair. "That's all very well, but what if something unexpected has occurred? You've no way of knowing, so I think it's best if I—"

"No," I leaned forward in my chair and cut off his words with an emphatic sweep of one hand. "I'm the big dog with the brass collar here. This is my game and I say how we play it. You're only here as a favor to your master by the grace of mine."

Usara's lips thinned with irritation as a faint wash of color rose on his high cheekbones. I thought it wise to give a little carefully judged ground. "We'll give Sorgrad and Sorgren until tomorrow evening to contact us. If we've had no word by then, we'll think again."

The annoyance faded reluctantly from Usara's pale complexion. "What now?"

"We eat," I gestured to the maidservant waiting patiently by the hatch to the serving room. I could see a wonderful range of delicacies brought up from the kitchens being suitably plated up and garnished and our table was soon spread with an elegant array of creamware dishes. I savored the enticing aromas, always gratified to be eating the sort of food I'd grown up seeing carried up the back stairs by footmen and the house steward. The girl brought fine white bread, the first, sweet, grass-fed mutton, seethed pigeon breast with its broth thickened with egg and herbs, a grand salad of spinach and cresses, decorated with nuts, raisins, pickled buds and crystalized flowers, lightly sauced with verjuice and green oil. Usara seemed rather less impressed than me, but he probably ate like this every noon, not just on high days and holidays like we lesser folk.

He wiped his mouth on a brocaded napkin. "What have you been doing this morning?"

"As I said, leaving word in likely places." I didn't see any need to tell Usara I was topping up my purse. I wasn't paying for any of this luxurious living but I needed a reason to be hanging around in the tap rooms, didn't I? "How about you?"

"I've been around every guild hall asking for entry to their libraries or archives," scowled Usara, "but the liverymen are entirely taken up with the fair."

That was chafing him like an ill-fitting boot, used as he was to instant respect and unquestioning cooperation. I stifled a smile with my own napkin. "The festival's only five days long. You can look at the archives or whatever after that. It's taken us the best part of a season to get here so a few more days won't tip the balance either way."

Usara nodded mutely but I could see dissatisfaction lurking in his warm brown eyes as we applied ourselves to our meal. I had better do something before he took himself off on his own initiative. I wasn't having him toss a random rune to spoil my plans.

Using a licked finger to collect the last sweet crumbs of a curd tartlet, I pushed aside my plate. "Let's see what kind of show this city puts on."

"You think we'll find these friends of yours in these crowds?" Usara would never have been so openly scornful when we'd started on the long journey from Toremal. Well, it was about time he felt at ease with me.

"There aren't that many Mountain Men in the cities, so I suppose we might," I said. "They mostly just trade with villages on the edges of the uplands. But no, Sorgrad and 'Gren prefer to go unnoticed. You don't get far in our line of work if you stick in people's memories."

Usara looked skeptical for a moment then favored me with a sudden bright smile. "It's got to be more interesting than sitting here all afternoon. As you say, we don't see spectacles like this in Hadrumal."

His words were lost in a carillon of bells from every side of the city. We hurried out to the broad front steps of the inn and found the flagway packed tight with people. Watchmen burnished for the festival were clearing stragglers out of the way. Standing on my toes, I could just see the first of the huge guild symbols being carried high by journeymen of the trade. Then a heavily built man with a lavishly plumed hat blocked my view entirely. I tugged at Usara's arm. "Let's find somewhere better to stand."

Not much taller than me and scant measures heavier, he was similarly struggling to get a sight of the procession. Judicious use of elbows and brooch pin helped us to an alley entry where the jutting foundation stones of a Tormalin-built hall gave us a vantage point. I gave Usara a hand up and we saw a massive pair of scissors bobbing down the high road. Made of wood painted and gilded to look like metal, they incidentally demonstrated the wealth of the Tailors' Guild, of course. Liverymen bowing and waving in fur-trimmed robes followed the journeymen sweating under the honor of their burden. Finally the warden of the guild appeared, carried aloft in his padded chair on the shoulders of apprentices, presumably chosen for even height and stout muscles. Louder cheers identified loyal craftsmen keen to show allegiance and have their fealty noticed by the masters of their trade.

Fullers and dyers followed with an unexciting display of cloth on tenterhooks teased and harried by rising breezes. The skinners and furriers came next, garnering far more approval from the masses with journeymen wearing monstrous heads: wolves with mad silver eyes and crimson tongues lolling over bloodstained teeth, bears with snarling, foam-flecked jaws. One lithe figure dressed as a cunning marten, complete with mask and tail, dodged among them, while another in the long leather apron of his trade pursued him with a knife as long as my arm mocked up out of wood and paint. I laughed along with everyone else.

"This makes festivals in Hadrumal look a bit staid." Usara bent close to my ear to make himself heard.

"Selerima puts on nearly as good a show as Vanam," I shouted appreciatively.

Tanners followed next, then leather workers. The procession wore on, each guild's standard raised above the Great Gate before they dispersed to feasting at their own audit hall. The banners proclaimed the myriad skills and trades earning coin for the cities of Ensaimin strung along the rivers, bringing valuables from mountains and forests and dotted the length of the Great West Road that carries all manner of staples and luxuries to the ancient Kingdom of Solura in the west, to the diminished Tormalin Empire in the east and for anyone in between with silver to spend. Saddlers, fusters and lorriners gave way to coopers and joiners; pewterers and cutlers were followed by blacksmiths who disdained the counterfeits of the other guilds. Journeymen carried a massive hammer wrought of polished wood and gleaming steel between them, muscles rippling.

The goldsmiths alone of the crafts allowed women in their procession, prosperous wives and haughty daughters on the arms of the liverymen, decked out with rings by the handful, necklaces and earrings jingling, brooches and pins securing dark blue gowns and head-dresses. To my mind the effect was rather spoiled by the glowering of heavy-set apprentices marching alongside, before and behind, each swinging a hefty cudgel. I don't suppose it was any coincidence that the bladesmiths followed, daggers, swords and steels bright in the sunshine as apprentices brandished their trial-pieces in flourishes threatening to take off any greedy hands. I wondered idly if the ladies would be still wearing their finery at the guild feast and how hard it might be to find a maidservant's dowdy dress.

Finally the fitful breeze brought a tempting scent over the heads of the throng. Silversmiths and copper workers got scant attention as the crowd turned expectantly to the bakers and brewers, the butchers and grocers. A massive loaf carried high above the heads of the throng was an impressive sight and the heady smell of yeast from vats of ale being wheeled along even managed to outdo the sweaty odors of unwashed bodies. Links of cooked sausage joined buns and sweetmeats tossed out on either side, and cheap earthenware beakers of beer were handed around. The crowds began to move again, people filling the road as the last craft passed, eager to get a share of the largesse and save the price of a meal. Peddlers and pie men appeared with jugglers and entertainers. All were looking for a share in the festival pennies hoarded through the latter half of winter and the first half of spring. Some canny minstrel raised a boastful song proclaiming Selerima's might and bright pennies pattered into his upturned hat.

It was pleasant to stand aloof, no need to scramble for bread and meat, the days long past when I would salvage a meal from the gutters, brushing off the soiled straw and nameless filth. "Come on," I caught at Usara's sleeve as he stared, rapt, after the parade. "Let's get down to the fairground and see the fun there."

Selerima, Western Ensaimin,
First Day of the Spring Fair, Afternoon

"Where do we go next, Jeirran?"

"You've tried every assay house, every tinsmith?" Jeirran planted booted feet firmly on the cobbles, defying the stream of locals flowing past intent on holiday amusements. "What about pewterers, there must be plenty of those?"

His three companions were less certain in their stance. Both men and the woman had the fair hair and pale eyes common to Mountain Men but their faces showed shared blood as well, the same solid features and sturdy frames.

The two men exchanged a somewhat hesitant glance before the elder spoke up. "Three places out of five are shuttered up for festival. Where we can get an answer, no one will do business." Irritation overcame his reluctance to speak. "Not with us anyway. They all say the same thing,

Jeirran; they buy their metal from the traders who come down from the hills."

"And did you find out what prices they're paying? Five times what Degran and his cronies are paying us, I'll wager," interrupted Jeirran, exasperated. "You explained it exactly as I told you to, Keisyl? We can deliver finer ingots for a fifth less cost?"

"And they say show us your ingots," the older brother retorted. "No one's interested in ore samples. We need to bring down metal—"

"The ore samples show the quality of what we offer!" Jeirran broke in. "We'll smelt the ores and deliver the tin, but we need coin to meet our needs. Are you sure you explained it properly?"

"Yes, Jeirran, we're sure." The younger broke off to scowl after a burly fair-goer barging past with scant apology. "Those that didn't laugh in our faces told us to talk to the metalworkers' guilds, said they might be interested in staking us for a share in the profits."

"The guild halls are shut for the festival but it might be worth staying on—" Keisyl lifted his voice above the hubbub of the crowds. The girl hushed him but he patted her arm. "There's not one in a hundred here understands what we're saying, Eirys. Don't fret."

"The whole point of dealing direct with the lowlands is to keep all the profits for ourselves." Jeirran did not bother to hide his contempt. "We could find three trustworthy kindreds inside a day's travel who'd be more than happy to take a share in return for timber props and furnace charcoal, spare sons to dig the ore like as not. Make a deal like that and you sign away any hope of filling your coffers or making a decent marriage before Maewelin claims your bones!"

"A half-share in worked metal has to be better than whole claim on ore ten measures underground and no way to reach it!" the younger brother objected with some heat, folding muscular arms over a brawny chest.

"Do you ever listen to a word I say, Teiriol?" Jeirran

turned on him. "If we can be sure of selling the metal down here, we can buy in what we need to put in a deep mine ourselves, hire in labor like the lowlanders. That way we keep all the profit."

"I don't like discussing our business in the open street like this!" In the girl's face, the broad foreheads and square jaws of the men were softened to an appealing oval framed with delicate curls artfully drawn forward from the knot of her golden hair, but her lip was quivering in an ominous pout as she drew in her skirts, trying to keep the others between herself and the townsfolk. "I want to go back to the boarding house," she burst out. "I'm fed up with being jostled and stared at. You shouldn't treat me so, Jeirran, I'm your wife and I deserve better. It's downright disrespectful and—"

"Very well, as you wish." Jeirran clasped his hands behind his back, knuckles white as he sought to contain his frustration. "Keisyl, take your sister back to our rooms, if you please."

"I want Teiriol to come with me," the girl interrupted petulantly.

"As you wish. Keisyl and I will see you at sundown. Oh, Eirys, don't start crying!" he snapped with exasperation.

"I'm sorry." Her flower-blue eyes brimmed with tears, the pale rose of her complexion vanishing under an unappealing bloom of scarlet. "I'm sorry, but I don't like it here. It's noisy and dirty and the people are rude and—"

"Come on." Teiriol put a comforting arm around his sister's shaking shoulders and led her away on the inner side of the flagway where she was protected by the buildings on one side and himself on the other. Eirys pulled up the hood of her fur-trimmed cape and clutched it tight. Teiriol spared a fulminating backward glance at Jeirran. Keisyl watched them go, his expression a mixture of relief and concern.

"Why did you insist she come?" sighed Keisyl, running a hand over close-cropped blond hair. He loosened his own cape with blunt-fingered hands to reveal a creamy linen shirt bright with embroidery. Weariness shadowed the pale skin beneath his azure eyes. "I'm sure it's not fitting to expose her to all this barbarity."

"I wasn't about to leave her at home," spat Jeirran. "Your mother's spent every day since Solstice telling Eirys any three men she could name would care better for her lands. Give Ismenia half a chance and she'll be telling Eirys to repudiate me inside a half-year of marriage." Rising color threw his golden beard into unflattering relief. Neatly trimmed around full lips, it did little to soften a square jaw set above a bullish neck. Jeirran's hair was longer than Keisyl's, swept back from a wide, high forehead to curl down to his collar in wiry yellow waves. For all the bluntness of his features, he was undeniably handsome and carried himself with that knowledge.

"I don't think Mother will be any too impressed if you bring her home with some foul lowlander disease." Keisyl glared at Jeirran, sufficiently taller to make it an effective tactic. A couple of seasons' seniority added to the harshness of his tone. A ragged lad with startled eyes ducked past, clutching a loaf to his chest.

"There's no reason to imagine dangers like that, not this early in the year." Jeirran forced himself to a more conciliatory stance. "We're keeping ourselves to ourselves and we'll be back in our own air soon enough. That should cheer Eirys up."

"And what will we have to show for our trouble?" demanded Keisyl. "You've been telling us all winter this fair was the only place to come and trade for better prices. So far no one will even take a look at our ores, let alone discuss a deal."

"So these people are too stupid to see buying without a middleman adding his profit saves them coin! I'll try some of these so-called smiths myself tomorrow. I speak lowlander tongue better than you and it's about time you tried to entertain Eirys. Today we find a buyer for the furs. If necessary we'll use that coin to buy what we need. We can drive a decent digging into the back of the lode and make a start ourselves." Jeirran nodded firmly. "We'll bring ingots next year, so fine even these clods can't ignore them. There's more than one way of snaring a coney."

A child bright in her holiday best turned her beribboned head at meaningless words in unknown accents. She tugged at her mother's skirts, but the woman bustled her away, sparing a glance of surprise and suspicion at the men.

Keisyl smiled at the child. "How do we go about that, when every furrier will be as intent on his holiday as everyone else?"

"There are plenty of merchants dealing in hides and skins at this fair," Jeirran stated confidently. "I was talking to some while we waited to pass the gates."

Keisyl's expression brightened. "Why didn't you make a deal there and then?"

"None of Degran's men wintering in the valley bottom thought to mention a ban on all trading before the official opening of the fair." Grievance soured Jeirran's voice.

"So when is that?" Keisyl's question was lost as a heedless group of youths chased a stray dog past. Even the shortest of the ebullient boys was a good head taller than either Mountain Man, though not the tallest was as broad in the shoulder. "When is that?" he repeated.

"The man at the rooming house said it's after the guilds' procession is done." Jeirran set his jaw and forced his way through the busy street, upland muscles earning him irritated glances that he ignored. "The fairground's down by the river, this way."

Moving with the flow of the crowd soon brought the Mountain Men to the Water Gate. A sudden surge carried them through the clogged arches and they found they were outside the walls. Jeirran's expression cleared a little to see blue sky uncluttered by looming buildings. Scant moments later the crowd ground to a halt and a fierce scowl carved its habitual lines between his pale eyebrows.

"What now?" he hissed at Keisyl's shoulder. The other

man muttered an oath and lifted himself on the toes of his boots to try to see, but the expectant throng hemmed them in uncomfortably. The murmur rose to a new pitch of excitement before a shrill of brassy trumpets demanded silence. By the waterside, an unseen fruity voice was lifted in formal declamation.

"For-Spring is past; we give thanks to Halcarion for the renewal of seed and beast. Aft-Spring is coming; we beseech Arimelin to send us good luck and good counsel. Remember this feast is sacred to Raeponin and let every man deal fairly or face due judgment."

A great cheer rang out, startling a flock of mottled birds from the willow-crowned islets barely visible in the broad, spring-swollen river. A great leather glove, tall as a half-grown child, bobbed and waved above the heads of the crowd until its pole dropped home into the waiting socket. The people surged past into the fairground, eager for bargains from brightly colored booths and gawking at entertainments offered on all sides.

"See a wonder or two, my lady? You look like a daring young man! Spend a copper to see creatures half man and half beast?" A crier hovered in front of a gaudy tent painted with improbable scenes of forest and mountain, darting this way and that. "Freaks of magic or of nature—you decide! Sir, how about you?"

"Come on, we're here to do business, not put copper in some charlatan's purse." Jeirran caught Keisyl's arm as he wavered. "We don't have coin to waste gawking at misbegotten lowlanders." Jeirran glared at a hawker waving crudely carved puppets bright with tatters of cloth.

"Have you any idea where we should go?" Keisyl looked down the five already trampled lanes spreading out from the fair's standard. Each was lined with eager sellers, merchants working from the back of wains piled high with wares, modest traders with barrows and tables, peasants looking to sell the paltry fruits of winter evenings' labors from threadbare blankets spread on the damp ground.

"We'll try down here," said Jeirran decisively, pointing to stalls groaning beneath bolts of fine cloth, peddlers touting ribbons and lace, beads and buttons busy in between. He pushed through smartly dressed women toward larger, more somber booths beyond. Stern-faced men were examining piles of hides and furs laid on broad trestle tables, sharp scents of dye and tanning rising above the green odor of crushed grass.

Jeirran spared Keisyl with a nod of satisfaction. "Here, tell me, what is the price you ask for these skins?"

"What's that you say?" The skinny stallholder turned from a customer, cupping a hand as tanned as his wares to one prominent ear.

"I thought you said you spoke lowlander tongue better than me or Teiriol." Keisyl stuck his hands through his tooled-leather belt and scowled at the Seleriman. Jeirran repeated his question carefully and the leather merchant flipped the edge of a skin to show figures chalked on the underside, looking down his long nose with faint contempt.

"See, this is three, five times what Degran Lackhand pays in the valley bottom," Jeirran hissed to Keisyl, stabbing a finger at the numbers. He checked quickly through the heap of hides, shoving the top ones aside as they slid and hampered him. "The quality's nowhere near as fine as ours."

"What's that you say? Not got a civilized tongue in your head?" The lanky trader planted hands on the hips of his buff jerkin with some irritation. "Are you looking to buy or not?"

"Where do you purchase your hides?" demanded Jeirran, brushing chalk dust from his fingers.

"None of your business." The merchant scowled under black brows but a prosperous townsman claimed his attention with a wave of a jingling purse and a ludicrously low offer for a russet and white cowhide.

"It's just as I've been telling you. One winter's worth of trapping sold direct to a merchant here will net more coin than we'd get in three seasons waiting on Degran." Jeirran crossed to a stall heaped with soft bundles of rolled furs. "Look! Your mother wouldn't use this to line a hound's winter boots, I'd scarce bother bringing it in from the hills. Down here, it's fetching more than Degran pays for miniver!"

"That's no great deal if we have to waste half a season tramping all the way down here and back again." Keisyl shook his head. "We agreed to help you on the snare lines over winter as long as you helped us at the diggings in the summer. We should be clearing the workings by now, not haggling with lowlanders."

Jeirran ignored him. "We'll get a good price then use some of the coin for trinkets and fancies. Eirys is always nagging for treats from the traders. Enough gewgaws will shut your mother's mouth as well." He turned on Keisyl. "Otherwise she'll be looking around for a husband for Theilyn, like as not, walking her around this coming Solstice."

"Theilyn's too young to marry for a good few years yet." Keisyl shook his head but a shadow of concern darkened his blue eyes.

"But she's not too young to be betrothed," Jeirran insisted. "What if your mother finds some family with a gang of sons all eager to offer their labor to help the one who's going to be getting the prize? Who's to say she won't let them start working the diggings instead of you and Teiriol?"

"We have the right to those workings until Theilyn's wed, no day less," objected Keisyl.

"Then you'd better make sure you're bringing in enough to keep your mother sweet. And you need enough coin in hand to woo a girl with decent lands of her own once Theilyn's eye does start looking out a spot to set her own hearthstone, you and Teiriol both. You won't get that scratching pits where the lode surfaces. Stripping out easy tin and cutting trees to smelt it may have been good enough for your father but there are no more surface seams to be

had, are there? You need to dig deep ore and you need fuel.
It'll be thrice three years before there's any new growth to
speak of in your coppices and you're not touching the old
growth, not while I'm husbanding them. Those woods are
Eirys' endowment; it's my duty to provide for our children
out of their bounty. You could show a little gratitude; I
should be concentrating on Eirys' business, not spending
time and effort helping you two make something of
Theilyn's portion. You need to drive in a proper mine and
that means shoring and charcoal furnaces and if you're not
going to strike a shares deal for what you need, you'll have
to pay coin on the settling stone. Where are you going to get
that gold, unless I'm willing to come in with you, for Eirys'
sake?" Jeirran's eyes burned.

"So find someone to buy the furs." Keisyl clenched
empty hands eloquently. "Do something besides just telling
me things I already know!"

Jeirran dug in the satchel slung beneath his cape. Pulling
out a handful of neatly trimmed squares of fur and leather,
he caught at the moss-colored sleeve of the man across the
trestle. "Here, what do you think of these?"

"I think I'm selling, not buying, friend." The busy merchant swept a meaty hand across his board. "Get your
moth-bitten rubbish off my goods."

Jeirran stooped to recover his sample pieces, face scarlet
with indignation. "Your loss, fool!" Pushing through the
jostling masses, he headed for the next fur trader, a hatchet-
faced man with a shock of gray hair swept back from
shrewd hazel eyes.

"What can I do for you, friend?" The man spared Jeirran
a quick glance as he rummaged in the pocket of his calico
apron, brushing stray hairs from his jerkin sleeve with the
other hand.

"Would you like to buy fine furs?" Jeirran proffered a
silky white strip. "Better quality than anything you've got
here."

"Mountain fox is it?" The man took the fur and sniffed at

it, turning it over to see how well it was cured. "What are you asking?" His eyes scanned the crowd.

"Ten Marks the pelt and we have a good supply with us." Jeirran nodded triumphantly at Keisyl.

"Guild rate is five Marks the pelt and that only for top quality. There you go, mistress, that will trim a gown or a hood to perfection, fair festival to you." The merchant abruptly turned his back to sell a fluffy red squirrel-skin to a sharp-eyed woman in blue whose maid was already laden with purchases. "Anyway, Mountain Man, I don't do deals outside the audit hall! Do you think I'm some kind of idiot? Yes, sir, what are you looking for?"

Eager customers forced them away from the busy trader and his unmistakable dismissal. Keisyl looked puzzled but Jeirran set his jaw obstinately, smoothing the ruffled fur around his hand. "Come on, let's try over there."

Selerima, Western Ensaimin,
First Day of the Spring Fair, Afternoon

"I've seen everything I want, unless there's something else you're interested in." I turned to Usara, who smiled a little shamefacedly.

"There was a man back there claiming to have a cockatrice," he began.

"Let's see it," I said obligingly. Let's see if he could work out how that old trick's done. A surge of bodies nudged me into the shadows between two rows of booths. I tried to retrace my steps but a bulky body stopped me edging back to the main walkway.

"Hello, pretty!" it leered. "Fair festival to you."

"Fair festival," I nodded a tight, polite smile and tried to side-step past.

"Here for the holiday, are you?" He stretched one

grubby, nail-bitten hand toward me. "Hair like autumn leaves, eyes as green as grass, that makes you a Forest lass."

A necessary step back took me deeper between the muffling canvas walls. "Just a traveler, passing through. Let me about my business, friend." Folding hands together in a demure gesture, I loosened the cuff of my shirt, ready to reinforce my point with the little dagger I keep sheathed on my forearm.

"What do you say to a little celebration of our own?" The bumpkin licked fleshy lips, lust gleaming in his close-set eyes like the sweat on his unshaven face. "Show me what you girls know to give a man and I'll buy you a bunch of ribbons as a fairing?"

"Thanks all the same but I'm here with friends." I tried to look regretful. That came easier when a quick glance showed me that carousing apprentices watching one of their number being comprehensively sick had blocked my escape to the rear.

"Why—" Whatever temptation the lout thought he could offer was lost in gasps and applause and I saw my would-be swain outlined against flaring yellow fire. He turned; I ducked rapidly around his blind side and dodged between two stalls. Jumping over a blanket of trinkets with a hurried apology, I would have gone farther but the way was blocked by people agape at Usara juggling handfuls of flame, his lean face alight with unaccustomed mischief. The fires changed hue, yellow to orange to crimson and back again, soaring higher and higher. He wove the burning colors into dazzling patterns, setting the crowd blinking and cheering. I snatched up a cracked bowl discarded beneath a potter's bench and pushed my way through.

"Fair festival to you." As I proffered the bowl, the appreciative audience began reaching for purses and belt-pouches with gratifying haste. Some took the opportunity to discard coin halves and quarters cut for change but more found the performance worth whole pennies, even if mostly copper.

"Forest Folk are you?" One mild-faced tradesman in sober gray slipped a doubtless unintended silver penny into my open hand, unable to take his eyes off the spectacle.

"He's my brother, good sir." I ran a hand over my own head and gestured to Usara's sandy if sparse hair. His being able to pass for Forest blood at a pinch was one of the reasons the wizard was here. I slurred my voice into the softer mumble of the eastern cities where I'd wintered, exotic enough to local ears to mark me as a foreigner. "We have come to delight you with our mysteries."

"How does he do it?" A matronly woman breathed, one hand resting on the lace at her ample cleavage, her eyes as wide as the child's clutching her ocher skirts.

I swept a low bow. "The ancient magics of the wildwood, my lady, brought to illuminate your festival!" It was nothing of the kind but no one here would ever know that.

I saw the plumes of a Watchman's helmet bobbing toward us and tossed a copper cutpiece through the middle of Usara's increasingly complex pattern. "Stop," I mouthed.

He tossed knots of flame high with a flourish before snuffing them with a clap of his hands. A final incandescent flare left his audience blinking and rubbing their eyes. I had been looking the other way so grabbed Usara's sleeve and moved him away toward the waterside before anyone could gather their wits and wonder which way we went.

"You looked like you were enjoying yourself." I emptied the crock and rapidly tallied our earnings, sparing an eye for anyone taking too close an interest.

"You know, I was rather," he said with satisfaction. "What are you doing with my coin?"

I looked up, eyes wide with patent surprise. "Half-shares, of course."

"I'll allow you a tenth-share," suggested Usara. "That's fair, since I was the one doing all the work."

"And if I hadn't had my wits in hand, you'd have nothing

to show for it and be paying a Watchman out of your own purse besides." I managed a show of injured indignation.

Usara made a convincing pretense of considering this. "A fifth-share, then, since I'm feeling generous."

I stuck my tongue out at him as I poured pennies and cut-pieces into his cupped palm. Some was silver minted here or in Vanam, more were crudely struck copper faces with the boasts of minor lordlings together with a fine mixture of local trade tokens. "I thought all your dealings were with princes, councils and scholars. You've got the measure of my world well enough for someone used to staying on the sunshine side of the laws." I slid the few enough Tormalin-minted pennies into my own purse. I had more need than a mage of sound coin that passes pretty much anywhere. The mongrel currency of Ensaimin can be regrettably worthless five leagues beyond the town where it was struck. Usara could find that out for himself.

"Thank you, my lady," Usara swept me an elegant bow. "Let's just say I'm a fast learner."

I had to laugh. "Well I'm glad to see you've got more between your ears than arcane learning and library dust. I think the locals were suitably impressed."

"Fire's not really my element, but it's close enough to the earth to give me a fair talent with it. I have a sound enough skill with water as well, but don't ever bet your purse on my abilities with air. That's been a scourge to me ever since I was first apprenticed." Usara offered me his arm and we made our way along the riverbank, picking a careful path past the barges and wherries unloading their bales and bar-rels, merchants and lightermen all intent on the serious business of commerce. "I know it's not exactly the done thing, but I think wizards should be allowed to have a little harmless fun now and again, don't you?"

I feigned surprise. "That would be frowned on in Hadru-mal, would it?" It was no news to me that mages had no idea of fun.

"Where exactly are we?" Usara frowned and looked
around.

I pointed at the Conclave Tower, tallest of the turrets
watchful over the parapets of the wall. "This way." The
open postern of a small sally-gate let us back into the city
and we walked past shops shuttered for the festival. The
owners were doubtless selling their usual goods for a price
and a half in some booth down at the fair.

"You can see the Conclave Tower from pretty much anywhere in the city," I explained to the wizard. "If you get
lost, head for it and then take the road to the Great Gate.
You can't mistake it; it's the only one with strips of flags in
the cobbles to ease carriage wheels. Either that or find a
shrine. I expect a priest would take pity on you and set you
on the right road."

Usara nodded. "Selerima's a lot bigger than Hadrumal."

I laughed out loud. "Usara, most two-mule towns are
bigger than Hadrumal! It wouldn't warrant its own mill or
market on the mainland."

"Trydek, the first Archmage, founded our island city for
the contemplation of the elements and serious study of the
complex arts of wizardry." Usara attempted a stern frown.

"Did he?" I clapped a dramatic hand to my breast. "So,
what would happen if you tried a trick like that back home?
The Archmage would ceremonially snap your staff over
your head?" I paused to get my bearings but decided
against a short cut. It wasn't as if the Watch were actively
seeking me, not like the last time I'd been here, and I was
still getting the measure of obstructions around the back alleys. It was a good few years since I'd been in Selerima and
these things change more than most people realize.

Usara was chuckling to himself. "Planir? No, he'd see
the joke well enough, but he'd let me know it isn't quite
what he expects. We do get the occasional new apprentice
showing off though. Given how potentially hazardous untrained magic can be, it is something we discourage," he
added in more serious tones.

All magic is downright dangerous as far as I'm concerned, but I kept that opinion under my tongue. "If you want to play that game again, you should add a smell of hot oil, perhaps let the cuffs of your shirt scorch a little."

"Why?" queried Usara. "It's a very minor magic after all."

These wizards might learn all about magecraft on their hidden island but they can be precious little use around ordinary folk. "Remember how seldom these folk see a real mage. Don't take offense but a lot of us commoners find wizardry rather worrying. If people want to believe it's magic, they can, but you want to give the meddlesome enough to suggest it's just a trick. Then we won't find ourselves up in front of the festival assize answering a lot of awkward questions."

"Up in front of the what?" asked Usara.

I stifled a sigh of irritation. "The festival assize. The guilds run it for the duration of the fair rather than tie up the regular courts and advocates. It deals with merchants who evade selling tolls or cheat customers, people caught stealing or getting too drunk and starting a fight, anything really. Anyone profiting by the fair falls under its jurisdiction for the duration of the holiday. By rights, we should be paying a cut of what we just took for your little show, so if a Watchman comes asking the next time, we just hand over the coin and let it go."

"And he gives it to the assize?" Usara sounded rightly doubtful.

"What do you think?" I grinned at him. "Don't worry, it only happens if a Watchman manages to catch you." Which, in a nutshell, is why I was playing the squirrel game in grubby taverns rather than more profitable diversions like runes or Raven. Both take too long to bring in the coin and you can't just walk away from your play pieces and buy them afresh from the next hawker's tray. I wasn't risking coming across some Watchman with a memory going back more than the last couple of years. There was a little matter of a robbery suffered by the richest liveryman in the city where the apparent culprits had broken out of the lock-up and fled. Not that there was any need to bother Usara with that.

My smile faded. "Now I come to think of it, we might take a look at the assize tomorrow evening, if we haven't had word from Sorgrad. If 'Gren's landed himself in trouble, that could explain why they haven't got any of my messages."

I stepped around a knot of women pinning little bows of ribbon to the doorpost of a shrine to Drianon. The usual tokens of festival pieties fluttered bravely, gold in gratitude that the fruits of last year's harvest had seen them through the winter, white in hopes that sons wouldn't come home with a dose of the itch. With the lesser moon at dark and the greater waning through its last quarter, the older people on the road had been muttering about ill omens. Even the rest of us who barely spare the gods a thought from day to day tend to hedge our bets around festival time. I decided to find time to make a decent offering to Halcarion and one to Trimon as well.

"Is it likely they've fallen foul of the authorities?" inquired Usara disapprovingly.

"It's possible," I said shortly. I hoped I was wrong; the success of my plans depended on Usara and the brothers working together and I was already concerned about Sorgren's admittedly volatile personality starting him off on the wrong foot with the sedate wizard. Even after a season's traveling together, I was still getting Usara's measure; I couldn't see the mage being any too impressed if he learned about some of 'Gren's more notorious exploits. Even I'd been startled to learn he'd burned down an apothecary's shop after the owner made some disparaging remarks about Mountain blood.

It wasn't a subject I wanted Usara to pursue. "I'd rather not find myself trying to explain our little sideshow to the liverymen on assize duty, so perhaps we'd better try and stay inconspicuous. Not that I'm not grateful for your help, of course," I added hastily.

"I wasn't sure what was going on when I lost sight of you, but I didn't fancy my chances of taking that brute on in a fist fight." Usara shrugged his undeniably scrawny shoulders.

"It was an excellent diversion," I reassured him. I've had plenty of practice of getting myself out of awkward corners but having to cut my sweaty suitor's ardor down to size risked causing more problems than it solved. We came to a crossroads and I checked the skyline for the Conclave Tower before turning past a marble worthy brandishing a scroll.

"What exactly did he want?" asked Usara hesitantly.

I looked at him, surprised. "What do you think? Just another one who thinks that all Forest girls are a carpenter's delight."

"A what?" The mage's bemusement was plainly genuine.

"Lies flat as a board and waits to be nailed?" I giggled as Usara's fair skin betrayed his blush. "You wizards do lead a sheltered life, don't you?"

"I heard you telling those people we were both Forest Folk." Usara halted. "Do their men have a similar reputation?"

"Forest minstrels are reckoned to be able to charm their way inside most bed-curtains, if they put their mind to it." Which was what had happened to my mother, leaving her with me to hamper her skirts and ensure she was never going to make a respectable match. I'd been barely as high as her waist before I understood the pity in the eyes of her family and friends, the strictures confining her to life as a housekeeper. I shrugged. "Don't feel obliged to try living up to the ballads, Usara."

A group of youths dashing out of a side street nearly bowled us over, dodging to either side, muddy boots skidding. "What's your hurry?" I called to a straggler hampered by a large, fetid sack.

"Wardmote offenders are about to be pilloried," he shouted with evident glee.

"That's something we should take a look at," I said to Usara.

"You enjoy seeing people pelted with dung, do you?" His distaste was apparent.

"No," I answered a little reluctantly, "but 'Gren does. He has rather straightforward notions of entertainment."

Usara let out a long resigned breath. "Very well."

We followed the eager youths and soon found ourselves in the long paved precinct before the law courts. A tall frontage of new stonework, proud with a pediment of statues, disguised the jumble of mismatched roofs that I had once scrambled over to freedom. The first handful of wretched men shivering bare-arsed in their shirts were about to be locked into the unforgiving jaws of the pillories and face the punishment their peers deemed fit.

"In the name of Raeponin, I call all gathered here to give balanced judgment to the offenders presented." The first of the ward constables claiming citizen's rights by serving his year keeping order in his neighborhood stepped forward. He opened a substantial ledger, imposing in his cockaded hat, scarlet sash of office bright. "Markel Galerene, for selling bread loaded with alum." The pillory snapped shut on its struggling victim, the scales of the god of justice burned crudely into the wood.

A roar went up from the crowd and a scatter of decaying carrots came shying in to batter the disgraced baker, one vindictive stone gashing his cheek amid turnips foul from the store at the end of a long winter.

"Ansin Shammel, for giving short weight." The luckless Shammel looked to be a butcher and suffered accordingly, bombarded with the knuckle ends of old bones, scraps of hide and fat, finally getting the noisome entrails of some family's festival mutton full in the face, which raised a cheer to echo all around the square. Some housewife must have felt revenge was worth more than a sheep's paunch pudding.

"Is this really necessary?" murmured Usara with discreet contempt.

"Ask these women what being cheated a pennyweight of meat for every Mark they spend means." A stout female beside me flung a handful of nameless filth, face ugly with outrage. "It's their children who go hungry." Hard times in my childhood had wrung double duty out of every penny before my mother swallowed her pride and hired herself out as a maidservant. As far as I was concerned, these thieves deserved every chime of their five days of humiliation and pain. When necessity obliges me to relieve someone of coin or valuables, I make sure that those who suffer can stand the loss, and not just to avoid loading Raeponin's scales too heavily against that day when I answer to Saedrin for passage into the Otherworld.

Usara's lips were pursed with that unconscious air of wizardly superiority that so irritates me. I ignored him and scanned the intent assembly for blond heads, not just pale or sandy hair but the true corn-colored locks that denote undiluted Mountain blood.

The pitch of the clamoring crowd rose as a man whose name escaped me was pilloried on account of a vicious dog, but more insults than missiles were flung at him. As we waited, all of those who'd failed to abide by the laws of the city were duly chastised, the last man choking in a cloud of ash and clinker, since he'd allowed a fire to spread from his property. The crowd drifted away to other amusements, leaving the square to relatives of those pilloried offering comfort or water while a few persistent accusers harangued them with further rebukes. Beggars twisted with injury or disease scurried to glean the best of the spoiled food that now littered the pavement, glowering at the ragged paupers who challenged them.

"Why are these unfortunates scavenging like this?" The

outrage in Usara's voice startled me. "There should be no need for this! Who takes care of such matters?"

"People are hard enough pressed to keep their families fed and warm without worrying about beggars they don't even know." I suppressed my irritation at his naïveté. "Shrines give alms to the needy, same as everywhere else, and the guilds run their own charities. Beyond that, they're on their own. This isn't Hadrumal, spells to solve your problems or earning coin for any lack."

Usara opened his mouth for some heated reply but frowned over my head instead. "Isn't that a Mountain Man over there?"

I turned to follow his gaze. A glimpse of golden hair made my heart skip a beat but when the throng shifted I saw a man in stout leathers, face dour and defensive, guarding the woman on his arm with all the jealousy customary in the uplands. Drab and incongruous among festival finery on all sides, the pair stuck out like the stones on a stag-hound.

"No, that's not them." I sighed. Was I ever going to get my game together?

Selerima, Western Ensaimin,
First Day of the Spring Fair, Evening

"We've tried every trader down to that rancid dealer in half-cured coneyskins." Keisyl stepped into Jeirran's path and folded his arms. "No one's buying, not from us."

"We haven't spoken to that man yonder." An obstinate light burned in Jeirran's eyes. "He's sold most of his stock, so he'll want more and have the silver to pay for it."

Keisyl heaved an exasperated sigh but followed Jeirran toward a burly man in a beaver-trimmed jerkin of mustard broadcloth who was bending down to an urchin hopping urgently from foot to foot. The lad shot the two Mountain

Men a startled glance and melted away while the fur trader
rested his hands on his paunch. "What can I do for you?"

"We have furs to sell: fox, hare and otter, fine elk hide
and some deerskins—" began Jeirran in an ingratiating
tone.

"Guild-stamped, are they?" snapped the trader. "Paid
your tenth at the audit hall, have you? No, I didn't think so."
He raised his voice. "I wouldn't disgrace the guild by trading behind their back, do you hear? Who do you think I am,
offering me such insult? I've never seen you before neither."

"Don't," Keisyl caught Jeirran's arm as the shorter man
took an angry step forward, beard bristling on his thrusting
chin. As Jeirran stopped, indecisive, a reveler stumbled into
him, unaccustomed ale sending the youth sprawling loose-
limbed to the ground. Jeirran loosed frustrated rage in a
savage kick that set the unfortunate lad spewing up. Passing
fairgoers too slow to keep boots or skirts clear exclaimed in
annoyance.

"Come on!" Keisyl dragged Jeirran over to an open space
where stilt-walkers were entertaining the crowds. A pair
painted like butterflies swooped and fluttered vast wings of
sapphire silk, capering ungainly to amuse a wide-eyed child
but deft enough to wrap their pinions around some giggling
girl. A third in more conventional motley of scarlet and gold
came after them, a hopeful bag-puppet on one hand, its
maw greedy for small coin.

Jeirran shook free of Keisyl's hand and stepped into the
path of a passing dame. "Here madam, fine furs, smooth
and supple leathers, fairer prices than anyone else will offer!" The woman shook him off, affronted and coloring beneath the frills of her cap.

"Sir, that's a fine cloak you're wearing," Jeirran darted in
front of a prosperous merchant. "Think how a fur trim
would improve it, let me show you!"

The man's florid face darkened, indignation warring with
consternation in his deep-set eyes. "Be off with you,

vagabond," he spluttered, drawing the lavender folds of his mantle around him.

"Here, you!" One of the stilt-walkers loomed over them, annoyance clear beneath his garish paints. "You're queering our pitch, pal. Go and make a nuisance of yourselves somewhere else!"

"If you've got something to sell, go pay for a token like the rest of us!" called a nearby stallholder, safe behind cheap, speckled plates and green glazed pots under a brightly striped awning. Even Jeirran's belligerent self-assurance wasn't proof against hostile eyes on all sides.

"Let's get something to eat." Keisyl looked around and beckoned to a lad who was carrying a savory-smelling basket.

"Lamb pasty, mister, with a bit of this and that." The boy looked from Keisyl to Jeirran, eyes wide and wondering at the oversewn seams on their embroidered shirts, at the stamped patterns on their short capes and the long leather trews gaitered into sturdy boots.

"Four, how much?" Keisyl held up his fingers.

"Two copper, mister," stammered the boy.

Keisyl frowned as he rummaged in a pocket. "That's the last of my coin, Jeirran. Teiriol has our purse."

Jeirran was looking dubiously inside the pastry, picking at a stringy piece of grayish meat with a fingernail. "This is no more lamb than my boot soles." He chewed slowly with an expression of distaste but the lad had already melted away into the crowd, leaving a faint smell of leeks fried soft in rancid fat.

Keisyl swallowed a stubborn mouthful. "I've eaten worse at the diggings. If you've got some coin, we can find a drink to take the taste away. Do you suppose they brew mead anywhere down here or will it still be that goat's piss ale?"

"I've only got a few silver on me." Jeirran reached inside his cape. "I didn't want to risk having my purse cut, so I left most of the good coin in Eirys' coffer."

He spread his hand to count the paltry pennies, worn almost anonymous, edges bent and nicked. As he did so, a mailed gauntlet landed heavy on his shoulder and half the flimsy coins jumped from his hand to vanish into the crushed grass.

"You muck-footed fool! Can't you people ever look where you're going?" He turned furiously and found himself facing a bronzed breastplate, freshly polished with festival zeal. The gauntlet tightened its bruising grip on Jeirran's shoulder.

"I'd keep a civil tongue in my head if I was only arse high to a short horse," sneered the Watchman. He shook Jeirran by way of emphasis, demonstrating muscle beneath his flab. "Let's have a look in that bag of yours, shall we?"

Jeirran ripped the gauntlet from his shoulder with an ease that clearly disconcerted the bigger man. Keisyl moved to pick up the fallen coin but another official planted a hobnailed boot on the pennies, an unfriendly smile creasing his unshaven face, fingerless leather gloves with studded knuckles gleaming on both hands. Jeirran turned but a third Watchman in a leather cuirass blocked his way with a metal-bound stave as thick as his bony wrists. The first Watchman tugged Jeirran's satchel roughly from around his stiff neck and unbuckled it, grunting.

"Looks like them's our pigeons, lads." His chapped lips curved in a satisfied smirk. "Right, you pair come and explain yourself to the festival assize."

The thin Watchman with the quarterstaff brought it level in both hands and gestured at Keisyl, whose fists were now clenched and raised. "I don't think you want to make a fight of it, corn-poll. I'll cut you down to the stubble if you do!"

Keisyl spat an incomprehensible Mountain oath that sent a rustle of apprehension through those fairgoers clustering behind the protection of the Watchman's stave.

"You tell your friend, any trouble and I'll put you both in irons," warned the first Watchman, jingling the manacles at his belt in emphasis.

"What right have you to detain us?" Jeirran glared at the man, refusing to acknowledge the faces whispering and gawking on all sides.

The Watchman brandished a handful of fur and leather, white, russet and black. "We've had complaints. Some reckon you're in the pay of the guilds, trying to tempt them to break the laws. Some tell us you're trying to gull them into paying out for goods you ain't got. I just think you're uplanders with no more wit than your goat. Got a fair token to show us, have you?" he demanded sarcastically.

"I don't know what you mean," answered Jeirran warily.

"Then you haven't paid your guild fee, have you, cully? Else you'd have bought the right to trade like an honest man and have the token to prove it. You're coming along with us!" The Watchman nodded to his subordinate with the stave who brandished it in unmistakable threat.

"I'd check their purses, boss," the one with his boot still resting on Jeirran's fallen coin spoke up with an innocent air. "If they've not got the price of a meal and bed on them, they're vagabonds, ain't they? That's the law, ain't it?"

"You thief—" Jeirran took an ill-judged step toward the unshaven man.

The Watchman with the manacles moved swiftly to grab Jeirran's arms, pulling them up behind his back with a painful twist of the elbows. "That's enough from you. Rif, check his pockets."

The man leaned forward awkwardly to stick intrusive hands into Jeirran's cape and trews, glowering at an urchin eagerly hoping he would step away from the fallen silver. "No, nothing beyond what he's got in his hand, boss," he said with satisfaction.

"What about you?" The one with the quarterstaff thumped its butt on the ground and held out a hand to Keisyl.

"I have no coin," Keisyl said, the foreign words halting on his tongue but the wrath in his face speaking clearly enough.

"Then it's the lock-up until the assize calls for you." The leader snapped black iron fetters on Jeirran's wrists, the smaller man too startled to resist. Keisyl raised his fists in fury but a sweep of the quarterstaff behind his knee sent him sprawling to the ground. The Watchmen hauled him to his feet, deftly manacling him as they did so.

The one called Rif hastily scooped what coins he could from the tangled grass, the urchin scrabbling eagerly for any the Watchman missed. The boss sent Jeirran on his way with a shove past fairgoers exclaiming at the unexpected diversion. "Get moving!"

"So we had to pay some toll to trade?" Keisyl hissed furiously at Jeirran. "Something else Degran's man didn't tell you? Did he make any mention of this assize or whatever they call it?"

Jeirran twisted around to face the Watchman pushing him along. "What is the penalty for simply making an honest mistake?"

"Mistake or no, your goods will be forfeit, I reckon," Rif replied with happy malice.

"Well done, Jeirran!" Keisyl's indignation halted him until a blow from the quarterstaff sent him on his way again. "We'll be going home with no goods, no deal, nothing to show for the trip at all. That'll fulfill Mother's every expectation of you!"

"That's enough of your barking, cully." The Watchman with the breastplate shoved Keisyl's shoulder. "Talk like a civilized man or not at all, none of this yapping like dog-foxes."

The humiliation choking Jeirran prevented him from answering Keisyl or the Watchman and fury stained his face scarlet as the pair of them were driven through the busy streets. People stopped to stare open-mouthed, to catch a neighbor's arm and point, to whisper behind lifted hands. After what felt like an eternity, the Watchmen dragged them up steps of reddish stone to a solidly built hall.

"Knock 'em up, Neth," ordered the leader. The one with

the stave hammered on the stout door with its butt. A bald
ing man little taller than Jeirran slid a metal squint aside
and peered out.

"Fair festival to you, Vigo." He stepped back to open the
door. "What have you got here?"

The one called Neth gave both Jeirran and Keisyl a shove
with his stave. "Mountain Men, still with the snow on their
boots and trying to trade in the fair without a token."

The little man nodded unsurprised as he turned to make a
note on a lengthy parchment.

"And they'm vagabonds," added Rif suddenly. "Not got
coin on them for a bed and a meal, that's the law, that's two
offenses."

The clerk looked up, a smile lightening his somber face.
"You and Westgate Ward got the usual wagers on, have you,
Vigo?"

"That's right," grinned the burly Watchman. "You make
sure it's all recorded straight and there'll be a drink for you
if we come top of the tally."

"I'll hold you to that." The clerk stuck his quill back in
his inkpot. "Right, leave them with me." He nodded to a
well-muscled man lounging against a wall who stepped forward to glower at the two Mountain Men.

"Let's see what other game we can spring, shall we?"
Vigo led his men away, picking up more manacles from a
basket with an optimistic air. The clerk closed the door
carefully behind them.

Jeirran and Keisyl stared in all directions, wondering
where they had been brought. Scuff marks and dents on the
dusty floorboards showed the room had been cleared of
substantial furniture for its temporary duty as a place of
judgment. A stale smell of food and wine suggested some
kind of dining hall. Black oak hammer beams soared above
their heads, dusty pennants hanging motionless in the
heights. Narrow lancets just below the roofline let in the last
of the evening light but tallow candles were already burning

in sconces set into the windowless walls lower down. A handful of Watchmen with staves and cudgels guarded a disconsolate group of men and women hunched on the bare floor.

"If you give me your word that you'll behave, I'll take those chains off and you can wait here until the assize calls you." The clerk nodded to three prosperous townsmen seated behind a long table on a dais at the far end of the hall and looking unfavorably on a ragged beggar being dragged up the steps. "Give any trouble, you get chained in the undercroft with the barrels and the rats and like as not you earn a kicking from those nailers who'd rather be out looking for fun." This nod indicated the two Watchmen either side of a menacing arch over dark descending steps. "What's it to be?"

"We will abide quietly here," Jeirran forced the words out.

"You swear it?" demanded the clerk.

"We swear," said Keisyl in clipped tones. Jeirran echoed him.

"Good enough." The clerk took a key from his belt and removed the manacles which his thick-set assistant tossed into the basket of identical restraints. "Right, there's nothing I can do about the trading offense, but you don't look exactly like vagabonds to me. If you can show means of supporting yourselves, we needn't take up assize time with that nonsense. Have you got a lodging paid for? Is there anyone who can vouch for you?"

"We'd better send word to Teiriol, get him to bring a purse down here," Keisyl said firmly.

Jeirran opened his mouth to object but finding it empty of any argument closed it again.

"What's that you say?" The clerk looked suspiciously at them and the heavy-set man loomed over his shoulder.

"If we can send a message to our companions, they can bring money," translated Jeirran in resigned tones.

"Good enough." The clerk made another note on his parchment and used his fingers to whistle up a lad from a bench by the dais. "Tell the boy where to go."

Jeirran gritted his teeth and gave the youth directions to their rooming house. "Tell Teiriol to bring the hazelwood box from Eirys' coffer."

"Get on with you," the clerk gave the lad a copper penny from a bowl on his table and opened the door to let him out. "Right, you pair sit over there. Make any trouble and it'll go harder when you come to be heard."

Jeirran walked briskly to a space against the wall, glowering at any curious faces turned their way, but most of the petty offenders were content to sit and keep their own counsel. Jeirran flung his cape down and sat on it, arms around his knees, brooding blackly with his eyes fixed on the door.

"Why did you ask for the hazel box?" Keisyl demanded in a curt whisper, cross-legged beside him. "Teiriol's purse will be good enough to prove we're no beggars."

"There's gold coin hidden in the base of the casket, part of my patrimony," hissed Jeirran. "I want to buy our way out of this. The last thing we need is to forfeit those furs. If we go home with nothing to show for them, we'll never hear the last of it. We'll have to sell them at one of the towns between here and home and make the best of it. That's going to give your mother a big enough stick to beat me with as it is!"

Keisyl grunted. "And what's Eirys going to say? That gold's supposed to be your earnest of managing her lands competently for her, providing for her children. Come to that, it should all be safely under the hearthstone at home!"

"Eirys doesn't have to know about it," spat Jeirran.

"You think she'll sit still when Teiriol gets that message and starts taking things out of her coffer?" Keisyl's voice rose, incredulous. "She'll be here and madder than a scalded cat!"

"She doesn't have to know it's part of my patrimony,"

Jeirran insisted. "I'll tell her I did some trading last year, before we were wed. I'll find a way of earning the gold back before Solstice, and Eirys need never know it was missing."

"On your own head be it," snapped Keisyl. "If anyone asks, I'm saying I knew nothing about it."

Jeirran nodded, his eyes still fixed on the door, humiliation souring his stomach and shortening his breath. He sought vainly for any hope of salvaging something from the wreckage of his hopes. Hot fury welled up within him, at all these lowlanders, with their incomprehensible guilds and secret rules, conspiring together to keep every trade for themselves. It was all the same, this deceit, the way Degran and his like cheated the Mountain Men. When had any up-lander last seen a just share in the profits, a fair reward for the dangerous work of wresting metal from barren reaches or furs from the forested heights? It was all of a piece with the way lowlanders were setting their filthy villages ever higher, seizing the best grazing for their mud-caked cattle and greedy sheep, claiming the right to buy and sell the very land itself, haggling over blotted parchment they said could outweigh rights of blood and lineage. Jeirran's burning eye lit on the heedless clerk, on the three men sitting in smug judgment as they robbed their victims of coin and dignity.

The main door swung open but it was only some immodest red-headed female in close-cut breeches peering in past the clerk. Scowling at her, Jeirran returned to his angry thoughts.

How could he have known that there was no chance of honest dealing here? He had come in all good faith. Degran and those others, they must have known this would happen. They'd all be laughing up their sleeves at him, wouldn't they? Jeirran set his jaw, beard bristling wrathfully. These smug lowlanders, with their tricks and deceits; he'd find a way of making them pay, every last one of them.

Selerima, Western Ensaimin,
First Night of the Spring Fair

"It's not them," I told Usara regretfully. "Just some pair
fresh off their mules who gave the wrong Watchman a
funny look."

"So where next? Oh, your pardon, madam." The wizard
stepped aside as a painted lass sauntered past, scarlet skirt
hitched high on one hip to show off snowy petticoats, an inadequate shawl draped over barely covered shoulders. With
the sun setting over the fairground, the other sort of flower-
sellers were out looking for trade.

I looked after the whore. "If 'Gren's found himself a blossom ripe for plucking, we've not much chance of finding
them tonight. They've probably not even arrived yet. We'd
have found them at the smithing stalls being sarcastic about
the quality of the metalwork. I'd have put money on it."

Usara looked at me quizzically. "Tormalin coin or one of
these local pennies?"

"All right," I amended, "maybe just an ale-trader's token."

The clash of cymbals and a thrum of strings announced a
small band making up with enthusiasm for their lack of
numbers and skill. Their leader put his battered pipe to his
mouth and blew a squeaky flourish. "Good folk of Selerima
and honored guests at our feast, I invite you to view a masquerade of rare talent and no little beauty! The Martlet
Players will be giving their rendition of *The Gulf Traders* at
the Fleet Hound, commencing at the second chime of
evening." He turned to his motley musicians and they struck
up a ragged fanfare before launching into one of those tunes
that everyone knows a different set of words to. With the
piper leading, they set off down to the next junction to make
their bold declaration again.

I looked at Usara. "Fancy an evening at the masquerades?"

"I'm not sure," he replied cautiously. "There are masquerades and masquerades."

I laughed. "The Fleet Hound is a respectable house, right up on the market square. When did you last hear of a brothel with a name like that? If you want girls wearing nothing but a few silk flowers and a winning smile, you'd better try down by the waterfront."

"I'll resist the temptation," said the wizard dryly, "unless you think we might find these elusive brothers somewhere around there."

I shook my head. "If 'Gren's in a brothel, he won't be wasting his time looking at the posies, he'll be busy hunting the honey. But Sorgrad certainly likes a good play. It's worth taking a look around the masquerades." And since those of us who live the traveling life, masqueraders, confidence men, and gamblers, nearly always pitch up at the same big festivals, I reckoned I could put a decently minted silver penny on my chances of getting word of Sorgrad at very least. With luck, I could leave a few messages with people who actually knew him.

"So whereabouts is the Fleet Hound?" Usara was looking vainly for the Conclave Tower.

"This way." I led him down a side street that took us to the marketplace. With bawdy amusements down at the fairground getting ever more raucous as the night deepened, the worthies of the city were holding more sedate celebrations up here. The centerpiece was a blazing fire roasting an ox, courtesy of the Butchers' Guild if the flensing knives on the pennants all around were any indication. A priest was invoking Ostrin's blessing on the gathering and everyone was listening attentively, the older people even joining in the liturgy. The priest looked delighted, as well he might; this was the most attention anyone was going to pay to him between now and Solstice. Braziers made bright dots in the gathering darkness as the chill of the evening belied the sunshine of the passing day. Chestnuts were roasting to warm the hands and the belly, a reminder of how early the season still was.

"Hot wine, my lady?" A girl with flushed cheeks and bright eyes proffered a tray of steaming horn goblets. "Compliments of the Vintners' Guild."

"Thank you." I passed a cup to Usara and sipped at my own, finding the spices and warmth good enough to mask the inadequacy of the vintage. "Over there," I pointed to the far side of the busy square. "That's the Fleet Hound."

Usara drank thirstily, grimaced and looked distastefully into his wine before pouring the dregs onto the cobbles. "Where else do you suppose masquerades will be playing? Does this city have a purpose-built playhouse?"

"No," I said scornfully. "The Looking Glass in Vanam is the only one of those this side of the White River. Selerimans make do with inn courtyards, like everywhere else."

We made our way over, pausing at my insistence to accept coarse bread rolled around meat and crackling hacked from a plump porker halved from snout to curly tail and spitted either side of a searing fire. A queue was already forming outside the Fleet Hound; a few doors down, beneath the sign of the Swan in the Moon, two masqueraders in bright costumes were taking silver pennies from those keen to get in early enough to secure a good view.

"Livak!" One of the pair pushed up his mask and hailed me in delighted tones.

I laughed with equal pleasure. "Niello, how good to see you!" I grabbed Usara's sleeve to drag him after me. "I'd have come sooner if I'd known you were here, but I thought you were fixed in Col for good. What happened to Lord Elkith's Players? Wasn't he buying the lease of an inn for you?"

Niello shrugged the exaggerated shoulders of his gaudy

doublet. "The usual, my dear, a masquerader, a lady, a misunderstanding."

"His wife," I guessed.

"His sister," grinned Niello wolfishly, running a hand over immaculate chestnut locks.

There was doubtless more to it: rows over money, takings spent on ale instead of paying the reckoning, costumes ruined or distrained for debt. None of that was my problem. "So, who are you playing with now?"

Niello swept a low bow with consummate grace. "We are the Brazen Bell Troupe." His companion gave his hand bell a vigorous shake by way of illustration, which turned heads all around the square. "I joined them when they came to Col for the Winter Solstice."

"I take it you two know each other," said Usara in an undertone.

"We've had some dealings in the past." I dimpled a coquettish smile at Niello, whose hazel eyes brightened hopefully. "You might be able to help us, Niello."

"How?" he asked a touch warily.

"Do you remember Sorgrad and Sorgren? They were at the Cavalcade with me and Halice, Winter Solstice a year back?"

Niello frowned in thought. "Mountain Men, brothers, the little one rather unpredictable, as one might say?"

I nodded. "That's them. You haven't seen them, have you?"

"Not so far, though I have to confess, I could have missed them easily enough."

"Could you look out for them?" I gave him a hopeful smile with all the wide-eyed charm I could muster. "We have some business to discuss with them."

Niello looked fondly at me. "I can do better than that, Livvie. Reza's here with me, the lad who was my runner in Col? He'll remember that pair well enough, so why don't I send him around a few of the other inns and masquerades to see if he can find them for you?"

I blew Niello a kiss. "You're a treasure, do you know that?" And Reza now had an excellent excuse for spying out the competition.

"That's what all the girls say, my pet. Now, get inside, you're holding up paying customers!" He raised an arm to let the pair of us through and I led Usara to a table at one side of the courtyard.

"Livvie?" queried Usara with something perilously close to a smirk.

I raised a warning finger. "He's the only one I let get away with that, and don't you forget it. If I find anyone else calling me that, I'll know who's been talking out of turn!"

"How do you come to know him?" Usara twisted on the low bench to look back at Niello, who was coaxing a blushing youth to bring his wide-eyed companion in for the entertainment.

"I've been traveling the length and breadth of Ensaimin for ten years and more; I know a lot of people." I turned to look for a serving wench. That was enough truth for Usara. In fact my friendship with Niello went back to my heedless girlhood in Vanam, when I spent my free time roaming the city looking for any mischief to enliven the tedium of life as a housemaid. Niello had been a lowly runner in those days, hanging around the Looking Glass and the lesser companies of players who played the inns and temple courtyards, carrying messages, mending costumes, standing with his spear on the edges of the big scenes and hoping for that one chance to take up a mask, to play the part to perfection.

The courtyard was filling up, people packed tightly at the sides of the stage lashed up out of planks and barrels. Rows of benches were set out in front, spectators rolling up cloaks to pad their seats as they prepared to enjoy the spectacle.

"Have you seen this one? *The Back Gate Gossips* they said it was." Usara looked expectantly at the scenecloth obscuring the doorway into some back room of the inn where the players were busy organizing masks and costumes. It was painted with a bold portrayal of two improbably colored gardens separated by a looming wall. Two iron gates all wrought with curlicues stood on little platforms on either side of the stage, things that wouldn't keep out a cat with theft on its mind but that would happily symbolize all manner of barriers for the willing playgoers.

I shook my head. "No, but it'll be the usual kind of thing, young love frustrated by a stern father or an ambitious mother, a couple of comic bits about a pig and everything coming right after some wicked series of coincidences." I beckoned to a maidservant who was wandering around looking vacant. "Wine for me and my friend and a flagon for the players, compliments of Mistress Deft."

The girl looked uncertainly at me. Mistress Deft was an elderly scold from *The Orphan's Tears*, a gloomy piece that had blighted every troupe's repertoire a handful of years ago. "It's a private joke," I explained, "Niello will know what it means."

"Some of the apprentices put that one on for Winter Solstice a couple of years ago," said Usara unexpectedly.

"Do you have masquerades in Hadrumal then?"

"Only attempts got together for one performance, usually. Proper troupes don't ever accept invitations, not even from the Archmage." Usara sounded genuinely puzzled.

"Are you surprised?" I asked, incredulous. "When you mages have spent Saedrin knows how many generations building up your terrifying legends, your hidden island locked away in enchanted mists, powerful sorceries holding the very stones together? What player's going to take on an audience like that? People throwing fruit if they don't like the play is bad enough, never mind risking being turned into blackbeetles!"

Usara looked faintly affronted. "People don't believe those old stories nowadays."

"You'd be surprised," I said darkly. Not that I had any intention of dispelling the rumors. If I wanted to impress people by casually mentioning that I had been to the mystical city of the wizards, I was hardly about to tell them it was a staid and tedious place full of self-absorbed scholars and pompous mages. "Remember what you thought before you proved mage-born and were sent off to be apprenticed."

Usara shook his head. "I'm Hadrumal born and bred, a fourth generation on my mother's side, five on my father's and mages borne on every branch of the family tree. For me it's the mainland that's where all the mysteries lie!" He grinned and I smiled faintly back at him. How had I managed to travel so many hundreds of leagues with the man and never find that out? I chided myself for that slackness; I'd better be on my guard in case his ignorance landed us in some bear-pit, for all his native wit and subsequent learning. Just how shrewd was he? "So, what did you think of the cockatrice?"

Usara frowned. "It started life as an ordinary cockerel, obviously, until someone cut off its spurs and comb. What I don't understand is how that man set the spurs growing on its head instead."

So he'd seen nearly all the trick. "You have to castrate the bird first, so I've been told." A chorus of horns ended all conversation and the Explanatory in his plain white mask and unadorned wig stepped out from behind the backdrop. He gave us the set-up for the tale and the usual broad hint of what moral we might expect to improve us, harking back to the days of pious plays performed in the shrines. As was modern custom, half the audience listened attentively to find out who was who and the other half stirred restively, wanting the dancing girls and the comedy with the pig. I sipped my wine as our hero, a rich youth from the nearside house, came on to declaim his love for the virtuous daughter of the warden of his guild. This paragon was apparently and somewhat improbably off traveling with her aunt. There were jokes about the warden hating anyone who didn't make coin through honest trade and a few mild sallies about his girth, which must have been written in for local color, given the immoderate laughter they provoked.

The cook of the neighboring house spent a lengthy passage complaining to the hero's housekeeper about how badly her miserly master treated her and then, to everyone's relief, the messenger came rushing in with muddy mask and windblown hair firmly set with flour paste. After stressing how private his news was, he proceeded to tell all and sundry how the virtuous maiden had been abducted by hired bravos. As those of the audience who'd failed to see this coming gasped, the band struck up and dancers came skipping out from behind the backcloth.

I nudged Usara. "I'll have to tell Niello upper-house servants would sit naked on the rooftops before so much as commenting on the weather to a cook!"

The mage didn't answer, leaning forward for a better view of the girls, whose shapely legs were barely concealed beneath muslin skirts bright with ribbons. Gaily colored half-masks hid their eyes, but not their enticing smiles. After an energetic song, just the tasteful side of bawdy, it was time for the clowns, one hook-nosed and the other moon-faced, so no surprises there. They were playing tradesmen this time, their problem a guard dog who attacked anything in breeches. One clown was a knife-grinder wooing the cook, with all the jokes one might expect about blades and scabbards and we soon learned that the dog was keeping him from getting a regular sharpening. I recognized Niello's voice behind the hook-nosed mask and he played the scene with a relish that set me giggling.

As the hero came on to lament the loss of his love in tedious detail, a stir ran through the crowd behind me. I turned quickly in my seat but Usara's attention was still fixed on the stage. My instinctive trepidation was replaced with delight as I saw two blond figures pushing toward us, heads at shoulder height to most of the men, one with the unmistakable stocky build of the mountains, the other slighter, long hair tied back with a braided leather knot.

"Make some space, Usara." I dug an elbow into his ribs and he shuffled along the bench with courteous apologies to some apprentices on his far side. 'Gren grabbed a stool from behind someone unwise enough to stand up for a better view and passed it to Sorgrad, who promptly settled himself at our table as if he'd been there all evening.

"We got word you were here." Sorgren slipped in between me and Usara, helping himself to the last of my wine with a cheeky grin. "That's welcome; I'm dry as a limeburner's hat."

Sorgrad pulled a little silver goblet from his pocket and I filled it from our jug. "I've been leaving word everywhere I could think of. When did you arrive?"

"Just after sunset." Sorgrad drank thirstily. "We've just come up from Col."

"Do I owe you money or something, Sandy?" 'Gren challenged Usara's inquisitive face with a bold stare of his own. "Want to try minding your own mutton?"

"This is Usara and he's with me." I reclaimed my cup from 'Gren and looked around for the serving girl. "We'll get to that later. What were you doing in Col?"

"Keeping out of trouble." Sorgrad smiled contentedly at me and I noted the fine wool broadcloth of his maroon jerkin, skillfully cut in the very latest fashion and expensively tailored to flatter his barrel of a chest. Silver ornaments on his belt and purse were plentiful and untarnished, the leather still shiny and new. His fine blond hair was neatly cut beneath an elegant cap in the new southern style. Even over stable smells and the sweaty mass of revelers, I could smell the lingering perfume of expensive bath oils.

"So your little project in Draximal went well?" I inquired innocently. The last time I'd seen the brothers, they'd been full of a madcap plan to steal a mercenary pay-chest, gold intended to finance a further season of the interminable civil wars in Lescar.

Sorgrad nodded. "We found some old friends who fancied getting paid up front for a change and not spilling too much blood. We picked the right spot on the road through the hills north of Sharlac and it was easy as clubbing a roosting bird."

"So what brings you to Selerima?" Usara had to raise his voice as the dancers came on again to some lively pipe music.

"We thought a certain Cordainer might be here for the festival." Sorgrad's blue eyes burned dark with a promise of vengeance. They don't say Mountain memories are carved in stone for nothing.

"Who?" Usara looked to me for explanation.

"Later." Perhaps, if I could come up with an acceptable way of explaining that Arle Cordainer had masterminded that robbery I didn't want to discuss with any Watchman. He'd recruited our services but had then found a way to leave the city with all the proceeds while the rest of us faced a climb up the gallows, almost certainly on account of him laying information. I turned to wave at a potman, summoning more wine and an extra cup.

The action resumed with a new maidservant appearing in the miser's house. Unsurprisingly she wore the delicate mask and ringletted wig of the mislaid heroine. I poured more wine for Sorgrad since there was no point trying to get 'Gren's attention if there was a trim female to look at. That was fine by me; as long as he was occupied, he couldn't be getting into mischief.

"Will you be staying hereabouts after the festival?" I asked Sorgrad. "I take it you're keeping clear of Lescar for the summer."

"We didn't leave anyone alive who could identify us," he shrugged. "But yes, once we'd shared out the coin we thought it best to put a few leagues between the others and us. There are a couple with mouths no safer than a torn pocket and if they find themselves facing a swing on the nevergreen tree, they'll speak up smart enough to save their necks."

I nodded and chose my next words carefully. "Charoleia said that she'd heard a couple of men had been taken for the robbery and the Duke of Draximal is out for their blood." Usara leaned forward, trying to hear what I was saying, but

'Gren pushed him back with an impatient hand as his view of the players was blocked.

Sorgrad looked at me sharply. "When did you see her?"

"Just before the turn of Aft-winter, me and Usara were on our way here," I told him. "She's been in Relshaz as usual; that's how I knew you were planning to come here for the festival. She said she'd seen you at Winter Solstice?"

Sorgrad frowned into his goblet. I knew he wouldn't question any word I claimed to have from Charoleia. Given she makes her coin talking gullible people into plausible schemes, her network for gathering information is second to none. She spends her winters in one of the biggest ports on the Gulf of Lescar, and everyone knows that if they send her information she can use, gold will eventually work its way back to them. In this case, the news happened to be true.

Usara said something to 'Gren that I didn't catch but that went unanswered in any case as the clowns were back on. The eager knife-grinder planned to get past the guard dog by wearing a dress. This naturally led to Reza under ragged fur and floppy-eared dog's head chasing Niello around the stage, the latter wearing no more than mask and skin-tight, fine-knitted wool.

"How dare he pad himself like that!" a blushing girl behind me gasped, intent on Niello's hose. I knew better than she did and allowed myself a quiet moment of nostalgic reflection.

"We're far enough away to be safe," Sorgrad's face was untroubled when I looked back to him. "No one's going to hunt us clear across Caladhria and four-fifths the way through Ensaimin."

"They might if the reward were large enough," I said slowly. "I heard the Duke was offering a tenth-share of what was stolen."

Sorgrad's sapphire eyes looked speculatively over the rim of his silver cup. "That's what you heard?"

I shrugged. "It could just be tavern talk but it might be

prudent to take a paying proposition elsewhere for a season or so."

"Which you just happen to have to put to us?" Sorgrad raised an inquiring eyebrow. He nodded at Usara, who had given up trying to talk to 'Gren and turned his attention to the masquerade. "Where does he figure in the game?"

"Never mind him for the moment. Yes, I do have something in play and I think you should hear me out." I smiled at him. "We could both come out ahead of the game."

Sorgrad's laugh momentarily turned a few nearby heads from the stage, where hero and heroine were clutching tearful hands through one of the wrought-iron gates. Sorgrad leaned closer to me.

"So what's the offer? No offense, Livak, but the last I heard you'd gone off with Halice to work for some wizards again. I can't say I fancy that. Charoleia told us she'd had a letter from Halice all the way from some new land clear across the ocean. The Archmage discovered it?" He gestured toward the stage where the heroine was now weeping alone. "People sleeping in a cave for thirty generations, heartless villains trying to steal their lands, wizards raising dragons to drive them off; Niello couldn't make a masquerade out of a story like that and expect people to swallow it!"

"I know it sounds incredible, but those people in the cave were the Tormalin colony that Nemith the Last lost track of just before the fall of the Old Empire," I explained.

Sorgrad looked more interested, despite himself. "We've all heard the stories about that lost colony, rivers running over golden gravel, diamonds loose in the grass. People have been trying to find it again ever since the Chaos."

"I don't know about any of that, the gold and the gems, I mean," I said hastily, "but do you remember those islands out in the eastern ocean, the ones where I was taken when I was forced into thieving for that wizard?"

Sorgrad nodded warily and I strove to keep my voice level, ignoring memories of that ordeal. "Don't forget how much coin I brought back from that trip, Sorgrad. Say what you like about wizards, they certainly pay well." If you come back alive, I added silently to myself. "It was these Ice Islanders—well, their forefathers—who stamped the original settlers into the mud. The ones that managed to escape hid themselves in a cave, wrapped themselves up in enchantments and the Archmage sent an expedition to find them last summer. That's what Halice and me got ourselves mixed up in. These people had magic, 'Grad, old magic, not the flash tricks of the Archmage and his like, but lost enchantments that put them to sleep and kept them safe while all these generations passed. Truthfully, I saw it with my own eyes, saw them roused."

I paused, expecting a scornful response from Sorgrad, but he was looking thoughtful. "So the Archmage woke these people up and now they've got their colony back? It still sounds like some bad masquerade. Why are you still bothering with any of this?" he demanded with uncharacteristic sharpness. "You used to keep as far away from magic as you could, same as the rest of us, and from what Halice says these Elietimm have enchantments to turn your hair white! You said yourself you've no real idea how it was you managed to withstand them. I know you were blackmailed into that first job for the Archmage, there was no helping that, and as for last year, I suppose you owed Planir something for saving your skin, but I don't understand why you're putting your neck in a noose of your own free will again! Is it something to do with this Tormalin swordsman of yours? Charoleia was telling us you've been letting him pick your pocket willingly enough."

"That tongue's too long for your teeth, Sorgrad," I warned him. There are times when the efficiency of Charoleia's network can be less than welcome and I wondered what else Halice had put in her letter. "I'm working for a Tormalin prince now, not the wizards. Yes, the Elietimm scared the shit out of me and I still wake up sweating at the memory and that's one reason why I'm heading as far away from the ocean coast as I can. Hear me out. The way Messire sees it, it's clear these Ice Islanders have had enough of their freezing rocks and are looking for somewhere warm and dry for a change. Planir threw them out of the colony and we found their footprints in Dalasor and Northern Tormalin the year before last—"

"I've heard no word of any such threat," interrupted Sorgrad skeptically.

"That's because Planir and Messire have put their heads together and decided to keep it all quiet until they've got some plan in place." Ryshad and I had argued ourselves breathless over that one, advocating instead the circulation of detailed descriptions of the Elietimm in their distinctive liveries, so that they'd stand out like the stones on a stag hound if they ever tried to make landfall again. I still thought our so-called leaders were wrong. "Sometime soon, the Emperor and his cronies will be facing organized soldiery backed by enchanters who can pull the wits out through somcone's nose from half a league away," I continued. "My master knows he'll need magic to fight back."

"So what does this prince want you to do?" Sorgrad was still looking as darkly hostile as someone with such a fair complexion could hope to. "Who is he, anyway?"

"Messire D'Olbriot. You've heard of him, surely?" It was a gold Crown certainty that Sorgrad would have heard of arguably the most important noble House of the Tormalin Empire.

He nodded. "Word is he's virtually running the court, what with Emperor Tadriol still being so green. What are you doing for him?"

I held Sorgrad's gaze with my own. "Messire D'Olbriot wants to understand this old magic, ideally before anyone else thinks to start looking, to know what he might be up against. It gets better. The Archmage wants to learn all about this old magic as well. Artifice, that's what they're calling it now, or aetheric magic, take your pick. The point

is, the wizards of Hadrumal can't use this old magic, don't
ask me why. That's got Planir worried, so he's doing everything he can to find out what he might be facing."

"So your patron, if he has the information the Archmage
is so keen on finding, he can trade it for some mages to start
throwing fire and lightning at any Ice Islander who wants to
come ashore without paying his harbor dues?" Sorgrad was
still looking thoughtful but less hostile. "That makes sense."

"I knew you'd see it," I grinned. Messire D'Olbriot
hadn't, not until I put it to him, for all his years of shuffling
the pieces around the games of Tormalin politics. The
whole notion of getting involved with mages and wizardry
was still about as welcome in Toremal as dancing with a
pox-rotted whore. "As I say, this is a job that could pay very
well indeed. We might even be able to play both ends
against the middle and double our winnings."

"So how do you get to be drawing a rune in the game?"
Sorgrad asked.

I could see curiosity beginning to get the better of him
and breathed a little easier. "The word is Artifice came from
the ancient races originally; the Plains People, the Mountain Men, the Forest Folk. That's where the Old Tormalins
got it from."

"Along with their lands, their wealth and their stock,"
grunted Sorgrad.

I pressed on. "Tormalin scholars and Planir's wizards
have been rummaging through archives and libraries for the
last half-year or more, looking for clues. I've done a little
looking around myself and come up with something interesting"—once the scholars had recovered from their aston-
ishment that a commoner like me might actually be able to
read more than a laundry list and let me in to fossick
through their dusty tomes. "I found a song book, going
back to before the fall of the Empire, lots of old songs from
all the ancient races, full of hints of aetheric magic."

"This is interesting?" Sorgrad's tone suggested it was
anything but.

"I think so, and if we can get all the songs translated from the original, I think Planir and D'Olbriot will agree, especially if the songs actually hold some of the incantations to work the magic."

"How likely is that?" frowned Sorgrad.

"Not so long odds as you might think," I assured him. "I've seen this aetheric magic worked and I'll wager any coin minted that there are Forest rhythms in their enchantments. I'm a minstrel's daughter, Sorgrad, you know you can trust my ear."

"So why aren't the wizards looking into this for themselves?" Sorgrad demanded.

"The particular wizard Planir has coordinating the scholars is a small-minded cloak carrier called Casuel," I explained tartly. "His plans and method are carved in stone and he wasn't about to listen to my theories, especially when he couldn't carry a tune if it was knocked down and tied up!"

"And you didn't just pull a case of books down on his head to get him out of your way?" grinned Sorgrad.

"Don't think I wasn't tempted!" I took a sip of wine. "No, I just went around him. There's a favorite nephew of the House who owes Ryshad a measure of respect, Esquire Camarl. I persuaded him this book was worth investigating and he suggested to Messire D'Olbriot that they pay me to go and get the songs translated."

"And you've had to come all this way to find someone to do the work? I take it that's what you want me for?" Sorgrad didn't sound impressed. "I appreciate you wanting to share a fee with your friends, Livak, but there must have been someone closer to hand!"

"Actually, no." I shrugged. "The scholars could manage the Old High Tormalin but they don't trouble themselves with what they call lost languages. We found a few nobles who'd spent time up in Gidesta, but Mountain speech sufficient for ordering wine, bed and a whore in the mining camps wasn't much use with archaic sagas."

"So you're looking for someone closer to the old ways to translate them?" Sorgrad ran a pensive finger around the rim of his finely engraved goblet.

"I am, and from every inquiry I've made that means going into the wildwood and up into the heights. There's no one I've found between here and Toremal can be sure of all the words." I'd learned enough to convince me these songs rang with Artifice, though.

"Are you getting paid up front or on results?" demanded Sorgrad suddenly.

"I got a handsome retainer before I set out," I assured him, "and I've authority to draw funds on D'Olbriot reserves in all the major cities hereabouts." The bronze amulet bearing the D'Olbriot seal hung warm and solid beneath my shirt, but I wasn't about to attract unwanted attention by showing it to him here. "Final payment depends on exactly what I find out. Yes, I want the songs translated, but with any luck anyone who can master the ancient tongues will point me toward people with useful knowledge of old aetheric lore or some such. I can get myself to the Forest, being half-blood and using my father's name to vouch for me. Once I find some real Folk, I should be able to talk someone into helping me. What I need to get me into the Mountains is someone who knows how things work up there, who can speak the language, who can make the right introductions."

"What you need is me and 'Gren." Mischief lurked in the back of Sorgrad's eyes. "It might just be worth doing, if we can agree a decent price."

His amusement was unnerving me and I realized I'd never quite learned why the pair of them had left the mountains in the first place. "We're not going to be running into handfuls of people eager to skin you for some price on your hide, are we?" I asked sternly.

"No, not as long as we steer clear of a few places." Sorgrad looked into his empty goblet, thoughtful again. I poured him more wine. "Let me think about it," he said at length. "I'll need to talk to 'Gren."

"Come and see me tomorrow morning. I'll show you the book."

I turned to the stage, where dancers were flirting their garters at the audience again. There was no benefit in pressing Sorgrad; he'd give his answer in his own good time and then 'Gren would do what his older brother recommended. 'Gren didn't concern himself with much beyond taking on life with an eagerness that frequently slipped into recklessness. That was doubtless why they had left the mountains; 'Gren had done something without thinking through the consequences and they'd had to get clear. They'd have worked their way to Lescar, like exiles from every corner of the map. 'Gren's propensity for casual violence would have soon proved an asset in the mercenary life, rather than the liability it can be elsewhere, so they would have stayed on, seeing that rich pickings could be made from the endless circle of civil wars.

The dancers left the stage to the masqueraders and I soon caught up with the plot. The miser who aimed to marry her money had abducted our heroine and he was working her as a scullery maid until she agreed.

"Why doesn't he just force the issue by raping the silly poult?" Sorgrad murmured quizzically.

"She doesn't look as if she could fight off a winter cold," I agreed. The cook and the housekeeper came on for another of those convenient masquerade conversations, where two characters tell each other things both of them already know. "There's your answer!"

"The old man in *The Orphan's Tears* was impotent as well." Usara leaned around behind 'Gren to speak to me, looking puzzled.

"It goes with a droopy-nosed mask as a rule," I whispered. Saedrin save me from these wizards with their sheltered lives.

Next for a turn by the garden gates were our hero and heroine. He was all for calling the Watch and simply having the old wretch arrested.

"First sensible thing I've heard him say," Sorgrad whispered with a grin. "An honest citizen should always turn to the Watch, after all."

"Bet you a silver Mark she won't," I replied. My coin was safe as our heroine replied with undeniable truth and convincing histrionics that no one would believe the old skinflint hadn't had a finger in her purse, her reputation would be ruined, and our hero's parents would never allow them to marry. I beckoned for more wine as we sat through the usual romantic nonsense that followed.

I found myself thinking about Ryshad, the Tormalin swordsman Sorgrad had mentioned. Our paths had crossed when he'd been pursuing Ice Islanders on Messire's account. Elietimm had been sneaking ashore to rob and kill in Tormalin through the last couple of years, stealing the valuables that they hoped would lead them to the lost colony of Kel Ar'Ayen. I'd been after those self-same valuables, reluctantly thieving at the behest of the Archmage.

A fire of sudden passion and the sensual delights that followed were nothing new to me but the real surprise had been the unwelcome sense of loss when Ryshad had returned to his patron. I'm not inclined to pine over men or anything else as a rule—the runes play themselves out and I move on—but I began to suspect we'd become one in more ways than just between the sheets. When chance and the Archmage's connivance brought us back together, I'd found myself compromising and yielding so Ryshad and I need not part. I wasn't dressing up my feelings in scented, senseless words like the heroine fluttering about the stage, but I'd finally had to admit I wanted to be with Ryshad and not just until the turn of the year nullified all deals. At least I had learned he was as set on me, a discovery that left me both elated and wary.

I looked up at the artificial lovers with faces of wood and

paint and lives drawn from the masquerader's stock of characters: the noble lover, the lost heir, the wronged beauty, the cheerful rogue, the wise old man, the comic artisans. Their predicaments and the solutions fitted like pieces in a child's puzzle box; not so, life for Ryshad and me. We'd reconciled my flirtations with necessary dishonesty on the road with his duty as sworn man to a noble House, largely by ignoring the subject, if truth were told, but finding any hope of a future together, for however long we might want one, was proving mightily difficult. Whatever else I might tell Sorgrad, Sorgren, the Archmage or D'Olbriot, that was what all my present contriving was aiming to achieve. But that was my secret.

Niello's ringing tones dragged my attention back and I realized the two tradesmen were offering to steal the heroine out of the miser's house, so she could be found wandering in the woods by our hero and returned to her loving family.

"And what am I supposed to be doing in the woods?" the hero asked in puzzled tones.

"Picking pretty flowers?" leered the moon-faced clown with a meaningful gesture at our hero's hose, which was definitely padded. "What else would a young man be doing in the springtime?"

Laughter swelled. "I don't think Daddy's little treasure will be coming home untarnished," I commented to Sorgrad with mock disapproval.

The masquerade romped down comfortably predictable paths: the improbable lovers chasing in and out of the back-cloth with the clowns, the dog, the cook and the miser raising ever louder laughter as the double-edged jests flew thick and fast. The miser made the mistake of trying to enter his own house by the back gate in an attempt to foil the heroine's escape and was duly stripped of breeches and, shirt tails flapping, was chased off by his own dog. The knife-grinder seized his opportunity, first to rescue the heiress and then to get his boots under the cook's table. The dancers came on to draw down the pace with a sedate display of lace and ankles and the piece ended with our hero and heroine emerging from the backcloth in their wedding clothes, her hair duly cut and laid on Drianon's altar.

The Explanatory raised his voice determinedly above the people stirring and calling for ale, proclaiming the moral conclusion, even if the tales would have shocked any priest who stumbled across the threshold by mistake. I was quite surprised that Niello hadn't cut that, as so many companies do nowadays, but this was a festival after all, when people like to see the old ways duly observed.

As the company came out to take a bow, Niello waved and mimed taking a drink, pointing at our table.

"Are we staying?" I looked at the others.

"Definitely," answered 'Gren promptly. The dancing girls were emerging from the backcloth in twos and threes, slippers in hand, warm shawls draped over their costumes. "It's too early to go to bed, without company anyway."

He strolled toward the stage, collecting a pitcher and a handful of cups from a serving maid. The dancers barely registered him at first, a slight figure in nondescript buff jerkin and breeches like half the men in the city. I watched as the girls' heads turned one by one, golden ringlets brassy next to 'Gren's flaxen head. Curious glances were replaced by demure giggles and 'Gren ended up sitting on the edge of the stage, four lasses around him sipping their wine and giggling flirtatiously as he praised their performance with flattering detail.

Niello sauntered over, swinging his hook-nosed mask idly from its ribbons, a tattered rainbow jerkin unbuttoned over a sweaty shirt. The masculine scent of him wasn't un-pleasant as he dropped onto the bench and gave me a warm smile. He ran a hand through the tangle of his chestnut hair and heaved a gratified sigh. "So, what did you think?"

"Most entertaining," Usara pushed a drink toward him. "First rate."

"Good enough for the Looking Glass," I agreed.

"Hardly that," shrugged Niello but his expression betrayed his pleasure. "I think we could still make more of the business with the dog."

"Not without you stripping naked and really giving the girls an eyeful," I retorted.

"Is that a sacrifice I could make?" he mused, mock serious. "Perhaps not; I don't think the Watch would see the funny side of it. What did you think of my scene with the cook?"

"Where was the letter?" demanded Sorgrad.

"What letter?" Niello was perplexed.

"The letter that either has some crucial significance and gets mislaid, or that brings a vital piece of intelligence to solve everyone's problems." Sorgrad's smile teased. "Every good story has to have one or the other, surely?"

We discussed the masquerade in general and Niello's part in particular for some while. Gradually the courtyard emptied until only we four were left with the players as they relaxed. The five chimes of midnight sounded from some distant tower.

"So whereabouts are you staying?" Niello's eyes slid from me to Usara with an obvious question.

"We have rooms at the Six Stars," I laid a gentle emphasis on the word "rooms."

Niello whistled soundlessly. "You've come up in the world, my dear. I'll escort you back when you're ready to go to your bed."

I smiled but shook my head. "No need, thanks all the same."

His hazel eyes clouded with enough disappointment to flatter me but he recovered his poise in the next breath. "If you'll excuse me, I really should speak to some of the company. It was a good performance, but there are always improvements to be made."

We watched as he went straight as a scenting hound for the lass who'd played the heroine, her own face showing none of the innocence of the mask she'd worn earlier.

"You turned him down last time as well," observed Sorgrad slyly. "Keeping yourself free for your swordsman?"

"Keeping myself free of the itch," I replied with some asperity. "That's what I got the last time I let him talk me into a tumble."

I caught an expression of frozen distaste on Usara's face and was about to challenge it when commotion erupted by the stage. 'Gren had his arm around the waist of a pretty dancer whose face glowed with the vacant sensuality that so often causes trouble. The second clown, his own face nigh as fat as his mask and red with wine and anger, was reaching for the lass's arm. "Come on, Lalla! I said we're going. You're coming with me tonight."

'Gren swung the girl backward out of the clown's grasp. "Lalla wants to stay, don't you, pet?" He tightened his arm around her waist and smiled up at her.

"Go away, Vadim," one of the other girls interrupted unwisely. "Lalla's no more your property than any of the rest of us. When are you going to get that into your wooden skull?"

Vadim thrust a warning finger in her face. "Shut your mouth, Kelty, unless you want me to shut it for you."

I saw 'Gren's expression harden. With all the delight he takes in the company of pretty girls, he has an exaggerated sense of the courtesy due to women. He lifted Lalla up and sat her on the edge of the stage, his unexpected strength surprising her into a witless little giggle.

"I don't think these ladies require your company any further this evening." 'Gren squared up to Vadim, mocking him with the accents of the masquerade. "Why don't you take yourself off?"

It took Vadim, a man of Col by his accent, a moment to grasp the meaning of the north-country obscenity. Lalla was a breath quicker and giggled but Kelty and the others had the wit to get 'Gren between themselves and Vadim. The fat clown's face twisted in a furious scowl and he lashed out at 'Gren with a fist the size of a donkey's hoof. 'Gren avoided the blow with ease, dodging around to land a mocking slap on Vadim's back. "Over here, lard arse!"

Usara braced his hands on the table, rising and ready to intervene. "Don't," I laid a firm hand on his arm.

"Oh come on," objected Usara. "It's hardly a fair fight, is it?"

"No, it's not, but the fat man started it, so he'll have to take what's coming to him." I tightened my grip.

The wizard sat down, bemused face begging an explanation. I directed his attention to the fight. 'Gren was deftly evading Vadim's clumsy swings, landing stinging slaps on the clown's puce face. The idiot girl Lalla was fluttering with distress, trying to catch the sleeve of either one despite the urgent hisses of Kelty and the others telling her to get clear.

"I'll throttle you with your own tripes, you little shit," raged Vadim, grabbing a stool to fling it at 'Gren, who dodged it easily before throwing a platter of bones and scraps back to catch Vadim full in the chest, spattering him with grease. Enraged, the big man lunged forward, mad as a taunted bear. A fruit rind under 'Gren's foot betrayed him, dropping him to one knee. With a roar of triumph, Vadim swung at the side of 'Gren's head. Moving away even before the blow connected, 'Gren had an arm out to cushion his landing and rolled with a grace most tumblers would envy. Back on his feet, he split Vadim's lip with a lightning punch before the fat man knew what had hit him. A second blow to the gut doubled the clown up. He'd made the same mistake as so many others, thinking 'Gren's size meant an easy mark. I'd lost count of the men who'd learned to their considerable cost that skinny frame was strong as seasoned wood and whipcord. There was also the fact that 'Gren never imagined he could be beaten. I caught Sorgrad's eye and he nodded; we'd both seen 'Gren was upping the pace.

'Gren took a step backward, ready and waiting. When Vadim straightened up, he promptly kicked the big man in one shin. I winced, knowing 'Gren still favors the steel-capped boots of the sensible miner. Vadim howled and hopped as he clutched his leg, as comic as anything he'd shown us on stage. The witless Lalla was stupid enough to laugh and with a speed he'd have been better employing against 'Gren, Vadim lashed out, knocking the daft blossom clean off her feet. Kelty darted forward to drag the weeping chit clear.

The mocking amusement on 'Gren's face was lit with bright anger and a blade glinted steely in one hand.

"He won't kill him, will he?" Niello tapped Sorgrad on the shoulder, faint concern wrinkling his forehead. "I'll have no end of trouble finding another clown who knows that part, now the festival proper has started."

Sorgrad didn't answer and I was watching the fight. Vadim was moving more cautiously now, eyes flickering to 'Gren's knife hand. 'Gren was coming closer, eyes shining with a pale blue fire and a faint smile curving the corners of his mouth. He was enjoying himself and my heart sank; that made him so very dangerous. The two of them circled around and around, feet scuffing up the rushes and rubbish. Vadim spread his hands, checking behind for tables and benches at every other step. 'Gren followed, poised like a cat.

Usara made some faint murmur of frustration. "Can't we put a stop to this?"

"You won't succeed, and if you spoil 'Gren's fun you'll make an enemy for life." The mage's mouth hung open with questions he couldn't quite frame. I spared a glance for Sorgrad, to reassure myself he was ready to intervene. He was the only one who could stop 'Gren killing the idiot now.

Vadim made his play in that same breath, fat face creased with vicious cunning. He edged around a table where lamb bones lay in a puddle of sauce. Snatching up a carving fork, he lunged at 'Gren, a swerving move to stay beyond the sweep of the smaller man's knife. What Vadim didn't expect was 'Gren instantly swapping the knife to his other hand, a sideways step taking him out of danger and around to Vadim's unprotected back. The knife flashed in the lamp-light, the swiftness of the move deceiving my eye and I had been watching for it, knowing it of old.

Vadim's yell mingled pain and outrage and blood oozed between his fingers as he clutched a deep gash in the meat of his shoulder. Stumbling around in shock, he gaped at 'Gren, who was grinning broadly, daggers in both hands now. Vadim dropped his weapon from nerveless fingers, not the only one to see his death in the Mountain Man's bright eyes.

"Nia mer es! Als verget." Sorgrad's curt command in the Mountain tongue cut through the tense silence. The fire in 'Gren's face faded and he looked at his brother, puzzled, then at Vadim, almost as if seeing him for the first time. I breathed a quiet sigh of relief.

"I think you owe these ladies an apology, friend." Sorgrad's voice was genial enough but the glitter in his eyes told a different story. Vadim curled his lip and drew a deep breath on some defiant retort.

Niello stepped forward making a wary bow to 'Gren while prudently keeping out of range of his knives. "That's enough, Vadim. You've had your lesson in manners, so get out of here and clean yourself up."

I couldn't ever recall hearing such authority in Niello's voice and it certainly brought Vadim to heel. The clown drew himself up and spat bloody phlegm into the rushes at 'Gren's feet. He left the yard, all eyes on him in silent hostility, no one offering so much as a handkerchief to staunch his oozing wound.

As soon as Vadim's back was turned, the girl Kelty was at 'Gren's elbow, offering him wine, dabbing delicately at a bruise on his cheekbone now darkening impressively under his fair skin. He sheathed his knives and submitted meekly to her ministrations. She shot a proprietorial glance at the other dancers, who had to content themselves with helping the grizzling Lalla back into the inn. 'Gren gave me a wink over Kelty's shoulder that suggested his energies were far from spent.

"Come on, Usara. It's time I was off to my bed." I stood up and gave Sorgrad a brief embrace. "Call on us in the morning."

"We'll do that, first thing. Well, as soon as we're out of bed." Sorgrad's gaze was resting on the erstwhile heroine, now standing looking rather impatiently after Niello, who was trying to excuse the fight to the innkeeper.

"Come on, Usara." The wizard followed me out with an air of confusion that kept him silent all the way back to our inn, up the stairs and into our respective bedchambers.

Two

I learned this song as a young bride, when my husband's cohort was stationed in defense of Selerima. Small groups would gather in the islands in the river at equinox and solstice, unmistakably descendants of the People of the Plains. This song makes it clear that Arimelin has been granting her gift of dreams to all races for uncounted generations.

> *Sal Ar'Imela, the goddess has made*
> *Your woods and your waters,*
> *Your groves and your shade.*
> *River and tree meet in endless embrace,*
> *May lovers be fruitful*
> *When joined in this place.*
> *Send wisdom in sleep to those bold ones who lie,*
> *Where two realms and neither*
> *Rule under the sky.*
> *Let heartsore lay burdens beneath bow and leaf*
> *That cleansing oblivion*
> *May wash away grief.*
> *Sal Ar'Imela, your blessings we seek*
> *For newborn and dying*
> *For mighty and meek.*

"I don't think they're coming." Usara stalked over to the window to look down at the street for the third time since the second chime of the day. Below Selerimans were walking off last night's excesses or setting off to haggle at the fairground.

I helped myself to fine white bread and lavender-scented honey cleared of every speck of comb. This wasn't a morning for anything greased or spicy. "Sorgrad'll keep his word," I said stickily. "Even if he's decided against helping us."

Usara picked up a tankard of small beer and set it down again untasted. "You don't think they will?"

"I have no idea," I replied, exasperated. "I reckon the chances are better than even but Sorgrad will have a sight more questions before he agrees to work for wizards."

"Sorgrad does the thinking for both of them?" asked Usara with a faint sneer.

"You'd better keep a civil tongue in your head," I warned. "Mountain Men are no more stone-skulled cave dwellers in bearskins than Forest Folk are heedless songsters living off nuts and berries. Relax and eat your breakfast; they'll have had a late night last night."

"I'm still not convinced we need involve them," said Usara testily. "Be careful how much you tell them; you know Planir and D'Olbriot are agreed we need to keep word of the Elietimm very close, until we have a definite means of countering their enchantments."

"You can swear every mage and esquire to secrecy on pain of death, but you won't stop word getting out. I spend more time around backstairs than you do, wizard, and rumors were running around the kitchen yards of Toremal last winter." I waved the honey spoon at him. "I'll tell Sorgrad what he needs to know. I don't think you realize I need the pair of them a cursed sight more than I need you, just at present. They know people and places and all manner of useful things besides the Mountain tongue. You may have your magic but that's precious little value most of the time."

"I think you found it useful enough yesterday." Usara's words were clipped and haughty.

"Fair comment." I sweetened my tone. "It's just that it's important you get on with them. You have to understand how Sorgrad and Sorgren think. It's very straightforward; the world is divided into people they are for and the rest. If they decide to call you friend, they'll take a dagger in the ribs before they'll let you come to harm. If you don't measure up, they won't piss on you if you're on fire in the street. Can you understand?"

Usara opened his mouth, changed his mind about what he was going to say and turned to look down along the high road. I continued my meal and wondered about a few things. Hopefully Vadim hadn't been stupid enough to catch up with 'Gren this morning. I'd yet to see anyone get the better of 'Gren and wasn't about to wager a Lescar cut-piece that I ever would. Countless men had thought they could take on some scrawny son of a fatherless goat and ended up mixing blood with their wine. I wiped my fingers on my napkin. If there had been any trouble, Sorgrad had the wit to keep out of it and send word to me. If worst had come to worst, Reza knew where we were lodging; he was a bright lad.

A maid knocked and opened the door of our private parlor, bobbing a curtsey. "Beg pardon, but there are two gentlemen to see you." She covered her breath of hesitation over the word gentlemen with creditable aplomb.

"Fair festival to you." 'Gren breezed cheerily in while Sorgrad swept the maidservant a courteous bow and sent her on her way with a silver penny to tuck into her bodice.

He was dressed in willow green today, another expensively tailored display of understated elegance.

"Good morning." Usara's nod mixed welcome with a nicely calculated hint of his rank in relation to theirs.

"It will be when I've eaten," 'Gren took a seat and reached for the last soft roll. "My throat's full of cobwebs." Doubtless wakeful until nigh on the last chime of the night, he looked remarkably lively, washed and brushed in clean linen and plain leather.

Sorgrad settled himself on the window seat, speaking without preamble. "So, who's this, Livak?"

"Usara?" I spread an inviting hand.

"I'm here to represent the Archmage's interests." The wizard drank small beer with an expressionless face. "I am a mage with a principal talent over the earth beneath us and skills with the other elements supporting it. I have the honor to be pupil to Planir the Black."

"Pupil? Cloak carrier, bag man, something like that?" Sorgrad's skepticism was a shade the polite side of insulting.

"I have been privy to the Archmage's councils for some years." Usara looked down his nose with an air of condescension.

"Not much experience of the world beyond your halls and courts then?" Sorgrad tilted his head on one side.

"If you lot were hounds, I'd expect to wait around while you all sniffed around and cocked a leg on the fence posts," I commented idly. "Since you're not, could we just get on?"

Sorgrad and 'Gren laughed and after a moment Usara's severe countenance lightened with a rather sheepish grin.

"You always give peasants something to look at while you're busy with your other hand, don't you?" I pulled my gaudy ring out and waved it at Sorgrad. "Planir keeps everyone trying to follow his fancy footwork while Usara here does the business, no one any the wiser."

The brothers looked at the mage with the first faint stirring of respect.

"That's probably about right," Usara nodded, neck less stiff.

"So now we can all be friends. Are you two going to help out or not?" I demanded briskly.

'Gren looked at Sorgrad, who swung his highly polished boots up into the window seat. "I think we might come along if you're going to the Great Forest for a while. Even Niello had heard talk about the Draximal pay-chest and he barely listens to anything beyond people admiring his wonderful performances."

"And if your retainer that keeps you in this kind of style, we could just about suffer it along with you." 'Gren reached for a plump bottled cherry, dripping juice staining the snowy cloth.

"Good." I saw a degree of relief on Usara's face that reminded me the wizard wasn't stupid. Good, indeed; if he knew his own limitations, he'd be less likely to drop us all in some privy pit.

A clangor of bells outside was echoed within by an elegant silver timepiece on the mantel. The narrow pointer halted on its progress down the engraved scale, newly turned for the longer days after Equinox. A costly piece, I noted absently, separate faces for every season, not just different scales on the same one.

"Third chime of the morning?" 'Gren looked up from the cherries with dismay.

"Is there some problem?" Caught unawares, Usara betrayed some consternation.

"Second day of a fair is always the horse races."

'Gren grabbed his cloak. "If I'm going to turn some coin, I need to see the beasts showing their paces."

Usara frowned. "Isn't that a waste of time? Surely we should—"

"Horse racing is never a waste of time, as far as 'Gren's concerned." I caught Usara's attention with a stern look. "I don't know how you wizards do things, but when we work together, we all make time for each other's priorities."

"You go on," Sorgrad spoke up from the window seat. "Me and Livak need to talk."

I dismissed Usara with a gesture. "Go with him. We'll catch you up."

'Gren was waiting impatiently by the stairs, so after a last, faintly suspicious look at me, the wizard found his fur-trimmed cloak and followed.

"Do you think they can keep out of trouble, the pair of them?" I wondered aloud.

"If we don't give them too long." Sorgrad came to join me at the table. "So, where's this book of yours?"

I went to my bedchamber and took the closely wrapped bundle from the bottom of my traveling bag. Laying it on the table, careful to avoid any spills, I untied the silken cord securing the layers of linen. Sorgrad ran a delicate finger over the embossed leather covering the boards of the cover, the original creamy hide yellowed by time. I opened the book carefully, using fingertips to turn the pages, their edges dark with use and age. The neat script was faded and brown but the illustrations down each margin and bordering top and bottom were bright and vibrant with color, even hints of gold leaf defying nigh on twenty-five generations. Animal heads peered from precise leaves and hedgerows, birds soared above delicate vistas and small figures worked diligently at their trades in little oval panels.

"It's a beautiful thing," remarked Sorgrad absently. He peered at the sweeping script and frowned. "Cursed hard to read though, even if it wasn't so faded. You want Charoleia for this; she's the best I know for the Old High Tormalin."

I slid a sheet of parchment over the tablecloth, which bore Charoleia's distinctive Lescari hand in new, black ink. "That's why we came by way of Relshaz. I wanted a second opinion, given the scholars were apt to bicker over who had the right of it."

Sorgrad laughed. "What about these wizards? They're supposed to have powers over all the elements. Couldn't they do anything to bring up the writing more clearly?"

"According to Casuel, he had far more important things to do, beyond telling me the ink had faded because it was made with oak gall and iron, that is."

Sorgrad looked up at the sarcasm in my tone. "He sounds like a real prize."

I didn't want to discuss Casuel. "Can you read any of this?" I turned the pages carefully to a leaf decorated with a mountain peak, the angular script below a harsh contrast to the smooth regularity of the Tormalin.

Sorgrad bent over it. "I can't read it all but I can make out enough to recognize the tale. It's the saga of Misaen and the wyrms. I can tell you the version I know."

"I want to read that version." I tapped the book. "The Tormalin songs in there differ quite a lot from the ones I learned as a child. Curiosity gets Amit into the Empress's bedchamber all the same but he doesn't end up hanged, he makes himself invisible and sneaks out again."

"Can't Planir's wizards do that?" Sorgrad leaned back in his seat. "What's to say that's aetheric magic?"

"That's what Casuel said." I shook my head.

"I presume something besides determination to prove him wrong brought you here?" asked Sorgrad dryly.

"The colonists tell us it was aetheric magic held the Empire together." I turned to the book's preface. "Look here; Nemith the Wily was six generations before Nemith the Last. No one had ever heard of elemental magic, the kind that Planir's wizards use. That only emerged after the Chaos and anyway, if there's magic in the Forest or the Mountain songs, it has to be Artifice, surely? No mage-born from either race has ever come to Hadrumal."

Sorgrad grunted. "If we're coming in with you, what's our next step?" he demanded abruptly.

"I wanted to be sure of you two before I started planning. The first thing to decide is whether we go to the Forest first or the mountains." I knew what I intended but wasn't about to ride roughshod over Sorgrad this early on.

"We start with the Forest, that's obvious," he replied

firmly. "Once the fair ends, there'll be plenty of people going out along the western high road, heading through the
Forest for Solura or back to villages along the edge of the
wildwood. We can hook up with someone who knows
where to find a band of the Folk at this time of year."

"I was thinking of asking a Forest minstrel who's come
in for the fair," I suggested. "For a start, someone like that
might be able to read the songs for us and then, if they
vouch for us, we'll get more cooperation once we're in the
wildwood."

Sorgrad pursed his lips. "Assuming you find someone
with ancient lore, why should they trust you with hidden secrets?"

"How many men won't trust me, if I put my mind to
charming them?" I gazed at him with wide-open eyes.

"Me, for one," he said tartly.

"Apart from you? No, it's a good question. I was thinking
it might be easier if I had some lore to trade." The best way
to get Sorgrad to do what I want is to show him a logical
reason. "Isn't it better to try the uplands first? You're Mountain blood so anyone with something to tell will be more
likely to speak to you. We take what we learn down to the
Forest after that." I tried to read his mood; Sorgrad's one of
the few people who ever takes my coin over a game of
Raven.

"You can play that rune reversed," countered Sorgrad.
"You're Forest blood, that's your introduction to the Folk."

"Half-blood," I reminded him, "born and raised outside
the Forest as well. I barely even speak the tongue." Besides,
I had just about made up my mind that the benefits of success to Ryshad and me outweighed the hazards of claiming
kinship with my long lost father but I still wasn't about to
risk it, if I could find another way of hitting my mark.
"You're full blood and Mountain bred and we can reach the
mountains sooner than the wildwoods, if we go north from
here."

Sorgrad looked at me for a long moment, his bright blue

eyes as unrevealing as the surface of a sunlit lake. He took a stick of charcoal in a silver holder from a pocket and uncapped it, turning Charoleia's parchment over. "Yes, the mountains are closer to the north, but do you want to walk into endless rows over mining rights and grazing? You've got Wrede over here, Tanoker, Dunsel and then Grynth." He sketched lightly as he spoke. "When were you last up this way? Not since that business with Cordainer? A lot's happened since to leave ill feeling brewing on all sides, ready to bubble right up into trouble. The lowlanders are pushing farther into the foothills each season, with wool prices going so high in the south. The smithing guilds from Wrede arc taking over any mine they can claim a sniff of a title to and sinking new shafts all over. If the locals object, the liverymen hire ruffians out of the gutters to break heads and shut mouths."

"That's what working for wizards does for you," I muttered, annoyed. "Messing around with quests and mysteries, you lose track of what's really important. How bad is it?"

Sorgrad shrugged. "Worse than any time in the last ten years, maybe fifteen. There's always been bad dealing up that way, on both sides. Add in the old rows over who exactly owns what in the Ferring Gap and the usual quarrels over just where Mandarkin territory starts and ends. I wouldn't travel up there without hired swords at my back. Any Mountain Man up there will most likely throw rocks at you before you can ask the way to the nearest well."

I looked doubtfully at his precise map. "Are we going to have to go right over to the east? I know the Gidestans aim to keep things peaceable but it's a cursed long hike on lousy roads. And it'll take us just about as far from the Forest as it's possible to get!"

"We should try the mountains between Solura and Mandarkin." Sorgrad drew in the westerly road and the edge of the Great Forest. "The Solurans leave the Mountain Men alone, keeping them sweet so any Mandarkin thrust south runs backward off a cliff edge, helped along by an axe. West of the Ferring Gap, the Mountain Men keep pretty much to themselves. If anyone has old lore, they'll be your best bet. Anyatimm in Gidesta have pretty much abandoned the old ways, marrying out and settling in the villages with the low-landers."

I looked at the map and then up at Sorgrad. It was un-usual to hear him using the Mountain name for his people, Anyatimm. Besides teaching me Mountain script and a few words like the ones for "horse," "gate" and "sunset," so we could pass messages between ourselves, he'd never shown any link to his origins. "So where exactly do you two come from? I don't recall you ever saying."

"That's not important." He tapped the map. "Look at the lay of the land. We go to the Forest first, find out what we can and head over into the fringes of Solura. We can avoid the Gap completely if we make our way up the Pasfall and reach the sokes, the valleys that is, that way." He looked up. "It was Soluran mystics healed Halice's leg, wasn't it, with lots of mumbling and incense?"

"Planir's sent his own men to make inquiries there," I said absently. "It's a cursed long way around, 'Grad. It'll take half the season."

"How long could a run-in between lowlanders and east-erlings delay us?" Sorgrad demanded.

"That's hard country," I said doubtfully. "I've heard sto-ries and they can't all be fireside fantasies."

"Another reason why we should go to the Forest first and wait for better weather. Spring down here can still be winter in the uplands." Sorgrad had the air of a man laying the winning rune in a spread.

Make a living out of gambling and you learn when to lay your pieces and when to hold them in your hand. I still wanted to take the mountains first, reckoning Sorgrad and Sorgren's blood and breeding were better bones for a win-ning hand than my uncertain birth. Perhaps we should trust to luck; every rune falls with two faces uppermost, after all. "Why don't I take a turn around the taverns and see if I can

get a promising tune out of some minstrel. You and 'Gren
see if you can find anyone who might let us travel north
with them. When we know what our options are, we can decide."

"Good enough," Sorgrad nodded. "Now what about this
wizard of yours? You don't think we might do better without him?" He looked sideways at me. "He'd be easy enough
to lose with the city so full for the festival. Won't he be
passing any information straight to his Archmage? You'll
get more value for any learning if you keep it to yourself,
until you know who it's worth most to."

"Messire D'Olbriot made the deal with Planir." I
shrugged. "He agreed a wizard should come to send any
news back straightaway. If we find aetheric magic, Messire
wants it fast enough to be some use if Elietimm boats turn
up now the winter storms are over. Getting letters back,
even by courier, would take half a season. Pay a merchant
to carry it, he'll like as not forget it; hire a messenger and
he'll either get lost or hit on the head for his satchel. No,
Planir knows he's beholden to D'Olbriot on this and D'Olbriot knows he's beholden to me."

Sorgrad was patently curious. "So what do you get out of
this?"

"You know that one deal, the one that sets you up for
life?" I drew a teasing breath. "This could be it, 'Grad, this
could just be it."

Sorgrad laughed. "Like Cordainer's offer? Like I don't
know how many other schemes Charoleia's suggested over
the years? You don't take lead coin any more than I do!"

"We'll just have to wait and see, won't we?" I laughed.
"There's got to be profit to be made from holding a marker
with a Tormalin prince's name on it."

Sorgrad nodded and I was satisfied. As long as he
thought I was just playing a speculation, I wouldn't have to
explain myself. Time enough for that when I claimed my
pay-off from Messire. How best to make sure that debt
would be a sizeable one was my current concern. "Let's not

waste daylight." I stood up. "I'll see you all back here at noon?"

"As long as 'Gren and that wizard haven't landed themselves in too much trouble," grinned Sorgrad. "No, this is a bit too rich for 'Gren's blood. We'll meet at the Swan in the Moon."

I stifled a qualm as I followed him down the stairs. 'Gren could take care of himself and if Usara made a misstep Planir could bail him out.

I decided to start with the market square. There was no indication of last night's bounty from the guilds now; all had been swept clean and men and women waited in long patient lines. The women were chatting, swapping opinions on erstwhile employers and comparing rates of pay; housemaids with their mops, weavers with the distaff no one uses these days if there's the chance of a spinning wheel, dairymaids whose stools at least offered a seat to save their legs. Fresh-faced girls with hopeful smiles stood next to others with harder faces and wary eyes, those who'd made a bad bargain for their fastening penny the year before. The men weren't talking so freely, eyeing up potential competition. Carters stood with a twist of whipcord pinned to their jerkins, grooms carried a hay wisp, shepherds had wool tucked in buttonholes and hatbands, a tuft of brindled hair for cowmen.

I made my way to the Swan in the Moon, wondering about enlisting Niello's aid. Minstrels would be contacting him, looking for a hire to take them east across the Old Empire, traveling through the spring and summer seasons. Then it would be back to Col to squander their earnings at the autumn fair, one last celebration before heading back to the Forest with the songs and little luxuries they had gathered. I'd heard the same hopeful patter from three such on the road from Relshaz, all eager for a patron to pay their way but unable to shed light on my tantalizing song book.

I looked idly at the maidservants waiting for some offer of a fastening penny and, with luck, an advance on their wages for some festival fun. The older housemaids were about my own age, hopefully clutching their feather dusters. Who knows, if my mother had let me prove my independence by taking a stand at the summer fair of my fifteenth year, it is just about possible I might still be in Vanam. I could have been diligently saving my wages for linen and plate, sewing neat seams for a well-filled dowry chest, waiting for some tradesman at the servants' door to woo me away to a respectable match that even my grandmother couldn't scorn.

I laughed out loud. Only if I hadn't taken to my heels with some glib charmer like Niello, after a few seasons polishing up fire irons and blackleading grates had driven me demented with boredom. I stuck my head through the gate of the courtyard and realized none of the masqueraders were around; doubtless all still abed and likely to be so for a good while. I'd come back later.

Music drew me into the tap room of the Fleet Hound but all I found was an impromptu gathering of local lads doing their best to impress their sweethearts. They were all fresh-faced girls; hair modestly braided and skirts decorously hiding the tops of their boots. One looked askance at my breeches and I grinned at her. The winter past had cured me of any lingering notion Drianon ever meant me for domesticity.

I had tried my best in Ryshad's Zyoutessela home. I'd smiled politely at his mother, taken an interest in the doings of her sewing circle and changed the subject every time she mentioned the neighbors whose daughter would be laying a wedding plait on Drianon's altar come Solstice. I had even spent more time in skirts than in breeches for the first time since I'd left home, until desperation had driven me out to hang around the D'Olbriot citadel in hopes of seeing Ryshad and curiosity had lead me to the vast, echoing library, the shelves of books reaching so high they had their own ladders attached.

At least my own mother had never smothered me with

the suffocating, uncritical affection of Mistress Tathel. She'd taught me to read and reckon, encouraged me to think for myself, to acquire skills to offset the disadvantage of my birth, though she'd been thinking more of clerking rather than honing my talents with a bag full of runes. I'd grown fond enough of Ryshad's mother but she reminded me of the white-banded eaves-birds I could see building nests under the gable of the inns that ringed the square. They always return to the spot they'd used the year before and the year before that. My sympathies lay with the ring-necked hawk I could see scanning the roadside, ready to stoop on any prey flushed out by a passing wagon, taking whatever Talagrin sent it.

A wain trundled past, rumbling over the cobbles, leather creaking as the harness horse strained against his collar. I hadn't been the only squeaky wheel on the wagon that winter. Ryshad soon realized there would be no going back to his father's trade. His brothers were doing well; an ordinance the previous year banning wooden porches as a fire hazard had given them all the work they could wish for, and they adorned all the fashionable houses with smart stone pilasters and canopies. But now that work had largely dried up, three stonemasons in the family business was as much as the trade would bear. His elder brothers made it quite clear.

I hadn't taken to Hansey or Ridner and the feeling had been mutual. Both expected demure obedience and home-embroidered linen from decent girls. Each was courting a tedious lass with wooing so lackluster any woman with a pennyweight of spirit would have been looking for a better offer. I'd said as much one evening, patronized beyond endurance.

I sighed, missing Ryshad, his ready wits, his certainty, his strong arms around me and the warmth of his loving. What we needed was some way of keeping ourselves in coin that we could both accept. His sense of honor wouldn't stand for living off the profits I could turn with a rune and I couldn't settle with him taking up some tedious trade, living in a neat little row house three streets from his mother and dining with the family every market-day evening.

A troop of dancers came out of the Bag of Nails. I waved to one. "What musicians have you got playing for you? I'm looking for a Forest minstrel."

The girl shrugged. "Keep looking then. All we have are a couple of halfwits from Peorle." She went on her way, a dancer's grace in her steps for all her sensible shoes and warm cape.

Winter Solstice had brought Martel, Ryshad's next eldest brother, to Zyoutessela. Home from his law studies in Toremal, he'd had a curvaceous masquerade dancer on his arm wearing less in the depths of winter than Mistress Tathel did at the height of the southern summer. Poor Mistress Tathel had desperately sought to be welcoming, imperfectly concealing her hopes that this lass's lustrous locks would stay uncropped. Hansey and Ridner were torn between disapproval and envy and under the cover of the ensuing uproar Ryshad and I had found time to examine our prospects for the new year upon us.

D'Olbriot had offered Ryshad the title of chosen man, an undeniable honor. A sworn man making the step to chosen man and then rendering sound service could justifiably hope for a later commission to watch over D'Olbriot lands and tenants in some city or province. A stewardship, its stipend, independence to live our lives as we chose; it sounded promising. Ryshad saw it as the soundest foundation for our life together but I wasn't about to sit on my hands for the next fifteen years waiting for that apple to fall in my lap. We needed some way of putting Messire D'Olbriot so deep in our debt that his gratitude favored Ryshad at once.

What were the patron's pressing concerns? Firstly, securing the Archmage's assistance without being obligated to Hadrumal. Secondly, ensuring the House of D'Olbriot retained its position as the sole conduit of influence with the

colony of Kel Ar'Ayen, or Kellarin as more modern inflex-
ions had it. Which is why I was here in Selerima working
on the former while Ryshad was busy in the temporary
service of Messire's nephew Camarl, securing the latter. I
still missed him though. Had I talked myself into a pointless
quest when I might just as well have stayed at his side? I
heaved a sigh.

No. If you don't throw the runes, you can't win the wager. What did 'Gren say about a seemingly impossible task?
"You eat an elk one bite at a time," usually adding, "and you
start with its balls if it's fighting back."

Selerima, Western Ensaimin,
Second Day of the Spring Fair, Afternoon

"I hardly think you are in a position to be making demands!" Eirys folded her arms and her indignation echoed
around the bare white walls of the little room.

"I don't think I should have to be asking," Jeirran replied
icily. He emptied his purse onto a dresser with chipped
paint and a crooked hanging door. "A wife shouldn't need
reminding of her duties in bed or out of it."

Eirys sniffed crossly. "If you had any consideration,
you'd think of the consequences. What if I were to catch
down here, in this rancid air? The babe would probably slip
before we were halfway home." She ran an unconscious
hand over her slim waist.

"Aren't you making a rather big assumption?" Jeirran
turned with a sneer. "It's been the best part of half a year
since we were shackled over Misaen's anvil. When's
Maewelin going to give you sons to work your land with
me? Perhaps you should try and find a holy place if these
profane lowlanders have such a thing, ask for her blessing."

"Perhaps she's waiting until you've proved yourself able

to provide for me," Eirys retorted acidly. "All your great plans have come to naught so far. All you've managed is disgracing my brother by getting yourselves locked up. I don't know what Mother will say!"

"She won't say a thing because you won't tell her." Jeirran raised a warning hand and Eirys took a hurried step to put the narrow bedstead between them.

"She'll ask how we prospered," she insisted nervously. "When we've been away so long, when you promised—" She fell silent as Jeirran took a pace forward.

"You go out shopping today," he forced a smile. "Buy yourself a couple of nice dress lengths, some of the fripperies and fancies. Get your mother some Caladhrian lace, that should please her." His tone hardened a little as he filled a small pouch with copper coin. "Find something that'll have her well enough satisfied to keep her nose out of my business." He tossed the purse onto the bed.

Eirys nodded, a smile brightening her face as she tied the purse at her waist. She picked up a warm embroidered shawl from the tattered counterpane, tucking it around her as she made for the door. Jeirran caught her with a powerful hand. "You needn't hurry, sweetest." He brushed a wisp of golden hair from her cheek and kissed her, lightly at first, then with more force, an insistent hand at the back of her head.

"It's already late." Eirys pushed ineffectually at his broad chest and twisted her face away coquettishly. "The best goods are to be had in the mornings—"

"And the best bargains are to be had in the evenings." Jeirran's forceful embrace startled a faint exclamation from Eirys but she yielded to his kisses readily enough. Jeirran's murmurs of satisfaction were answered by her stifled giggles, his breath coming faster and one hand untucking the blouse from her waistband before an abrupt knock startled them both.

"Tidy yourself up," Jeirran snapped, adjusting the set of his trews. "Who is it?"

"Us," came the tart reply through the rough wooden door. Jeirran untied the latchstring to let Keisyl and Teiriol enter. Teiriol gave Eirys a sharp look seeing the high color in her face but she shook her head minutely, silent appeal in her cornflower eyes.

"What have you two been doing this morning?" asked Jeirran with a creditable assumption of ease. "The maid said you'd gone out at first light."

"We thought we'd try our luck at the races," Keisyl shot Jeirran a meaningful glare. "See if we could find another way to turn up some profit on this trip."

"You should have woken me. What's the horseflesh like down here?" Jeirran demanded with genuine interest.

"Bigger," answered Teiriol with a bark of laughter. "Faster, sleeker, they race like dogs after a hare."

"Lovely to watch but no earthly good on a steep track or for packing more than Eirys' weight." Admiration gave the lie to Keisyl's contempt.

"You must have got their measure easily enough." Jeirran looked hopefully at them both.

"After handling hill ponies all my life?" Keisyl snorted. "I could have told you which were the likely winners before the grooms got them saddled—"

"—but none of the touts would take our coin," Teiriol burst out. "Apparently they'd heard about the likes of us. Mountain folk aren't to be trusted, so they tell us!"

"You're saying they wouldn't even hold your stake?" Confusion drove the optimism from Jeirran's eyes and a dark scowl settled on his brow.

"Not one of them," confirmed Keisyl with cold anger. "No explanation, no apology, just thinly veiled hints that we were somehow going to cheat them."

"I don't understand these people," Jeirran shook his head in wonder. "How can they be so wrapped up in their own conceits?"

"It's because there are so many of them, just as we heard on the way down here." Teiriol crossed the little room in two paces and peered down out of the clouded and ill-fitting window. "Look at them, busy as beetles in a muckheap. They have their own kind to buy from and sell to and that's all they need. Drefial was right. If two of them cut each other's throats over a deal, ten more step up to take advantage before the blood stops flowing—"

"All right, Teir, enough." Keisyl nodded sourly.

"I need some fresh air." Jeirran heaved a sigh "Keisyl, you take Eirys shopping. Teiriol and me will see if we can find someone from these all powerful guilds willing to give us the nod today."

Keisyl looked doubtfully at Jeirran. "Shouldn't I come with you?"

"It's your turn to chaperone Eirys," protested Teiriol. "I did spend all yesterday looking at beads and buttons," he explained with an apologetic glance at his sister.

Eirys looked uncertainly at the men. "I could just stay here."

"No, come on," Keisyl offered her his arm. "We've got to make sure you're looked after."

Eirys gave Jeirran a quick peck on the cheek. "See you later, my love." Before he could respond she was out of the door, her stout leather boots echoing on the bare wood of the stairs.

"I'll bring her back at sunset," Keisyl called back over his shoulder.

"We'll give them a few moments to get clear and then we can be off," said Jeirran quietly to Teiriol.

"What's the point of trailing around after more guildsmen, cap in hand and begging their indulgence?" demanded Teiriol. "I've had enough of that, thanks all the same."

"That was just to keep Eirys quiet," said Jeirran scornfully, watching from the window to see his wife reach street level. "You don't suppose everyone pays up for these trade tokens do you? No lowlander's more honest than a peddler's dog, if they think they can get away with it. There'll be someone willing to save the cost of a guildsman's bribe by buying direct from us."

"You could be right, at that." Teiriol nodded slowly. "So where do we start looking?"

"Degran Lackhand and his cronies always want a cockfight, don't they?" Jeirran slung his cloak over one shoulder. "You were saying you'd like to see a real cock-pit for a change, birds reared for sport instead of the dunghill. There was talk yesterday in the tap room about a bull-baiting."

"No wonder you didn't want Keisyl along. All right Jeirran, I'm your man. I'd like to see a baiting," said Teiriol avidly.

"I knew I could rely on you." Jeirran slapped the youth on the shoulder in a show of good fellowship but contempt shadowed his eyes as he followed him down the narrow stair.

"So where do we go?" Teiriol halted on the step, turning to look expectantly at Jeirran.

"This way." Jeirran walked around a corner to a wooden barn with an array of discarded horseshoes nailed on its wall. "I thought we'd ask in here."

A wiry man, clothes dusty with chaff, was holding the head of a fretful pony while a well-built girl carefully picked inside a hoof resting in the lap of her calico apron.

"Good day," the man said cordially. "Your mules are keeping well. Are you here to check on them or maybe looking for a day's hire? We've two well-rested saddle horses ready for work."

"No." Jeirran waved a dismissive hand. "We want to know where to go for the bull-baiting."

"All that goes on down by the Southgate. The baiting will be at the slaughter yards and the best bird-pit is at the Hooded Crow, just by the gate-house," answered the horse trader readily enough. "Fair festival to you," he called out but Jeirran and Teiriol had already turned their backs on him. The girl looked up to share a resigned glance with her father.

Jeirran strode out with a confident step. Teiriol followed rather more slowly, looking all around at the gaudy effigies set above the shopfronts.

"I can understand a cobbler hanging out a boot," he said, amused by a vast, gaudily stenciled and improbably high-heeled offering, "but what under the sun is that supposed to tell anyone?" He pointed out a brazen eagle frozen in mid-stoop.

"Who cares," said Jeirran, eyes fixed on the middle distance. He kept up the same brisk pace all the way down through the city, unwavering even when a clash of shoulders sent some passer-by stumbling into the gutter with an outraged oath. Neither was showing any sign of exertion when Jeirran finally halted. They looked up at the forbidding redstone bulk of the gate to the southern road. It loomed over the ramshackle houses run up against the city walls on either side, a vast three-story affair, parapets and embrasures alert in all directions, the gates below of black and ancient wood bound with straps and bolts of hammered iron. In the gloomy maw of the entrance, the sharp teeth of a portcullis showed like a hound's warning snarl. An ill-defined space opened before it, patches of cobbles here and there, a crumbling wall all that remained of a fallen building, all useful bricks looted. From the empty niches still visible, it looked to have once been a shrine.

The bustle of the city was drowned out by a rising discord of bloodlust. Jeirran and Teiriol tried in vain to see past taller men as the commotion rose to a new pitch of excitement. Sharp yelps rose above vicious growls and the lower bellows of an enraged bull. The last agonized roar of the tormented animal was lost beneath a great cheer and the comparative silence fell, broken only by the frantic whimpering of an injured dog. The men drifted away in small groups, exchanging opinions, settling wagers, heading for ale at the rough and ready taverns doing a brisk trade all around the long rank-smelling lines of slaughtering sheds.

"We missed it," lamented Teiriol, crestfallen.

A grim-faced man was unbuckling the studded collar of a brindled mastiff. The dog struggled vainly to rise, hind legs limp and useless in the foul mire of blood and dung. Its owner rubbed a roughly tender hand over its ears before lifting its muzzle. The dog's eyes were trusting and warm, the man's red and squinting as he slit its throat with one swift stroke of his belt-knife and stepped back from its final throes.

"Good day to you," said Jeirran, raising his voice above the frenzied snarls of the rest of the pack, now ripping into gory hunks of their late adversary. "Will there be another baiting today?"

The man looked up, brutish face doleful. "No, not today, well, not with my dogs, anyway." He looked over at the powerfully built animals, tan, black and brindled, tearing into their meat, and his expression lightened a little. "Artel! Show them the lash or you're going to lose a hand. Talagrin's teeth, don't you know anything?"

He moved rapidly to snatch a dog whip from a nervous-looking lad who was only too happy to step back from the insistent demands of the mastiffs. The dogs crowded around their master, bloodied all over their blunt faces and down to their massive shoulders.

"Those are impressive hounds," commented Teiriol, tucking his hands through his belt. One of the mastiffs caught his eye and rumbled menacingly deep in its throat.

"Which drinking house is the Crow?" Jeirran asked.

"Yonder," the lad replied. "I could show you, if you like—" He looked uncertainly at his master.

"You go on." The man brought an errant dog back with a sharp whistle and growled a command that had all the heavily jowled heads looking up obediently.

"Come on," said the boy Artel. He led them toward a tav-

ern with an open frontage of rough-sawn deal, none too recently painted over with pitch. Pushing the men drinking
idly around the threshold, he left Jeirran and Teiriol to pick
their own way to the counter past broken stools and tables,
the sawdust on the earthen floor many days old and
clumped with spills of beer and blood.

"Two, here," Jeirran raised a hand to an overworked tap-
ster by the row of casks behind the trestle. "We were told
this was the place for a cockfight?"

A leather flagon and two horn beakers were shoved toward him. "Out the back, that's three copper." The man
didn't even look at Jeirran's face, taking his coin and turning to the next thirsty customer.

"Come on," Teiriol tried to keep from slopping the ale
down his shirt as he was jostled. "We should see some sport
here, shouldn't we?"

The rear door opened onto a deafening scene of heated
anticipation, shouted conversation and a powerful smell of
ale, sweat and chicken coops. Men and women crowded
around the broad wooden steps rising all around the sunken
round of the cock-pit, eyes bright. Newcomers waited for
their chance at a place as those who'd already cheered
themselves hoarse went in search of ale or wine.

Jeirran leaned forward to hiss insistently in Teiriol's ear.
"We've got to sell those pelts or your mother will be flaying
the both of us."

The thrill in Teiriol's eyes dimmed a little and he sipped
his ale. "This isn't half bad," he said with some surprise.

"So you can addle your wits till you can't tell a cock
from a hen," Jeirran told him scornfully, drinking deep from
his own cup nevertheless. "The innkeeper takes a margin on
the betting, I'll warrant."

"Shall we have a wager?" Teiriol stepped forward eagerly as two birds were being readied for the pit. Jeirran
pushed his way through to the rail. A strutting cock with
scarred wattles and glossy copper plumage was already

coming up to scratch while its smaller speckled opponent was still having brightly polished spurs fixed to its scaly legs.

Jeirran smoothed a reluctant hand over his beard. "Better not. If we lose any more money, Eirys'll save your mother the bother and skin us herself!"

Teiriol gave Jeirran a sharp look but the two birds were released to fly at each other in a flurry of dust and feathers. Boastful crowing shrilled above the rising murmur of the onlookers and the fight was joined. The speckled bird made up for its lack of size with startling ferocity, launching itself upward, wings flapping and spurs raking forward at its opponent's head and eyes. The bigger cock was driven backward, its handler hurriedly getting clear, but it crowed defiantly before charging back into the fray, wings wide and baiting as it clawed and pecked. The little cock, feathers ruffed around its neck, moved nimbly to avoid the copper cock's vicious beak. It darted in to stab its head forward and scatter orange feathers beaded with scarlet drops of blood onto the raked sand. Not so deft on its feet and heavier in build, the bigger bird was soon on the defensive, vainly trying to protect itself from increasingly frenzied assaults.

Jeirran looked on as the smaller cock, comb proud and defiant, left its opponent crestfallen and dragging one crippled wing in the scuffed and bloodstained circle. People laughed as it went strutting and crowing its triumph before its handler could retrieve it. The defeated bird was carefully examined before being swathed in a soft cloth bag and taken away by its scowling owner.

"That speckle won't amount to much if it doesn't learn to go in for the kill," Jeirran observed to Teiriol.

"There wasn't much blood," complained Teiriol, dissatisfied. Movement on the far side caught his eye. "Look there, Jeir, those two are Mountain blood or I'm a lowlander. Mother can't say it's only the muddy feet who like this kind of thing, can she?"

"They're dressed like lowlanders." Jeirran frowned.

"They could be easterners, three-parts true blood maybe, from some kin that had a daughter marry out." He stared and got a challenging gaze back from the shorter of the two.

"I'd rather deal with our own, even with mixed blood," said Teiriol urgently. "Would they take our pelts?"

"Depends what they're trading for," Jeirran replied slowly.

"Where did they go?" Teiriol looked around but the moment had passed. The two were gone.

"No matter." Jeirran surveyed the room. His eyes returned to a handful of men on cushioned chairs set against the far wall. A small but respectful distance held steady between them and the close-packed crowd. Jeirran ignored the noisy contest beneath him as a couple of newcomers spoke to one of the seated men, handing over coin to receive a folded and sealed parchment, departing without so much as a glance in the direction of the cock-pit. "We want to fall into conversation over that way." Jeirran nodded his head meaningfully.

He stepped back from the rail and Teiriol reluctantly followed him, looking backward as he did so. Jeirran stopped abruptly and Teiriol trod heavily on his heels. "What is it?"

"See that fat son of his grandfather over there?" Jeirran's lip curled. "That's the pig's pizzle who took up me and Keisyl at the fairground yesterday."

Teiriol looked at the man whose back was turned toward them. "And the others?"

Jeirran looked casually around before nodding slowly. "Yes, they're all here, wasting our coin on birds better off in the pot."

Teiriol laid a warning hand on Jeirran's arm. "If we're going to replace that coin, we need to sell those pelts, for all that we owe those scum a debt," he pointed out reluctantly.

"True enough," Jeirran turned his attention again to the hard-faced men sitting against the far wall and then to the heavy-set entourage drinking their ale with watchful faces by the way out. "Let's see what that cloak carrier has to say for himself."

The man in question, burly arms folded over a substantial gut, looked at the two Mountain Men with an unspoken question as they halted in front of him.

"Will you share a drink with us?" Jeirran offered his flagon. The man wordlessly held out a battered pewter tankard and Jeirran poured a generous measure. "Where might we find an honest businessman hereabouts?"

The big man looked contemptuously down at the pair of them.

"A man who prefers to deal direct, none of this nonsense over guild considerations and fair fees," Jeirran explained genially. "We don't do things that way in the uplands, you see."

"What's your business?" Interest sparked in the man's hard eyes.

"Furs, pelts, better than half the stock on the stalls at the fair," Jeirran raised his chin in unconscious defiance.

"Talk to Harquas, that gentleman."

A heavy-set, silver-haired man with a crooked nose and sharp eyes turned his head toward them. "You want me for something?"

Jeirran stepped forward boldly, Teiriol rather more hesitant at his shoulder. "Good day to you. Your colleague suggests that you might be interested in mountain pelts."

"I might, at that." The man Harquas relaxed but his eyes were acute beneath bushy brows. He wore slate gray broadcloth, conservatively cut, bulk suggesting muscles relaxing into fat as he left enforcement of his dealings to younger men. "Are you looking for a regular trade or a one-off deal?"

"For the moment, just the one transaction," replied Jeirran cautiously.

Harquas pursed narrow lips thoughtfully. "You'd be the two Mountain Men I've heard tell of, then, trying to sell

your goods at the fair without paying your dues?" He nodded to someone.

"Where we come from, men only take a profit from work
they've had a share in," Jeirran said stiffly.

A mirthless smile curved Harquas' bloodless mouth. He
turned his head slightly as a potman came and whispered in
his ear. "Excuse me." Harquas leaned sideways in his chair
to the man next to him, another thick-set type missing the
forefinger on his near side hand and with a wicked scar running the length of his jawbone, as if some attempt to cut
his throat had come in just a little too high. Harquas hid
his words behind a raised hand. Jeirran folded his arms
with a cold air of confidence. Teiriol's attempt to copy this
was rather less successful, as he realized he now had three
villainous-looking men breathing heavily down his neck,
all topping him by more than head and shoulders.

Harquas nodded as his companion murmured something,
shooting Jeirran a suspicious glance. "Well, friend," Harquas smiled at Jeirran with all the warmth of a pig on a
butcher's hook. "I'm in something of a fix here. You seem
like an honest man to me but Lehrer tells me you got taken
up by the Southgate Watch at the fair. I can see for myself
that Vigo and a couple of other nailers have been wasting
their coin on these cocks since just after midday. If I were a
suspicious man, I could think you getting taken up to the assize were just a ploy. Suppose I strike a deal with you, am I
going to find guildsmen kicking in the door to my ware-
house and you identifying the furs you sold me to some
nosy Justiciar?"

The three men at Teiriol's rear stirred with a creak of
leather and the soft rasp of metal as one rubbed at a brass-
knuckled glove.

"If that's what you think, we won't waste any more of
your time." Jeirran was unmoved. "There'll be other people
I can trade with in a city this size. I'm not interested in your
guilds and your rules and your Watchmen," he continued,

not concealing his contempt. "I just want to sell my furs for a decent price and get back to my own affairs in the uplands."

Harquas raised an eyebrow. "That's very plain talk for a man outnumbered and out of his way. Am I supposed to be impressed?"

"I don't give a donkey's hangdown if you're impressed or not." Jeirran shrugged. "Are you buying?"

Harquas exchanged a glance with his neighbor, who in turn looked beyond Jeirran for some signal. Whatever he saw satisfied Lehrer, his scarred face nodding to Harquas.

"If you're prepared to do something to establish your good faith, I'll buy from you," said Harquas slowly. "If some misfortune lands on Vigo and his little gang, then I can be sure they're not nosing around my business, do you see? If you were to be that mishap, then I'd know you weren't hand in glove with them, wouldn't I?"

"Why should we do your dirty work for you?" Jeirran ignored the rumble of annoyance behind him.

"Do you want to sell your furs or not?" inquired Harquas with silky menace.

"You want us to kill them?" asked Jeirran baldly.

Harquas frowned. "A dead Watchman gets the Justiciary unduly stirred up, in my experience. But they have to accept that every so often a nailer takes on a man just that bit too strong in his drink and gets a beating."

"That's the price of doing business with you?"

Harquas nodded. "Tell me where you're lodging and if I hear the right word I'll send someone to look over your stock at noon tomorrow."

Jeirran shook his head. "We'll meet at the market square, by the fountain." He turned and glared up at the bull-necked man blocking his way.

"Let our friend pass, Teg," said Harquas smoothly. "We'll talk tomorrow, Jeirran."

Teiriol followed Jeirran out of the cock-pit and back to

the rowdy tavern. Jeirran's eyes flickered from side to side until he saw Vigo, the Watchman, plump red face glistening with uncomplicated delight as he cradled a tangle-haired girl on his knee. Her unlaced bodice showed off heavy breasts to any who cared to look while Vigo hitched up her skirts to reveal bare and grubby legs beneath her tattered petticoats.

Jeirran pushed Teiriol into a gloomy corner and shook his head in disgust as the Watchman's hand slid up and around the girl's thigh. "Lowlanders. No more sense of fitness than dogs rutting in the street."

"Never mind that," Teiriol dragged his wide eyes away reluctantly. "How did that Harquas know your name?"

"How do you think?" replied Jeirran scornfully. "He'll have men all over this city, won't he? If he got word of our arrest, he'll have had our names from the assize, maybe even our lodging." He glowered darkly. "If his brutes come near Eirys, I'll gut them, assize or no assize."

"What are we going to do about these Watchmen?" Teiriol looked back at Vigo, whose head was now cradled in the girl's arms, her wriggles feigning pleasure but her face bored.

"I can't see him tupping that whore in full view. They'll want a back alley at very least," said Jeirran thoughtfully.

"We catch him with his trews around his boots?" Teiriol laughed a little nervously.

"Fair recompense for the way he nailed me and Keisyl yesterday," answered Jeirran with cruel satisfaction. "Come on."

Outside, the afternoon light was softening and a handful of wrestling bouts were being contested inside roughly marked-out circles of sand. Teiriol looked toward them regretfully but followed Jeirran obediently to a dark corner behind a gibbet. The wood was blackened with old blood and noisome corpses of rats dangled.

"Watch for him and for the others," Jeirran ordered. They

did not have long to wait. Vigo soon appeared with the whore hanging on his arm, Rif and Neth trailing after with expressions of eager anticipation.

"Are they all going to do her?" Teiriol wondered, startled.

"Like I said, they rut like dogs." Jeirran moved cautiously as the Watchmen headed for the narrow entry between two dilapidated houses. "And they're stupid enough to take their bitch down a blind alley," he added with satisfaction, taking a pair of gloves from his belt and nodding to Teiriol to do the same. "Careful. We don't want to start a fight anywhere we'll be seen."

Teiriol loosened his knife in its sheath as they crossed the open ground but Jeirran shook his head. "We're not looking to kill them. We don't use knives, not unless we have to." He paused to pick up a stave from a broken barrel dumped outside a doorway and peered down the alley. "She's taking them into that stable. We'll give the fat one a few moments to get busy stuffing her. The other two will probably have their tools in their hands by then, so we can drop them before their boss gets himself unknotted." Jeirran's eyes were hard with a savage anticipation. Teiriol ran his own barrel stave through his hands, hefting the wood with a grin.

"Leave your cape here and tie something around your face." Jeirran untucked his shirt and tore a wide strip of linen from the hem, suiting his actions to his words. "All they can claim is Mountain Men did for them, and if anyone comes looking at us we swear blind it was those other two we saw. When we get in, you bar the door."

The alley was not long but gloomy in the double shadow of the city wall and the houses looming on either side. Refuse was piled high, discarded sacks, boxes and household rubbish mingled with old bones, nameless peelings and moldering muck, a fetid ooze seeping along a rough drain scraped into the bare earth. Teiriol and Jeirran moved silently forward, eyes fixed on the stable door dragged ajar on broken hinges. Jeirran brought his barrel stave up and back, nodding to Teiriol, who did the same. They paused, one each side of the doorway, but Vigo's groans of pleasure and the whore's practiced responses were enough to drown any footsteps.

Jeirran rushed inside, Teiriol a pace behind him, kicking the door shut with an ominous thud. Neth turned, face flushed, eager expression changing to startled horror. Jeirran's stave scythed in to catch him under one ear. The impact sent him staggering into Rif, who clutched at him in confusion. Teiriol jumped forward and brought his club into Rif's unprotected flank. Mountain-hardened muscles landed the blow squarely in the man's kidney, forcing a yell of agony from him. Neth was still dazed but Rif threw him off and turned to rush at Teiriol. It was an unwise move. The Mountain Man sent him reeling back with a merciless jab to the gut.

Jeirran swung at Neth again, landing a vicious strike on the outside of his knee. The Watchman went stumbling sideways. Jeirran discarded his club and moved forward, gloved hands hammering face, ribs, gut and groin with a flurry of punishing blows, blood from the gash in his head soon coating the Watchman's shirt and jerkin.

"What the shit—" Vigo had abandoned the whore and was scrambling to his feet. The Mountain Men ignored his impotent curses as he clutched at the breeches hampering his feet.

Rif had a stall to his back now, rocking from foot to foot, clenching his fists. Teiriol sneered at him and feinted with his stave, first to one side, then to the other. Rif was forced back against the splintered wood, painful blows punishing shoulders and thighs. He hunched in a vain attempt to protect himself, spat at Teiriol and snatched for a hanging harness strap. Teiriol brought the age-hardened stave up in a swift move to smash his forearm.

Rif's yell of agony mingled with the crack of bone. His cry was drowned out by Vigo's howl of outrage as he threw himself on Jeirran's back, Neth lying limp and helpless in a mire of blood. The Watchman tried to get his broad hands around the Mountain Man's thick neck but Jeirran was too quick, ducking his chin to his chest and hunching his shoulders. Jeirran stepped forward and sideways in one fluid move, dropping one shoulder and sending the unsuspecting Vigo clean over his head to land him into the slime of the stable drain.

Vigo was gasping at Teiriol's feet, all breath knocked out of him. Teiriol used his boots, heavy leather reinforced with metal and nails going in hard to leave studded prints on Vigo's shirt, his half-laced breeches, stamping on his hands and ankles, ripping open one cheek with a sweeping kick. The Watchman could only roll and twist in the muck, vainly trying to get away from the torment, curling around a blow in the stomach only to have his back arch in the agony of a boot to the base of his spine.

Rif tried vainly to intervene, one arm dangling uselessly. Jeirran dropped him with one iron hard punch to the short ribs and grabbed Teiriol's arm. The younger man's breath was coming quick and harsh through the cloth around his face, his kicks ever harder and more cruel.

"That's enough. You don't want to kill him, just make him useless for work. Didn't your father teach you anything about fighting?"

Teiriol struggled for a reply, gave up, and bent down to spit full in Vigo's face, now a mask of blood and filth.

Jeirran nodded with satisfaction. Rif was hunched on his knees, choking as he struggled for breath. Neth's tears thinned the blood dripping down his broken and oozing nose as he slumped in a corner.

"What about her?" Teiriol gestured at the whore crouched in a terrified huddle of petticoats on a heap of musty hay. Daring warred with distaste in his face and he licked his lips uncertainly.

The girl tried for a smile but could only summon a ghastly grimace, ashen with fear. "You can take your pleasure for free, just don't hurt me," she begged, opening her blouse in a parody of seductiveness, hands trembling.

Jeirran wrinkled his nose. "I wouldn't touch a festering trull like you with a stick of firewood!" He picked up his barrel stave and took a menacing step forward. "Or maybe I'll come and find you, give you some of this, if I find anyone coming after us. You're the only one to have seen, so you're the only one can tell tales. You do and I'll be back to spoil your looks, you hear me?"

The girl whimpered incoherent promises of silence.

"Come on!" Jeirran dragged the stable door open. He shoved Teiriol through then wedged it shut with his stave. Stuffing his stained gloves into a pocket, he put on his cape, securing the front to conceal the blood on his shirt. He looked cautiously out from the mouth of the alley. "We need to get clear and quickly."

Teiriol caught up his own cape, pausing to splash his boots through water gathered where some cobbles had been dug up. "That should show our man Harquas we mean business," he observed with satisfaction. "And I can tell Keisyl I've settled his debts in full."

"You'll say nothing of the kind, not a word to him nor to Eirys," snapped Jeirran. "Anyway, it was hardly a fight to boast of, was it? They call these Watchmen tough? They wouldn't last three days in a mining camp!" His eyes rested briefly on the wrestling matches still being hotly contested. "We leave swiftly but calmly and we don't look back. We came to watch the wrestling, we found nothing to interest us and now we're going back to our lodgings. That's what we tell Eirys and Keis and anyone else who comes asking. Do you understand?"

"Of course," Teiriol couldn't resist one glance over his shoulder as they left the slaughter yards behind them. "So what now?"

"We clean ourselves up before the others return. We eat whatever that thief of a landlady claims is a four-Mark din-

ner and then you and Keisyl take yourselves off for whatever entertainment you fancy. Eirys and I deserve a quiet
evening in, just the two of us," announced Jeirran, eyes
bright with anticipation. "I think it's about time she showed
me some appreciation."

Selerima, Western Ensaimin,
Second Day of the Spring Fair, Evening

The runes finally rolled my way when I reached the
Crackwillow, a tidily kept eating-house on the corner of the
Audit Way. The resonant song of a lute floated out through
an open shutter. Childhood recollection stirred to Forest
rhythms and I pushed open the door to find a neatly furnished room where respectable worthies were entertaining
wives and daughters over sumptuous pastries and expensive
wines. It was several breaths before the servitors noticed
me, all eyes turned to the minstrel sat by the stairs, his own
closed as he lost himself in the melody.

He was no new traveler, fresh from the Forest and eager
to taste adventure. This man had been pacing the roads that
knit together the Old Empire for nigh on a generation, if I
were any judge. Of a little less than common height, his angular face was weathered, hair no longer the red of autumn
leaves but faded amber streaked with white, receding at
temples and crown and cropped close. His long-fingered
hand on the frets of his lute was bony, the other plucking
the strings in the Forest manner was deft with the thickened
nails and calloused tips of a lifetime's playing. His voice
had the rich timbre of a double-reeded flute and the depth of
a thousand leagues' experience. His clothes, unremarkable
in color or cut and showing signs of wear at knees and elbows, had once cost good coin paid to a master tailor. He
was unmistakably of the Folk but old enough to be wise and

spend winters traveling where inns offered warm beds and hot food, returning only when the woods were green, the living easy in the fruitful days of summer. A heavy gold chain around his neck was threaded through a handful of rings and each ear was pierced several times, gems catching the candlelight. Forest Folk, like pied crows, have a taste for such things.

"Can I be of service?" A youth in a spotless apron hovered politely at my elbow.

"I wish to speak to the singer." I rolled the Forest cadence off my tongue, my father's accents vivid in my memory.

"He takes his break in the back yard." The boy looked uncertain. "Would you care to wait there?"

"Thank you." I hardly expected the usual dumping ground for broken crocks and empty casks, given the good order of the house, but the yard still came as a welcome surprise. The gray paving was swept clean and pots of herbs were ranged around the walls, warm in the late sun and sweetening the air as I brushed against them. A bower seat's roses were scarcely more than bare stems at this season but still made a pleasant place to sit and wait and admire a carved statue of Halcarion. The goddess gazed at her own reflection, combing her hair over a broad marble basin. I recalled I'd wanted to find a shrine for an offering.

"She's a pretty thing, isn't she?" The minstrel's voice sent a thrill of recognition through me as he stood silhouetted against the early lamps behind him. I recalled a garret bedroom, my father halting on the threshold after singing me to sleep with songs of a heritage so long lost to me. But this man was not my father, so I got myself in hand at once.

"If you see the Maiden tending her hair and biding her time until Drianon calls her to motherhood. For myself, I prefer the tales where she makes men and moons alike dance to her tune." I realized I was gabbling and shut my mouth.

"That'll be your blood talking, given the color of your hair." The minstrel said something else in the fluid tongue of the Forest, the stresses suggesting some proverb or truism but the words meant nothing to me.

"I'm sorry, I don't understand." I shook my head in apology.

The minstrel leaned against the flecked and crumbling orange brick of the wall and raised an eyebrow. "You have all the pieces, and if you want to talk to me, I assume you want to play, but you don't know the rules?"

"That depends on the game," I countered. I can do this kind of banter readily enough but wondered what his point was.

"Life is the game, my dear, the whole round of it." He smiled at me and this time a light that I recognized well enough lit his copper-colored eyes. "So if you're not of the Folk, how do you come to have all the pieces that make a Forest maid, and such a very fine set at that?" He looked me up and down with that slow intensity many women find flattering.

"My father left me the outer shell." I tried to convey polite disinterest. Luckily another concern diverted my companion.

"Where and when were you born?" he asked, a faint worry wrinkling his brow.

"In Vanam, in the Aft of Autumn twenty-seven years past, to a servant girl called Aniss," I replied, my smile broadening.

He evidently ran rapidly through his memories of travel and conquest and his expression soon cleared to share my amusement. "In that year, at the relevant season, I was in Col, my dear," he said with a formal bow. "If you are seeking a lost father, I am afraid I do not have that honor."

"That's not what I wanted to talk to you about, don't worry." The door opened with a timely interruption as the lad came out with a tray of fancy pastries and an etched glass jug of golden wine, moisture beading the sides as it carried the chill of an ice cellar.

"Here's to our common blood in any case." The minstrel

poured me a glass and raised his own in salute. "What is your name?"

"I'm Livak." I toasted him in turn.

"And I am Frue," he responded. "Your father left you with a fine Forest name, at very least," he observed before hungrily biting into a flaky shell crammed with spiced apple.

I accepted his mute offer of an apricot tart, curiously remembering how my mother had resisted every blandishment and threat my grandmother could summon in her various attempts to rename me after my father's periodic visits ceased. "His name was Jihol," I volunteered, surprised by my own unbidden words.

"Of what kin?" Frue cocked his head to one side. "Do you know?"

"Of the Deer, I think." I drank some wine and cast around for some means of ending this fruitless conversation.

Frue's stillness was broken with an abrupt shake of his head. "No, don't know him, not to my knowledge."

"It's not important," I said with relief. In fact, I'd probably take some pains to avoid my long absent parent, if the breezes brought any scent of him. I had enough uncertainties to juggle in my life at present.

"So what are you looking for?" Frue devoured a second pastry and I waved away his offer of another, realizing this was likely part of the payment for his music.

"I have a book of old songs, collected by a Tormalin noblewoman in the latter days of the Empire. They are from all the ancient races, Mountain, Plains and Forest. I'm trying to find people who can translate them for me."

Frue looked up, clearly interested. "I'll take a look for you, willingly."

That had been a certain bet, hadn't it? Old songs could offer a minstrel something new for his repertoire without all the effort of composing it himself. "I'd welcome your thoughts, certainly. The thing is, I'm traveling with a scholar and he's bound to want more than one opinion, so

I'd really like to show them to more Folk of the true blood as well. Are you returning to the Forest? May we travel with you?" I refilled Frue's glass.

"I am heading back to my kin, as it happens," said Frue with caution, wiping his fingers on a well-darned napkin. "You and your scholar would be welcome to take the road with me."

"We have two other companions, old friends, men of the mountains." I hoped Frue hadn't heard the faint hesitation in my voice.

"What do uplanders want in the wildwood?" Frue seemed more curious than concerned, which was a relief.

"They travel, like me, playing the runes and White Raven where it's offered. Raven was a game of the Folk long before it traveled east and north, so I think they are hoping to find some trick or strategy to give them an added edge." I made a mental note to warn Sorgrad of his new interest.

"You play White Raven?" Frue was looking at me with interest again.

"My father taught me as a girl," I replied.

"Then you know that the game relies on the balance between the protection of the woods and the strength of the birds, as they try to drive the Raven away." Frue's eyes were bright. He came to sit beside me under the bare thorns of the bower and leaned close. "Every exchange must be even-handed between the Folk. What have you to offer me, in exchange for escort and introductions?" His voice was soft and caressing, fingers brushing lightly on my breeched knee.

"Songs that no one has heard since the days when the greenwood reached to the very gates of Selerima?" I delicately lifted his hand from my leg. "A romp for a night is all very well, but a good song lasts forever. When they're heard anew, it'll be your name associated with them."

"If they are truly unknown. You'd be surprised how far back down the Tree of Years some of our songs reach." He laughed and I realized with relief that part of the game was done, with no ill feeling on either side.

"What's amusing you out here, Frue?" The door to the yard flung open to reveal a well-rounded lass in grass green draperies glaring at me with ill-disguised suspicion. She had a childlike face, round and soft with a turned-up nose and pretty eyes but with a sulky downturn to the corners of her full-lipped mouth. "Tris said you were out here." Her silent question was unmissable.

"Zenela, this is Livak," Frue smiled with a hint of lasciviousness. "She's been tempting me with the prospect of an intriguing lay."

That set Zenela's nostril's flaring. "That's lay as in music, not as in bed. For the moment," I added, giving Frue a flirtatious smile to shake her a little.

"Bring your song book over tomorrow morning and I'll see how I can help you." He pulled Zenela close as her outraged breath threatened the low neckline of her dress. "Let's sing for our supper, sweetest." Frue sauntered through the door and, after shooting me a look sharp with warning, Zenela hurried after him.

Chuckling, I took the tray back to the kitchen. "Can I listen from here?" I asked the broad-hipped woman everyone was deferring to, her snowy apron smudged with honey syrup and face flushed beneath a no-nonsense cap.

She lifted a tray of pastries from a vast range that wouldn't have disgraced Messire's kitchens. "Just keep out of the way." She busied herself with powdered sugar and crystalized fruits.

I found a quiet corner by the door and made myself useful passing empty plates to the lank-haired youth up to his elbows in the vast wooden sink. The bustle of the kitchen stilled momentarily as Frue struck up a lively roundelay. He finished with a flourish and then Zenela began to sing, the soft chords of the lute underscoring her melody. I moved closer to the door for a better view.

Her voice was pure in the higher notes, rich and resonant in the lower. Thrilling with emotion over a song everyone must have heard a double handful of times, she made it sound as fresh as the first time of hearing. Standing beneath a double branch of candles, her bright auburn hair owed more to herbal rinses than Forest blood and her eyes reflected the green of her dress and the subtle cosmetics on her lashes. I wondered idly what her story was. She was maybe a handful of years younger than me and looked still to have a number of lessons to learn. I watched as she sang of love and loss and let myself be caught up in the glorious harmony of voice and lute.

An idea was slowly forming in the back of my mind. What if I offered Frue a new story as well as the old songs, something never yet set to music, a tale of recent events that stirred the highest powers of Tormalin and set girding their arms for a challenge not seen since the fall of the Old Empire? Minstrels spend their lives looking to be the first to weave tale and melody into new enchantment and this was festival time, when every tuppenny ha'penny warbler churns out the same old tunes just when people are looking for new diversions. The threat from mysterious islands in the ocean, the discovery of the lost colony and its sleeping survivors, all that would make a ballad to seize the attention and grip it till it cried for mercy.

The ten chimes marking sunset and the end of the day floated in through the back door and I chided myself for self-indulgence. "Tell Frue I'll call back tomorrow," I caught the serving lad's arm and slipped him a couple of copper for his trouble. Back at the Swan in the Moon, I found Sorgrad sharing a companionable meal with Usara in the tap room.

"Where's 'Gren?" I pulled up a stool.

"Giving Kelty some color in her cheeks before the masquerade starts." Sorgrad poured me a drink. "How did you get on at the races?" I asked Sorgrad.

"Well enough," he grinned. "None of the tally-touts knew your man here so he was able to play the innocent abroad. We were laying bets at good long odds and taking their coin." Usara smiled modestly.

"Where did you get the tips? Did you meet someone we know?" There was no way the brothers could know the current word on the local breeders, not when they'd been in Col all winter.

Sorgrad smiled sunnily. "Our good friend here was able to tell us all about the state of the earth beneath the grass when the horses were showing their paces and when they were running. Once we had the measure of that and 'Gren could tell which beasts liked the wet side or the dry, we had an edge to shave the odds off the risk."

'Gren's always had this theory he can tell what a horse is thinking, just from its expression. As far as I'm concerned, a face that long, hairy and inflexible can't have an expression beyond putting its ears back because it's about to kick you.

I narrowed my eyes at Usara. "The Archmage would approve of that, would he?"

"Planir appreciates I may have to use my talents in somewhat unorthodox ways, to further our researches." He smiled blandly as he reached for more bread.

That was a different song to the one he'd sung yesterday. "How did you get on?"

"I've found a minstrel who could be able to make some useful introductions," I let myself sound a little dubious. "How about you?"

Sorgrad shook his head. "Not a trace of a scent. There were a couple of Mountain Men at the cock-pits but they were with Harquas."

I grimaced as I helped myself to some of Sorgrad's bread and scooped a piece of the seared fish he was carefully easing away from its bones. "What were you doing at the cock-pits?"

"Sandy there said he wanted to take a turn around the guild halls again and told us to go and amuse ourselves." Sorgrad smiled at Usara but the wizard didn't rise to the new nickname. There was definitely something awry there.

"Is this Harquas someone significant?" Usara looked at us each in turn.

"He's one of the biggest villains in this city," I explained. "Anyone working with him will be as false as a pawnbroker's welcome, not someone we want to travel with."

"Order your food at the kitchen door, my girl," said Sorgrad as he moved his plate out of my reach. "No, this pair looked fresh off their donkeys, all dressed up and sticking out like a cut finger."

"Then Harquas will have them stuffed like squabs from a dovecote before the festival's out." I munched on some cress filched from Sorgrad's plate.

"Are there likely to be other Mountain Men in the city?" inquired Usara.

Sorgrad shook his head. "Very few. It's only the bigger valleys, the kindreds with labor to spare can afford to send their goods all this way. For all the profit you can make, you lose so much time on the trip—"

Movement by the door silenced him. I looked over to see Reza hurrying toward us. "Niello said to give you this, soon as you come in." The lad pulled a twice-folded and sealed note out of his overlarge and shabby jerkin.

I signaled to the potboy before cracking the wax. "Sit down, Rez, have a drink."

He smiled at me, exposing the toothless side of his mouth, permanent legacy of the hunger and beatings that had been his lot before Niello picked him out of the gutters. I winked at him but my good humor faded as I read Niello's unpracticed scrawl gracing the back of some ancient masquerade dialogue.

"What's the problem?" Sorgrad was reading my face as closely as I was studying the parchment.

"Did you and 'Gren run into any bother this afternoon?" I asked casually.

Sorgrad shook his head, unconcerned. "No."

"And was 'Gren with you all the time?" I inquired.

"Until we got back here and he spotted Kelty adjusting her garters at him," he grinned. "He's never one to find fault with a fat goose."

I nodded slowly. "According to Niello, they had the Watch in here asking questions earlier. Seems they want to talk to a pair of Mountain Men on account of a beating they gave some nailers."

Usara opened his mouth and if I could have I'd have kicked him under the table to shut it. "Is this likely to be a problem?" His tone was both courteous and conciliatory.

I tried not to show my relief he hadn't implied doubt in Sorgrad's word. "Yes, to be honest. Niello wouldn't have bothered straining his wits with this," I waved the note, "if he hadn't reckoned it was serious."

"They cursed near tore the stage apart, in case anyone was hiding under it," supplied Reza. "Emptied out all the costume baskets."

I laid my hands on the table in front of me. "If their own have taken a hammering, the Watch will be pulling in any-one who fits the cry and like as not giving them a kicking for good measure. That's the way of it here, the same as anywhere else. At any other time of year, we could find our-selves an advocate and argue the case in the courts, get a few witnesses to swear for us. Kelty for instance, she'd be good for convincing a judge 'Gren never left her bed." I shook my head. "Not at a festival. The assize will father the bastard on the first face through the door and that will be that."

"I don't think we want to come to the attention of the Watch, do we?" I saw the face of Arle Cordainer reflected in Sorgrad's eyes. Another consideration to add to the balance.

"Niello says Vadim took one of the nailers off into a cor-ner," I said to Sorgrad, ignoring the others. "Close as a miser and his money."

"We can shut his mouth for him," shrugged Sorgrad.

"If he turns up dead before the end of festival, that'll just cause more trouble," I warned.

"He won't turn up," Sorgrad grinned evilly.

"Why don't we just leave?" asked Usara in some alarm.

"Because no minstrel is going to hit the road until the

very last moment of the fair." I hid my annoyance. There's no point in trying to buck the run of the luck so I had to play these runes as best I could. "You could play the second clown, couldn't you Rez?" The lad nodded hopefully.

"Then Niello can tell Vadim to take his coin and be on his way or we'll use it to buy his ashes a niche in a shrine," I said firmly. "He won't argue. His type are all bark and no bite."

"Who plays the dog?" asked Sorgrad.

" 'Gren?" I suggested. There'd be no holding him back.

"So we're going to the Forest, not the Mountains?" asked Usara, looking from me to Sorgrad and back again. "At the end of the festival?"

I nodded. "Do you have any problem with that?"

"No, none at all," Usara spread his palms in a placating gesture. "I am bound to follow your lead." He smiled with self-deprecating modesty.

I wasn't fooled; he'd used magic to bespeak Planir in Hadrumal some time during the afternoon. It was a safe bet he'd been told to chain up his dog and make himself agreeable. That was all very well—at least he'd be likely to get along with 'Gren and Sorgrad—but I wasn't about to trust a wizard, not completely, not even when he sat eating his supper, demure as an old whore at a wedding.

"What shall we do tomorrow?" Sorgrad asked. "The shrine confraternities will be playing at piety in the morning but the tumblers and animal trainers will get their place in the sun after noon."

I shook my head. "I'm going to see this minstrel about a song or two." And not just about the ancient songs. Usara could keep his secrets and I'd keep mine. I'd been thinking about songs, their power and their persistence. Learning the secrets of old aetheric magic was all very well but perhaps I could make more prosaic use of a good tune and rousing words. If Frue could set some song doing the rounds that warned people about the Elietimm threat, word would spread faster than fire in a thatch. If I was careful to tell the tale so I didn't feature at all, no one would be able to trace it back to me, either.

Kehannasekke, Islands of the Elietimm, Spring Equinox

He was so absorbed in distant contemplation that he did not register his father's soft-footed entrance, not until a breath stirred the hairs on the nape of his neck with a question. "Eresken?"

Startled, he could not prevent a sharp intake of breath, his shoulders tensing involuntarily beneath his unadorned tunic of undyed wool.

"How do you fare?" The question was genial enough; the older man was in a good humor and Eresken breathed more easily.

"Badly, sire," he admitted frankly. "I have spent night and day in the search and might as well be wandering lost in fog. I had hoped the stasis of Equinox might aid me, but so far I've felt no advantage."

The white-haired man snorted and crossed to the narrow window, where iron bars laid black stripes of shadow across his plain dun garb. The pale sunlight forced its way past, only to be reflected back from the bare white walls and floorboards scrubbed to the color of straw. He looked down into the courtyard four stories below, where black-liveried men-at-arms moved with set purpose and servants in drab cloaks hurried out of their path. "Perhaps we should make an example of some wrongdoer, kill a bantam to cow the rest of the flock." He glanced sharply at his son. "What do you think?"

"I don't feel the problem is a lack of commitment among our people," Eresken replied carefully. "I sense their strength well enough and the focus of the stones is as strong as ever. It is rather that Tren Ar'Dryen is somehow shielded, barriers ranged against us. Even with the clarity of the balance, I cannot penetrate the deceptions."

Admitting failure was risky but he had no option. If anyone could pierce the unholy miasma defeating him, it would be his father. Then he would show Eresken how it was done.

"You are correct," his father nodded slowly. "How do you account for this?"

Eresken took a moment to think; that was allowed. He was careful not to show he realized he was being put to the test; that was not permitted, on pain of punishment or worse, dismissal from his father's counsels and instruction. "In reviving the hidden ones of Kel Ar'Ayen, the false magicians of Hadrumal will most likely have found practitioners of true enchantment," he began cautiously. "If Planir has suborned these to his own ends, he may be using their skills to deny us."

"Good," said his father approvingly. "You are correct again."

Emboldened, Eresken leaned back in his chair, hands relaxing on the parchment-strewn table. "Perhaps Kramisak—"

"Kramisak is not your concern," snapped his father. "Kel Ar'Ayen is not your concern. If I feel you straying from your allotted duties, I will chastise you in no uncertain measure, do you understand me?" His anger came and went with all the instant violence of winter lightning but the cold threat lingering in his voice was infinitely chilling.

"Of course, sire." Eresken slowly laced his hands together, stopping them from shaking. "My task is to work around these obstructions. I will apply myself more diligently."

"What have you been doing today?" The white-haired man crossed from the window to begin leafing through Eresken's parchments, frowning at notations in margins and neat additions to the bottom of texts written in several different hands, the oldest lines blurred where the ink had rubbed away. A few bright lines of illumination here and there were the only specks of color to disturb the neutrality of the stark room.

"I have been looking for priests." Eresken spoke with more confidence.

"Explain your reasoning," his father demanded curtly.

"Equinox comes for the lands of the west as well as for us and some of their traditions reach back to the days before the Exile. I looked for those cities that hold religious gatherings to mark the quarter-year." Eresken turned his notes to a relevant page and proffered it. "We know their priests hold the last remnants of true enchantment in the lands of the west; that's why we were killing them. Now I think they might be more use to us alive than dead. I hope to find one with some vestige of piety turned to their gods that will leave his mind open to mine. It has always been easier to contact a mind with some training than an unwilling one."

"A sound enough argument," noted the old man. "What progress have you made thus far?"

"At the moment, it's like trying to hear a single voice shouting in a storm." Eresken could not disguise his chagrin. "Luckily, the strongest barriers are set in the east, so I have been following a chain of recollection and anticipation woven from the unguarded thoughts of merchants and the like traveling west. There is a great fair in this city, Selerima, and there must surely be some shrine where the devout will gather, even if it is only to pay duty to their lesser gods or goddesses."

His father studied a map. "At such a vast distance, you cannot hope to influence a mind that is not actively cooperating with you."

"I will do my utmost," said Eresken stoutly. "With the strength that abides in the stones, I believe it will be possible."

The white-haired man threw the parchment down on the table. "You should be searching for wizards at their false conniving. We know that leaves them vulnerable as new-born babes to us."

The old man must be tired, Eresken thought discreetly. This was too obvious a snare to step into. "Planir knows that too, none better. The mages are the most closely shielded of all. I am not even attempting to touch them, not until they grow idle from lack of threat and relax their vigilance. Even then, while killing the mages is gratifying, it would be a shortsighted act, merely enraging the Archmage. I am looking for means to attack on a wider front."

A half-smile quirked the corner of the old man's mouth. "And what of those whose minds you have already touched? The redheaded bitch, the swordsman? Have you sought them?"

"I have, but on no more than a superficial level," said Eresken slowly. "Anything more would risk alerting them to our continued interest in their downfall."

"You're afraid, that's plain enough," his father said softly. He leaned forward, hands on the table, and stared deep into Eresken's grass green eyes.

Denial was useless and Eresken hastily emptied his mind of any thought he wished to keep to himself as his father's opaque brown eyes held his own in unbreakable thrall. Eresken forced himself to concentrate on the face before him, to stop unbidden feelings or opinions intruding themselves. His father's face was lean and taut, crowned with dead white hair, faint lines showing the scour of wind and years and the few scars mute testimony to lessons learned from rare mistakes. Eresken forced his breathing to a slow and even pace and laid his mind open. It was better this way, less painful. He'd learned that lesson long ago and now passed it on with the same merciless sting when opportunity presented itself.

The old man laughed but not unkindly. "They humiliated you, didn't they? Jumped you, knocked you senseless and hauled you away like a seal trussed from the hunt. You don't want to risk that happening again. Well, I can understand that. You're not alone, boy. The slut held her own against me with no more than inborn defiance and a flood of doggerel."

Eresken gaped. "I had no idea—"

"No, neither did I." The white-haired man's laughter rang unexpectedly light against the whitewashed walls of the room furnished only with a single table and chair. "It's one more of the ironies of our present situation that some ignorant bitch could light upon a pattern of half-remembered song and gibberish that could disrupt our practiced incantations so thoroughly! One is prepared for challenge from an equal, not from some misbegotten sneak-thief."

"They were none of them worthy foes," spat Eresken with rising anger. "All they had was brute strength and savagery, too stupid to recognize their fate and submit!"

"Do not give way to your frustrations," warned his father, speaking softly. "Emotion will restrict you, limit your effectiveness. But on the other hand," he turned away abruptly, "you need to feel that anger, that outrage, that spur to set you looking beyond the confines of these islands, when so many others are content to see no farther than the horizon. That vision is what marks you as my son and makes you worthy of my time and trouble. You must learn to recognize such contradictions and master them."

"But why—" Eresken spoke before he could stop himself.

"A child who simply asks 'why' shows an aptitude for training. A man who does the same is mistaking trust shown him for license to dissent."

"I meant no disrespect," insisted Eresken. Never that, not so long as he could reap the rewards of his sire's favor. The truth of his words and his thoughts hung in the tense silence.

"You should be able to answer such questions for yourself, as I have done. All these things are tests set for us, to

prove us worthy of reclaiming our lost lands and more besides. As we master one challenge, another arises, para-
doxes that make no sense testing our resolve. I am the
richest man on these islands, my revenues the sum of any
five others you could name, yet I am a pauper against the
meanest lordling of the Tormalin." He began pacing, speaking as much to himself as to his son. "With sacrifice and
discipline, we finally raise our enchantments to a pitch that
allows safe crossing of the ocean currents. We find Tren
Ar'Dryen is a land overrun by the feeble of body and of intellect, morally corrupt and wholly contemptible. But these
dross have a strength in numbers that we cannot match, we
who have been refined in the crucible of these islands, tem-
pered in the harsh cold. How can we be stronger, yet
weaker? We find these people have lost nigh on all true
magic, so should be open to our attack, yet that lack has
meant false magicians meddling with the visible and tangible have flourished, even reaching an arrogance that en-
courages them to challenge us. How can this be so?"

Eresken knew better than to answer; his role as passive audience while his father rehearsed a speech was well understood. These words would be used to turn the thoughts of the
lesser folk more closely to their allegiance, loyalty focused
through the prism of the stones so that the power of the men
who ruled them would burn ever brighter, ever more fierce.

"So we decide to turn our attention south, to Kel
Ar'Ayen, the land so nearly held yet let slip by our forefathers' forefathers. But somehow, our interest alerts the villains of Hadrumal and they are able to snatch that prize
from our open hand." The white-haired man broke off to
narrow his eyes. "For the present, at least.

"So now we must answer paradox with paradox. We fight
by not fighting; we make haste to our goals with painstaking slowness. We have the enchantments to carry us over
open ocean yet we keep our boats safe in harbor. We bide
our time, and because of that our victory will come all the
swifter and be all the more complete."

The door slammed as he left without a backward glance. Eresken sat for a moment, looking at the disarray of parchments on his table. Sorting them methodically, he restored his original piles, each aligned precisely with the edges of the table and equally spaced from the next. The growl of his hungry belly sounded loud against the muted rustle of documents, but Eresken ignored it. A passing desire for water to freshen his stale mouth diverted him for a moment, but he thrust the idle thought hastily aside. It was many seasons since he'd had proof that his sire observed him from afar but the punishments for idleness were not something he was anxious to experience again.

There would be no respite until his father took some refreshment. As hard as Eresken was applying himself, sequestered in this lofty room, devoid of anything to distract the eye or the mind, his father was working three times as hard, thrice as long, Eresken knew that. He asked nothing of his son that he did not demand of himself in triple measure.

His sire was a great man. The whole of the great, square keep knew that, down to the lowliest scullion. The grim-faced men who paced the parapets and guarded the sanctuary of the harbor knew of their lord's commitment to their advancement. Those wresting food and necessities from this grudging land and sheltering in their meager villages beneath the ever vigilant watchtowers knew they owed him loyalty to their last breath for his defense of their pitiful lives. Beyond, past the bleak gray ridges of rock and ice, down the length of the cold sea strands, across the inlets and boundary cairns, those who enviously watched his success knew it too and gnawed their nails as they tried to outguess and outmaneuver him.

Eresken's duty and privilege was to support and assist his sire. That knowledge warmed and soothed him. His lips moved in soundless incantation as he ran through disciplines drilled into him through endless repetition and fear of failure. Few had the stamina, the commitment, the wit to reach his mastery of these arcane truths. He owed it to those who could not to use his strength to their ultimate advantage. The common flock owed him the unquestioning loyalty that underpinned his supremacy. Determination smoothed his face into a pitiless mask.

Eresken spun his mind into the maelstrom, violence wrought to bend the external world to his will that thrilled the blood to the edge of ecstasy. Seizing the heart of the vortex, he refined silence in the midst of fury, reveling in sublime consciousness that freed him from the tyranny of the visible and tangible. From that transcendent awareness, it was a comparatively simple task to concentrate the chilling assault, the unstoppable sweeping domination that paralyzed the lucid mind and stripped naked the innermost secrets of the unconscious. The next step was the greatest challenge, the discipline that eluded all but the most adept. Eresken did not falter. He melted ice into gossamer mist, a whisper of unobtrusive charm that warmed the chill of terror into the caress of seduction. No mind would recoil from this touch, few would even note its passing, those that did would find soothing release from cares and worries ample recompense for the knowledge unwittingly exchanged.

Eresken reached for his parchments, green eyes distant and unblinking, hardly glancing at the map beneath his hands. He ran light fingertips along the length of the road running west, his mind's eye seeing sights unknown to the lesser people of his barren homeland. He listened to the hubbub of humdrum minds, searching this way and that. Patience was what was called for. If he had to spend days in this room, seasons, mark the cycle of one year's sun to the next with these labors, he would find a foothold in the minds of Tren Ar'Dryen. Once he had that foothold, he would make a bridgehead. Once he had a bridgehead, the invasion would begin.

Three

As the game of the White Raven is becoming ever more pop-
ular, I have included this amusing song of the Forest Folk.

> Raven heard the whispering wind,
> Beguiling words to snare the fool,
> Seek out wisdom, it did say,
> For the wisest he shall rule,
>
> Raven flew into the wood,
> And looked among the laughing trees,
> They hid their lore beneath their leaves
> Where no one looks, so no one sees.
>
> Raven flew into the peaks,
> And dug among the icy snows,
> But wisdom lay beyond his reach,
> Buried right beneath his nose.
>
> Raven flew back to the plains
> Came croaking loudly in despair
> The grasses told him, "Do not weep,
> Risk the rainbow if you dare."
>
> Raven flew into the storm,
> Until the sunlight split the rain.

He crossed into the Otherworld,
Wisdom stole, flew back again.

But where had Raven's color gone?
Where once his wings were black as night,
The rainbow claimed its due from him,
Raven now was hoary white.

Raven said to every bird,
"Now I am wisest, bow your head!"
The birds all cried, "We know you not!"
And pecked poor Raven till he bled.

Poor Raven fled their savage beaks,
And wept with long and lonely tears,
Pursued until he came to rest,
Sheltered by the Tree of Years.

Now Raven sits and holds his tongue,
Until his counsel may be sought.
That wise birds must earn their respect,
The last thing that his wisdom taught.

Medeshale, Western Ensaimin,
12th of Aft-Spring

"I appreciate this is as far as carrier's coaches go, but do tell me we don't have to walk all the way to Solura up to our ankles in dung?" Usara stopped to scrape a noisome lump from his boot. This early, with the cool of the night still lingering, the smell of the ordure was fortunately muted.

"No, don't worry. This lot's for fattening on summer grass hereabouts." I was glad to be back on my own two feet again. Usara could grumble if he liked. I'd had more than enough of jouncing along a high road in the musty interior of some lord's cast-off coach that was now reduced to wearing a regular rut between the little towns of western Ensaimin.

"Some will be pasturing on the edge of the wildwood." Sorgrad had purchased a dark gray donkey the previous evening. He secured my stout leather bag to its harness with an air of satisfaction. "Let's get ahead of any droves."

I looked at the young stock penned with hurdles on all sides, lowing for their morning water and jostling for a taste of old hay and wormy turnips. I wouldn't be traveling this road in the autumn, not with these droves half a year grown on good grazing, churning the road into morass as they headed back to Selerima for sale and slaughter. "Where's 'Gren?"

Sorgrad shrugged as he settled Usara's valise between two of his own. The donkey shuffled its neat black hooves on the hard-packed earth, grass pounded into oblivion by the countless white and russet cattle.

"There he is." Usara pointed and I saw 'Gren coming out of the brick and flint inn looking mightily disgruntled, his own bag under one arm and one of Sorgrad's on the other.

"Where did you get to last night?" I asked.

"Cattlemen are supposed to be good for a game of runes," 'Gren grumbled, handing the baggage to Sorgrad and getting a reproachful look from the donkey.

"That's when they've sold their stock and the coin's wearing holes in their pockets," Sorgrad reminded him. "This lot's wealth is on the hoof."

"You should have tried singing for your supper," Frue appeared from somewhere, Zenela hanging on his arm. "We did well enough." He patted the plump purse at his belt.

"Fancy throwing a few hands tonight?" 'Gren asked hopefully.

"You never know your luck," grinned Frue. I noted Zenela looked less than pleased. Maybe she was just tired; she must have been up before dawn and the kitchen maids

to heat her curling irons to make such a complicated
arrangement of hair and ribbons.

Dusty-coated stockmen were busy around their kine,
moving them with a slap on the rump or a shove to the
shoulder, checking for injury, dull eyes or dry muzzles.
Voices lifted above the lowing and joined the swelling noise
of the little township setting about its morning business.
Medeshale was a place of tidy houses built of cheerful
ruddy brick beneath sturdy roofs of mountain slate. The
scent of baking bread drifted from a bakehouse chimney
reaching high above the rooftops. Children were scamper-
ing home with the morning's loaf past women opening
shutters and sweeping steps. A gang of men headed past us
on their way to the clay pits and I heard one whistle a snatch
of melody. It was the refrain to Frue's song about the Elietimm. I smiled to myself. It had been a resounding success
last night in the tap room and, better yet, Zenela had let slip
a letter-press man had paid the minstrel a tidy sum for the
right to print ha'penny sheets of the words to sell around the
inns of Selerima. Frue was welcome to the coin, as long as
word condemning the Elietimm was spread wide.

"Time's wasting." Frue looked on with amusement as
Sorgrad settled his final bag onto the donkey. The animal
laid its large furry ears back and startled a passing pony cart
with indignant braying. Frue slung a leather strap, tied to a
roll of stout blanket holding his few possessions, over his
shoulder.

Zenela wore a gown more suited to taking the air in a formal garden than a day's hard walking but at least her boots
looked sturdy. I rocked on my heels and the shiny leather of
my new footwear creaked. The coin for good fit and new
socks had been well spent; this was no time to be crippled
with blisters. Zenela clearly wanted to load her own bulky
satchel on the donkey but Sorgrad made no offer, hardly
surprising given the way she'd been patronizing both brothers. She was going to have to ask outright but I couldn't see
her doing that.

Shouts suggested a drove was about to set out.

"Come on," I said hastily. "I don't fancy picking a path through cow pats."

Frue led the way, Zenela still hanging on his arm. 'Gren and I followed, Sorgrad and Usara behind, disputing the history of Col either side of the donkey's head, something they'd been scoring points over for the last three days.

I'd given up trying to follow either argument. So had 'Gren. "You don't fancy trying your chances there?" I nodded at Zenela's fussily crimped head.

"After that song of hers?" 'Gren's lip curled. "If she wants lovelorn suitors admiring her from afar, that's her look-out, but I'm not playing her games."

I chuckled. My mother had taught me the touch-me-not song, along with every other goodwife in the street keen to convince her daughter to save her maidenhood for a worthy suitor, but Zenela was the first I'd heard sing it with such obvious reference to herself. So she saw herself as the bloom whose perfume would only delight as long as it were left unplucked? I'd been a girl who'd never seen the point of keeping boys at arm's length, finding them much more interesting close at hand.

"Where's she from, anyway?" 'Gren was still looking at Zenela with an intensity that belied his disinterest.

"Her father is an innkeeper in Kadras," I told him. "Frue said he's been visiting their house for years. He knows her voice is her only hope of fortune, so he asked Frue to take her to Selerima in the hopes that someone of wealth or influence might hear her."

"She'll hardly find a wealthy patron warbling in the wildwood," 'Gren said critically.

"Nothing to do with us," I shrugged.

On our way down the high road we passed farmwives and their maids coming to the pannier market in Medeshale's paviored square. Some carried laden baskets; others had broad yokes across their shoulders swinging buckets stacked with covered crocks. Frue stopped to buy a round of cheese, fresh in its muslin. I did the same while 'Gren flirted with a pretty maid, her cheeks as round and freckled as the eggs she carried in a careful trug.

"Thanking you." The goodwife nodded a farewell, a good start to the day's coin in her purse. "Come on, Tila."

'Gren swept Tila a bow and blew her a kiss that won him a giggle. I caught Zenela's bafflement. Why were none of these men giving her the adoration she was accustomed to?

I moved to walk next to Frue. "The Serpent's Tale was a fine inn, a good recommendation. Do you pass through Medeshale often?"

"From time to time." Frue's face hardened a touch. "A handful of years since, it was just a hamlet hacking at the edge of the wildwood. A generation ago, all the cattle marts were back down the road at Brakeswell." He gestured at spring flowers dotting the grass, mostly yellow, here and there a soft blue or vibrant pink. The air was none too warm but the climbing sun dried the dew and warmed the flowers to lift their scents to the breeze. Spinneys here and there broke up the pasture, birds rustling and darting and their trills lightening the air. "When I was a boy this was all cob trees and red hazels. The nut harvest was quite something." He gave me a sly glance. "Many a maiden went home with a full apron."

Zenela hurried up to stake her claim on Frue's arm again. "Will we be safe, traveling the road alone?"

"I'll protect you, sweetheart." I heard a hint of mockery in his tone.

I didn't reckon we had much to worry about; any cover for would-be footpads was hacked down for a plow length either side of the highway. "There aren't the lordless or landless men in these reaches of Ensaimin that make places like Dalasor or Gidesta so chancy." Let Zenela chew on the fact I'd traveled five times the leagues she had.

"The Forest Folk take care of bandits using the wildwood as cover to prey on the road," Frue added. "And we have

common blood. Any Folk out to settle scores with the cattlemen won't trouble us."

"But what if—" Zenela tried to break in.

"Who takes it up if there's a fight or a killing?" I rode
over her words. "Lord Whatsisname at Brakeswell or the
Solurans?"

"Things settle themselves." Frue shrugged. "Cattlemen
don't welcome officialdom this side of the wildwood and
the Solurans' only concern is keeping the road open. Castle
Pastamar sends out men once a season or so; they cut back
the growth and mend the worst holes."

Losing interest in the not very challenging game of ruf-
fling Zenela's feathers, I looked ahead as the road wound
slowly toward the dense green line thickening the horizon
of the undulating plain. Through an uneventful morning of
steady walking, waving at the occasional farm cart or standing aside to let some urgent carriage rattle past, I gradually
realized why the Great Forest is called simply that in Soluran, in Tormalin, in the tongue of the Folk and probably
every other language. There are no other words for it. I've
been in other wildernesses; they've had gullies, hills and
rivers. If trees hem you in, you know they will give way
soon enough. This forest hid any such hope beneath an impenetrable cloak of leaves. Ahead it blocked the view, an
unsmiling barrier. Unbroken green marched away to the
south, fading to a distant blur that promised unbroken ver-
dant leagues beyond. North and west it ran up to distant
mountains still capped with snows. Shading my eyes with
my hand, I saw the brighter green of broad-leafed woods
darken to somber shades of fir and pine, broad swathes of
drab rock and ice stark contrast beyond.

"That's the mountains," Sorgrad stood at my side, face
somber.

"They're very big." I couldn't think what else to say.
"How far do they go?"

"All the way from the eastern ocean to the wildlands west

beyond Solura." Sorgrad smiled but his eyes were unreadable. "And these are the low ranges. A few hundred leagues farther north there are the high peaks."

"These look high enough and cold enough for me." I shivered. "You're right. It's still winter up there."

"Maewelin made the land and Misaen made us fit for it, that's what they say," Sorgrad murmured thoughtfully.

"All the world is made up of the same elements: air, earth, fire and water," said Usara, his voice startling me. "It's just that the arrangement differs."

I imagine he was trying to be reassuring. Unfortunately he just sounded dismissive and Sorgrad scowled with unexpected affront.

'Gren came up behind us. "Are we stopping for lunch?"

We ate looking at the tiny trees holding the grasslands at bay. The road wound inexorably on through the afternoon, the one highway that cut through the secrets of the wildwood.

I told myself not to be fanciful. My Forest blood was mere accident of birth. I knew my father's name, that he was a minstrel and if Drianon had been paying attention the goddess would never have let Halcarion's fancy tie such an unsuited couple together. I had left concerns over birth or parentage behind me in Vanam. A chill blew down from the hills toward evening as we entered the Forest proper. Tender leaves showed Maewelin's black touch and the shadows under the trees were damp and chill with the memory of the Winter Hag's slow step.

"Will it freeze tonight?" I asked Sorgrad, who had spent the day unusually silent. He's always had the best weather sense I know.

He looked up at the sky. "Probably not but it'll be cursed cold all the same. Do you reckon her ladyship is much used to sleeping outside an inn?" He coaxed his donkey through an uneven stretch where frost had broken up the surface to catch at wheels and hooves. "The Solurans had better send out a few wagonloads of gravel before midsummer if they want to send their wool clip east," he commented.

"How come your boots aren't thick with mud?" demanded 'Gren suddenly, staring at Usara's feet.

The wizard looked slightly taken aback. "I've been using a cantrip."

The rest of us just stared at him, each several fingers taller than usual by virtue of gluey clods stuck to our feet and sapping our strength with every step.

"I can dry out a path a little, if you all walk in my footsteps," he offered hastily.

"We'll manage, thanks all the same," Sorgrad said curtly. I wondered how to go about reminding the wizard that we were singing a round song here, not out for solo admiration like Zenela.

Even with the trees hacked back to let in wind and sun, the ground was still sodden with the winter rain. We picked past heavy vehicles, mud clinging ever thicker to their wheel rims. None were stuck, which was a relief. I know we all owe Trimon a duty to help out and you never know when you'll be the one being hauled out of a ditch, but wherever possible I find it best to keep myself to myself on the road. People had been spreading out onto the cleared land on either side of the highway in an effort to find a dry path, cutting a tangle of new tracks. Zenela and the donkey picked their way daintily through the morass with identical expressions of distaste. My scowl equaled theirs when we reached the first bridge.

To be precise, we reached the bridgekeeper's hut and the little shrine to Trimon beside it where a tattered flag with the waterwheel device of Brakeswell fluttered above a wooden shield bearing a boar's head emblem. The river swirled dark and turbid around a wreckage of wood and twisted iron, wedging a storm-felled poplar tree against the doughty stone pillars. The tree must have hit the bridge with the force of a battering ram and done just as much damage. The bridgekeeper was sitting outside his thick walled hut, sulking under the mossy thatch while a group of Solurans stared helplessly into the roiling water or berated their hapless leader. With angry gestures he turned to the bridgekeeper, who responded with spirit.

"You go tell Lord Pastiss. You risk the ford and may the Master of the Road help you! Whine to his lordship all you want, and while you're at it ask him how he spent all these tolls he's so keen to claim. If he'd sent timber and nails along with his tally-reeve back end of last year, you'd be getting over dry shod!" A short man with reddish hair, he reached for a handy-looking quarterstaff lying beneath his bench. The Soluran prudently backed off.

"We'd better not try any ford till this river drops a little, not tonight, not tomorrow," Sorgrad said firmly.

Usara joined us and peered up at the sky skeptically. "I don't think there'll be rain tonight."

"If only we had horses," I sighed.

Sorgrad shook his head. "I wouldn't risk a horse in that."

"I'll gauge the force of the water in the morning," offered Usara. "If it keeps dry we should be able to cross without too much trouble."

"I doubt it very much. Rain's not the issue at this time of year," Sorgrad told the wizard firmly. "It's snowmelt."

Usara looked at him and then around at the dark, leaf-strewn ground. "Any snow hereabouts is long gone." I stifled a sigh at his unconscious arrogance. One thing wizards never seem to learn in Hadrumal is tact.

"And what about the snow in the mountains?" Sorgrad said, combative. Whatever had been galling him during the day, he'd found a vent for his resentment now. "This warm spell is just right for a thaw."

"A thaw will be a gradual process in this weather." Usara shook his head. "I can feel it in the air."

"I've lived in these mountains and I've seen a snowfield disappear overnight," retorted Sorgrad.

"Let's claim a dry spot for a fire before too many other people turn up." I spoke up before either could take further umbrage. "We're not going to be the only ones stuck here for the night."

"We want to be well back from the water," insisted Sorgrad. "This way." He dragged his donkey over to an uncomfortably exposed knoll.

"The sky is clear and we've had a run of fine days. I really don't think there's any likelihood of a storm," protested Usara.

I followed Sorgrad reluctantly, for all that he's always had the best weather sense I know. "We'll be right in the teeth of the wind coming down the road here. It'll be cursed cold."

Usara was clearing dead wood from a smooth patch of turf in the lee of the rise. "There's shelter from the breeze down here."

"Which means that's where frost will fall," Sorgrad retorted.

"Which means we'll be able to keep a fire in without it being fanned so fast we spend half the night gathering firewood." Usara straightened up. His commendable determination to get on with everyone was clearly not proof against being contradicted on matters of element.

Sorgrad looked at him with contempt and stuck his donkey's picket spike in the stony earth of the knoll. I looked for a spot somewhere midway between the pair with the least ruts and stones to cripple me in my sleep. I didn't want to fall out with either of them, but both were raising their hackles over nothing. Hopefully a good night's sleep would put them both in a better humor.

By the time the sun finally sank over the shoulder of the high ground to the north, a double handful of little fires were bright in the gloaming between us and the riverbank. Knots of disgruntled travelers hunched in cloaks and blankets, sharing the shelter of their vehicles and the warmth of their fires. Ours was spitting sparks, damp wood cracking in the fierce, uneven heat. I jumped as a sudden gust scattered a flurry of hot ash.

"I cannot understand what is making this fire so erratic." Usara poked at the embers with an impatient stick, as if at some personal affront.

"Leave it alone," growled Sorgrad, scowling into the flames. "You're just making it worse."

'Gren passed me a split and rather scorched half of wood-fowl. "Here you are, young enough to be tender unhung."

"And lost its chance to grow old enough to learn caution." I smiled at him as I ate the crunchy skin. 'Gren's always had the knack of taking a roosting bird. I prefer to pluck a different breed of pigeon and looked over at the other travelers who'd fetched up here. A couple of families had been on their once-a-generation trip to Selerima. Pack-men were traveling in twos and threes, heading for the scattered villages of Pastamar to sell on trinkets they had bought at the fair. A few more solid merchants guarded loaded carts with roped canvas covers. None looked eager for a hand or so of runes.

"So, do you think we'll be crossing tomorrow?" I asked the world in general.

"Quite probably," said Usara confidently.

"Most unlikely," stated Sorgrad in the same breath.

I exchanged a resigned look with 'Gren, who snorted around a mouthful of leg meat. He chewed and swallowed. "Water's an element, isn't it, Sandy? Can't you make us a path across it or something?"

"Sorry," Usara sighed. "Were I a Stone-Master with a nexus to support me, perhaps. The momentum—"

"You're a mage?" interrupted Zenela, eyes wide. At least she spoke over Sorgrad's mutter of contempt.

"Indeed," Usara replied with mild amusement. "Of Hadrumal."

Frue glanced briefly at me. "I thought you were a scholar."

"That as well, an historian primarily," nodded Usara. "Hence my interest in Livak's song book."

Frue seemed well enough satisfied with this explanation, Halcarion be thanked for the habitual tolerance of the Forest Folk.

The conversation flagged after that. Sorgrad was brooding and Usara's air of injured dignity was getting wearing. I didn't fancy being stuck here with the pair of them for too long. Where was the bridgekeeper? I looked toward the little shrine to Trimon. Someone had lit an offering fire in front of the weather-darkened statue of the god. The Master of the Roads hereabouts had a definite Forest cast to his wooden features, his harp a small affair tucked under one arm. A sudden flare of flame silhouetted two heads close in conversation.

"That pair have been looking our way a fair deal and I don't think they're just admiring the lass's legs." 'Gren moved to sit next to me.

"They've been taking the measure of everyone here." I glanced idly around the camp. "Who are they traveling with?"

'Gren covered his nod by rubbing his hands over his face. "Those two over there, picketing their ponies." Sturdy hill ponies, fast enough on the flat for short distances, small and nimble enough to dodge through trees and take rougher, steeper ground where lowland horses would balk and slip. Raiders' beasts.

"Four lads, no goods to speak of but double-buckled saddlebags with shiny locks to them," I commented speculatively. I saw one of them near the shrine glance at Sorgrad's donkey, securely hobbled and dozing placidly with a mouthful of grain from its nosebag.

"The moons are both waxing to a double full," 'Gren pointed out.

"Thieves' season, isn't that what they call it in Col?" I looked speculatively at him. "They'll be setting a watch, if they've got a pennyweight of sense."

"A guard can always be distracted," said 'Gren with undeniable truth. "Zenela would be out of her blankets fast enough if a spider tried a fumble in her shift. Sorgrad can take care of her, that should cheer him up."

"What's the burr under his saddle, anyway?" I asked softly.

"Ask him yourself. I can't say." 'Gren shrugged. "He'll get over it. Now, are we going to take them before they take us?"

"It would be the surest way to find out if they were honest men," I allowed. I'd promised Ryshad to avoid thieving, unless out of direst necessity, but relieving dishonest men of ill-gotten gains could hardly be called stealing, could it? And it would certainly improve Sorgrad's mood, even more so since Usara could be counted on to disapprove.

"A few trinkets to trade couldn't hurt," murmured 'Gren. "All Forest Folk have an eye for nice jewelry. They could be carrying just what we need to trade for a sing of your songs."

I looked at him. "Let's see if anyone's wakeful enough to make difficulties come midnight. If so, we leave it."

'Gren smiled, teeth white in the deepening gloom. "It'll be easy as feeding cherries to a donkey."

A chord from Frue's lute ended our conversation. The minstrel had left the intermittent warmth of our sulky fire and his arrival prompted a gathering around the largest fire. Old favorites were sung with gusto and so was Frue's new song, much to my satisfaction. Zenela sang, her rich voice spiraling up to the bright stars and sending every nightingale within earshot off to its roost in a huff.

The bridgekeeper started a move to settle by putting up his shutters. The wagoneers disappeared beneath the shelter of their carts, horses secure behind an improvised quickthorn stockade. The packmen talked for a while, wrapped in their cloaks, low-voiced over the embers, but by the time Halcarion's Crown showed me midnight the camp was silent and still. The rushing chuckle of the river was the only sound beyond the occasional stir of a horse or some rustle in the underbrush.

I watched the arc of stars move slowly across the sky, the colorless light fading as the moons both followed their courses down behind the trees. Rolling over, I found myself face to face with 'Gren, his eyes lively with mischief. "Have they set themselves a watch?"

"Not last time I went for a piss," he replied, barely audible. "They're trusting to the fellow by the carts."

"And he's asleep?"

"Snoring like a cottager's pig," confirmed 'Gren. He unwrapped his blanket from ready-booted legs.

"Where's Sorgrad?"

"Next to Zenela," 'Gren smirked. "Ready to invite himself into her blankets if we need a distraction."

"You'd better find something worthwhile," I warned. "She'll black his eye for him."

"He said she shouldn't show off the goods if she's not selling," 'Gren whispered.

A lesson better learned at Sorgrad's hands than others' I could think of. "Which way are you going around?"

"Yonder." 'Gren passed his hand low over the ground between us. "You see any of them stirring, sit up and cough."

I rolled over again and pillowed my head on my arm. The four we suspected were shapeless huddles of blankets in the darkness. Their ponies were picketed and dozing to one side, harness and the baggage sought stacked between the sleeping men. That wouldn't deter 'Gren. Nothing would, not when a fancy took him.

Over by the carts, the merchants' supposed guard rested motionless against a cartwheel, chin on his chest, still snoring. Faint rustles suggested no more than branches swaying on the night breeze or some foraging woodland animal.

Movement beside me had me nearly bite my lip through. Sorgrad sat bolt upright, face ashen in the moonlight. Usara opened perplexed eyes and sudden fear ran cold fingers down my backbone.

"The river—" Usara's words were drowned by a roar shattering the stillness of the night. A brutal gust of bitter air surged through the camp, ominous with a stink of weed and water. Birds erupted from the trees, shrieking in alarm, and unseen shapes came crashing through the spring growth. Rabbits and weasels fled something more terrifying than any bigger beast. A spotted deer ignored the fires and unfamiliar scents of our campground and raced through, head back, tail high in alarm. As the hind vanished, the ground vibrated beneath us, as if something huge and untamed drummed frantically high on the hillside.

"Everyone, away from the river," bellowed Usara but he took a pace toward the ruins of the bridge. Shouts and questions roused half the camp, scrambling free of their blankets, but others were scarcely registering the commotion as they raised sleepy heads. In a rumbling rush of sound and fury, a torrent crashed down on us, foaming up out of the riverbed. Water came surging through the trees, fallen timber slamming into beasts and people, tossing them helpless in the grip of the flood.

"Get behind me!" Usara yelled, turning to face the riot of water and debris racing toward us. I grabbed frantically for my bag with the precious book inside it. Sorgrad seized my arm with iron fingers, his other hand knotted in the donkey's bridle. The animal's rolling eyes were white-rimmed in terror so I flung a blanket over its head and held it close. I gritted my teeth and waited for the impact—but a shimmering wall of emerald light defied the flood.

It rose from the ground, seeming no more substantial than a curtain of shot silk the width of Usara's outspread arms. It was strong enough to send the greedy torrent skittering sideways. Spray stung my face, needles of icy fire, but the killing rage of the water could not touch us. It could only fall away on either side, boiling with fury as we escaped its ravenous clutches, dirty froth blown on the wind like the spittle from a mad dog's mouth.

Usara stood, feet braced and hands wide, effort twisting his face as a new ripple of amber fire ran from his fingers to the ground. The magic raced toward the river, a spreading tracery, shining through the muddy water racing ever higher crested with choking foam. Sorcery clawed at the banks on both sides, earth and grass cracking like ice trodden under a boot heel, great chunks carried away on the water. As the land fell away, the torrent was sucked inexorably back into the riverbed it had abandoned, leaving us gasping with the shock of such unexpected devastation.

For half a breath, maybe less, there was utter silence, then the frantic neighing of a horse broke the thrall and shouts came from all directions.

"Sorgren!" bellowed Sorgrad.

I couldn't have heard an answer if one came. I was wrestling with the cursed donkey, shins and toes smarting with its kicks and stamping. I shook its halter furiously. "These are new boots, curse you!"

Soaking wet and hands trembling, Frue appeared from somewhere and helped me tie the recalcitrant beast to a sodden tree trunk.

"Zenela?" I demanded.

"I had her hand." Unbidden tears welled in his eyes. "She was trying to run the wrong way, it all happened so fast, it all happened so fast—"

"Help us, for pity's sake, help us!" a man roared, slipping in the mud ankle deep all around, vainly trying to brace himself to get a shoulder behind one wheel. The heavy wagons, dragged askew by the strength of the water, were shoved in a muddle like children's toys. One was completely overturned, bogged down in muck and debris and defying all the efforts of the carters to move it. A man moved feebly in the mire beneath it, pinned across the thighs, hands pushing ineffectually at the weight as agony twisted his face.

Blue light coalesced around him and everyone froze, even the trapped man. "Get ready to drag him out!" All heads turned to see an azure nimbus surrounding the mage. "Get ready," he repeated with a touch of anger. Everyone bent to add a hand instantly.

Usara set his jaw. "Now!"

Sapphire light flared and lifted the cart, no more than a handspan but that was enough. We pulled and the carter came free, biting his lip on a howl of pain, legs limp and broken. I shared a glance of pity with Sorgrad. That man would be lucky to walk again. "So the wizard is good for something," he commented and without too keen an edge to his voice.

Usara was breathing heavily. "Start gathering wood, everyone who can!"

"It's all wet," protested someone weakly out of the gloom. "It'll never burn, not—"

"That doesn't matter." Usara flung a scarlet gout of flame from one hand into a tangle of mud-covered brush. It burned as if he'd smashed a flagon of lamp oil on it. Awestruck, people gazed for a moment before throwing splintered branches and the wreckage of a carriage on top.

"He's a good man for a bad day, your wizard," 'Gren commented cheerily.

I rounded on him. "Saedrin's stones, where did you get to? I thought you were drowned!"

"Not possible." 'Gren winked at me. "Sheltya said I was born to be hanged."

"Over here, over here!" Shouts of exultation and anguish came from the far margin of the forest. I ran with 'Gren, slipping on silty grass, stumbling on nameless debris. Soaked and filthy people were trying to pull apart a weed-wrapped mess of muddy cloth washed up against the broken body of some hapless horse. A child was pulled free, crying and bloodied, passed to its distraught mother. Two more coughing figures were being helped up by kindly hands, then led away vomiting and stumbling on shaking legs. Zenela was at the bottom of the heap, face pale and still, carried off by the flood like a drowned kitten.

"Get her to the fire." Sorgrad pushed past me, digging
Zenela's limp body free of the clinging soil. The reluctant
earth released her with a sucking noise of disappointment
and muddy water oozed from her mouth and nose. We carried her to the fire and laid her gently down. I wondered if
we should be laying her out.

"Usara!" yelled Frue, cradling Zenela's unresponsive
head in his arms.

"Where did you find her?" Usara knelt and put one ear to
her mouth, light fingers on her neck to measure the beat of
her blood. He grimaced and briskly ripped open her bodice,
one impersonal hand on her breast above her heart. "Lay
her flat."

Using his other hand to tilt Zenela's head back, Usara
closed his eyes in concentration. Her skin was still stark
white in the firelight. Usara lifted his hand and her chest
rose slowly, following the wizard's movement. Her bluish
lips parted, a faint radiance showing air at the mage's command forcing itself down her throat. The rest of us held our
breath. Usara continued, moving the girl's ribs for her, reminding her body how to breathe. A warm glow settled over
her, coaxing the chill from her bones.

"Rub her hands, her legs." The mage nodded abruptly at
Sorgrad and me. I hurried to comply but Zenela's wet fingers felt dead between my palms, cold and unresisting. Sorgrad chafed her feet, face emotionless. Usara looked up
sharply to stare at him before fixing his attention on his
task.

After half an eternity, Zenela coughed, her eyes rolling in
her head.

"Keep her sitting up and wrap her warmly," Usara told
Frue.

Zenela coughed again and suddenly spewed great gouts
of fetid water over both of them, racked with spasm after
spasm. I moved hurriedly backward.

"Will she be all right?" I caught at Usara's arm.

"Perhaps." He looked grim. "Her lungs might fill with

water again, it can happen after a drowning—" He shook his head. "Let's hope she has a strong constitution."

"What about Castle Pastamar? The Solurans have this aetheric lore in their healing." Zenela hadn't exactly endeared herself to me but I wasn't about to risk Drianon's disfavor by not doing my part to help her.

"We can't get anyone to Pastamar unless we can get across this thrice-cursed river," scowled Usara.

I gazed at the torrent. The sturdy pillars once carrying the last ambition of the Tormalin Empire were ragged stumps of broken masonry. The bridgekeeper's hut was a roofless ruin of tumbled blocks, the man assuredly dead within it, and the little shrine to Trimon had been completely washed away.

"Will the water rise up again?" I heard a tremor out of my voice that demanded a comforting arm.

"It shouldn't have risen in the first place!" Usara glared angrily upstream. "I simply don't understand it. I took soundings from the river, I included the rate of snowmelt, the fact that the ground is so saturated—" He broke off, shaking his head. "It's all so different out here—you'd be better served by a water mage."

"You're the only wizard we've got," I said rather more forcefully than I intended.

"Yes, I suppose I am." Usara's narrow shoulders sagged a little. "I should certainly have worked a more effective defense—"

"That's not what I meant," I objected.

"Who died and got you elected king?" demanded 'Gren in the same breath, draping my own good cape over my shoulders, ruined, filthy but warm from the fire.

"Those of us with magical talents have a responsibility to use them for the greater good," said Usara, faint hurt in his voice.

"So you stopped me and Sorgrad drowning like mice in a drain," I said robustly. Drianon save me, these wizards did take themselves seriously.

"Come and get something warm to drink," 'Gren urged us both.

Usara shook his head. "I need to see how the water's affected the ford." He rolled a weave of ocher light between his hands and stared at the water. "This simply should not have happened." He stalked off, muttering to himself.

I found the wizard's uncertainty profoundly disturbing and found a handy target for my irritation in 'Gren. "Where did you get to?"

He gave me a friendly hug. "See that outcrop? Up like a rat on a granary wall, that's where!"

I looked at our raiders, three dispirited figures trying to pick apart a sodden tangle of harness. Two filthy and sweating ponies were hobbled alongside them.

"The flood washed their baggage clean away," said 'Gren with spurious innocence.

I narrowed my eyes. "Where to?"

"A handy crevice up yonder," he admitted.

"Did you get a chance to look inside?" I couldn't help asking.

'Gren smiled sunnily. "Let's just say that if they're honest men, I'm the Elected of Col."

"So the night's not a total wash-out," I joked feebly.

"You need a hot tisane," said 'Gren critically.

"Of course," I agreed, "and white bread to go with my roast dinner, and tell the maid not to call me too early in the morning." I've always found it impossible to stay cross at him for long.

I allowed him to lead me back to the fire, where a couple of women were scolding the merchants into broaching their remaining supplies. No one had salvaged any juniper liquor so I had to settle for a cup of newly boiled water bitter with the tang of steeped herbs. It could have done with a spoonful of honey but this was hardly the time to complain about trivialities.

"How are you feeling?" I sat next to Zenela, who was propped up against what remained of Sorgrad's valises.

"My chest hurts," she said hoarsely. A massive bruise was purpling across her forehead and a deep graze under her chin would leave her marked for a long while. Her hands were scratched, her nails broken and her long hair was a tangled rat's nest. Her chin quavered and tears blurred her eyes. In no mood to sit doing nothing but get miserable myself, I pulled a comb from my pocket and began teasing the snarls out of her hair. Frue sang a Forest song, the chorus a meaningless litany, pleasant enough to listen to and soothing. Zenela's breathing came a little easier as we sat, people all around us seeing what could be salvaged, anxiously checking over their horses and mules, a chill in their spirits as well as their bones.

Frue struck up a new song and one name among the otherwise unknown Forest words caught my ear. "Is that a song about Viyenne?" A ridiculous notion teased me.

He nodded. "Do you know it?"

"I think I heard it, once, long ago." More importantly, I'd recognized the name in one of the untranslated Forest songs in the book. I itched to get it out but dared not risk the precious thing in the midst of all this muck and damp. "Remind me of the tale." Perhaps I'd remembered wrong.

Frue smiled. "Viyenne had left her lover, Seris, to travel for a season or so and learn new songs. She traveled for a while with Regere, the weaver of trees. He became besotted with her, was outraged when she decided to return to Seris. Regere had the willows knot themselves into a cage to keep Viyenne with him, but her tears dropped into the river and it rose up to sweep away the barriers and set her free." Frue looked at the desolation all around us. "It seemed a timely tale."

So I had remembered right. Uncertainty nagged at me, no longer so ridiculous. Looking over to the riverbank, I saw Usara still prowling, frowning and gesturing with his hands as he argued with himself. Sorgrad and 'Gren had joined a gang trying to get into the demolished hut. I got up and made a tisane, trying to ease the stiffness in my back and legs as I walked over to the wizard. "Drink this," I ordered.

"I need to—" he protested.

"You need to take some time to gather your strength, or you'll be no use to anyone," I told him firmly.

He sighed and sipped at the steaming cup. "Thank you."

"So are you satisfied this was just happenstance?" I was cold, damp and tired, and I wanted reassurance.

"Frankly, no." Usara scowled at the waters rushing past in the pale light of a warming sky. "Oh, perhaps, I really can't say. There's certainly something awry with the elements hereabouts but that could just be coincidence, a result of some peculiarity of the weather, an effect of the sudden warm spell." He yawned. "With access to a good library, an apprentice or two to set researching and a week's sleep I should be able to tell you one way or the other." He managed a thin smile. "Theory and practice are proving rather more widely separated than I had imagined. I think I owe Sorgrad an apology."

I wonder what odds I'd have got against a wizard ever admitting he'd been wrong?

"Is there any way the flood could have been summoned with Artifice?" I asked abruptly. I'd been trying to find a less obvious way of phrasing the question, but I was tired and Frue's reminder of Viyenne's story had me more nervous than I cared to be. In a city you can tell where the threats are coming from, out of doors or down clear paths, and when you're up against other people you know you're matching your speed and wit against theirs. Out here in the wilds, danger could come from any direction and with any manner of magic; it could be invisible, inaudible and biting your ear before you knew it.

Usara was looking perplexed. "I've no idea. What makes you say that?"

"One of the old songs, it talks about a flood coming out

of nowhere. That might have been aetheric magic." I realized it did sound unlikely, even as I said it.

Usara did me the courtesy of taking me seriously. "I could ask Planir to inquire of Guinalle, next time I bespeak him, but I think you're just seeing Eldritch-men in the shadows."

Perhaps, and perhaps the old tales about little blue-gray men using the darkness of chimney corners and attic rooms to travel instantly from place to place held their own hints of ancient aetheric magic. I rubbed a hand over my face and shivered in the predawn chill. This whole quest had seemed so straightforward when I'd come up with the notion over a flagon of wine by the fireside of a comfortable Tormalin tavern with Ryshad.

A shout went up from the ruins of the bridgekeeper's hut and we looked over to see men springing aside as the remains of the chimneybreast fell with a sullen thud. Sorgrad and 'Gren came away, shaking their heads and I went to make them each a tisane.

"So that's six dead for Poldrion's ferry in all," said Sorgrad bitterly.

"Maybe the Ferryman'll give the bridgekeeper a free journey, on account of them being in the same trade," 'Gren quipped, but his heart wasn't in it.

I handed them each a drink, having nothing useful to say.

"Perhaps if I'd listened to you, we could have done more, got them away from the bank," Usara said with honest regret.

Sorgrad looked sharply at him, face drawn with exhaustion. "There's no saying they'd have believed us. Anyway, it's a rune that could have rolled either way. Flash floods are like that, unexpected, catching everyone out."

Deliberate noise at the edge of the trees brought heads up all around the campground. A handful of men stepped forward, dressed in leather and fur, two with short bows ready to hand, one with an array of throwing knives in a crossbelt. They were muscular, lean of face, all shorter than me, but just as redheaded. I wondered how long they'd been watching us.

The Wedge and Hammer Tavern, Grynth,
12th of Aft-Spring

"Don't you think you've had enough?" Keisyl's voice was affectionate but Teiriol colored all the same as he looked up muzzily from his tankard. Keisyl stood by the table, where the younger man slouched over sticky spilled mead and an untouched bowl of pottage.

"No, I don't think so." Teiriol spoke with precise enunciation, blinking as he concentrated on emptying the last of the flagon into his cup. He rubbed an unsteady hand over his sweaty face, hair sticking up in unruly yellow spikes. "Mother will be fit to chew an iron bar and spit out tacks when we get home, so I'm going to make the most of this trip. Another, here!" He waved the empty jug at the potman, who looked at Keisyl, brows raised in unspoken question.

"Not until you've had something to eat." Keisyl caught the eye of a serving maid. "Bread and meat here, if you please." He handed her the congealed bowl.

Teiriol looked unpleasantly belligerent for a moment but the defiance in his eyes sank beneath a sudden rush of sentiment. "You know what's best, don't you, Keis? You look out for us all. I should listen to you, shouldn't I? Not like Jeirran, drown him—"

"What about Jeirran?" Keisyl sat down and unobtrusively moved Teiriol's drink to one side.

"Where is Jeirran?" Teiriol's head lolled a little as he peered around the common room of the inn. "Where's Eirys? We must look after her, Mother said—"

"Jeirran's taken her to a dance in the market hall," said Keisyl.

" 'S'about flaming time he started being good to her," Teiriol scowled. "Dunno what Mother's going to say. Eirys got no prize insisting on that one, for all his fancy promises." He looked perplexed at the coarse brown bread and succulent mutton that appeared in front of him.

"Eat up, Teiro," said Keisyl, tone casual but eyes intent. "Jeirran never did tell me exactly what happened when you sold those skins." He ate neatly with knife and fingers. "You went off to find a cockfight or something? Don't worry, I shan't tell Mother."

Teiriol's curse was stifled by his mouthful and he choked. "Do you know what he was paid?" he demanded when he could speak again, red-faced and not just from coughing. "No more than twice what we'd have got from Degran. After all his promises!"

"Didn't he bargain hard enough?" Grim satisfaction lurked beneath Keisyl's brows.

Faint bemusement drifted over Teiriol's face. "Didn't get a chance to bargain. That Huckus, he says that's the price and we're to take it or he'll have that whore laying information with the Watch it was us kicking the shit out of their mates." He sounded puzzled and aggrieved.

"Jeirran got you into a fight with some lowlanders?" Keisyl's knuckles shone white for an instant as he gripped the hilt of his knife.

"He said it was part of doing business with that Huckus." Teiriol wouldn't meet his brother's eye and shuffled a sturdy boot in the herb-strewn rushes on the floor. "It was a fix, all right," he continued indignantly. "That whore, she was working for that Huckus, I'll wager any money. Must have been looking out for those Watchmen, unlaced to her waist and legs as bare as a skinned rabbit—"

Keisyl shook his head. "Forget the whore, she doesn't matter. Keep your voice down, we don't want everyone knowing our business. You're telling me Jeirran got gulled?"

Teiriol looked around vaguely for his drink. "That

Huckus, he turns up with a bag of coin and five bully boys wide as a barn door with studded boots and clubs to match. Jeirran doesn't even count the coin before he's arguing but these two, they're already taking the hides off on a hand-cart. Jeirran starts making a noise and Huckus threatens to call the Watch then and there." His tongue stumbled under the double burden of outrage and alcohol. "All this way for no more than we'd have got if we'd sold the hides at By-tarne, like you'd said. That's no return for Mother spending both halves of winter curing and caring for them. What's Eirys thinking of—"

"Enough," Keisyl said firmly. The door opened to admit a cheerful group of revelers followed by faint chimes from the timepiece in the tower of the market hall. The men were proud in new hats, feathers still crisp and colorful. Their ladies had furbished up their workaday woolen gowns of blue and madder with new silk ribbons, azure and rose trimming bodices and sleeves to give a festive air. One dark-haired girl was carefully teasing out the long fringe on a fine shawl of soft goat hair, embroidered with mountain flowers.

"Didn't you buy one of those for Theilyn?" Teiriol peered over with difficulty.

Keisyl looked at him with a measuring eye. "More mead, a full flagon," he called to the potman, who shrugged and turned to the barrel resting on the counter behind him. Keisyl took a scant half-cupful for himself, but filled Teiriol's tankard to the brim. Grinning broadly, Teiriol nearly emptied it before he took a breath. He frowned, an ominous gray pallor supplanting his previous pinkness.

"I don't feel so well." He swallowed uneasily. Taking another sip, he put the tankard down hastily. "I think I could do with some air." A fresh outbreak of sweat beaded his forehead.

"Come on." Keisyl got his arm under his brother's and they headed for the door, the potman watching them anxiously. Halfway there, Teiriol's legs gave way and he folded his arms over his stomach, jaw working in distress.

"Move!" Keisyl got an arm around Teiriol's waist and half dragged, half carried him out. He let Teiriol fall to all fours in the narrow, uncobbled street. Teiriol vomited convulsively, spewing up meat, mead and bread in a revolting mess. Keisyl's face twisted in distaste, but when the wracking nausea abated he raised Teiriol up to walk him slowly to the town well with gentle encouragement. "Just sit there a moment, my lad."

Teiriol's knees obediently buckled to drop him on the cold stone steps. Keisyl briskly wound up the pail and dashed the chilly water over Teiriol's head, repeating the process over Teiriol's incoherent protests before using his kerchief to wipe the droplets from his brother's shivering face.

"I'm soaked," protested Teiriol, teeth chattering, ashen in the uncaring light of the moons high above.

"Drink, just a little."

Teiriol cupped some water in his shaking hands, looking mournful now, chin wavering.

"You want to drink till you puke, that's your right and I won't tell Mother," Keisyl said, "but you're not sharing a bed with me smelling like something the dog sicked up."

Teiriol simply sat there, wet and woebegone.

"You need some sleep, my lad," said Keisyl affectionately.

"Better in the morning," mumbled Teiriol, still pale but looking less pinched around the mouth.

Keisyl didn't bother dashing that forlorn hope. He helped Teiriol along the street to the low-roofed hostel where they were staying.

The grim-faced doorkeeper opened to his knock carrying a smoky tallow candle. "Drunk is he? I'll not have him puking in my bed—he can sleep it off with the dogs."

Keisyl had his hands full supporting Teiriol who was fading fast. "We've hired the room and we'll be sleeping in it," he snapped.

"And what about them as comes next? There's more than you heading back to the hills after festival!" the doorkeeper complained.

Keisyl ignored him, propping Teiriol against the wall as he unlatched the door to their narrow room. "Come on."

Teiriol lurched forward and collapsed onto the rough pallet, groaning as Keisyl yanked off his boots. Cursing under his breath Keisyl stripped off Teiriol's wet cloak and the shirt beneath it. "Little fool." Loosening his collar and unlacing his breeches, Keisyl rolled his now inert brother onto his chest, wedging a rolled-up blanket beside him and covering him with another. "Right, now for you, Jeirran." The menace in his face silenced the old woman sulking with her sewing by the door.

The market hall was bright with candles within and braziers outside. Groups of men taking a rest from the dancing shared chewing leaf and one was roasting a few nuts in a skillet set on the glowing coals.

"Evening," one nodded to Keisyl, licking his fingers as he peeled a hot kernel. Keisyl acknowledged the greeting with a curt nod, but he was already looking in through the open door, searching out Jeirran and Eirys. There was a good sprinkling of fair heads in the company and plenty darker with the shorter, stocky build of upland blood.

Eirys was in a set forming for a round dance, eyes bright with enjoyment and a pretty blush on her cheekbones. Her dress of embroidered linen was the only one of Mountain style in the wide room but Eirys seemed entirely content to be noticed for it. Respectably high-necked and long-sleeved, it was cut to her curves to flatter her and drew irritated glares from a couple of local beauties affecting boldness in low cut and sleeveless gowns.

Eirys would still have drawn all eyes, had all the other girls been stripped naked, Keisyl thought with a private smile, even if she hadn't a jewel on her. Eirys was wearing a necklace of interlaced gold chains, rings on each finger catching the light with their deep engraving and a filigree net with crystal drops glittering against her blond braids. The jewelry Jeirran had given her in earnest of his pledge to wed her made a good show, Keisyl reflected. He'd given her precious little since though.

Around the edge of the dance floor the matrons of the town were exchanging gossip over tisanes and well-watered wine. One glanced curiously at Keisyl as he made his way past them. "Who is that young man?"

Her companion peered short-sightedly after him but shook her head. "Just some uplander passing through." The women returned to topics of more compelling interest.

Keisyl stood for a moment, looking at the four musicians sitting by the shrine to Larasion. The statue of the goddess was decked with a spray of pink and white blossom and looked with blank marble eyes at the red-faced man puffing out his cheeks as he led the melody on a double-reeded flute. His companions, brothers by all appearances, filled out the tune with a bowed lyre and a dulcimer while a double-headed drum carried the beat.

"Shouldn't you be dancing with your wife?" Keisyl took a chair without ceremony. Jeirran was sitting by a screen set to baffle the draft from a rear door, eyes unfocused as he sat deep in thought.

"What?" Whatever Jeirran was thinking, it was putting a smile on his face. Already one of the most handsome men in the room, he was attracting a share of speculative glances from the girls currently sitting hoping vainly for a partner.

"I said, shouldn't you be dancing with your wife?" Keisyl's emphasis was little short of a challenge.

Jeirran looked at Eirys with proprietorial satisfaction. "No, she's safe enough on the dance floor and she's hardly likely to go outside with one of these muddy-boots. Can you see any of them thinking he could risk it without me breaking his face? I'm joking!" he added hastily, seeing

Keisyl's unsmiling face. "What are you doing here? You don't like capering like a spring-giddy goat any more than me." He smiled fondly at Eirys as the girls whirled past in a quick exchange of partners. "You don't have to put up with her nagging like a hooded crow."

"Did you give Teiriol the coin to get puking drunk?" Keisyl looked hard at Jeirran who shrugged.

"He's a man, he can do what he likes."

"He's not of full age for another five years, as you cursed well know. You're married to his sister, you owe the duty of care that I do," stated Keisyl.

Jeirran looked around with the first stirring of concern. "What's he done?"

Keisyl's eyes were midnight blue in the shadowed corner. "He's been telling me about the wonderful deal you struck in Selerima, for a start."

"Deal? It was little more than robbery," snorted Jeirran. "A nest of thieves, like all the lowlanders, that's what Teiriol led me into. You're right, he's nowhere near full grown, not yet awhile."

Keisyl scowled. "Teiriol said you suggested looking for a trade around the back gates."

"It was Teir who wanted to see a cockfight."

Jeirran's confidence dared Keisyl to deny this. "He says you got a piss-poor price," insisted Keisyl grimly.

Jeirran's expression turned belligerent. "I got the best price I could and I'll knock down any man saying otherwise." He ran an unconscious hand over his beard. "Anyway, what's done is done. Dogs barking at a moon don't stop it setting."

"You can quote fireside wisdom at me? After all your promises to make us rich are dust and ashes? Teiriol said it was little more than robbery!" Keisyl retorted. "We can be cheated by lowlanders in the valley bottom back home, thanks all the same. And you've got more losses than either of us to make up! Where's the gold coming from to replace your patrimony? What's Eirys going to find under her hearthstone come Solstice?" He kept his voice low beneath the jaunty music but the anger in his unintelligible words was still attracting curious glances.

Jeirran folded his arms over his burly chest with an air of satisfaction. "Eirys will be thanking me for more than tainted lowlander coin in her coffers by Solstice. We can forget that stinking Harquas and his gutter curs." He drew back his feet as a couple of dancers strayed out of their set.

"What are you talking about?" Keisyl's irritation was replaced by plain bafflement.

"Would you like to find a means to put these lowlanders in their place once and for all? Don't we need a way to regain what's rightfully ours and be cursed to anyone who tries to do us down again?" Jeirran stretched his arms over his head and smiled broadly at Keisyl as he folded them again.

"You're deeper in your cups than Teiriol," said Keisyl crisply. He reached for the green glass goblet by Jeirran's hand and sniffed at its dregs.

"I'm not drunk on almond sweet-cup," sneered Jeirran.

Keisyl gave him a steady look. "Then explain yourself."

Jeirran's desire to share his discovery overcame the temptation to hug it to himself for a while longer. "See those musicians over there; they're just back from Selerima."

"So?" Keisyl barely spared a glance for the players lustily raising a new tune.

"So, they've got a new song. The drummer was singing it earlier."

Keisyl sighed. "Either tell me straight or I'm going back to look after Teiriol."

Jeirran's good humor faded a little. "They had a ballad, about Tormalin men sailing across the ocean to unknown lands, finding a powerful race of men. Powerful in magic, Keis, using it to cross the seas and attack Tormalins in their own homeland."

Keisyl shrugged. "The lowlanders drove their wizards into the sea, didn't they? So they've come back to make a fight of it."

Jeirran looked smug. "According to the singer, these folk are called Elietimm."

"Should I know that name?" Keisyl knotted his brows. "It sounds familiar—"

"Alyatimm?" suggested Jeirran.

Keisyl's mouth opened in sudden surprise. "But that's only a fireside tale for winter nights."

"What if it isn't?" Jeirran demanded. "What if these folk, wherever they are, are born of that blood?"

The two men fell silent as the music swelled and the dancers swirled past them.

"Do you think they could be?" Keisyl pondered this startling question, antagonism forgotten.

"This ballad speaks of fair-haired men," Jeirran told him.

"That just makes us the villains of the piece again," Keisyl said slowly. "That's no news. Half the lowlanders' tales have yellow-headed thieves raiding Grandma's chicken run."

"The peasants hereabouts, true enough," nodded Jeirran, "but why would a song from down and east say that? The ballads we heard in Selerima mostly warned of shoeless barbarians raiding up from the far south."

Keisyl spread his hands. "So that's your answer, isn't it? They're islanders, aren't they, the barbarians from the Southern Seas?"

"And dark of skin and eye," Jeirran pointed out. "This tale can't be about them."

Keisyl chewed his lip, puzzled. "But do you think they could really be Alyatimm?"

"The song spoke of Men of the Ice," Jeirran told him. "That can't be coincidence, surely?"

"No," breathed Keisyl. "I don't suppose it can." He looked at Jeirran. "What should it mean to us, beyond mak-

ing history out of a tale? And why would we want to find
Alyatimm anyway? They were exiled because their leader
tried to make himself sole ruler of all the sokes!"

"These people have magic, Keis," Jeirran said, eyes intense. "They have magic enough to cross the ocean, to
travel unseen among the lowlanders. If that song's any
guide, the lowlanders are running scared of these Elietimm.
Think about it, Keisyl. If these are Alyatimm, then this must
be true magic, not perversions of lowland wizards. Real
power, rooted in the mountains of old and not locked away
in Solstice secrets by Sheltya. If these are Alyatimm, then
we have common blood, no matter if it's countless generations divided. What if we could claim kinship and help?

"Think on tales you've heard around the hearth of a sun-
less Solstice. What if the Wyrm of Ceider could be summoned up again? That would get lowlanders out of our
mines faster than firedamp! What if the wraiths of Morn
could be sent down the sokes? Let them chase the stupid
cows clean over the nearest crag! We could maze the feet of
the thieves setting traps in our woods couldn't we? Kell the
Weaver did it!"

"But those are just stories, Jeirran," objected Keisyl, but
his voice was uncertain.

"Are they?" Jeirran countered. "So are the Alyatimm, or
so we've always been told, but how else would lowlanders
know of them if there weren't some truth in it?"

Keisyl was confused. "It's just a song, Jeirran, just some
balladeer making up a story to give the lowlanders a thrill.
Tell me, what happens to these Elietimm?" He stressed the
word. "I'll wager my best shoe buckles they come to grief,"
he snorted, looking with hostility at the unheeding dancers
weaving a complicated figure down the length of the hall.

"Not so you'd notice," replied Jeirran with satisfaction.
"These Tormalin men went to these islands, so the song ran,
to steal back a hostage—"

Keisyl drew a sharp breath.

"—that's right, Keis. What lowlanders would understand

the folly of that?" Jeirran pressed on. "They went to steal back the hostage, so naturally he was executed. The others were hunted as proved vermin, stole a boat and somehow managed not to drown, were washed up home. That's as far as their victory goes and piss poor I'd call it."

Keisyl shook his head. "It's just a song, Jeirran. It's some tale of adventure stitched together out of half-remembered scraps of saga. Some easterner who married out has passed on the legend to some lowlander wife and their half-breed children. That's all it can be."

"What legend?" demanded Jeirran stubbornly. "You tell me what saga this is cobbled up from. How could easterners come up with a tale like this, when they have fallen so far from the old ways? They can scarcely recite three degrees of their kindred!"

"Oh, I don't know," Keisyl conceded. "All right, but what good does it do us, even if there's some truth at the bottom of it? These people might have the power to raise Varangel and his ice demons, but it's half a year's journey to the ocean and you're saying they're on the far side of that!"

Jeirran leaned forward to speak softly. "If they have true magic, Sheltya should be able to reach them."

Keisyl started as if he'd been stabbed in the leg. "You're not serious!"

"Why not?" Jeirran demanded, face bold. "Don't you think Sheltya should be told?"

"If this song is doing the rounds, they'll get to hear of it soon enough and they don't need to hear it from me," said Keisyl with consternation. "I don't want that kind of trouble."

"I want that kind of power, if these Alyatimm have true magic and are willing to share it," Jeirran said grimly. "Let Sheltya cling to their wisdom and get driven back farther every year. I want to walk Eirys' lands without putting a foot in some thief's spring-trap. I want to sell the metals I win from the earth by the sweat of my back for a fair price, not to be undercut by some lowlander whose mines run with the blood of slaves, tainting the earth with their misery. I want to move from soke to soke in safety, claiming shelter when I need it, not finding doors barred against lowlander robbers who dishonor the truce of the road so often it's worthless."

"You've no way of knowing these people have true magic, even if they exist," protested Keisyl, but his words lacked their earlier force.

"Don't you want to find out?" challenged Jeirran.

"Perhaps, now you've set your maggot in my brain with your fancies," Keisyl sighed. "But not at the price of getting myself shunned by Sheltya!"

"I think I know one we can trust," said Jeirran slowly. "My sister."

"You have no sister," Keisyl looked sharply at him. "She's Sheltya now. Her blood is theirs and you have no claim on it."

Jeirran ran a pensive finger through his beard. "I think I could persuade Aritane to keep this to herself."

"She better had, else you're neck deep in trouble," said Keisyl dubiously. "What do you think she will say?"

"I have no idea," admitted Jeirran. "I'll sound her out, see if she's willing to listen to me."

"You keep us out of it," Keisyl insisted. "If you do end up shunned, at least we'll be able to take care of Eirys."

"Eirys is a large part of why I want to do this." Jeirran's eyes burned. "I want to give her everything her little head fancies, I want to give her daughters standing enough to claim back every right on and under the land that has fallen away to others of their blood. I want sons with a patrimony to catch every mother's eye, to link our blood, yours and mine, to every soke west of the Gap, so we never have to deal with lowlanders again unless we choose to."

His voice turned calculating. "And of course, you and Teir will be the first to benefit. Given your father died be- fore he could leave you a respectable coffer, no one will quibble if Eirys chooses to endow you. You could be taking a confident stand at Solstice, not like last time. I heard you claim not to be seeking a bride just yet, hoping all the while some girl with a decent holding would fall for your charms and insist on having you."

"You managed it," Keisyl replied cynically. The dance music concluded on a triumphant chord.

"Doesn't Teir deserve a chance at a decent match?" Jeirran ignored the jibe, glancing at Eirys acknowledging the bow of her erstwhile partner.

"If you want to pursue this, I won't stop you," decided Keisyl. "I won't tell anyone and neither must you, especially not Eirys. If anything comes of it, good or bad, that'll be time enough to explain."

"Fair enough," Jeirran offered his hand and Keisyl shook it briefly. "As soon as we're home, I'll send word to my sister as was."

"She won't come," predicted Keisyl.

"We'll see," said Jeirran. Eirys walked toward them. "My love, you shine like a swan among these wood pigeons." He rose to brush her cheek with a kiss.

Eirys curtseyed as she giggled. "Will you dance with me now?"

"Of course, my dearest." Jeirran offered her his arm. "To remind these lowlanders that you are my wife, before they all lose their hearts to your beauty."

Keisyl watched them join a circle with a faintly mocking smile. His face turned somber for a moment but then he rubbed his hands together in a decisive burst of energy and stood up. Crossing the room, he bowed low before one of the provocatively dressed girls, looking up and down her brunette prettiness with admiration tinged with insolence. "May I have the pleasure of your company in this dance?"

The girl was a little disconcerted but, seeing the envy of her more modestly shawled and petticoated friends, could not refuse. "You are welcome, sir," she said boldly.

The musicians struck up a lively tune and Keisyl swung
the girl into the dance, broad hand firm on her narrow waist.

Erdig's Bridge, the Great West Road,
13th of Aft-Spring

"Do you need assistance?" The man with the throwing
knives stepped forward. The copper in his hair was fading
to a middling brown and, allowing for the weathering of his
skin, I guessed him about Ryshad's age, maybe a handful of
years older than myself.

Frue spoke briefly in the Forest tongue, which sent a fris-
son running through the other travelers, faces a mix of hope
and apprehension.

The knifeman spoke briefly to his companions. Two of
them vanished back under the trees but the other two went
to assess the state of the river. "What's the plan, Frue?" I
smiled politely at the knife man, who gave me a heartening
grin.

"They'll help people cross the river." He stood, brushing
ineffectually at the mud dried on his breeches.

"What about Zenela?" I asked. "Do we take her to Castle
Pastamar or back to Medeshale?"

Frue nodded toward the tree line. A Forest woman of
about my own age and with a deerskin bag slung across her
body was approaching with one of the bowmen. She knelt
beside the man with the broken legs. Uncovering the
wounds with careful hands, her expression remained noncommittal despite the mess of torn flesh revealed. She took
from her bag a small pottery jar, stoppered and sealed with
wax. Cracking the seal with a thumbnail, she began spreading something on a length of clean linen, nodding as the injured man talked to her.

"What do we do now?" Sorgrad was poking wood into

the embers of our fire and setting the kettle to boil on its tri-
pod while 'Gren rummaged in an unregarded pack, un-
earthing a muslin-wrapped ham. He sliced me a chunk and
I chewed hungrily, despite the musty taint of river water.
Sorgrad unearthed his personal tisane case from the depths
of a valise and checked the little jars were still tightly sealed
against air and damp. "Should we offer to help? We might
find out what's going on."

"Let's see how the runes roll." I watched the rest of the
camp gaping at the visitors in our midst. A couple of the
packmen were inclined to be disagreeable but the wagoneers and the families welcomed the newcomers readily
enough. A matron with a manner as robust as her forearms
soon had one of the Forest lads laying aside his bow to fetch
her firewood. The woman with the herbs went to talk to her
and the matron dispatched a lass to poultice the injured
man's wounds. The other travelers soon moved closer to the
reassurance of this brisk organization.

The water was scarcely hot enough for Sorgrad to make a
tisane when enough Forest Folk appeared to have me wondering just how close they had been. At least, I assumed
they were Forest Folk; they didn't share any startling resemblance, certainly none of the stamp of common blood
marking Sorgrad and 'Gren. They were all men and women
grown, no children or elders, who worked together with an
ease suggesting long familiarity. One woman with an impressive array of rings and earrings, chains of silver and
gold close around her neck, unwound a thin rope from
around her waist.

"That's not stout enough to hold anything," 'Gren observed dubiously, assessing the rope with an expert eye.

"Look over there," nodded Sorgrad, pouring boiling water on herbs in a twist of muslin. Three others had unslung
ropes and were deftly twisting them into a stronger cable.
Once done, they knotted theirs securely to a similar length
made by another trio and stood waiting for a third to twist
into a still thicker cable.

A whistle too deliberate to be a bird turned my head and I saw Folk climbing an oak tree on the far bank of the river. One stepped forward and clapped his hands and the taller of our original bowmen loosed an arrow with a fine line tied to it. It nearly spitted the feet of the man waiting on the far bank.

"He's got steady nerves," murmured 'Gren appreciatively. He wrinkled his nose at a sodden heel of bread and tossed it aside.

"The one shooting or the one waiting?" I quizzed him, picking a thread of tough meat from between my teeth.

A cord was tied to the line, heavier rope to the cord and, after a flurry of activity up a tree on our side, a substantial cable swung above the water. The river skulked below in sullen muddy eddies.

"They look like they know what they're doing," Sorgrad observed. Two more cables were strung to join the first, one hand-high and the other chest-high. The Forest Folk began to cross the river, blithe as if they were on a four-span bridge.

"How's the minstrel's lass supposed to manage that?" 'Gren raised an eyebrow.

I looked for Frue. He was talking to the girl with the deerskin bag as she laid a silver-ringed hand on Zenela's bruised forehead. "I'll bet he'd welcome a tisane to wake him up. Have you any mariseed?"

Sorgrad obliged with an unappetizing cup, scummy with dull green dust.

"I'll take some wine if you can find any, with a little hot water and honey," I added hopefully.

"My dear girl, how terribly old-fashioned." Sorgrad shook his head in mock horror. "Everyone of discerning taste drinks tisanes nowadays." But he turned to investigate a stack of bottles laid carefully aside by a merchant.

I crossed the bustling campground, careful not to slip. The surface of the mud was drying out but the ooze beneath was treacherous. I nearly lost my footing when a fu-

rious argument broke out behind me. The three we reckoned were raiders stood nose to nose. Two were shoving
the third man away, threatening words backed up by gestures.

"What's their quarrel?" I asked one of the packmen.

"They just found their mate," he told me somberly.
"Throat cut, not drowned."

I shook my head and went on my way. Pulling a knife on
'Gren is generally the last mistake a man makes. I looked
around the remaining travelers. The merchants and wagoneers were busy making beasts and vehicles fit, but the
rest were staring at the rope bridge with dismay, slow to
shake off the shock of the flood.

Frue was talking to a Forest lad, speed and accent defeating my slight knowledge of the tongue. The lad's green eyes
darted to me several times, warming with a hint of admiration. He was a good-looking boy, at that age where height
outstrips strength but with a promising width to his shoulders. Freckled like a throstle, his hair caught the frail sun
shining through the tops of the trees with a gleam like burnished copper. A necklace of white and red gold twisted
around the base of his throat.

I realized the woman with the deerskin bag was looking
at me with an amusement that I didn't entirely like. She
was about my own height and build but looked as if she
needed more meat on her bones. No-nonsense eyes, dark
beneath heavy brows and unremarkable mid-brown hair
studied me.

The boy asked her some question and I was gratified to
find I could understand her reply, slowly spoken with a distinctly different accent.

"She needs rest and careful nursing if she is not to suc-
cumb to the rot in her lungs. The more she is moved and
distressed, the weaker she will become."

Zenela was an unhealthy color in the strengthening daylight, struggling to suppress a soft, persistent cough. Her
bruised and bloodshot eyes were wide and fearful as she

glanced from Frue to the woman, unable to follow their conversation.

"Where's the closest place we can get care for her?" I wondered if we would have to part from the minstrel.

"Orial will nurse her." Frue's surprise was close to a rebuke. "I am born of the blood and those in my protection are treated as such in turn."

"I'll go and make ready." The woman stood up and brushed the dirt from her leather leggings. "In the meantime, steep these thoroughly in boiled water. Have her drink it hot and tell her to breathe in the steam." She unfolded a small oilskin packet and handed Frue a handful of dried flowers, nothing more enigmatic than cowslips. I remembered the bitter taste all too well from childhood rheums, when tisanes were something you took when you were sick or not at all, not an elegant fad.

I handed Frue his tepid tisane. "May we stay with you for a day or so? We could do with some rest before moving on."

"You're of the blood, you'll be welcome enough." Frue looked at me with some asperity. "Can you save your questions about old songs for later? The sooner these outdwellers are got over the river and sent on their way, the sooner Zenela can be moved to shelter."

"Of course." I gave Zenela an encouraging smile and made my way over to Usara.

"What of the beasts and the goods?" A balding carter was looking dubiously upward at Forest Folk above his head weaving thin ropes around the cables of the bridge to give an illusion of sides. "We can't carry them over that!"

"We should probe the ford," Usara replied with an innocent air. "The bridge pillars will have spared the riverbed from being too badly scoured."

"I'll cut a pole," the carter muttered unconvinced as he walked away.

I looked pointedly at Usara's freshly damp and dirty sleeves. "And how is the ford?"

"Sound enough for the wagons, if they take it slowly;

harness up an extra pair of horses." Usara heaved a sigh. "At least whatever was awry yesterday has abated so the water isn't fighting me."

"Don't take too much out of yourself," I warned him.

He smiled thinly. "If anyone else has the skills to rebuild a riverbed, then I'll be delighted to accept their help."

His gaze moved to a point behind me and I turned to see Sorgrad approaching. "Ravin says to get this lot moving. The Folk will help out travelers caught in the flood but they're not about to take on bridgckeeping for the summer."

"Ravin?" I asked.

"With all the knives," explained Sorgrad.

I climbed up to test the bridge for myself. Cautiously getting the measure of the sway and the flex, I walked toward the river. I looked down to a circle of upturned, curious faces.

"It's all very well for her, she's one of them, climb like squirrels, everyone knows that," said a Soluran woman, her Tormalin with the lilt common to both sides of the border. Despite the mud crusting her gown, she had found a lace cap from somewhere and made time to comb out and pin up her hair. I recognized her as the woman who'd taken charge by the fire.

"That's hardly true of me." Sorgrad appeared at her elbow, words thick with the accents of Col. "If I risk it, perhaps you'll try?"

He climbed up with a convincing air of uncertainty. I offered him my hand as he got to his feet with a suitably nervous smile.

"Follow me and try not to look down," I advised reassuringly. I walked slowly, feeling the bounce of Sorgrad's clumsy steps behind me. "This isn't going to work if they see 'Gren going across like a startled ferret," I murmured. "Where is he?"

"Gone to get whatever it was he hid last night," Sorgrad replied easily. "Will that be enough to convince the goodwife?"

"Do we tie a bell around her neck, to make sure all the rest follow?" I smiled down at the open-mouthed crowd.

Sorgrad turned around with exaggerated care. "It's a sight easier than it looks," he said loudly, "and I'll go for crossing dry shod than risk a second soaking!"

"Come on, Ma." An eager lad was urging the woman on; he was nearly grown but his face had been scoured pink and clean by his mother, same as any other morning. His sisters were rolling over a sprung cask of wine discarded from a wagon, practicality doubtless learned at their mother's knee.

The goodwife looked up, face grim but determined. Tucking the hem of her skirts into the sash at her waist, she climbed onto the cask and hauled herself clumsily onto the bridge. A timely boost to her rump from a carter surprised an oath from her that set her daughters giggling.

"Get your balance." I gave her an encouraging smile. "Take it very slowly, one step at a time, don't look down, that's right, look at me, just one hand or one foot at a time."

I continued this litany of reassurance as the woman planted one sturdy shoe in front of the other, dirty stockings over thick ankles wobbling a little, knuckles white as she gripped the ropes. She murmured a stream of prayer to Drianon as we proceeded. I added a brief request of my own; if she slipped, there was no way I could hold her.

"That's fine, just keep going, we'll be over the river in no time." She glanced down for an instant at the turbid ocher waters below. "Don't look down," I snapped. That brought her head up in indignation. "If you don't do this, no one will," I told her. "You'll be stuck for Trimon only knows how long. It'll be days before that ford's low enough to risk your children in."

She drew a deep breath, moving slowly but not faltering until she reached the far bank and helpful Forest hands helped her down to the safety of the grass.

"I'd rather risk childbed five times over," she said with

feeling, fanning herself with the edge of her wrap. Still, her voice was firm as she shouted back to her children. "Mirou and Sarel, get your skirts up well out of the way. Go on, this is no time to be coy about men seeing your legs, you silly girl! Esca, you follow your sisters. No, one at a time, I don't want you all over the water at the same time. Show some sense, Mirou, use both hands!"

She kept up this stern encouragement until they were all safely on the ground, where she hugged them as if she would never let them go. "So, what are you lot waiting for?" the goodwife called over their heads to those still dithering on the far bank.

Drianon grants mothers a tone of command second to none. By the time the sun was fully clear of the treetops, everyone was across the river bar the carters waiting with their vehicles. We all watched the first wagon edge into the water, men cursing as the water splashed up around them. The river was still running strong enough to tug at the wheels and rock the cart bed alarmingly.

"Get on, get on!" The driver lashed at his lead pair, whip merciless around their ears as the horses shied from the assault of the icy water. Men leaned into ropes twisted into the harness of each beast to drag the horses onward. The animals plunged forward, straining at their collars. With a mighty effort, they hauled the heavy cart clear, shaking and sweating, rewarded with slaps of delight, soft words and handfuls of fresh grass. The carter was soaked, but beamed with relief. His livelihood was across the river intact.

As the rest of the wagons made the crossing, I noticed Usara arguing with the merchant waiting by the last cart and I ran back across the bridge. "What's the problem?"

"I don't think we should risk this man in the cart." Usara's displeasure was clear beneath his tight politeness.

"Hory can't take the bridge," protested the merchant.

Hory lay on muddy blankets in the bottom of the wagon, both legs now crudely splinted, thick bandages holding green-stained dressings in place.

"You'll use magic to get him across the water, won't you?" I queried mildly.

"Of course," said Usara, exasperated. "Why ever not?"

I saw fear darken Hory's eyes. "You can trust him," I reassured the man.

Hory's mouth set in an obstinate line. "The ford's sound enough. I'll trust to that."

"Your choice." I took Usara by the elbow to force him out of the way. "Let the runes roll how they choose."

Usara's indignant reply was lost as the wagoneer whipped up the horses and drove them into the punishing stream. The cart slipped sideways at once with no weight of cargo to steady it. Hory clung to the sides, white with fear and cursing fit for a mercenary. The wagoneer lashed the beasts but the cart was increasingly dragged askew. If Hory went into the water, he wouldn't surface again.

"Do something, Usara," I urged.

"Why should I?" snapped the mage with ill-suppressed fury.

"Fair enough." I folded my arms. "It won't be the first time stupidity's been the death of someone."

Usara shot me a fulminating glance but shook his cuffs loose from his wrists. With a flash of golden light that left the sun colorless, he sent a shaft of magic into the water. The river seethed around the wagon in a boiling confusion of gold, azure and sapphire and the horses fought against their reins as the carter clutched them in shock.

"Get them moving, you fatherless son of a pox-addled whore," snarled Usara. Hearing him swear like that outweighed the treat of the magelight for me. The carter brought his whip down on the wheel horses, lashing until the weals on their rumps were edged with blood. I looked across the river to see open mouths and wide eyes on every face as the wagon hauled out onto the shallow slope, the last faint tendrils of magic light fading from its wheels with the water dripping onto the muddy turf.

"Me, I'd have let them drown," 'Gren commented. Sorgrad was a few paces behind.

"But you're not a mage of Hadrumal, trained to use your magic for the greater good, are you?" I gave Usara a friendly smile.

The wizard muttered something under his breath, gave Sorgrad an entirely unwarranted look of annoyance and stalked away. He was breathing heavily, cheeks sunken beneath his angular cheekbones and weariness plain in the sag of his shoulders.

"It really does take it out of them, doesn't it?" Sorgrad remarked thoughtfully.

"It does," I agreed. "Good thing really, given what he might be able to do if he put his mind to it."

'Gren had an unfamiliar saddlebag slung over one shoulder and I realized the raiders were nowhere to be seen. "Where did our friends go?"

"Took themselves off back toward Medeshale," Sorgrad replied.

With a burst of activity the other travelers departed, keen to make up lost time or anxious to get away from Usara's magic. The Forest Folk began dismantling their bridge and I saw Orial had returned with a litter of rough-cut branches and colorful cloth for Zenela.

"Your outdweller man is a mage?" The good-looking lad came over, eyes bright with curiosity.

"My friend," I corrected him. "Yes, he is a wizard."

"This magic, how is it learned?" he asked, evidently intrigued.

"It's a power one is born with." I turned my mind to my original purpose. Good deeds today might put me in credit with Saedrin; what I wanted for this life was credit with Messire and with Planir. "Do the Folk have magic among themselves?"

We walked behind four well-muscled lads supporting Zenela's litter.

The lad shook his head. "No, we have no enchantments."
I kept my tone light. "Not at all?"

"No. So, what brings you to the greenwood at this season?" He was looking hopeful.

"I have a book of ancient songs, some written in the tongue of the Folk." I smiled, encouraging. "I want to learn more about them."

If I could get Frue singing those old ballads, I could look for anyone showing any particular interest or recognition, I decided. We made our way through glorious spring green, creeping carpets of blue hornflower mimicking the bright sky above. Of course, in most old ballads the crucial revelation enabling the lost prince to prove his claim generally falls into his lap three verses before the end. Real life has never proved that easy in my experience.

The settlement Ravin led us to came as something of a surprise. I hadn't exactly been expecting savages sitting under the trees and waiting for the nuts to fall, but I'd been imagining shelters made of leafy branches or some such. We found a broad clearing and Folk busy around a loose scatter of round dwellings cloaked in thick mats of woven tree bark. A woman was hanging brightly patterned bedding out to air over a wooden frame polished with use and children were playing happily with some half-grown pups by her door. Another circle of women was sitting busy with leatherwork and sewing. The younger ones exchanged lively banter with lads stacking firewood in precise cones close by. All wore close-tailored leather leggings with tunics of varying lengths and cut. The younger men favored a sleeveless style displaying muscular arms to best advantage while most of the women opted for plenty of pockets. So much for the exotic mysteries of the wildwood. This was domestic enough for Ryshad's mother.

"That'll be for us." Frue nodded at a group busy making a new house. One girl was digging out a fire pit while another piled stones ready to line it and a third marked out a circle on the swept turf. Four older women were making a long, flexible lattice of fine wands pierced and tied with leather thongs while a couple more carried over rolls of woven matting.

"Bring her in here." Orial appeared at a door with a spray of greenery fixed above the lintel. The litter was laid down and Frue carried Zenela into the low house. Curious, I followed to see her settled in a bed frame strung with tanned skins and covered with a woolen coverlet that could have come from any town in Ensaimin. A paroxysm of coughing left Zenela gasping, tears on her cheeks and fear in her eyes.

"Sit her forward and unlace her gown," Orial ordered. Frue leaned Zenela against his shoulder and Orial rubbed an oily salve into the girl's back, pungent with garlic and something else that I couldn't identify. I coughed. There might be mysteries for apothecaries here but I saw no sign of the intense mysticism of the Soluran healers who'd mended Halice's leg.

"Breathe out, slowly and steadily." Orial bent her ear to Zenela's mouth, felt the beat of her heart in her neck and then pulled down her eyelids with a gentle finger to check the color of her blood. Just like any apothecary I'd ever visited. "Now, settle yourself and try to sleep a little." She shooed me and Frue out with one hand and I saw Zenela's eyes were already drowsy. I wondered just what was in that rub.

Frue pushed past me and went to speak to Ravin. Sorgrad, 'Gren and Usara were nowhere to be seen and I was uncertain what to do. I didn't like the sensation.

"You'll share that with your men." Orial's voice behind me made me jump. She pointed at the circle of lattice now roofed with stronger rods all meeting in the middle and socketed into what had to be an old cartwheel. The fire irons being fixed in the pit looked suspiciously like wellhammered wagon struts as well. I thought about going to help but everyone involved looked well used to sharing the task. I wasn't about to risk showing myself up by making some error.

I sat down next to Orial, who was pounding some hapless root to pulp with a pestle and mortar. Thick mats of coarse linen were wrapped around the walls of our new home, covered in their turn with stout woven bark securely lashed with ropes of twisted vine. "Do we thank Ravin for this?" I asked.

"Frue is of the Folk and as such can expect shelter in any campground." Orial's gaze was somewhat superior. "You are not of the Folk, even if you are of the blood, are you?"

"You're not from around here either," I countered. "Your speech is different from the rest."

"I am from the far south," Orial replied easily. "I am traveling to learn new wisdoms. I will return to my own people in time—for winter." I had the impression she might have said something else but her face was hidden as she searched in her deerhide bag.

"What kind of wisdom are you seeking?" I asked casually. "Something of the kind my friend Usara has? Magic or enchantments?"

Orial pulled a little knife from her belt and added flakes shaved from a leathery dried stem to her paste. "I'm a herbalist, as my mother before me and most of the women in my line. I look for new knowledge of roots and leaves, powers of flower and fruit to soothe and cure." She nodded toward the new house. "You should go and light the first fire in the hearth, for luck."

Like any new bride in Vanam, taking possession of the kitchen soon to become her whole world? Not likely, I thought. Orial was humming again, intent on her work.

"Frue was playing that tune last night," I remarked. "Do you know him?"

"Not beyond brushing shoulders today." Orial shrugged. "It's 'The Lay of Mazir's Hands.' All healers sing it, for luck."

"Could you sing it for me, please?" I sat on the damp earth, hugging my knees, all innocent appeal. There was something about the tune tugging at me like an importunate child.

Orial looked up at the sun, overhead now and dappling the ground with shadows. "I suppose I could spare a little while." Her voice was rich and full, her accent far closer to what I remembered of my father's than Frue's thicker, more fluid tongue and as the tune soared and dipped, I listened close for the words. Kespar, whoever he might have been, had been duped into a wager with Poldrion that he could swim the river between this world and the Other faster than the Ferryman could row his boat across. Unsurprisingly, the demons got him and Kespar went home to Mazir with pride and hide both in tatters. She healed him with love, herbs and teasing rebuke. That was the burden of the verses at least but the refrain meant nothing to me beyond a teasing echo.

"What does that mean," I asked, " 'ardeila menalen reskel serr'?"

"It's just jalquezan," Orial struggled for a translation as I sat looking blankly at her. "Word-music."

"But what does it signify?" I persisted.

"It's meaningless." She waved her pestle in a helpless gesture. "Nonsense, just word-music."

"You sing this for luck?" I itched to go and fetch my song book. After the delays of the journey and the reverses of the night before, it finally looked as if the luck was running my way.

"It's a tale reckoned to bring good fortune to medicine or poultice." Orial was looking perplexed.

"Are there other songs you sing for luck, especially for different things?" I asked with studied casualness. "Are there many with this jalquezan?"

"There's 'Viyenne and the Does,' " Orial said after a moment. "When she fled Kespar's advances, she had to turn herself into a deer and hide in the midst of a herd. Then there's 'Seris and the Bridge,' 'Mazir and the Storm.' They all have jalquezan but I don't know of anyone singing them for any particular reason. Why do you ask?"

I shrugged. "Just curious." I got up and headed for our neat new house, where Frue was unrolling his sodden blanket and spreading it on the roof to dry. Our other bags were stacked inside the door and I opened mine with trepidation. My clothes were damp and smelled like a bucket of frogs but the oilskin I'd added to the song book's wrappings had been coin well spent. The linen beneath was barely damp at the outermost corners and the book within was untouched. I heaved a sigh of relief.

Frue was looking at me with mingled irritation and amusement as he tenderly inspected his lute. Trimon only knows how he'd kept that safe from the flood. "What are you getting that out for?"

"Orial and I have been talking about songs and I'd like her opinion on some of these." I smiled at him. "She's been telling me about the jalquezan. That would be the bits you couldn't translate for me?" I was mentally kicking myself for mistaking Frue's meaning when he'd said that. "Mazir and the Storm," here it was. A tale of losing the path and finding it again.

"Of course," he nodded, unconcerned. "No one can, I told you."

I managed a casual tone. "You said there was no point singing these on the road, where no one would understand the words. How about giving Orial a song or two as she works? These Folk will be able to follow them and it would go some way to thanking them for their help today, their care of Zenela. We could both put something back in the balance, couldn't we? No time like the present, isn't that what they say?"

Frue looked around the glade where men and women were sitting over undemanding tasks or openly taking their ease in the thin sunshine. "You know, whoever your father is, Livak, I'll bet he's a man with a lot to answer for."

He picked up his lute nevertheless and carried it over to

sit by Orial. I followed with the precious song book and propped it in my lap so Frue could see the pages. He said something to Orial that escaped me and then struck up a jaunty melody. Forest words in his rich tenor were less easy to follow, but this was one he had already translated for me on the road. A man had gone wandering in the deep woods, finding a strange woman who—for some reason I missed— turned into a grotesque hag when he pursued her. Our hero declined her invitation to stay as her lover and tried to find his way back to his people, only to find himself lost among strange trees and stranger encounters, each taking him farther from home. When he eventually came full circle, he discovered he'd been absent five full years, not just the five days he'd lived through.

Now that I heard it sung for the first time, this jalquezan clamored for my attention, underscoring every instance of the man's lament over his plight. The underlying rhythms were increasingly familiar; Geris the gentle scholar had used aetheric charms with just such a beat. The Elietimm bastards who'd killed him and had done their best to pull my wits out through my ears had spoken foul enchantments ringing with just such a cadence. But what did the words mean? Was this Artifice or coincidence?

Frue finished with a flourish of chords and two women came over to join us.

"That's a tale I haven't heard since I was a little girl," one smiled.

"I have a book full of ancient songs." I turned the pages so she and her companion could see. "Are there any others you know?"

The women shrugged. "We do not read, me nor Serida," the first one explained easily.

"How about this?" Frue turned back a few leaves of parchment and frowned as he fingered the frets on his lute. His face cleared and he began a tune with a tricky shift of pitch in the middle of the verse. The women nodded with laughing eyes and joined him in a lively song about the

original White Raven. Orial looked up from her work and
added a descant and Frue slipped into a lower harmony,
blending and dropping away in elegant counterpoint. I listened intently, finding myself nodding to the beat, but while
the tune remained constant, the words dissolved into chaos
when they reached the refrain.

Laughing, Frue stopped playing and Orial chuckled. She
said something to the women and I cursed my lack of this
tongue yet again. Orial looked at me. "This is the problem
with jalquezan; everyone knows a different version!" She
repeated herself to the first woman, who nodded after a moment.

"Once again, then." Frue struck up the tune and this time
they all agreed on the chorus, their exuberant song turning
heads all around the camp. More Folk came over and joined
in the song, each adapting their accustomed words to the
majority.

The first woman looked at me when they finished.
"You've yet to light a fire in your hearth, haven't you?" Her
Tormalin was barely accented to my ears. "You should do it
before the sun begins to sink."

She stood up so I set the song book carefully on the
ground beside Frue. "Will you look after this, if I leave it
with you?" I asked nervously.

"Like a child of my blood," he promised. Since he'd
taken better care of his lute through the flood than Zenela, I
judged he meant that.

I crossed the open glade to fall in with the woman as she
emerged with a bundle of sticks from her shelter. "My name
is Livak."

"I am Almiar." With scant flesh on her bones and skin
tanned like fine kidskin, I couldn't put an age to her beyond
being of my mother's generation. Her russet hair was generously sprinkled with white and her eyes were a warm
brown, deep set in a lattice of wrinkles woven from good
humor. "You are very welcome here, my dear."

"I'm curious about the song you were singing," I said casually. "How is it that you all knew different words, especially the jalquezan?"

Almiar was laying a precise fire in the stone-lined pit, setting tight-pressed lumps of dried moss among the sticks. "You learn such things at your mother's side," she shrugged. "As she did from hers and so on, back down the Tree of Years. Everything grows and changes, words are no different."

In other words, with every shift and repetition, changes of emphasis and paraphrasing crept in, until what might once have been aetheric enchantment was now a myriad versions of nonsense. My earlier optimism sank like a stone; there was going to be no instant revelation to send me straight to the feast at the end of the ballad, was there?

Almiar offered me steel and flint and then peered up through the smoke hole at the center of the roof at the sun. "You could probably still use a burning-glass, if you prefer."

But the rhythm I was hearing from the songs outside still rang with the pulse of aetheric magic. I cleared my throat. "I have another way to light a fire." I knelt beside Almiar and took a breath to steady the qualms in my stomach. Artifice had invaded my mind and pursued me with merciless intent on more than one occasion. I was in two minds about ever using it myself, but this was a small enough trick, one of the very few I knew and harmless enough, no more than the festival trick I'd first thought it. "Talmia megrala eldrin fres."

Wouldn't the older women have the wisdom of the Folk in their keeping? If they saw I had some learning of such craft, they would surely share it.

Almiar looked startled as little yellow flames crackled among the sticks, setting the moss flaring. "How did you do that?"

"It's a—a charm of sorts," I told her.

"How clever." Admiration overcame her shock. "You are a mage then, like your man?"

"His magic is of the elements." I shook my head. "This is a trick of a scarcer magic, what they call Artifice. Don't you have similar charms among the Folk?"

"Oh no, I've never seen the like before." Almiar's eyebrows rose and I'd have wagered every coin ever passed through my hands that she spoke the truth. "It's a marvel, isn't it?"

I smiled to hide my disappointment. Almiar suddenly looked concerned. "You won't show the children, will you? They'll start making a nuisance with flint and steel and even with the woods so wet—"

"No, I won't," I assured her. "But you could use it for your hearth, tell it to your friends." If the little fire trick spread, perhaps it would spark memory or recognition somewhere. I was casting runes at a venture now, but couldn't think what else to do. "Try it yourself," I urged, brushing a bare patch of earth clear before making a careful pile of kindling. "Feel the song in the words."

"Could I really?" Temptation was warring with her natural inclination to prudence.

"Just concentrate on the words," I encouraged her.

"Talmia megrala eldrin free." At least Almiar's saying it convinced me the lilt of the Folk ran through the incomprehensible words. A faint flicker lit the kindling.

"That really is remarkable!" Delight at her success shone bright in Almiar's dark eyes. "Now, will you be cooking for your men tonight or would you like to eat at my hearth?"

"They're not my men," I told her firmly. If they were, they'd choose anyone else's cooking over mine. "We'd be honored to eat with you."

Almiar paused at the doorway. "You have the instincts of your blood, child, for all you've been reared as an outdweller." She ducked outside without further ado.

I looked around at the shelter hemming me in and sighed. This was all very well in the balmy days of spring and summer, but I'd wager a penny to a packload that it would be cursed cold and damp come the winter. I'd rather have a stout stone house and a broad hearth, preferably with the coin to keep a maid busy bending her back over the cooking and cleaning.

Wondering where the others had got themselves to, I went out into the sunshine, blinking. The Folk were busy around their homes; a woman came to leave a pile of cooking pots by our door with a friendly smile and a girl shyly offered me a bowl of cresses gathered from some nearby stream. I could have bought either within half a street from home in Vanam.

four

While a charming song, this favorite of Forest minstrels shows indisputably that however foreign that race may seem to us, we all give due reverence to the same gods.

> Trimon took his harp up,
> As he sang to greet the day,
> For the sap was rising in the trees,
> And the spring sun lit his way.
>
> Larasion was plucking,
> Pale blossoms from the thorn,
> When Trimon wooed her with sweet words,
> And she stayed with him till dawn.
>
> Larasion walked softly,
> Summer flowers in her hair,
> Chanced on lonely Talagrin carving wood,
> And she paused to ease his care.
>
> Talagrin went hunting,
> Through the autumn leaves bright gold,
> When he caught Halcarion dancing,
> In the moonlight, bright and cold.

Halcarion met his passion,
As he matched his step to hers,
Until Trimon's music to the frost,
Drew her to the year-green firs.

The Great Forest,
13th of Aft-Spring

"My thanks for a superb meal." Sorgrad bowed to Almiar with consummate grace, the sweep of his velvet-clad arm defying the mud staining the amber fabric. The doublet glowed richly as the setting sun filtered through the trees.

"You are entirely welcome," she replied, a little bemused.

"It takes no more than a good cook to satisfy hunger, but to delight the palate, that is the work of an artist." He sounded like one of the Tormalin lordlings Ryshad must be trailing after and I stifled a grin. I'd known 'Gren and Sorgrad in the days when they owned three pairs of breeches, three shirts, two jerkins and a threadbare cloak between them.

"Yes, thank you." I looked at the applewood bowl I was holding. "Can I help you clear away?"

"No," Almiar took the bowl from me. "If I invite you to eat at my hearth, I do not expect you to work for the meal."

I smiled at her; that was a civilized custom as far as I was concerned. "I want to check on Zenela. I'll see you two back at the—"

"Roundhouse," Almiar supplied, "sura, in the blood tongue." She stacked the bowls inside a larger one that had held a mix of green leaves, some familiar to me, others strange but all palatable enough. An earthenware pot had proved to contain the shredded meat of an old hare, well flavored with herbs and cooked slow and solid, covered with a succulent layer of fat. My mother at her most censorious couldn't have criticized the cook for sending that up to table. I didn't think they ate that richly all the time, though; all these Folk looked as if they went a few meals short of a full belly as a rule.

We walked toward our own sura, other circles of Folk eating by the doorways to their homes. I wondered what the plural of the word might be. Would that signify the settlement as a whole? I knew precious little of these Folk whose blood I supposedly shared, didn't I?

'Gren was still chewing on a piece of flatbread. "I don't reckon to eat leaves, not as a rule."

I grinned at him. "You'd better get used to it hereabouts."

Sorgrad was studying the sura closest to our own. "How long do you suppose they've been settled here? That hare had been hung properly for one thing."

I looked at the beaten earth between the houses and the lack of fallen wood beneath the nearest trees. "Long enough to be foraging farther afield for fuel."

Sorgrad shrugged. "So, what now? Do you want to pursue this business with the songs some more?" I'd told them both of my earlier experiences.

"Frue's still got the book and I think we owe him the time to get all he wants from it. We wouldn't be getting this kind of hospitality without him." I rubbed a hand over my hair, feeling mud still in it. "I reckon we need to find the nearest inn, don't you? Get ourselves a game going and work out who's going to be most usefully indiscreet in their cups?"

"And that inn would be, what, a couple of handful days' walk back that way?" Sorgrad and I shared a rueful smile.

"Everyone's friendly enough. Given a few more days, I'd say we could start asking a few more pointed questions." I looked around at the little dwellings, doors open to any who might care to enter. The Folk seemed mighty trusting, I mused. Or was it just that they had nothing worth stealing? Their jewelry was valuable enough but they looked to keep that secure around hands and necks. "Everything the wizards have learned says aetheric magic came from the ancient races."

"Who are you trying to convince?" asked 'Gren lightly.

As we passed Orial's threshold, Frue emerged followed by a drift of steam redolent of thyme.

"How's Zenela?" 'Gren asked a breath ahead of me.

"Orial thinks she will do well enough," Frue said cheerfully. He fell in beside us and pulled up the deerskin that covered our doorway. "Did anyone rescue Zenela's bag?"

We all shook our heads. "The river claimed that." I ducked inside and poked at the little fire, laying on more sticks to give us both warmth and light. At least the Folk had been building these shelters long enough to master ventilation for their fires; I'd half expected we'd be smoked like eels on a stick.

"What does the lass want?" asked Sorgrad.

"Jewelry," said Frue with some reluctance.

"Jewelry?" I echoed incredulous. "The girl gets half drowned, she's all wrapped up in Drianon only knows what stinking poultice, and she wants to look her best in case anyone comes calling?"

"There's a lot more to it than that," Frue said with some harshness. "As you would know if you had any knowledge of the Folk to go with your blood."

"There's no call for that," said Sorgrad sharply.

"No, it's fair comment." I hid an unexpected pang at the minstrel's words. "What does she need jewelry for?"

The firelight cast harsh shadows from Frue's face. "Zenela has a fancy to live among the Folk awhile."

"But she's not Forest blood," said Sorgrad doubtfully.

"That's no bar." Frue's eyes were hidden in the gloom but he sounded a little shame-faced. "She's taken a fancy to the ballads and tales, especially the more romantic ones."

The more fool her. I kept my face noncommittal. Another silly girl looking for love in all the wrong places was no concern of mine. "And the jewelry?"

"It's customary among the Folk for men to give the

women they, ah, favor, some token of gold or silver." Frue's delicacy was belied by his grin, teeth bright in the firelight. "For a woman to wear her jewelry signifies she is open to offers, and it's generally reckoned that the more experience a woman has, the better a wife she'll make."

'Gren grinned lasciviously. "So what's the going rate for a good favoring?"

"You outdwellers don't understand, do you?" Frue shook his head. "Never mind."

I wondered what the women were making of the fact that I wasn't wearing any visible jewelry. "I think we might be able to come up with something." I shot a meaningful glance at 'Gren.

Frue nodded without expectation. "Where's Usara?"

"He was invited to supper with Ravin," I explained. "Have you eaten?"

Frue nodded. "With Orial. You know you have to repay these courtesies at your own hearth?"

So that was the catch in all this cheerful open-handedness. "You'd better give it some thought," I said to Sorgrad.

"What makes you think I'll be cooking?" he retorted.

"You're the one tells me I can't boil water without putting out the fire," I pointed out.

Frue stood up. "I want to see Ravin myself." He left, picking up his lute from the pile of cheerful blankets we'd been given from various neighbors.

"See you later." I turned to 'Gren. "Right, what did we get off those pony-boys that might get Zenela noticed by some handsome young buck out to try his horns?"

'Gren opened his shirt, untied a length of linen from around his waist and unrolled it. "I don't know where they'd been hunting but the pickings had been rich enough."

I held a small brooch set with amethyst closer to the firelight. "Wrede work, do you think?" I passed it to Sorgrad, who's always had the edge on me over jewelry.

"Almost certainly. I'd say they'd been working the Lake

Road." Sorgrad was studying a necklace. "Coming down from Bytarne maybe. This is Lakeland-made, and so's that leaf-pattern ring."

I picked up the silver ring. "This would be about Zenela's size. Since we had no real work to come by this, why not let her have a couple of pieces?"

"Give me one good reason, beyond the obvious," challenged 'Gren.

"Sorgren! The girl's ailing and stinking of garlic. Anyway, you said you weren't interested," I reminded him.

"That was when she was preening herself silly," countered 'Gren, bright-eyed. "The boot's on the other foot now."

"We want to be on good terms with these people," I pointed out. "If we're to learn anything to turn to coin and advantage."

"We help Livak get inside D'Olbriot's favor, he'll convince Draximal to call off his hounds." Sorgrad fixed his brother with a stern eye.

"You don't want to spend the next five years of your life rusticating in Solura, do you?" I hoped a noble refusal wouldn't make a liar out of me. Ryshad would be best placed to broach such a topic, I decided. He could speak to Esquire Camarl, who was definitely edging ahead of the pack nosing around for favor with the Head of their House.

'Gren pretended to consider it. "No, I prefer my towns bigger and closer together and my women smaller and more open-minded."

"You can look into attitudes hereabouts, with a few tokens of your esteem to offer," Sorgrad pointed out.

'Gren laughed. "So how are we splitting this? A few bits for the lass and the rest three ways? I take it our mage doesn't bother with trifles like this?"

"I don't think he needs to be worried with such things," I agreed.

Sorgrad rapidly sorted the spoils into three piles evenly

matched for value and content. He set aside a gold necklace, the leaf-pattern ring and a copper bangle set with polished amber. "Zenela can have those."

"That's probably crediting her with more experience than she can boast," I commented.

"Miaow." Sorgrad grinned at me.

I scooped up my own portion and shoved it hastily in a pocket as steps outside brought a shadow to the threshold.

Usara lifted the door drape. "Am I interrupting something?"

"Did you have a good meal?" I adjusted my shirt casually to conceal the new fullness to my jerkin.

"Yes, very pleasant." Usara was looking at us all with faint suspicion.

"Can you cook?" demanded Sorgrad, effectively quelling any question. "Does your magic extend to mundane tasks?"

"It can do, but my talents aren't primarily with fire and its associated skills," Usara replied cautiously.

"Are you saying fire mages are good cooks?" I interrupted, intrigued.

"As a rule," Usara nodded.

"Then you're in charge when we come to pay these folk back for the meals they've given us," said Sorgrad firmly.

'Gren got up. "I'll go and call on Zenela," he said with a predatory smile and left.

"It's her own fault for playing the unattainable fair maiden," observed Sorgrad. "Tell 'Gren he can't have something and that only makes him want it the more. He's just been waiting for a chance to get her off guard."

"True enough," I admitted.

"So, what were you talking about just now?" Usara looked from me to Sorgrad.

"Did you know that Forest girls expect jewelry in return for their favors?" I asked him.

"Oh, no, I didn't know that." A blush was visible on Usara's high cheekbones even in the firelight. He'd never have made a living from gambling, with that coloring to give him away so easily.

Sorgrad saw something I didn't. "Have you been getting the eye from one?"

"A couple of the younger women have expressed interest in my magic." Usara tried and failed to look unconcerned.

"Your magic?" repeated Sorgrad with delicate skepticism.

"That's right." Usara cleared his throat. "They seem quite intrigued by it, not like those mistrusting peasants." That clearly still rankled with the mage.

Sorgrad tossed over a necklace of silver interlaced with diamond-shaped links, which the mage caught with a surprised reflex. "Something to brighten a girl's eyes with, when you've given her a taste of your talents." His meaning was as obvious as a pig in a priest's robe.

"I don't make a habit of casual conquests, thanks all the same," replied Usara frostily.

"Do you have someone back in Hadrumal or—" I hesitated, " —are your tastes the same as Shiv's?"

"I beg your pardon?" Usara looked startled. "No, no, my—tastes—are for women, when I choose to indulge them. And no, I have no particular understanding with anyone, not that I see that is any of your business."

I raised a hand. "I didn't mean to offend."

"The disciplines of study in Hadrumal leave little time for indulging other appetites." Usara tried to look forbidding but just sounded prissy.

"And it's a small town so you don't foul your own doorstep?" Sorgrad hazarded with a grin. "Why not enjoy yourself here while you've got the chance. Some girl might share what she knows, if you show her—your wizardry." He got up and brushed at a stain on the front of his doublet. "If I can make myself presentable, I'll go and see if these Folk are as handy with the runes as rumor claims."

I looked at Usara as Sorgrad left. "Where did you get to this afternoon?"

"I was talking with Ravin, among others." The mage sighed. "We've got Folk here from a handful or more distinct lineages, did you know that? This isn't family in the usual sense of the word. These people might settle for the winter somewhere, different groups deciding to work together for a season or so. Come the spring, they split up, make new alliances, and move on. Some stay with their blood kin, others join troops traveling any amount of distance. None of them have any notion of a permanent home. Some of these Folk have been with Ravin for years, others joined him last autumn, this spring, even within the last few days."

"Life is growth and change; bud, blossom and fruit." Some long-ago words of my father came to me and before I realized I had spoken them aloud. "Sorry. Your point?"

"I really don't see how you can expect to learn anything of value here," he said dubiously. "There's no continuity, of kinship or custom or history from what I can make out. I sat with Ravin and three others for most of the afternoon, discussing floods and such hereabouts. Even where they agreed on some particular incident, they all had a different version of events. How are we to tell what are additions or omissions, even completely false elements in such a story?"

"We're not here to write a new chapter for the Annals of Col," I reminded him. "We're looking for any lore hidden in the songs." I hid my own doubts firmly beneath an optimistic face.

"Have you found anyone to translate the pieces Frue failed with?" He sighed again. "From what I am seeing, these Folk travel so widely the current generation barely even speak their own tongue."

"The older ones have been helpful," I countered. "I'm not about to give up just yet."

"There are precious few here beyond their second generation," commented Usara with a shake of his head. "Dwelling in the wildwood means short measure in the cup of life from Misaen. If there are any wise ancients sitting

over mysteries of lost magic in hidden glades, I'll eat that
song book."

"Not all wisdom and learning has to be set down with ink
and shut up in libraries," I told him firmly. "If you make up
your mind you're going to find nothing, that's just what
you'll do. You never know; the only certainties in this life
are sunrise, sunset and Saedrin's door at the end of it."

The more defeated the mage sounded, the more determined I became to prove him wrong. "I'm going to see if
Sorgrad's found a game worth a gamble."

Leaving the sura, I looked around the campground.
Small children were being rounded up for bed, and some
adults already sat by fires handily placed to rebuke small
faces peering around door curtains with hopeful requests. A
group of tired women relaxed over drink and conversation,
needlework laid aside now that the light had failed. A knot
of men with heads more white than copper were sitting by a
rack of spears, expansive gestures doubtless recounting
some notable escapade of youth.

It was a cozy scene and I felt utterly out of place. Fleeing
stifling domesticity in Vanam and more recently in Zyoutessela, I'd hardly expected to find it in the wildwood. What of
the songs my father taught me, of high adventure, untamed
spirits, mischief and merriment pursued in equal measure?
What of the ancient Artifice I'd been so certain would be at
the root of such tales? Had I talked the others into chasing
shades in the fog?

I set my jaw. I'd better find out and if so, we'd move on.
Nor was there any profit in getting all regretful because the
reality of life among the Folk didn't match up to my idle
fancies. I'd never pined over leaving Vanam behind so I
wasn't about to start hankering after a life I'd never even
known. I looked around for the good-looking lad with the
twisted necklace. He was nowhere to be seen, nor were his
cheerful fellows. Nor were the brightly decorated girls
who'd been carrying wood and water with gossip and flirtatious glances.

A snatch of music drifted along on a lazy evening breeze. I followed it into the darkness of the night-time Forest and smiled with faint humor. At least my Forest blood gave me better night-sight than the outdwellers, one useful legacy from my father in a traveling life. Beyond a gentle rise in the land, I saw a golden glow of firelight caged in a complex ring of tree trunks and picked my way cautiously toward it.

Alone in the gloom, I fingered my share of the raiders' booty. I could deck myself out with choice enough pieces to reflect my conquests, but what would that achieve? I'd just jingle like a festival rattle and I wasn't open to offers, was I?

I pulled out the leather thong I wear around my neck and weighed the rings on it in one hand. One gold ring was a boring piece, won from a particularly stupid cousin of Camarl at Solstice, nothing beyond a weight of sound metal to buy me out of trouble that I couldn't talk my way clear of. The other was a narrow band of red gold, delicate beading on either edge, finely incised with the stylized wave patterns that the southern Tormalin are so fond of. Ryshad's Solstice gift to me.

My conceit was hardly flattered by these people thinking Usara was the best I could attract, but if I wore this, as a remembrance of Ryshad, no one here would know what it signified. I hid the rings back beneath my shirt and stowed the other jewelry in my purse. Let these Folk think what they like about me; I had more important fish to fry.

The leaf mold of the Forest floor yielded to a soft carpet of fallen brown needles and the green spring undergrowth no longer brushed my legs. Moss clung to gnarled and twisted roots that grasped the swell of the earth like ancient fingers and I put one hand on the rough and flaky bark of a yew tree. This was a younger tree, upright and firm, heartwood strong and resilient. I moved closer to the light, where the trees bent beneath the weight of years, split to empty hearts where time and decay had eaten the dead wood away. But the outer shells grew strong and vigorous, new wood flowing like clay over the old. The firelight was brighter now, and I heard voices and laughter.

In the center of the grove was the oldest tree, a stumpy half-circle, deep fissures in the hollow wood, branches arching outward to curve back down to the soft layer of needles. Some were rooting themselves afresh to send out bright shoots, while fallen wood lay dead on either side. The central tree was crowned with spring green, feathery sprays of glossy needles rising from the ancient wood. I breathed in the resinous scent and childhood memory stirred. No, this untamed place bore scant resemblance to the groves maintained and trained for bow staves in the cities of Ensaimin. I'd once asked my mother why the mysterious trees were so strictly fenced, disappointed by her explanation of poisonous berries. Looking at this mighty tree claiming its ground and extending its domain with seedling and branch, I felt my childhood fancy had been justified. Those trees had been fenced to stop them getting loose and driving out the tyranny of stone and brick.

But that was just a child's notion. For the moment, I'd found what I'd been seeking. Folk sat where fallen branches offered handy seats, or where the living arms of the tree dipped down to offer their embrace. Loose groups around the fire fed it with dead wood granted by the great tree and her lesser daughters. The flames burned bright yellow, white at their core, crackling and shifting like a living thing.

As I was wondering how to insinuate myself into the gathering, one of those closest looked around and I recognized the good-looking lad.

"Join us." He extended a welcoming hand.

"Good evening to you all." I sat next to him and smiled, friendly and unremarkable, that's me. Three sets of female eyes examined me for adornment and I was flattered by a hint of disappointment in the men's gazes.

"You are Livak?" one asked politely. "Of the blood but an outdweller?" His hair and close-trimmed beard looked brown rather than red, though that may have been the light. You could find his face anywhere in eastern Ensaimin, round-jawed with heavy brows, but his vivid green eyes were unmistakably of the Folk.

"That's right." I remembered a phrase from an old song. "My father cast his dreams upon the wind and followed them. He was a minstrel and he paused a while to sing for my mother who lived in a city of Ensaimin." Who had never taken pleasure in music since his departure. I discarded that sudden, irrelevant thought.

The girl beside him said something that escaped me, her smile so sweet it was probably none too polite.

"I speak little of the tongue of the Folk." I dimpled some charm at the man.

"Don't concern yourself. We all learn the tongue of the outdwellers, for trade and travel. Folk who come from far distant can have speech strange to our ears as well," he smiled back. "I am Parul."

"I am Salkin," the good-looking lad with the necklace offered and the rest introduced themselves. Nenad was a skinny youth with a raw-boned face and freckles more affliction than adornment. The girls, sisters with well-formed figures and tightly curling auburn hair, were, from youngest to oldest, Yefri, Gevalla and Rusia. All wore a couple of unremarkable trinkets and discreetly hopeful expressions.

"What are you doing?" A square of leather on the ground had a set of runes spread on it, wooden and each half the length of my hand rather than the finger-joint lengths of bone I carried. Three triangles made of three runes joined to make a large one, creating a fourth in the center, just like a birth sigil.

"Seeing what the fate sticks show us of the future," one of the girls, Gevalla, giggled.

"How very interesting," I said slowly.

"Do you do this, beyond the wildwood?" Salkin asked. I could smell the spicy scent of new sweat on his clean body.

"We game with runes, sometimes for coin," I replied cautiously. "Do you?"

Parul nodded toward a lively circle on the far side of the fire. "Certainly."

I looked over and saw two bright blond heads among the range of russet and brown. So 'Gren had decided to pursue more promising game than Zenela. That was probably just as well, because I couldn't see her romantic virginal notions surviving an encounter with him.

"Do the fate sticks show you the truth?" Looking no more than idly curious, my thoughts raced; aetheric magic is a magic of the mind. I've seen enough fortune-tellers to know the charlatans deduce four parts from five in any prediction from clothing or accent or demeanor, but did the Folk somehow hold the missing fifth? Perhaps there was some Artifice hidden in the wildwood. I held my excitement firmly in check but wondered where I might find a less precious book for Usara to choke down.

"If you truly want to know, the runes will speak to you." Rusia took the sticks, fitted the three-sided rods into a larger triangle and tapped their ends level.

"How?" A woman in Col who claims to be Aldabreshin does good business weaving mystery over a spread of colored stones. Her trick is statements so vague they answer any query.

"You can ask particular questions," Gevalla volunteered, her face eager, "or lay the sticks for a foretelling."

"Or for a picture of where you are and where you are going," added Yefri.

"Are they an accurate guide?" I made sure my skepticism didn't show.

"It depends." Salkin spread his hands. "Those who trust the sticks are shown truth. For those who doubt, the runes fall without meaning."

A convenient explanation for errors. "Who lays the sticks?" If the results were to be manipulated, there had to be a guiding hand.

"The seeker," Yefri said, as if it were obvious.

"Would it work for me?" I asked slowly. "As an out-dweller and unsure of it?"

The two girls looked at Rusia, who rolled a rune stick between her fingers like a professional fixer. "It's belief that governs the sticks. If you believe, they will speak true. I'll read them for you if you like."

"I'm curious," I said slowly, "and willing to believe. Is that enough?" I let a hint of a challenge edge my words.

Rusia's eyes shone dark and determined. She rolled the runes between her hands and pulled one free. "This is your birth rune?"

I held the polished yew wood between my hands, each image upright as I turned the three faces. The symbols were more fluidly carved than I was used to but were undeniably the Wellspring, the Harp and the Zephyr. I nodded slowly. "My father told me he drew this rune when I was born, that these are lucky symbols for me." Could she have learned this from 'Gren or Sorgrad?

"Rusia's always able to draw someone's birth rune," said Yefri with pride.

"Then he was truly of our blood," commented Salkin. "Only the Folk take a single stick and read the three sides together. Outdwellers have all manner of strange rituals."

"The Men of the Mountains draw a single rune," Rusia corrected him with a hint of rebuke.

One chance in nine was not impossible odds. I looked at Rusia and pointed to 'Gren. "You've not spoken to him?"

"No, not at all." She half turned in her seat. "Why?"

"Could you draw his birth rune, read something from it, even though you know nothing of him?"

Rusia nodded, a combative glint in her eye. "A test?"

"Go on, Rusia, we know you can do it," Gevalla urged. The others all nodded, entirely confident in the girl's talents.

Rusia took a moment to look thoughtfully at the nine sticks in her hand before taking a deep breath and plucking one from the bundle. "Are these his birth runes?"

"What do you read about him?" I countered.

Rusia pursed her lips. "The Storm is dominant of those three, a strong rune, masculine. He is inclined to temper and to trouble."

Which could be true of any man, in the right circumstances.

Rusia turned the rune. "Lightning, so he is given to sudden inspiration but—" she hesitated. "A lightning strike can be calamitous, it sets fires and great destruction can result."

I saw a curious detachment behind her eyes. The others were all intent upon her and I held my tongue. Rusia continued, her gaze fixed on something unseen. "The chime sounds as it is struck, so he has a reputation he does not care to deny or conceal. Striking is violence though—" She broke off. "I need his heavens sign." She reached for another rune stick and made an inarticulate noise of surprise.

"This isn't the heavens rune." Yefri took the stick from her. "How ever did you mispick?"

Rusia colored and reached again but suddenly stayed her hand. "What ruled the heavens at his birth?" she demanded.

"I don't know." The question had never come up.

Rusia's eyes were distant for a moment as she fingered the first stick she had drawn. "This is a rune of the mountains, linked to winds, to noise and disruption. There is something ill-omened—I cannot tell more without knowing his heavens sign."

The group all turned to look rather dubiously at both brothers, deep in a game with a gang of young men. I walked over to stand at 'Gren's shoulder. He turned his head briefly to acknowledge me.

"Your birth runes, 'Gren, do you reckon anything to them?" I kept my tone light.

'Gren glanced back to the noisy gambling. "Not beyond claiming that bone if we're drawing lots."

"What's the heavens rune for your sigil?"

"Empty." 'Gren turned with a wicked grin. "I was born at the dark of both moons." He opened his eyes wide, white all around the startling blue. "Born to be hanged, that's what they said."

"Who said?"

"So did Sandy go off to find a pretty neck for that chain?" Sorgrad spoke over his brother with a malicious grin.

"When I left him he was tucking himself up for the night." I looked at Sorgrad. "That was a costly gesture you made."

He grinned in the flickering firelight. "I'd pay twice over in solid coin for that kind of entertainment. And now we know how to drive the mage out of any conversation." He reached into a pocket and twirled an emerald signet ring on one finger. "What'll you put up against this if I say some girl has that collar around her neck and Sandy's got a spring in his step tomorrow morning?"

"No wager." I shook my head. "Watch that one with the chain bracelets," I whispered into 'Gren's ear before returning to Salkin and his friends.

I sat down by the leather square. "He was born under no heaven's sign, at the dark of both moons, Rusia."

She muttered something in the Forest tongue and I cursed my lack of the language again. "What does that signify?" I asked.

"It is . . . ill omened," Rusia said with a finality that forbade further inquiry.

Was this only superstitious nonsense or some lore shared by the ancient races?

"What could the runes tell you about me?"

She handed me the sticks with a challenge in her eyes. "Lay them as I tell you and we'll see, shall we? Don't look at them, don't choose, just set them down."

I took the runes from her and ran the smooth wood casually between my fingers. Polished from years of use, as far as I could tell there were none of the minute nicks or hollows that can tell practiced fingers so much more than the eye can see.

Rusia's eyes held mine. "One first, laid crossways," she

commanded, "then two below it, crossways again and three in a line below that." I did as I was bid. "The rest, one each at the corners of the triangle. No, pointing outward, like that."

I sat back. "So, what do they say?"

Rusia picked up the single rune, the first I had laid. She held it up to show me the sign on its base. "You were born under the protection of the sun."

"True enough," I admitted, curious to find that I had laid the heavens stick first.

"This second row speaks of your character." She looked at the two signs set upright beside each other. "Lightning, so you see yourself as creative, the Zephyr, so you consider yourself lucky." She looked at the reversed runes on the other visible faces of the sticks. "How do other people see you? The Storm suggests they find you difficult, prone to disagreement. The Wellspring? They think you conceal a great deal."

I smiled at her. She could try reading what I was concealing beneath my cheery unconcern if she liked.

She lifted the sticks to reveal the runes laid face to the leather. "And these speak of your true self. The Chime sounds for resolve, decisiveness. The Harp is a sign of craft, of skill, of cleverness."

So Rusia was a shrewd judge of character, even on slight acquaintance. And news of newcomers runs around any village like a dog with a bone in its mouth. She'd doubtless been listening to gossip all day.

"What about the rest?" I pointed to the bottom row of three.

"Your mother, yourself and your father," she said.

"Go on." We might as well see this through. There might be something to this if Rusia could tell me anything of significance about my parents.

She showed me the Pine, first of the runes set upright and facing me. "Your mother is strong like the tree yet flexible enough to weather a storm."

I'd certainly seen my grandmother's anger come down like summer thunder, my mother passive yet ultimately resisting her fury.

"But there's also adversity there. The Forest," Rusia frowned as she looked at the next rune along. "That's for resourcefulness but also for loss, getting lost. Reeds next, for flexibility but also for weakness."

I kept my face a mask of polite interest, ignoring recollection of my mother's laments, over being saddled with a minstrel's bastard and then over her cowardice in not following him. But surely any combination of runes could be interpreted to strike a resonance from any life?

"I've heard those traits linked to those signs but plenty of others besides," I said cautiously. "Tormalins call the Reeds Drianon's sign for faithfulness in marriage. In Caladhria they signify Arimelin's whispers carrying dreams."

"Rusia always knows which aspect applies," Yefri said, as if surprised I needed to ask. The others all nodded fervent agreement.

Rusia looked at me for a moment before considering the runes on the reverse faces. "For your father, the Wolf, that's ambition but also hunger unsatisfied. The Oak is strength, vigor in life, but also stubbornness, hollowness. The Salmon, for travel, for fertility." She smiled a little. "But also for a compulsion overriding all else. We can stop if you like," she offered.

She knew full well my father had been a traveling musician, there was no ingenuity needed for these so-called insights. I spread my hands. "May as well finish what we've started."

"Very well." She picked the runes up to look at the hidden symbols on the bottom-most faces. "As their child, you have the Mountain, endurance and vision but also a lonely rune. The Stag, that's for speed and courage, but can suggest running from things that you fear. The Sea, that's power, hidden depths, but a lack of direction as well."

I gave her a quelling look.

"The runes read your birth and family correctly, don't they?" demanded Gevalla.

I took a slow breath before answering. "Well enough, in some senses."

"Then let's see what your future holds." Salkin shifted his shoulder behind mine, keen to move closer. I smiled, a touch apprehensive, but I could hardly pull out now.

"Not just the future." Rusia pointed at the three remaining rune sticks, the ones set at angles to the original layout. "What is just past, where you are at present and what is to come."

Given the bizarre events I'd been caught up in over the past year and a half, any interpretation that even came close might suggest this was more than sideshow chicanery.

"The reversed runes are your recent past," Rusia explained. "Fire, a new passion, maybe even true love." She smiled at me and I grinned despite myself. "The Eagle, signs or omens, travel?" I nodded. "The Drum, secrets revealed, a break with something . . ." She looked uncertain.

I managed to look unconcerned. "I travel a lot, true enough." Maybe they did have the missing fifth here.

Rusia looked at the three upright runes. "The Ushal . . ."

"The what?" I queried. "We call that the North Wind."

"Outdwellers have lost much. Look at the rune, the wind coming off the mountains. It is the Ushal, the cold killing wind that comes off the heights in the cold days of winter." Rusia looked serious. "Opposite to the Teshal, what you call the Zephyr, the warm wind from the southern seas that brings rain and life." Her words tailed off, her manner distracted.

"So what does the Ushal mean for my present?" I prompted.

Rusia shook herself a little. "It's either a destiny or something missing. Are you seeking something? Broom, that's taking care of something, or maybe a blessing? The Calm, well, that could be a truth, study perhaps?" She looked frankly baffled.

"The mage and I have come to learn of Forest songs," I offered.

"These are your runes, not his," she said tartly. Again she fell silent, gazing perplexed at the symbols.

"So what of Livak's future?" Salkin was sitting so close I guessed he was keen to figure in my immediate fate.

Rusia lifted the runes with reluctant hands. "The Plains. A lifetime, more than that, endlessness, timelessness. Or maybe just an inheritance." She shrugged. "The Horn, a summoning, important news, but it might be for good or ill, perhaps a warning. The Earth, that's success, hard work, some grand event." She was speaking quickly now, running a hand through her hair. "You'll know better as the moons unfold the seasons, but these are powerful runes, the pattern suggests something important."

Doubtless I would, certainly it would be easy enough to find truths in such vague generalizations if I went looking for them. But what of her flights of fancy that had landed uncomfortably close to the mark?

Rusia was looking concerned again. "You are going to be moving on, aren't you? If you're going to be bringing down a storm on your head, I'd rather you did it somewhere else." She was absolutely convinced of the truths revealed in the patterns, I realized. So who was she deceiving, herself or me?

"Let me have them." Gevalla held out her hand. "I'm wondering whether I should travel beyond the wildwood this summer." She laid six sticks in two rows of three. "The positive signs in the top row are reasons why I should travel, the negative ones below are reasons why I should not," she explained.

"Is this just for journeys?" I asked.

"Or any question where you are looking for a yes or a no." Nenad spoke up for the first time. I saw him looking at Gevalla with hope in his eyes and listened to see if he tried to influence her reading of the runes one way or another as the six of them discussed the symbols and their relevance to

Gevalla's own wishes, her family, what travel might mean for her and for others. Nenad didn't seem to be pushing any particular course and they all seemed to be taking it very seriously. Rather than try to follow the intense discussion, I drew my own pouch of runes out of a pocket, a shorter set carved in bone in the Caladhrian style, and fingered the little charms.

"You can't lay a second reading in any one day." Rusia looked up. "And it won't work for you anyway, not unless you believe it will."

I sat and thought for a while longer about the various symbols, the interpretations Rusia had given for them, and did a few calculations on the likelihood of those runes falling in those places and aspect. Then I looked for all the reasons Rusia's guesswork could be intelligent enough to seem accurate. Did she have more than four-fifths on her side of the scale?

I felt suddenly tired, unsettled by memories of years and people long since discarded. "Thank you for sharing your skills," I smiled at Rusia, "but it's been a long day. I'll bid you good night."

"I'll walk you back." Salkin was on his feet, offering me his arm. I avoided meeting Yefri's chagrined gaze.

I didn't need the runes to deduce his intentions. As we picked our way through the trees, eyes adjusting to the gloom after the firelight, he took my hand to help me over some fallen wood. Then he put a companionable arm around my shoulders. When I did not object, he slid it down to my waist and drew me closer. The active life of the Forest kept him well muscled and lithe, the skin over his knuckles dry and rough as I laid my hand over his. Cold white moonlight was filtering down to the Forest floor through trees still to come into leaf. It leached all color, leaving ink-black shadows in hard-edged patterns.

Salkin stopped and turned to face me, bending his mouth to mine. He kissed me, softly at first, then with rising passion. I savored some unfamiliar spice on his lips and an answering heat rose deep within me. Opening my eyes, I saw his were closed, intensity in his face deepening with each breath. He pressed his hips to mine and I felt an urgency to match my own rising inclinations.

I broke away and took a pace backward, laying a hand on his broad chest. Fine auburn hair curled beneath my fingertips in the open neck of his tunic. "I don't think—"

Salkin clasped my hand and I felt passion drumming beneath the warm slickness of sweat. "No?" His disappointment was evident.

"We'll be moving on soon," I said slowly. "I don't want to leave unfinished business between us, so better not to start it, don't you agree?"

Despite some of my girlhood escapades, Halcarion graciously decided not to drop a star on my head for that lie, so I smiled winningly at Salkin. "For the present, can we just be friends?"

Hearing myself sound like one of Niello's less convincing heroines was almost too much. I was glad of the handy shadows hiding my smile. Men of sound character accept being turned down, be it with good or ill grace, but very few, even of the best, will take being laughed at.

Salkin heaved a sigh. "Then I'll see you back to your threshold," he said with a glumness that betrayed his youth.

"I can see the settlement fires from here." I shook my head. "You go back and enjoy yourself. I'm sure Yefri will be glad to see you," I couldn't resist adding.

"I'll see you tomorrow." He kissed me with an intent that promised further pursuit and retraced his path to the yew grove.

I walked toward the ring of roundhouses, my spirits absurdly buoyed, but when I arrived back at our sura, there was no one there to share the joke. Where had the wizard gone? Expecting to be disturbed before long, I claimed the softest and prettiest of the blankets and wrapped myself up. But by the time the camp had fallen silent, none of the others had returned and I was feeling a little piqued. No, curiosity and passing fancy are not sufficient reason to take a young man to your bed, even one as tempting as Salkin, I told myself firmly. If I had been irresponsible in the past, no harm had come of it, not to me anyway, but things had changed. Besides, Ryshad had spoiled me for anyone else. Getting a tune out of a second-rate fiddler would only leave me missing him more. I'd found myself better suited with him than any previous bedmate and I had more basis for comparison than most girls would consider respectable, I privately acknowledged. But no amount of moping would shorten the leagues between us, so there was no profit in that.

What about Rusia's little patter-game? But it wasn't a patter-game, was it? She certainly believed in what she was saying and so did the others. Was there any significance to that? Was there any significance to the few things she'd said that were close enough to the truth to make me increasingly uncomfortable? Curse 'Gren and Sorgrad both; where were they? Making some girl's eyes sparkle with a pretty trinket no doubt. I resolutely forced long-shunned memories of childhood, parents and everything else behind me. I was looking to the future, to new opportunities and hopefully sharing them with Ryshad. This was why I was failing to get to sleep in this uncomfortable, drafty, smoke-laden hole after all.

I nearly had myself convinced when unexpected slumber claimed me.

Teyvasoke,
17th of Aft-Spring, Late Afternoon

"What under the sun is that?" demanded Jeirran, astonished.

Keisyl squinted into the sun. "Carts, lowlanders,

smoke . . ." A sound of hammering echoed around the smooth slopes of the valley.

"How dare they!" Teiriol looked around for agreement.

Eirys bent down from her rough-coated gray pony. "Don't let's get involved," she pleaded. "Let's get to the fess. They'll be sorting it out, won't they?"

"If they've any mettle in their bones." Doubt shaded Jeirran's words.

"Come on." Keisyl pulled on the bridle of the pack mule he led. It followed him placidly, a string of others coming on behind. Jeirran and Teiriol were a little slower, glaring angrily at the activity they could now see clearly in a fold of land down by a stream. A handful of wagons were drawn up, awnings slung between them. Small figures were busy around a stack of fresh-felled trees, drifts of dust rising from a sawpit and one solitary man astride a massive log stripping bark and branches with an axe. Others were marking the unmistakable lines of a house with pegs and line in the muddied grass.

"Ho, you there!" The hail turned all their heads. A man in rough homespun came over a rise in the ground on a tall bay horse. "Where are you bound?" His tone was courteous but rang with unconscious authority that set Jeirran's beard bristling.

"Teyvafess," said Keisyl shortly.

The man shook his head. "What?"

"The fess," repeated Jeirran with annoyance. "The stronghold, you would say."

The rider nodded, absently wheeling his horse around. A bow was slung at his shoulder and a full quiver of arrows hung from his saddle. "You've no dogs with you?"

"No," said Keisyl slowly. "Why?"

"We're running sheep up by the river," explained the horseman. "I'll bid you good day."

"Wait!" Jeirran dropped his lead mule's reins and stepped forward. "What do you mean, you're running sheep? On whose authority and what are you building? How dare you fell in these woods?"

The lowlander rode away without answering, cresting the rise and disappearing from view.

"The thrice-cursed sister-whelped—" Jeirran gaped after him.

"Don't let's get involved," repeated Eirys. "The Teyvakin can tell us what is going on."

"Could they have sold a grazing term to some lowlanders?" asked Keisyl doubtfully.

"With a grant to fell and build?" scoffed Jeirran.

Keisyl yanked on his mule's halter. "Let's see what the Teyvakin say."

Their pace slowed as the long rise of the valley swelled up toward distant peaks. Bare rock crowned with shrinking snows split the forested glens, two long ridges enclosing a smaller shallow valley in watchful arms. A sturdy stone bridge spanned a rushing river foaming high over a stony bed, guarded by a solitary figure sitting kicking his heels against the parapet.

"Seric!" Jeirran tossed reins to Teiriol without a backward look and hurried forward. "What on earth is going on in the lower valley?"

The elderly Mountain Man looked dourly back down the slope and leaned on the shaft of the billhook he held. "Lowlanders, up from the Gap." He spat his contempt in a wadded lump of chewing leaf. "Turned up maybe a few days after you headed down. Reckon they're claiming all the land up to this bridge seeing as no one lives there!"

"But that's your winter grazing," protested Teiriol.

The bridge guard glared beneath bushy, snowy brows. "So you go and tell them that, youngling. Maybe they'll pay heed to you instead of ignoring us!"

"Why are you here, at the bridge," Keisyl nodded at Seric's billhook, "with that?"

The man heaved a sigh. "There's been trouble."

"Bad?" Jeirran looked belligerent.

"Bad as it can be," replied Seric morosely. "Gedres and his boy were coming back from the far woods when he finds all these sheep eating up the hay meadows. This Gap man, he tells Gedres to clear right out, curt as you like, get off his land. Gedres tells him to go tup his own ewes! Well, lowlander tries to fetch him a smack in the mouth so Gedres drops him. They'd been coursing, so he tells the lad to set the hounds on the misbegot and his sheep, see how he likes that. Lowlander whistles up a pack of thieves to help him." Seric shook his head. "The lad's none too clear on what happened after that but the long and the short of it, Gedres ends up dead with knife in his back."

"Oh," Eirys cried, distressed. "Poor Yevrein! Is there anything I can do—?"

Seric looked up at her, wrinkled face softening. "She'll be glad to see you, I'll warrant. Sheltya arrived this morning and they laid him out at noon so it'll be a hard day for her."

"How's the lad?" asked Keisyl.

Seric shook his head. "Taking it hard but no one blames him. How could he take them all on, barely two-thirds grown? Bastards took a whip to him!"

Jeirran and Teiriol burst out with furious exclamations but Keisyl overrode them with a shout. "Enough! We're doing no good here. Let's get to the fess and offer what comfort we can."

They crossed the bridge and made their way up a long valley where the wild beauty of trees and grass had long been turned over to ugly heaps of broken rock, the land scarred with diggings old and new. A few figures were busy damming a stream, diverting the water into a series of channels and sluices, and they stopped to watch the new arrivals. Teiriol's cheery wave went unacknowledged and the men soon turned back to their work.

Eirys kicked on her pony and was at the gates of the stronghold well before the others. The wall was twice the

height of any of the men—massive, irregular rocks fitted together with a precision that defied even a dagger blade to
slip between them, a maze of joints and angles baffling the
eye. Watchful figures patrolled the crenellated wall walk
and one, spear in hand, peered over to hail the girl. Eirys
stood in her stirrups to reply, and by the time Jeirran and the
others had arrived the mighty gates were opened just sufficiently to admit the file of mules each in turn. Keisyl led his
charges through the tapering tunnel made by the thickness
of the wall.

"There's room in the far stables." The gatekeeper nodded
to a youth who barred the heavy wooden doors at once.

"Hold there!" Keisyl braced himself as a mule backed
nervously from the gatekeeper's dog, a brindled animal
high as a man's waist with a questing face and lithe build.
The rangy hound's barks rose to a furious pitch, baying
erupting from a distant kennel in answer.

"You're keeping them hungry then?" shouted Keisyl.

The burly gatekeeper silenced his hound with a yank on
the chain he held wrapped around one fist. "Hungry and fit
for anything those lowland bastards might try."

Eirys swung herself down from her saddle and hastily
smoothed her skirts. "Where is Yevrein?"

"In the rekin." The gatekeeper nodded to the square
tower set in the center of the compound, narrow windows
watchful as they rose above the height of the surrounding
wall.

"Look after Dapple." Eirys abandoned her pony to an indignant Teiriol and hurried for the broad steps leading to a
wide double door.

"Take them around and get them settled." Jeirran
dropped his own reins and followed his wife.

The mules looked incuriously at Teiriol. "But—"

"Ask someone to help, Teir. I'll be around as soon as I
can." Keisyl clapped his brother on the shoulder. "I want to
hear the truth of this."

Leaving Teiriol muttering crossly, Keisyl ran lightly up

the steps of the rekin. Pushing the door open slowly, he slid in to stand silently behind Eirys. A single room took up most of the ground floor; sconces for lamps and candles were dark and all furnishings had been pushed back against the walls in disregarded confusion. The household stood in a loose circle, a discouraged sag to their shoulders, children huddling by mothers who held them close. Eirys clutched Jeirran's hand, tears sliding down her face, eyes fixed on the woman by the broad hearth that dominated the center of the room. Pale and hollow-cheeked, eyes red with weeping, the woman tipped a bucket of ash onto the fire, stifling the bright flames. A chill fell heavily on the darkened room.

Two men stepped forward with metal pry-bars and wedges to move a heavy slab of hot stone from the edge of the plinth. Bending to the hollow revealed, the woman removed a small copper-bound casket of black wood. Selecting a key from the bunch hanging at her girdle, she opened the coffer. The older man beside her held it as she counted out the thick gold and silver coins it held.

"This is your patrimony, Nethin." Her voice cracked as she turned to a youth a few seasons younger than Teiriol, gaunt with grief and guilt. The second man laid an encouraging hand on the lad's shoulder. "Use it well to honor the memory of your father. He would have given it himself, when you came of age . . ." Anguish choked the woman and her voice failed.

A tall man in a gray robe stepped forward, shaven face somber. "That is sufficient." He closed the lid of the casket and nodded to the older man, who replaced it beneath the hearthstone. The gray-robed man gave the weeping Yevrein into the embrace of caring women and gently led the boy Nethin out of the main door.

"Go on," Jeirran nodded as Eirys turned to him, a question in her tearful face. She hurried over to join the women in their sorrow.

Keisyl heaved a sigh. "It's a bad business, Jeir."

"And a cursed sight too common since our fathers' day," spat Jeirran. "Every soke is being straitened and plundered."

His word caught the attention of a man who turned to them. "Has the Othilsoke suffered like this?"

Keisyl shook his head. "Not thus far, but then we are that much farther from the Gap."

"It's just a matter of time," growled Jeirran.

Keisyl went to help the man drag a sturdy wooden chest back to its customary position. "What do you reckon to do, Alured?"

"We've sent word to the upper diggings and the summer pastures but I don't know what good that'll do. Bringing the men back is all very well but we'll lose the best part of the season's work." Alured took a stool from another man and set it down, his movement revealing a heavy limp.

"But you'll drive those vermin out of the soke?" demanded Jeirran, arms folded, aloof from the rest of the men busy setting the room to rights.

"Maybe," shrugged Alured. "If we can, but you're right to call them vermin. They're just like rats; for every one you kill, thrice three more are lurking unseen, just waiting to bleed you dry."

"But you can't just let them steal the land," protested Jeirran.

"Later," Keisyl scowled at him. "Make yourself useful."

Jeirran glowered at him but took a hand in moving chairs and furniture. Gradually the room resumed its normal appearance; plainer cabinets and work benches set around with stools to one side, chairs softened with embroidered cushions, work baskets neatly arranged on shelves beside crudely carved animals or clumsily woven strips of colorful wool. Keisyl watched three men carefully laying the body of a new fire on the hearth, remembered grief darkening his eyes.

"See what I told you," Jeirran began. "How many more—"

He fell silent as the gray-robed man entered the room and

clapped his hands. He was not overly tall and showed no muscle built by years of toil, but his piercing blue eyes were dark with experience beyond his years. Everyone turned, expectant.

"Gedres was a good and honest man, faithful husband and caring father. His death diminishes us all. Our grief has quenched the flame that was lit at his marriage. The last rays of the sun have lit a new promise of life by the hand of his son. The eyes of the moons will guard his daughters now and always."

Nethin stepped forward nervously, a burning smoky brand held in shaking hands. He thrust it into the heart of the hearth and something more potent than normal kindling caught in a burst of bluish flame. Muted cheers and a few handclaps brought a wavering smile to the lad's face before it crumpled to be hidden in his grandfather's embrace.

Jeirran sighed heavily and scrubbed an angry hand across his eyes.

"Time to drink to Gedres' memory." Alured's voice was rough with emotion as he came over with a green glass flask and a handful of rough goblets. Other men were doing the same, sitting around the tables and sinking their sorrows beneath hasty swallows. Women were lighting spills at the rekindled fire, setting lamps and candles to brighten the room. They took their own seats on the far side of the hearth, flagons and glasses soon set out in turn. A couple of girls came out of a far door and began laying bread, meat and other plain food on the long table that ran the width of the room beyond the hearth, but no one paid it much attention. A few men wept openly and most of the women clutched damp handkerchiefs and paused frequently to wipe their eyes. Gradually the stifled conversations grew more animated with a few shamefaced laughs to break the hush of mourning.

Teiriol came in a while later with a handful of other men, indignation and hesitation warring in his expression. "You didn't come," he complained in a low tone.

"They were quenching the hearth," apologized Keisyl. "Didn't you see Sheltya just leave?"

Teiriol shook his head.

"When do you ever?" sneered Jeirran. "They disappear as soon as they step over the threshold! A man dies, Sheltya come, lay his body out on the charnel crag, do the trick with the burning glass and say no more about it. Misaen's ravens do their work, Solstice comes, Sheltya lay the bones in Maewelin's embrace and all's done. How is that supposed to help Yevrein, widowed before her time and not even by honest accident? Where's the consolation for Nethin, poor lad, no one to guide him, wandering and wondering till he comes of age and can claim his patrimony."

"He's got the entire Teyvakin to guide and guard him, Jeirran!" Alured looked affronted. "Don't judge others by the failings of the Lidrasoke!"

Jeirran's feet scraped on the flagstones as he sprang to his feet. "You know nothing of it," he snarled.

"Enough!" Keisyl got between the two men. "Jeir, go and see if Eirys is coming down. Yevrein has plenty of sisters to console her and Eirys could lighten cares down here with news of the festival."

"How did you fare in Sclerima?" Alured looked up with interest.

Jeirran did not answer as he stalked over to the door leading to the stairs. It was some while before Eirys appeared, pink-faced and looking self-conscious. Keisyl watched her with half an eye, ignoring Jeirran, who appeared moments later and began to circulate, exchanging greetings and news. Satisfied Eirys was settled happily with two old friends and with Teiriol sharing nudges and low jokes with a gang of youths, Keisyl turned his full attention back to Alured, who was sharing a foaming jug with a new companion. "Hordist," he nodded.

"Keisyl," responded the newcomer, carefully lifting an earthenware beaker in hands bent by joint evil. "It's a bad business, this."

"True enough." Keisyl drained his own glass.

"So, what's to be done?" Alured looked dispirited.

"Did anyone ask Sheltya's counsel?" asked Keisyl slowly.

Hordist sucked at a swollen knuckle before answering. "Peider did. Sheltya said he'd ask the bones at Solstice, see what the light stirred in them."

"What use are dry bones?" Jeirran crossed over from another table, goblet of clear liquor in one hand. "What we need are strong arms to drive these bastards out."

"And when they come back from the upper diggings, maybe we will at that." Hordist looked at Jeirran with dislike. "In the meantime, all we've got are part-grown lads and the halt and the lame." He held up a twisted hand. "What am I supposed to do with Maewelin's curse on me?"

"Your feet are strong enough," said Jeirran with a harsh laugh. "You could kick the bastards to death."

"I might at that." Hordist drank noisily.

Alured refilled his beaker for him. "By the time the others are back, those vermin will have dug themselves in good and strong, felled half the woods, frightened every beast with fur on its back halfway to the high peaks and had their sheep crop the ground bare beneath them."

"At least the beasts can leave," grumbled Hordist. "Blood and bone bred to the soke can't just take flight."

His complaints were interrupted as the grandfather of the orphaned boy rapped a horny hand on a table. "I give you tales of fury," he proclaimed thickly. "When Ceider rode the north. His mail of dragonscale, his wrath as dragonsbreath!"

The four men sat and listened to the legend declaimed with burning passion. Evening closed in around the fess and the rekin as the old man retraced the steps of the myth.

"Shame Peider can't summon up Ceider from his bones and find out how to set about raising a dragon himself," muttered Hordist as the old man paused to wet his dry throat some verses later.

"No dragons nearer than the high peaks," said Alured morosely. "Lowlanders hunted the wyrms out of the eastern ranges in my forefathers' youth."

"The fess, its walls thrown down, was scorched by fury's flame. Vengeance true was claimed, ill faith was drowned in shame!" Peider's voice rose to a shout as he wound the tale to its triumphant conclusion.

Rousing applause filled the room and a new energy revived conversation on all sides.

"Fire," said Jeirran suddenly. His face flushed with excitement, eyes bright and not just from the alcohol he'd drunk. "Dragonsbreath, that's fire! We could drive the lowlanders out with fire!"

"Where are you going to get a dragon?" demanded Alured blearily. "Ask Misaen to lend one out of his forge?"

"You've got wood spirit, haven't you?" Jeirran turned to Hordist, whose slower pace of drinking had left him slightly clearer-headed. "Resins, pine knots?"

"Yes." Slow realization dawned in Hordist's lined face. "I can't hold an axe but I can throw a torch with the best of them!"

His voice was loud enough to turn heads at neighboring tables. "What do you say, Rakvar?"

"To what?"

"To burning out that nest of rats in the lower soke!" Alured said with growing eagerness. "They've cut us plenty of wood for a nice fire!"

"Green lumber won't burn," said a doubtful voice, but it sounded willing to be convinced.

"It will if you chuck a cask of stripping spirit on it first," riposted Hordist.

Harsh laughter all around gave temporary release to simmering anger.

"A good fire would send those maggot-eaten sheep scurrying all the way down to the Gap," commented another man with approval. "Let the lowlanders go chase them."

"Never mind stripping spirit," said a balding man with

scarred hands. "Get some acid from the assay shed and see how they like a faceful of that!"

A few looked shocked at his vicious words but more nodded growing approval.

"So what are we waiting for?" demanded Jeirran. "Wait and there'll be nine times their number by Solstice. Burn them out now and the bones will shout their approval to Sheltya when the sun strikes them!"

"It's the full of both moons," said the doubtful voice again.

"Good hunting light then," Rakvar turned to rebuke him.

Eirys and the other women looked on in some bemusement as the men rose, laced heavy boots and found capes and stout gloves.

Teiriol came over, face eager. "What's afoot?"

"We're going to settle the lowlanders," said Jeirran fervently.

"We're going to drive them off." Keisyl looked less zealous but more determined.

"I'll get my boots!" exclaimed Teiriol.

Keisyl looked after him with some concern; as the men began hurrying out of the door, he caught the younger man's arm. "You can come, Teir, but watch yourself. None of the younger lads though, no one not two-thirds grown. Tell them they are to stay behind and guard the fess and the women."

The compound was a hive of activity; workshop doors standing open as axes, picks and even shovels were passed out to impatient hands. Blades caught the light of torches raised high and shouts warned caution as small iron-bound barrels were loaded onto a bemused mule blinking at the dark sky above. The women crowded the steps of the rekin, shouting out endorsement of the plan. Two hurried out with a basket full of narrow-necked jars and another brought an armful of tattered cloth. A second mule was dusted with black from sacks of charcoal slung over its back, yellow streaks soon added from a sulfurous jar.

"Covered lights only," yelled Jeirran and there was a flurry to kindle lamps of pierced metal, slides lowered to mute their glimmer. The heavy doors of the fess were slowly opened and the mob passed beyond the wall. They moved slowly at first until eyes adjusted to the deep twilight of the spring night and the valley formed itself from the shadows hanging all around. Moving with the practiced stealth of hunters, the Mountain Men spread out and crept down the valley, over the bridge and past the unheeding sheep. A group split off in silent agreement and lay hidden in a hollow by the shuffling flock while the rest continued in small and furtive groups. Moving slowly, with halts and cautious pauses, they finally encircled the lowlander camp. A merry fire burned between the four wagons, an awning stretched between each pair of wains, men sleeping in shapeless rolls of blankets under each one. A single figure sat idly by the fire, throwing on scraps of wood.

"There are more than we reckoned," said Keisyl dubiously.

"It's all the ones in from the trees," commented Teiriol. "They'll have half the valley stripped before Solstice if we don't drive them out."

Keisyl nodded grimly. "True enough."

"Who's got the best throwing arm?" whispered Jeirran to Alured.

The older man thought for a moment. "Rogin. He can hit a single-stone from four score and one paces!"

Word was passed back and Rogin came forward, standing half a head taller than Jeirran with a beak of a nose and a shock of coarse hair. "Can you pitch this right into that fire?"

Rogin weighed the sloshing flagon bound around with lumpy resinous cloth in one hand. "No contest," he said readily.

Jeirran looked around to see crouching men wrapping charcoal in sulfur-coated cloth, filling jars with liquid and jamming their necks with rag.

"For Gedres!" bellowed Rogin, standing and launching the vessel in a soaring arc with one fluid motion. The watchman was halfway to his feet when his fire erupted in searing flames that set his clothes and hair alight, sending him reeling. Inside a few breaths he was a figure of horror, screaming blindly, hair flaring like tow, skin charred and cracking, face blistering into a featureless mess. As the other men leaped from their blankets, more bright missiles came sailing in. The canvas of both awnings bloomed with flame and liquid fire ate greedily into the wood of the wagons. With roars of fury, the lowlanders grabbed any tools ready to hand, spades, adzes and billhooks, heads snapping from side to side as they looked for their enemy in the darkness. Their blankets went up behind them in a stink of burning wool.

With yells of defiance on the far side, a gang of Mountain Men flung trestles, tools and wood into the sawpit, brands and a barrel of fir-spirit following to burn a smoldering scar deep into the grass. Flames exploded upward, gouts spilling over the rim of the pit, bright as sunlight. The lowlanders ran at them, weapons lifted high, but the Mountain Men vanished into the darkness. As the lowlanders hesitated, uncertain, burning jars shattered at their feet, scattering them cursing. They tried to gather themselves, shouting in dismay as the firing of the lumber pile sent all their hard work up in smoke. Timbers cracked as the fire took hold, fueled by torches and volatile liquids. Heat battered them like the blast from the maw of a furnace.

"Get them!" Jeirran raised his pickaxe and led a furious charge at the disordered encampment. The men of the Teyvasoke came roaring in from all sides, breaking heads and legs. The lowlanders fell back toward the wagons where their picketed oxen were bellowing and wrenching at their tethers.

"Roast beef when the work's done, lads!" shouted Jeirran. He swung at a shirt-sleeved lowlander who was thrusting a shovel at him. The tools met with a clang and the shovel went sailing away. Jeirran smashed the pick forward full into the man's belly, sending him backward onto his rump, all breath knocked out of him. The wedge end left the lowlander's skull dented to the depth of a hand, hair matted into the mess of brain and blood. The man fell lifeless as Jeirran left a boot print on his shirt front, spurning the twitching corpse in his eagerness to meet the next.

Keisyl swung his axe in a wide defensive arc, standing his ground as two frantic lowlanders tried to jab past his guard with their billhooks. "Too stupid to run for it?" he shouted at them, but his words were lost in the commotion shattering the night all around. One of the lowlanders, hair in a long queue, ducked to scythe at Keisyl's legs. Keisyl brought the flat of his weapon around to smack against the man's ear, sending him flying, blood streaming from mouth and nose, the shattered bones of his face white in the firelight as they pierced his pockmarked cheek. The second thought he saw an opportunity, but the returning blade bit deep into his armpit as he raised his hedge-tool. Weapon falling from limp fingers, the man folded over the gory gash in his chest, choking and writhing until Keisyl decapitated him with one swift stroke.

"Down is good as dead," snarled Jeirran, scorning this delay.

"Maewelin grants mercy to the merciful," spat Keisyl. He looked for his brother and saw he had a thick-set lowlander trapped by the burning wreck of a wagon. Teiriol was feinting with a long pry-bar, the heavy iron easy in his hands. The lowlander had a turfing spade, the keen edge gleaming in the firelight. The man raised it, two-handed, stabbing forward at Teiriol's face. The youth stepped back with contemptuous grace, shaking his head. The lowlander's knuckles were white on the wood of the spade, buck teeth gnawing his lower lip. He stabbed forward again; Teiriol swept the pry-bar under and around in one swift movement and smashed the man's elbow. Even above the chaos of the fight, Keisyl heard the sickening crack of bone. Blood spilled down the man's unlaced shirt as he bit his lip clean through in his agony. Teiriol hesitated for a moment but Jeirran came storming past him with a shout of triumph to smash the lowlander's face into bloody pulp, ripping his jaw half off with the fury of his pick.

A Mountain voice raised in anguish snapped Keisyl's head around. Alured came stumbling toward them, a feathered shaft sticking out of his shoulder. More arrows hissed out of the darkness, biting deep into the leather-clad attackers. Shouts of dismay came from Rogin and his companions as they found themselves suddenly assailed from the shadows beyond the blinding pyre of the lumber pile.

"Come on, you bastards, let's have them!" Jeirran turned in fury but could only peer vainly into the featureless blackness, unable to see anything beyond the circle of firelight.

"Ware behind!" Teiriol leaped forward to club down a lowlander, howling as he ripped an adze down at Jeirran's unprotected back.

"It's the shepherds!" someone yelled.

Keisyl squinted into the darkness. "We're easy meat against the fires," he shouted to Jeirran. "They'll just pick us off one by one!"

A scream drowned out his words and Rogin's voice lifted above the furor. "Fall back, fall back. Get out of the light."

Keisyl grabbed Jeirran's arm. "Move or do you want Eirys weeping with Yevrein?"

Mountain Men scattered into the darkness, leaving lowlanders dead and crippled on the blood-soaked grass. The fires burned on, consuming all within reach. Jeirran paused to rip a tangle of pegs and line out of the grass, flinging it away. "That'll teach them to try taking our lands," he cried.

Keisyl ignored him, one shoulder supporting Alured, whose cape was black with blood. "Are you all right?"

"Once we get this cursed arrow out," gasped the older man, "I'll be fine then."

"You won't feel a thing when you've drunk a few toasts to our success," predicted Jeirran, boastfully.

Teiriol yelped as an arrow bit deep into the ground beside him. "Where are they?" He looked around wildly.

"Keep moving and weave as you run," shouted Keisyl, virtually lifting Alured clean off his feet.

Jeirran cursed as he tripped over a body fallen just short of the bridge, hair fair in the moonlight, a curious breeze fingering torn linen, embroidery blotted and smudged with blood. Keisyl spared the corpse a regretful glance but saved breath and energy for the long haul back up past the spoil heaps to the shelter of the fess. Pursuit fell away once the Mountain Men were past the river, but several collapsed as they struggled up the long slope, companions unable to rouse them.

"Come on, come on!" Jeirran stood at the gate, waving exuberantly. "We've a victory to celebrate!"

Keisyl gave the white-faced Alured into the care of two women hurrying forward, pads of linen ready in their hands. Puffing as he walked slowly into the compound, he tallied at the number whose wounds were being tended by anxious women. The youths were busy bringing steaming bowls of water, carrying pots of salve and bandages, holding down those unfortunates struggling beneath the knife as arrows were cut from clinging flesh. In the shadows beyond the lamplight spilling from the rekin door, motionless figures were being laid in a row.

Eirys flung herself into Keisyl's arms. "Is Jeirran all right? And Teiro? Are you hurt, any of you?"

"No, kidling, no." He hugged her close. "We're all fine and fit."

"It was a success?" Eirys looked around with dismay. "You did win, didn't you?"

"Yes," said Keisyl slowly, "but many more victories like that and the lowlanders will be able to just walk up the soke and knock on the gates. They can stand their losses better than we can."

"Don't be such a doom-sayer," said Jeirran, pulling Eirys free of Keisyl's arms and folding her in a rough embrace. "We'll do better next time."

"Next time?" scowled Keisyl, incredulous.

Jeirran nodded firmly. "When we've allies to back us with real power."

The Great Forest, 18th of Aft-Spring

Sudden brightness woke me fully from the comfortable drowse I was enjoying among my warm blankets. I opened one eye to see 'Gren throwing the deerskin up onto the roof to shed some light inside the sura.

"Good morning." I rubbed the sleep from my eyes.

"Good morning," he yawned. "Do we have to start the day this early, or can I take a nap?"

"Haven't you been to sleep?" I asked critically. "Been emptying your pockets for some willing maiden?"

He shook his head, another yawn cracking his jaw. "With those lads and their runes. I thought I could spot every trick of the hand in bad light or snowstorm, but Saedrin's stones, I can't begin to see how they are doing it."

"You lost again?" I made no attempt to hide my incredulity.

"That's right." 'Gren pulled off his jerkin and dropped it to the floor. "Taken like some goatherd fresh off his mountain." He sounded more amused than annoyed so, with luck, he wouldn't go looking for a fight to console himself.

"Well, easy come, easy go," I commented.

"True enough." He shucked breeches and boots and rolled himself in a blanket. "I'd still like to know their tricks though. We could empty every strongbox between Vanam and Col."

"Who was doing most of the winning?" I wanted to know who to avoid.

"Barben, that bull-necked type with the ears like a startled mouse." 'Gren's voice was muffled as he pulled a fold of wool over his head. "They all said he's just lucky, known for it apparently. Lucky, my arse! The way the runes were running, Raeponin must have hung up his scales and taken a holiday."

I closed my eyes, but now I'd been woken up I found I couldn't get back to sleep. Sorgrad and Usara were still motionless heaps of frowsty blankets so I dressed, wrinkling my nose at wood smoke scenting my shirt. Outside, skeins of mists wove waist-high through the trees and the early sun hadn't yet beaten the spring chill. The camp was barely stirring and I cursed 'Gren roundly as I realized how early it still was. Two Forest women passed me with nods of good will, heading for the stream. For want of anything better to do, I followed them. The brook was still bitter with lingering winter and washing brought me fully alert.

Lighting the fire with the incantation that the Folk were finding so entertaining, I set water to boil. Sitting and sipping hot wine and water, I watched fires being lit and breakfasts made, children emerging to get underfoot, still well shy of what anyone civilized could call a reasonable chime for waking. Ravin went past and I caught an unexpected shadow of resemblance to my father. Abrupt realization froze the cup at my lips. Since we arrived, I'd been unable to shake the absurd notion that all these Folk were far too short. Why in Drianon's name had I been expecting these people to be taller than me when I knew full well all the ancient races were short stacks of coin? Because I had last seen my father as a child, looking up from a child's short stature, as I did now when I was sitting down. Unwelcome doubts assailed me. The squirrel game, the deceptions of masquerades, all such things rely on the fallibility of memory. Had that little girl's recollections, colored with wishes and longing, led me astray, convinced me the Forest must hold some wisdom unknown outside? In simpler terms, was I tying horns on a horse and hoping for milk?

No. I set my jaw. So far, I'd discovered jalquezan in songs the women used for lulling fractious babies to sleep, timing the boil of their cooking and when sitting their children down for a session with a fine-tooth comb. Unfortunately, given my lack of experience in any of these occupations, I was hard put to decide if the jalquezan was having a significant effect. These women might just be practiced nurses, experienced cooks and diligent in their pursuit of lice. None of these songs were ones in my book and, as with the Raven song, I'd found two or three versions of each.

I looked over toward Orial's sura. Zenela had been sitting outside, taking the sun yesterday. That lass was recovering faster and more fully than simples and herbs could account for; she'd have been ashes in an urn by now, back in Ensaimin. Convincing Usara of that was going to be a different roll of the runes, though. What was I missing? There had to be something.

My thinking about him must have set the mage's ears itching. Hearing a noise within, I looked into the sura to see him rummaging for clean linen and his razor a little self-consciously.

"You were back very late last night, again," I observed neutrally.

Usara smiled suddenly at me. "One of a mage's most important skills is discretion, Livak, and besides, my father always said an honorable man never boasts."

"All I have to do is look for that necklace," I reminded him.

"You do that," he advised with a chuckle as he departed for the stream and his ablutions.

I wondered what the joke was and then asked myself what to do for the best. The prospect of another day making myself agreeable to the women of the settlement didn't thrill me. What would today hold? Another tedious walk in the forest trying to disguise my utter lack of interest in leaves or plants I might gather to eat? The only firm fact I'd learned so far on this sojourn is that Forest donkeys are considerably smaller and darker than those used by the rest of the world and that they can be loaded with so much firewood they look like a stack of faggots with legs.

Frue emerged from a nearby sura. "Good morning!" For all his cheery greeting, he was looking considerably less lively than the other Folk. Life in Ensaimin had accustomed him to more comfortable beds and routines.

"Good morning." I hastily gathered my scattered wits.

"We're going after boar." He was carrying two spears and waved the thick-shafted weapons with their sturdy crosspieces. "If Sorgrad or 'Gren come, they can claim a share of the kill and then you can repay your dinner debts." This was the second time in as many days he'd mentioned this obligation.

"I'll come." After the last few days, no one was going to keep me away from excitement.

Frue rested his spears in the ground. "I didn't think— you're hardly a country girl, are you?" He fell silent at the irritation in my face.

"They're going along, aren't they?" I returned a wave from Gevalla and her sisters, all dressed for the worst the woods could do, hair braided close. Each had ropes slung crossways over both shoulders and they carried a roll of stout net. "Trust me, I can run, climb and hit a moving target as well as any."

"Yes, but—" Frue shrugged off his uncertainty. "Just don't get in anyone's way."

A reedy whistle sounded above the trills of the morning birdsong. "Ravin's leading the hunt," Frue said sternly. "If you foul the chase and he tells you to fall back, do it at once."

I nodded shortly. It was Usara's bad luck that he chose

that moment to come up, eyes bright with curiosity as he saw the hunting party assembling with bows, spears and long knives. "Hunting? Can I come?"

"No," I said repressively. "You're not dressed for it."

Usara looked at the skirts of his brown robe, unbelted over shirt and broadcloth breeches. "Someone could lend me a tunic, couldn't they?"

"There's no time." I waved a hand at Ravin, who was moving off into the trees. "Anyway, I'm not sure your kind of help would be appreciated."

"The right spell at the right time can drop an animal in its tracks, rope of air, for instance—"

"And what if these Folk consider that a capital offense against Talagrin?" I demanded. "Use the time to talk to some more of the elders. Remember what we're here for."

"Frue?" Usara appealed to the minstrel.

"You'd best keep to the camp," Frue replied apologetically.

I nodded my agreement. City bred I might be but at least I knew my own limitations and had the wit to keep out of trouble. Even though Usara was one of the best of the mages I had met, he still had as much common sense as a frog has feathers. The wizard claiming the quarry with some pit of magic would leave these men as useless as eunuchs in a brothel and as pleased as if they'd caught a dose of the itch.

"Oh, very well," Usara sniffed with audible annoyance. He stalked off toward Orial's hut and I followed Frue. Hunters were gathering, fired with the eager anticipation that townsmen slake with bloody pursuits like baiting. Some were singing extravagant invocations to the Master of the Hunt and I itched to get closer, wondering if this was some new jalquezan.

I went to stand with Rusia and her sisters. Other women had rough bags and sacking strapped close to their bodies, skinning knives at their belts. Several honed blades with casual whetstones, chatting in low tones.

"So how will this play out?" I asked.

Yefri pointed at a man with a mane of unkempt graying hair and pale, intense eyes. "That's Iamris. He'll be finding boars for us."

Ravin sounded a trill like a woodlark on a reed pipe and we moved into the woods.

"He's a tracker?" I whispered to Yefri.

"He's a finder of game," she shrugged.

Parul joined us, bringing several sturdy spears. "Do you want to share in the killing?" Yefri shook her head and I did the same. When the nobility in Vanam go pig-sticking in the streets to clear the feral porkers to feed the indigent at Ostrin's shrine, they do it from horseback. I reckon outdwellers have the right of it.

"I'll join you," said Gevalla abruptly. She took a spear and stepped close to Parul.

"Geva!" Rusia looked daggers at her sister, who lifted her chin defiantly.

"She can come if she wants." Parul put an arm around Gevalla's shoulders.

"Watch yourself!" hissed Yefri before a shrill blast on Ravin's whistle silenced us all. Iamris led us into the trees. I tried to take note of landmarks and to get a sight of the sun whenever I could, but after what felt like half a season moving slowly through the forest, I realized I'd need some notable favor from Trimon to get back to the settlement unaided.

I eased my way through early undergrowth and branches felled by buffets of winter storms. Skills I'd learned for moving noiselessly through someone's house uninvited were easily as good as the woodcraft of Salkin and his fellows. We became more scattered, but all attention remained on Iamris. He wasn't checking the ground or looking for spoor but then my notion of hunting for meat is limited to finding a butcher who keeps blowflies off his carcasses. Perhaps Iamris had been out scouting earlier. What he wasn't doing was singing, not that I could hear, anyway.

A loud crack betrayed someone stepping on a dead stick. As I looked from side to side with everyone else, I caught Frue's eye and he nodded approval at me. We crossed a little stream burbling its way between mossy banks and I lost the minstrel among the burgeoning woodland. Parul and Gevalla were no longer visible, so I made doubly sure I kept either Yefri or Rusia always in sight.

Ravin's whistle mimicked an apple thrush up ahead, catching me unawares in a long narrow clearing. I moved hastily into the cover of a youthful beech. A motherly woman with a plain, kindly face lifted a wooden pipe and returned the signal. More piping replies suggested everyone had taken prearranged places and I wondered what my group was to do. We were notably short on spears, which had to be a good thing, didn't it?

Rusia and the girls strung their long net across a gap in the trees. Others secured similar snares to branches and stumps. I put the net between me and the sounds of other hunters moving stealthily away from us. Whatever came down the track would hit the net before it got a sniff of me. I mentally recited a general supplication to Talagrin, hoping the Lord of the Wilds might turn an eye if something unexpected leaped out of a bush.

Yefri handed me the end of a rope. I joined her in stringing branches and greenery to fake a barrier to turn the quarry to the supposedly open space where the net lurked unseen. Sudden commotion erupted to the north of us; shouts, whistles, spears hammering on trees, driving the prey onward. Tumult headed for us, piercing squeals and menacing grunts, what sounded like a whole rampaging herd of boars. I checked a good sturdy tree was at hand for climbing and realized my hand was opening the belt-pouch that held my poisoned darts. I tucked it firmly through my belt. Never mind Usara; no one was going to be best pleased with dinner inedible because of an apothecary's best venom.

A massive boar came plunging out of the undergrowth,

black and hairy, snout low to the ground, heavy head swinging from side to side. A handful of arrows deep in either flank left a trail of red behind it. In the center of the clearing, it rounded on its pursuers with a bubbling snort of agony. Leaves and muck were stuck to brindled legs and belly, massive shoulders heaved as it gouged at the moss with vicious tusks. Bloody foam sprayed from vicious yellow teeth as it vainly tried to bite at the shafts dragging it down.

I moved closer to my chosen tree. Ravin appeared, moving slowly, planting the butt of his spear firmly against his foot and angling it lest the maddened beast run at him. At Ravin's command, two men darted forward to plunge their spears deep into its ribs. The force of the blows sent the pig sprawling forward, bright blood gushing from its slack maw. It screamed, writhing and thrashing, but the men stood firm, sweat dripping down their faces as they wrestled with its death throes. Finally it lay limp and Nenad ran in to set a hefty hook under the jaw of the carcass, dragging the beast away with a rope. Some of the women stepped forward but sudden shouts from up the path halted them. Nenad's mouth hung open as two youths came racing into the clearing, one white and wild-eyed, the other limping, blood all over torn leggings but running just as fast.

A younger boar was in hot pursuit, a clotted gash in the coarse hair of its flank showing where an arrow had failed to stick. The animal's back was arched with anger, the wound only provoking it further as it snarled with outrage. For a clumsy-looking beast, it was still a solid mass of muscle and fury.

"Nenad, leave it!" Ravin shouted at the boy frozen with fear and indecision. The newly arrived boar turned malevolent black eyes on him and saliva dripped from its scarlet mouth. Nenad took a pace backward, but the rope caught his foot and he fell to one knee. The boar charged the boy as he scrambled backward on hands and rump. The bristling black fury ripped into his legs with ivory tusks, blood and spittle spattering the turf.

Men and women raced forward, spears and skinning knives flashing bright in the sunlight, rising dripping red. Someone else's cries joined Nenad's screams as the boar died hard, taking every chance at vengeance offered it.

"Get clear, get clear!" More commotion was heading our way.

The Forest Folk scattered, two men dragging Nenad between them. Another backed toward me clutching a badly bitten arm. Iamris, leading a solid phalanx of Folk, drove an enormous sow out of the trees. Spears jabbed and harried her, Gevalla wielding one with grim-faced determination. Stripy piglets squealed and fussed around their mother's feet, her heavy teats swinging low. She snapped at the spears, huffing and snorting, the bite of the spears sending her back in baffled pain. In some instant of understanding between the hunters, two of the leaf-shaped blades plunged down either side of the sow's neck, slicing through tough hide to sever the great vessels. Crimson blood gushed all over her forelegs, sending frantic piglets dashing hither and yon. Some snared in the nets were dispatched with spear butts, others caught in swathes of sacking were held up by hind legs, wriggling until a cut throat silenced their squeals.

I hadn't realized I was holding my breath until the thudding of my heart and faint buzzing in my ears told me to release it. Thinking I'd better do something useful if we were to claim some of this meat, I joined Rusia untangling suckling pigs from the netting. She was struggling with a particularly stubborn knot.

"Here, let me help." I worked the point of the dagger in and twisted it to loosen the tangle. "Is Nenad all right?"

"Better than he deserves." Irritation didn't obscure her relief. "Freezing like a rabbit in front of a weasel, honestly!" The lad was sobbing as his wounds were treated on the far side of the clearing. I looked over to see the man with the bitten arm grimacing, tears running down his face as his wounds were roughly cleansed with spirit from a flask. I winced; the deep gashes were torn and filthy, dark red muscle bared beneath ripped, tanned skin, as likely to fester as any wound I'd ever seen.

"Has someone sent for Orial?" Gevalla appeared, blood on her leggings and a piglet dangling from her spear.

"Yes, Ravin sent Lisset." Rusia pulled the net free. "Get that suckler bled; you know better than to waste time gossiping."

The ringing sound of axe on timber echoed across the clearing. One cruck frame had already been lashed together and Ravin was directing Frue and some others in hauling the bigger boar up by its hind legs. Almiar pierced the neck vessels with a careful knife while two men caught the rich blood in waterskins. The sow was pierced through the hocks with a sharp stake and soon hung on a second frame, one woman making a slow incision down her belly while Ravin held the guts of the beast from spilling out too soon.

Rusia turned to ensuring all the other piglets were bled dry, briskly enlisting me for the smelly and unpleasant task. "Almiar says you've some knack for starting fires?"

I nodded and Rusia shouted to the lad passing by with his hands full of offal. "Etal! Give that to Dria and start finding lampthorn. Livak, light a fire and we can start singeing the hair off these sucklers."

I gathered kindling from beneath the bushes and found a dry patch of earth, happy to do any task that didn't involve getting up to my elbows in some animal's innards. "Talmia megrala eldrin fres."

The flames leaped up obediently and Rusia laughed. "Just like Viyenne in the Frost."

Before I could ask what she meant, the piglet lying behind her was abruptly snatched away. Rusia yelped as a bright blade appeared in front of her face. A tree was hiding me from the knifeman who'd sprung from nowhere and I rolled sideways beneath the concealing spikes of a flourishing broom bush. Kneeling with palms flat I shifted my position with excruciating care as I sought a better view from my hollow at the heart of Drianon's shrub.

A dirty gang of ruffians emerged on all sides, Forest Folk by the coloring beneath their mud and rags. I'd been wrong to think Ravin's settlement looked a little starveling; compared to these, Rusia and the rest had been living on the fat of the land over winter. Several newcomers had the sores of low diet plain on their faces, others wore stained bandages around arms and hands that spoke of wounds long in the healing, or carried open, festering scars. A chance breeze carried the stink of them and I was hard put not to gag.

A leader stepped forward, an undersized runt, beak of a nose prominent in a sunken face, cadaverous eyes red-rimmed and staring. I could not follow his rapid speech but the malice in his tone needed no translation. He brandished his knife, a long blade with a serrated back, the only clean thing about him, and spat full in Ravin's face. Parul took a half-step forward before a threatening spear halted him. Color rose in Ravin's cheeks, but he stood, impassive, as the slime slid slowly down his face.

I tried to work out who might still be at large. I could see Frue, weaponless as he backed away from a raw-boned youth looking for any excuse for a fight. Yefri and Rusia were doing their best to hide behind Salkin, who glowered impotently at three men menacing him with long knives.

Whoever these newcomers were, they'd sprung their trap with no little skill, backed by impressive woodcraft to get so close without being noticed. Most of Ravin's Folk had laid their weapons aside to deal with their kills but the thieves outnumbered the hunting party regardless. I wondered what to do for the best. The single-handed hero may do well enough in ballads, but this was real life. I moved closer to the tree trunk with agonizing care. Could I get away fast enough to foil pursuit? What good would that do, since I had no idea which direction to take? Getting help was one thing, getting lost in the Forest would do no one any good, least of all me. On the other hand, being found in hiding would make me a prime target for some additional punishment.

The skinny one with all the spittle had moved away from Ravin, insisting that Nenad be dragged to his feet and laughing at the bloody dressings covering both legs. He grabbed a spear to knock the supporting arms of his friends away, taunting the youth as his knees buckled under him and kicking him as he fell. The lad's sobs sent a bird squawking skyward from its perch above my head and I froze.

The distraction seemed to remind Skinny what his thieves had come for. He set his men about cutting down the carcasses, some slinging them on carrying poles, others gathering up the offal and the suckling pigs. Ravin and the hunting party were sat in a circle, facing inward with hands on heads and ankles crossed. I resigned myself to waiting this game out, watching with regret as the prospects of a pork dinner retreated. When the thieves were laden with their spoils, the leader returned to Ravin.

Skinny pointed at one of the girls and barked a sharp command. I bit my lip; I'd been wondering about this, given there were no women among the raiders. If this was about to get nasty, I couldn't see what I could do short of putting a dart into the little bastard's back. All that would get me was first place in line for any filth looking to take his pleasure, so I wasn't about to try that.

The girl stood slowly, head hanging. She was one of the youngest, a thin little thing with red-blond hair framing huge brown eyes in a pointed face white with apprehension. Skinny sneered at her and tears began to trickle down her cheeks. Raising her chin with the tip of his knife, he taunted her with something that provoked a furious blush. Laughing, he hooked the point under the binding at her neck, cutting it through with a quick flick of his wrist. Taking the edge in one hand, he sliced slowly through the leather of her tunic. I winced but the girl stood motionless as the razor-sharp metal slid slowly past her naked breasts.

She closed her eyes as the little turd stripped her to the waist and his cronies laughed appreciatively. I presumed they were admiring his bravery at taking on an unarmed lass a head shorter than himself.

All the raiders' eyes were fixed on the spectacle and I was gauging the distance between my broom and the closest thicket when I saw movement in the leaves owing nothing to breeze or passing bird. I glanced briefly at the game in the center of the clearing where the hero with the knife was still enjoying himself. His little display was far more about humiliation than lust thus far at least.

I saw a flash of golden hair and my spirits rose further. Skinny finished stripping the lass, mocking her among the ruins of her garments. He was just pointing at Yefri when fury like Poldrion's own demons erupted all around the clearing. As the grin vanished from the skinny man's face, Salkin launched himself upward, hands around that filthy throat in the next breath. Sitting astride his chest, Salkin was giving the bastard the beating he deserved as what looked like the entire rest of the settlement surged out of the bushes, spears, rough-hewn clubs and simple lengths of fallen timber in wrathful hands. Ravin's hunters joined battle, weaponless or not, and the thieves found themselves between hammer and anvil.

Before I moved, 'Gren came charging out of the undergrowth opposite my hiding place, eyes bright with delight. He swept a spear around to cut a raider's knees out from under him. Dropping the shaft, 'Gren caught the man by the collar as he fell, bringing a gloved fist in to smash stained teeth loose. The man's boots scrabbled on the mossy turf as 'Gren shook him like a terrier with a rat. Twisting his tunic ever tighter around his neck, 'Gren soon had the man beaten limply unconscious and tossed him aside with a satisfied air.

Sorgrad was watching his brother's back, long knives in both hands. The pair of them turned on a barrel-chested, bandy-legged robber with thick brown hair curling above a matted beard, bare arms furred like an animal. Sorgrad feinted to drive the man back, 'Gren blocked his escape and the pair of them drove him back, ever closer to my hiding place.

His stout boots made hamstringing Hairy problematic at best. Reversing my grip on the dagger, I picked my moment and stabbed him in the side of the foot. Rolling out and sideways, I was up before Hairy's howl was cut short by Sorgrad's club knocking the senses out of him.

"How did you know we were in trouble?" I smiled with relief. "What's-her-name must have got home quicker than a scandalous rumor!"

I saw Sorgrad shake his head out of the corner of my eye as we stood ready for trouble. "I'm not sure what raised the alarm. I was chatting to Sandy and all of a sudden the place was like a kicked anthill. Me and 'Gren came along to see the fun."

"What there is of it," 'Gren said glumly, seeing the last of the thieves disappearing into the sheltering embrace of the wildwood.

"What about Usara?" I looked around apprehensively.

"He should be somewhere about," Sorgrad said vaguely.

I saw a stand of tall trees suddenly crowned with fire. This conflagration was heading our way but was leaving the leaves behind it untouched. A scarlet lattice of burning red light doubled and redoubled its length inside a heartbeat, an aberrant red rather than the orange and yellow of natural wildfire.

As the flames ran around to join hands and encircle the glade, Skinny and his dirty gang soon came scrambling out of the bushes. One of the raiders stood his ground, jaw set as the crimson flames edged nearer and nearer. He stuck out a defiant, trembling hand and howled as the flesh was seared red and blistered, stumbling backward to join his friends.

"I hope Usara doesn't set the whole wood alight," I murmured to Sorgrad.

"You're a harsh, untrusting woman," he mocked me. "Look."

Through gaps in the flames I could see mist rising in defiance of the hot sun now bright above. The vapor was shot through with faint jade luster and moved without aid of any breeze to cling to the trees and bushes, coating grass and flowers, coalescing in any hollow or dip before flowing on.

"Very pretty," 'Gren said with approval as Usara stepped through the ring of magic, gathering the flames in his upturned hands. His eyes were tired but he looked extremely pleased with himself.

"That man never had much chance to show off as a child, did he?" Sorgrad commented with amusement.

"What happens next?" I wondered, looking at the thieves, now cowering in a ragged circle.

"Taking some recompense," answered Sorgrad, his tone thoughtful.

The runes were most definitely reversed now. Skinny was dragged roughly to his feet by Salkin, whose bloodied knuckles must have been aching fiercely. The thief was bleeding slowly from several gashes and a nasty cut below one ear. Ravin beckoned forward the girl who'd been subject to Skinny's little game. After a brief consultation, she stepped forward, her pretty face set hard for vengeance. A full-blooded kick in the stones certainly got a reaction from Skinny, however dazed he was. He doubled up so fast he left a handful of hair in Salkin's fingers.

Several of Ravin's people cheered and clapped, but were waved to silence. The drive of blood lust that might have left all the raiders dead on the ground had passed. Ravin took charge with a few curt orders and his folk dispersed to reclaim the spoils of their hunt, Salkin and a couple of others set about stripping the robbers, roughly handling the unconscious and beating any remaining defiance out of the rest. We were soon ready to depart, leaving the would-be thieves cowering in nakedness and humiliation. Rusia and the other women were bundling up the looted clothing though I wondered what possible use they could make of it, even if the knives and spears were worth having.

"Perhaps those fools will think twice about listening to that one's suggestions," said Ravin to Usara, shoving the still uncaring Skinny with a contemptuous boot.

As we moved off, I glanced back to see a few slowly getting to their feet, some attempting to shoulder the unconscious, no easy task without belt or breeches to get a grip on. I kept an ear cocked for any hint of pursuit but heard none.

"Life in the greenwood's not all nuts and niceness then," said Sorgrad as we walked.

"No," I agreed, thinking with some regret of the songs my father taught me. I abandoned that childishness when the settlement came into view. Orial and the other women were busy dismantling the roundhouses, packing frames, matting and everything else on the small donkeys brought in from their foraging in the woods by the lads who cared for them. "What's happening?"

Orial looked up from securing a roll of leather with a thong. "We're moving on."

"They'll come back, tomorrow or the next day." Yefri came to fill in the hearth pit with stones from the edge of the sura circle.

"You're not going to stand and fight?" I put a hand on the closest donkey's harness to stop it fretting.

Orial stacked a nest of iron pots. "Why? There's plenty of forest to be had with no vexation."

"But then they've won," I objected.

She regarded me with perplexity. "That ratshit gang? We could stripe their hides for them if we wanted, but why bother? Some of ours will only get hurt."

"If we move on, they'll find nothing and he'll look even more stupid than he did with the breeze fingering his spotty arse," grinned Yefri, lashing a bundle to the donkey, soothing its furry brown ears.

"Won't they just track you and hit the next camp you make?" This might not be cowardice but it certainly sounded like foolishness to me.

"Not with Ravin covering our trail," Rusia came to help her sister. "No one's better at him than hiding a path, not since Seris himself."

"Scavengers won't follow a loser," Orial folded a stack of blankets into an oiled skin. "That one will be foraging on his own, well this side of Solstice."

Zenela walked up with her hands full of freshly washed crocks, wearing a Forest tunic over a divided skirt. She looked pale and drawn, eyes a little fever-bright, but I still wouldn't have expected to see her up and about before the next moon turned dark. I turned to Orial but her eyes were on Usara as he talked with Ravin. I saw the diamond-link necklace shining in the throat of the herb woman's tunic.

"He'll be bound for Hadrumal again before the year's out. You do know?" I said quietly over the donkey's woolly back. "The Wizards' Isle?"

"As I will be bound for the southern reaches of the Forest." She was unperturbed. "With all manner of new cuttings to take root in warmer soil."

"Is that what you came traveling for?" I was increasingly curious about this woman.

"Among other things." She looked fondly at Usara's back, laying a hand on her belt. "A herbalist should always look to bring long separated strains back to her garden."

"That's—" began Zenela but a spasm of coughing cut her short. Orial pulled a little vial from a pocket and held it for the girl to sniff.

"Do you want help with your sura?" asked Rusia with a hint of impatience.

"I'll tell them to hurry." I realized Sorgrad was mixing tisanes while 'Gren foraged among the pots and pans for something to eat.

"We're supposed to be packing up," I announced as I reached them.

"Drink this." Sorgrad handed me a cup that I sniffed suspiciously. "Halcarion's Heal-All."

I drank it down and looked around. "Is there any flatbread left?"

"Stale as stones but you can have it if you want it," Gren offered generously. He was chewing on a strip of cold meat, dipping it in a bowl of congealed nut sauce. I took the flatbread, dipping it in the tisane to soften it.

Usara came over and Sorgrad wordlessly handed him a cup.

"Are you all right?" I looked at him with some concern, but his color was improving

Usara wrapped his hands around the warmth of his cup, breathing in the steam. "Well enough, just weary. I think I've done more magic since Equinox than in the past half-year," he said with a rueful smile. "It's really not the same as just exploring the theories of wizardry. Still, one of the reasons I wanted to come with you was to test my skills."

"We need to decide what we're about here," Sorgrad stated firmly. "Has anyone found so much as a sniff of aetheric lore among these folk?"

Usara shook his head. "Even supposing it was something they were keeping secret, I feel sure someone would have let something slip by now, given how open they are."

I studied my bread for a moment. "I still think there's something to this jalquezan. And there was the hunt today; that Iamris was finding game with something more than a good eye and a sharp nose, I'm sure of it. How did word of the trouble get back to the camp so quick? No one could have run that fast! What about Zenela? When did you see anyone heal so fast and so fully from putrid lungs? I've finally found someone who knows a ballad where someone uses a charm to light a fire like me—"

"Livak, I've spent the last three days listening to ballad after ballad after ballad," said Usara, exasperated. "Every second person has a different version, some minstrel's variant on the words or the order of narrative. It seems to be a point of honor to fiddle about with the tune and add embellishments. I'm sorry, believe me, but these stories are so fluid, so much changes from year to year, that whatever knowledge they might have once held is lost beyond retrieval. I could give you five different versions of 'The Hunt of the White Stag' for a start." He shut his mouth with an obstinate snap.

"We're not here to write a treatise on the history of the Folk." I tried to contain my own annoyance. "Stop trying to pin down facts and look at the stories! Look at the unexpected, the remarkable, and the impossible and tell me you don't think there's magic involved. And where there is magic, there's the jalquezan, every time."

"Perhaps." The skepticism in Usara's voice left little doubt as to his opinion. "But how are they doing it? How do we test their abilities, determine the efficacy of whatever lore they might have?"

"Why do you wizards always have to pick and pry and pull things apart? Can't you just believe it?" I glared at the mage.

"If we don't know how they are doing something, how are we to repeat it?" demanded Usara.

I waved him to silence as an idea jumped up and bit me. "It was your own work that identified the collective belief of a group of people as the source of the power that Artifice draws on, wasn't it?"

Usara looked perplexed. "The main credit belongs to Geris Armiger—"

I raised a hand, frowning as I struggled to find words for my new notion. "What if enough people believing a person can do something is enough to make it happen? What if that's sufficient to bring aetheric influence to bear on someone's abilities?" Now that I said it, it all made sense, the pieces falling into place like a child's puzzle.

"I don't follow you," said Usara in weary tones.

"Everyone tells me Rusia is the best at reading the runes. She believes it and so does everyone else. That belief is enough to make it true. Orial is a noted healer; she sings the songs that she believes will add luck to her medicines. The words of the jalquezan don't matter so much as the fact she believes in what she's doing. That's what makes it happen. Everyone knows that Iamris will find game, so he does. Every time it happens, it strengthens the belief, the expectation that it will happen next time, so it does!"

"Self-fulfilling prophecy," murmured Sorgrad thoughtfully.

"But Guinalle and her Adepts studied Artifice back in the Tormalin Empire's height," protested Usara. "Her skills are born of discipline, not just blind belief."

"Where does learning stop and belief begin?" countered Sorgrad. "Which comes first and then supports the other?"

I picked a twig from the ground, dead wood with a spray of parched and brown leaves still clinging to it. I'd spent too long with these mages with their questions and insatiable curiosity. "Talmia megrala eldrin fres." The leaves crackled as they were instantly consumed, the dry bark split, the wood beneath charred. I dropped the twig to the ground and stamped on it, grinding it down beneath the top layer of dry litter into the damp leaf mold beneath. The sharp smell of smoke hovered in the air. "That's Artifice. Tell me how I did it, wizard! I don't know how but I believe I can and it's never failed me yet."

Usara opened his mouth and then shut it again. The mage's essential honesty and scholarly training made it impossible for him to dismiss my idea out of hand, however much he might want to. "But how do we test the notion? We have to have some proof, if we're to take anything to the Council or the Archmage."

"Presumably, if someone started doubting their abilities they could lose them," said Sorgrad slowly. "A bit like losing your place in a dance when you suddenly become conscious of what your feet are doing."

I frowned. "How could you just choose to stop believing in something?"

"We could fuzz the runes in a game with Barben," said 'Gren with feeling. "Or break his fingers. I wouldn't mind seeing him learning it's possible to lose. Everyone's certainly convinced he can't be beaten."

"There's another one," I nodded to Usara. "He believes he's lucky, and all the others believe it too; that invokes some unconscious element of Artifice and the runes run his way."

"He's certainly not cheating," remarked Sorgrad. "Trust me, we'd know if he was."

Usara brought his hands together, fingertips touching, tucking them beneath his chin. His eyes were distant among the bustle of the disintegrating camp. "It's an interesting notion and who's to say it's wrong, we know so little of Artifice. But where's the proof, where's the trial?"

"Why do you need that?" I shook my head. "Does every mage in Hadrumal reduce a timepiece to cogs and springs before they accept it'll mark the passing chimes?"

Usara grimaced. "We could find ourselves risking apples against ashes, couldn't we? If we ask questions of Guinalle that start her doubting her own abilities, we've not only lost our most advanced practitioner of Artifice but also one of the main defenses the Kellarin colony has against Elietimm raids."

He jumped as two Forest men swept a sheet of woven bark past his head. Our sura was being reclaimed as we spoke. We moved to one side and left them to it.

"Rusia says that Ravin will be able to hide them from any pursuit," I said suddenly. "How about we test that?"

Usara looked blank for a moment. "How?"

"We let them go off, let them get a few chimes ahead, then see if we can track them." I was hard put to keep the sarcasm out of my voice.

"They're going to have far more woodcraft—" began the mage.

"We grew up spending half the year tracking fur animals

through thicker woods than this," interrupted 'Gren, scornfully.

I could see the wizard was still looking doubtful and that Sorgrad was thinking the same as me. "We will try our best, you know. We won't just lose them because we want it to be true!" Usara tried to look surprised but his fair color betrayed him with a blush of red.

"You'll be trying to scry for them, won't you?" Sorgrad was looking amused at something I was missing. "Artifice can hide from clemental magic, can't it?"

Usara looked at him sharply. "It has seemed so."

"Then put your money where your mouth is, mage," Sorgrad said softly. "You wanted a test, let's make one."

I could see Usara was still looking for some trick or deception. "You've got to trust us sometime," I pointed out. "You got close enough to Orial to be able to scry for her, didn't you?"

Usara threw up his hands. "Very well. Let's see where this takes us."

I didn't trust myself to talk to him for a while so busied myself helping the Folk dismantle their camp. 'Gren slipped away to bid some tactful farewells and I saw Sorgrad in seemingly casual conversation with Frue.

"Did you make our thank you?" I asked when he returned to my side. I wiped some sweat from my face with a rope-scorched hand.

He nodded. "Frue's going to share out our cut of the meat and he said to tell you he was grateful for the new songs, or rather the ancient ones."

We stood and waited in the middle of the trampled glade and watched as the Folk melted into the forest, leaving us and our donkey and a pile of baggage. I felt a pang I didn't want to examine too closely. I wanted them to be my kin, but then again I didn't. And wanting wouldn't make it so, in any case. I didn't belong here, any more than I belonged in Vanam. So it was up to me to make my own place, wasn't it? With Ryshad, and that meant showing these skeptical wizards that I had found something worth solid coin. My spirits rose as I realized the song various voices were raising as the Folk moved away was a tale of Seris evading pursuit by Mazir. That was in my book and it had the jalquezan in every second verse.

"How about a hand or so of runes, to pass the time while we wait?" I took the bones from my pocket and sat down. By the time I'd taken all Usara's small coin off him and what remained of Sorgrad's loot from the raiders, the sun had slipped down to skirt the edge of the treetops.

"Now Livak's got everything she wanted, how about we try to follow those Folk," suggested Sorgrad with a grin.

"I'm game!" 'Gren sprang to his feet and began quartering the edges of the glade.

"We know they went in that direction," pointed out Usara apologetically.

'Gren ignored him. "If we're going to do this, we'll do it properly," Sorgrad said firmly.

"I've some tracking skills of my own," I told the wizard. "You come last with the donkey so as not to foul the ground."

"Right, we have hoof prints plain enough here," called 'Gren. "Let's see how far they go."

The trail was plain enough and the brothers followed it with close attention. We moved steadily and silently, the two of them a way ahead, bending over scuffmarks, noting crushed flowers, bent twigs. I checked the sun and worked out we were bearing north and west. We'd be reaching the river soon, I judged. Usara walked behind me, idly plucking leaves from bushes and offering them to the donkey who mumbled them before letting the pieces fall to the damp earth.

'Gren and Sorgrad slowed and stopped, conferring in low voices. Separating, they cast about like hounds after a scent and after a while came back to Usara and me.

"Lost them," said 'Gren baldly. "The trail's been getting fainter and fainter and now it's given out altogether."

"Doesn't that happen anyway, if someone is being careful to avoid pursuit?" asked Usara, choosing his words with care.

Sorgrad stepped forward and pressed his boot into a mossy patch. "On stony ground, on hard mud, maybe even on thick litter, if you're very careful. Not on this terrain."

"And we can track mice over a scree, if we put our minds to it," added 'Gren with a hint of menace.

We looked at the deep imprint of Sorgrad's foot and then at the soft, unmarked ground all around. "They were singing 'The ballad of Mazir's Search,' " I pointed out to the mage. "I can find that in the book, if you want to read it."

Usara nodded. "Very well. Then let's see if my magic can do any better than your woodcraft."

I held my tongue and 'Gren and Sorgrad exchanged an amused glance. Usara dripped green magelight from one negligent hand and the boot print in the moss filled with water. Usara knelt, bending closer with a faint frown. 'Gren, uninterested, pulled up grass for the donkey, stroking its velvety nose. I watched Sorgrad, whose expression was a singular mixture of skepticism and curiosity. Birdsong fluted around and about as the creatures of the woods went about their business, unbothered by our arcane concerns.

I restrained my impatience with a firm hand. Usara had to come to this conclusion on his own, unhurried and unprompted, or he'd never acknowledge it wasn't his own. I shoved my hands in my breeches pockets and fingered my rune bones. Sorgrad winked at me when I looked away, in case my gaze scorched the back of the mage's neck. I stifled a laugh.

"I can't scry them." Usara sounded genuinely astounded. "I can find absolutely no trace!"

I bit my tongue.

"What else could explain that, other than Artifice?" asked Sorgrad in a neutral tone.

"At this distance, over this time, given the time we've spent with them—" Usara rubbed a thoughtful hand over his mouth. "You know, I really can't think of anything."

The arrogance that had these wizards thinking they could never be wrong was a coin with two sides, wasn't it? I released my breath slowly. "So now you believe me?"

"I think you've an argument worth further consideration," the mage admitted.

"So, what do we do now?" 'Gren had wandered back to us. He grinned. "You're prepared to admit these Folk have some Artifice, but now we've gone and lost them. Do we go looking for another gang of them?"

"I'll grant the Folk look to have real Artifice but there's still no clear lore or anything we could put to immediate use," frowned Usara.

"What about the song book?" I objected.

"Sing me something, make it work," challenged Usara. "Do you believe it wholeheartedly enough to harness the aetheric influence? Show me how to explain it to Planir, to the scholars studying with Guinalle. Show me how to use it against the Elietimm!"

"Sheltya could," suggested 'Gren obligingly.

"What?" Usara and I spoke as one, rounding on the Mountain Man who smiled cheerfully.

"That's why you wanted to go into the uplands, isn't it? To ask Sheltya's help?" 'Gren looked at his brother, faint puzzlement wrinkling his brow.

"What is it you haven't told us?" demanded Usara.

I stepped between him and Sorgrad. The only person who was going to take that tone with him was me. "Who or what is Sheltya? I've never heard the word before."

Sorgrad's face was a blank parchment, nothing to be read. "They hold the sagas and the histories of the mountains. If any Anyatimm know of aetheric magic, it'll be Sheltya. Those Solurans straightening Halice's leg after her breaking her thigh, even when it was half a year healed, that's the kind of thing Sheltya are said to do."

"Saedrin's stones, man, why didn't you tell us this earlier?" exclaimed Usara angrily. "Why've we been wasting our time here?"

"Because we were always coming to the Forest first anyway." I took a pace forward and forced the wizard back a step. "You don't head into the hills that early into the season and we needed to take the long route anyway to avoid trouble in the Gap."

Usara retreated prudently. "Then let's get back to the high road and get on our way." He caught up the mule's halter and set off determinedly. His scrying had at least given him his bearings.

I tried to catch Sorgrad's eye as we followed but he avoided my gaze. I held my peace; he'd tell me what this was all about in his own good time. Then I'd tear strips off him for not telling me sooner, as soon as I could do it out of earshot of the wizard.

Five

When the Emperor granted my husband Gidestan estates in recognition of his service in the west, I first met the Men of the Mountains and learned their grave sagas. This piece, much sung at Solstice, reminds us that life in the heights can be as harsh as the climate and we should perhaps be more understanding of their brusqueness in dealings with those bred in gentler lands.

> The wolves crouched on the crag
> And gazed upon the slain,
> The mighty in their blood,
> As one with weak in death.
> From those that yet stood tall,
> A man of might rose up.
> He set a wrathful axe
> Before him in the snow.
> "Bring him who wrought this wrong
> From lust to rule us all.
> Maewelin lend her hand
> To prove our cause is just."
> They brought the evil man,
> And threw him to his knees.
> The war host spat their hate,
> And scorned all ties of blood.
> "Misaen be your judge,

And those who heed your lies.
Go north into the ice,
Return and you will die."
The kinless ones were stripped,
And driven out with blows.
The ones not fast to flee,
Were slaughtered as they ran.
The gray and wise stood forth,
And mighty oaths they swore,
That power that they held,
Would never rule the peaks.
Their skills would serve and guide,
Their touch would heal not kill,
And those who would not yield,
Fell witless to the stones.
Returning to quenched hearths,
The host wept bitter tears.
The wolves crept from the heights
And gorged upon the dead.

Lidrasoke,
32nd of Aft-Spring

Jeirran tied his hard-ridden pony to a ring carved in a block of marble and poured water from the skin at his saddlebow into a dry hollow in the stone. He turned his back on the grasslands of the valley where new growth was vibrant with flowers turning faces to the warmth of spring. Red, yellow, blue and white, all strove to take what they could from the sun before the snows blanketed them once more. Jeirran stood motionless for a long moment before the forbidding arc of gray wall.

The stronghold rose up from a solid hillock of earth piled up to level an existing rise, claiming immediate advantage of height over any that might approach. The massive wall rose like an outcrop of living rock and the windows of the rekin within were paired like watchful eyes. The stone-crowned fess dominated the wind-scoured valley as the land swelled toward the encroaching mountains.

But this place was an empty boast. The great doors to the compound stood wedged open with rubble, the bar to defy all comers leaning impotently in the angle of the thick wall. The triangular space in the stones above the lintel, where the mighty emblem of the house had once been raised, was as empty as a blind socket. Jeirran kicked the pebbles away from the iron-banded base of the gate and hauled on it, pins in the sockets of the solid stone threshold grating on wind-blown dust. With a wordless exclamation, he sent the heavy barrier slamming into the carved stop of the jamb. The sharp crack echoed back from the gray cliffs rearing up to the north of the compound, stark in their snow-capped beauty.

Walking into the compound, Jeirran made a slow circuit, pausing to peer into every doorway and window of the stone-slated buildings that clung to the interior of the wall. All were empty, swept clean and tidy, every possession gone, hearths cold. The bitter scowl marking Jeirran's face faded, gradually replaced by a sadness that mercilessly stripped away the years, betraying a wretched youth.

He looked up at the rekin. The black hollows of the windows defied the searching sun, secretive, baleful. Jeirran entered, ignored the dismantled hearth, and crossed to the stairs. Walking at first, then moving faster, soon running through the dark shadows, he finally emerged onto the flat roof. The hardness returned to his eyes as he bent to take a sight along a groove in one of the stones of the parapet. It pointed to the distant cliff face, to a fissure whose regular sides and angular edges spoke eloquently of hammer and mallet. Jeirran's expression settled into its habitual frown. The steady breeze, ever present, lifted a stray lock hair from his forehead and dust swirled around his feet with a noise like a curious whisper.

"Are you going to ask me to go in there for the Solstice? To see what the bones of our soke say when Misaen sends the sun to illuminate the sanctuary of our blood? What questions do you want me to ask?"

Only a sharp intake of breath informed against him. Jeirran stood upright and turned slowly. "You speak of my family." He stressed the penultimate word lightly. "What interest have you in the blood that once dwelt here?"

"For a man who wants to claim a favor on the strength of past kinship, you go about things in a very odd fashion, Jeirran," the newcomer said critically from her seat on the wall that ran around the edge of the roof.

Jeirran dropped his eyes for a moment, scuffing at the solid slabs with the toe of his boot. "Hello, Aritane." He smiled at her with a charm that did not reach his eyes. "You're looking well."

"Marriage hasn't changed you," she commented with an enigmatic edge to her tone. "How is Eirys?"

Jeirran waved a hand dismissively. "Well enough."

"It's a shame she's not breeding yet." Aritane smoothed her dusky gray gown over her lap, drawing softly shod feet together in an elegant gesture. The color complemented the twilight blue of her eyes, deep set and dominating a narrow face with a long nose unflattered by the way her corn-colored hair was cropped short, combed back from a high forehead. Her lips showed a full sensuality, the clearest stamp of common blood with Jeirran. "I would like to see you secure your posterity in a child, preferably a bevy of them."

"No child of Eirys' blood would give me a claim here," Jeirran sighed.

"No," agreed Aritane softly, regret naked in her eyes.

"Is it a fair exchange then?" Jeirran demanded belligerently. "Are the arts of Sheltya fitting recompense for abandoning your blood and its land to be claimed by the daughters of our foremother's foremother's sister? Do you wield any more power than being able to tell whether or not my wife is finally going to prove herself fertile?"

"You always were a contentious brat, even as a child, Jeirran," replied Aritane with disdain. "I lost count of the times Father had to dump you into that water trough yonder to quench your temper."

They both glanced at the long hollowed stone down by the main gate, dry as a wind-scoured bone, a few leaves and fragments of blown grass caught in the unstoppered hole in its base.

Jeirran hung his head for a moment before lifting a challenging face. "So tell me, sister-that-was, what of your life?"

"I travel between the sokes, I give judgment and counsel, I spread news and share appeals for aid or alliance." There was a dry mockery in her words. "You know full well the duty of Sheltya."

Jeirran drummed his fingers on the wall, chewing at his beard. "We all know what Sheltya do. What interests me is what Sheltya are. What of the powers whispered of in corners at Solstice and Equinox? What of those times when one lone traveler in gray will become ten or twenty Sheltya, all appearing out of nowhere and closing a fess to travelers while they deal with a pestilence, a crime against the blood, some other offense that only they can see."

"You know full well that it is not permitted to speak of these things," Aritane replied in a level tone. "Why do you defy that? What do you want of me?" She might have been inquiring about the weather for all the concern in her voice.

"Have you learned the secrets of their power? Just what it is that Sheltya can do?" persisted Jeirran. "How they can leave behind them empty halls whose people are vanished or scattered mindless to the charity of others? Even when they move on and leave all behind them hale and hearty, why do none have any recollection of what has been done to save or succor them?"

"This is not your concern," said Aritane, icier now. "Such things are only the province of those of us chosen to serve."

"Chosen?" Jeirran folded his arms and looked at his sister. "Taken, perhaps. Better yet, stolen. I was only half a season short of my ninth year, old enough to remember your tears, your screams, your anger. I remember you clinging to your bed when they came for you, begging our mother to deny them, cursing her when she did not." He drew a slow, measured breath. "But then I suppose that proved the justice of their claim on you, didn't it? Your curse worked well enough; Mother dead inside a year and Father and the rest of us home from a hard season in the diggings to find all we had worked for now owed to some mousy-haired chit from the far side of the heights whom none of us had even heard of before then."

"Mother died in childbirth, a tragedy but not uncommon." Aritane's hands in her lap were white at the knuckles as she clasped them together.

"In childbed as she desperately labored for a daughter to replace you, to safeguard the lands she had inherited." Jeirran shook his head. "I did hear tell that she forbade Sheltya her bedchamber, terrified they would see true magic in the future of that child as well. Had she allowed them in, they might have been able to save both her and the babe."

Aritane stood up. "If you have only brought me here to scratch at long-healed scars, I'll bid you farewell, Jeirran."

"But Sheltya wouldn't force her, would they? They won't use their powers, whatever they might be, without consent, will they? Whatever they can do, it's always shackled and hedged about with secrets and mysteries and never used openly. What good is strength if it's never used?"

Aritane was at the top of the stairs now.

"What do Sheltya say of the Elietimm, Ari?"

Jeirran's taunting words halted her on the topmost tread. "What did you say?"

"Is that the correct way to say it? Shouldn't it be Alyatimm?" Jeirran took a seat on the wall now, legs outstretched before him, leaning on his hands.

Aritane turned her head slowly. "What have you heard?" There was irresistible command in her voice.

"I'm not some accused to warrant your compulsion to speak the truth." Jeirran spat and scrubbed a hand across his eyes. "I've just heard what half the lowlanders will be hearing in their ale-houses and taverns before the summer's out. Songs of these Elietimm, of the powers they wield, of the dangers they pose, of the might of their fighting men. How long do you suppose it will be before some greedy burgher of Wrede decides these blond men from across the ocean are no different from those blond men over the mountains? They'll seize on any excuse to steal more land, more wealth, to drive us back farther and farther from what was once ours. Maybe that's what befell the Teyvasoke. You must have heard about that from your new kindred." Jeirran laughed mirthlessly. "If they drive us back far enough, we'll all become Men of the Ice, won't we?"

Aritane's face was cold, eyes like the shadows in the cracks of a glacier. "You have no idea what you are talking about. The Alyatimm sought to use the powers of Sheltya to dominate and rule without mercy or consent."

"I know that these Elietimm, whoever they may be, use their powers to defend themselves. I know that they do not see true magic as something to be hidden and secret but a weapon to save their lands and their people from plunder and rape. I'll wager every coin of my patrimony that their wise are not taken away from land and family, lest they are ever tempted to use what they learn for their soke's advantage." Jeirran got to his feet and walked slowly around the roof, looking down into the compound and over the wall to the grasslands of the valley beyond. "Wouldn't you rather have had the chance to use your learning to benefit your blood, to take up your inheritance and make it prosper, rather than see our home left empty to shelter passing travelers now that those who claim it cannot even be bothered to dwell here half a season in the year?"

Aritane's face was bloodless and pale as the flagstones beneath her feet. "Why do you do this, Jeirran? Why stir up the long-dead embers of old wrath and bitter sorrow? Raise a fire like that and it will burn your hands. What's done is done and there is no way to change it."

"But what if there were?" Jeirran said softly, crossing over to her and taking her hands between his. "You cannot tell me you are happy with your lot, Ari! If you were, you would hardly have come to meet me here. I saw you at Solstice, in the Parthfess, having to dance attendance on that stupid old man. Everyone else may have thought his ramblings were the mystical wisdom of Sheltya but you knew full well it was just senile nonsense. I could see it in your eyes. They promised you power and knowledge in return for losing your home and family. What have they given you? The role of nursemaid to some incontinent old fool who still gets more respect than you when he's drooling gruel down the front of his night-shirt! How is it right that the powers of true magic are kept from desperate people by the fears and cowardice of the Elders?"

"By rights, I should denounce you myself," Aritane spat at him, "or very least wipe this conversation from your memory, together with all this festering hate and whatever half-truths you think you've garnered from lowland gossip!"

"Do so," shrugged Jeirran. "No matter, it won't change anything. Inside half a season, someone like me, someone selling his ingots or another trapper trading with the lowlands, he'll bring back these songs and tales. Yevrein will be wondering why these people, who must surely share our blood, why are they so feared by the lowlanders? Why are these Elietimm using all means at their disposal to protect homes and families, while we are robbed and assaulted at every season's turn? Peider and his friends will start wondering too, start asking questions of Sheltya, demanding answers too. Whoever among you decides to find those answers—well, that'll be the one who finally takes the whip out of the hands of the old and fearful, won't it? To govern how the true magic is used, to see that wisdom tempers raw power that the so-called wise are too fearful to use?"

Aritane looked down at her hands, still clasped between Jeirran's broad palms. "You said you had a favor to ask of me?" She looked up, her face emotionless but her eyes boring into his.

Now it came to the point, Jeirran hesitated. "It is said that Sheltya can speak to each other across the mountains and valleys, send word to their colleagues far distant, farther than a season's travel."

Aritane nodded slowly. Jeirran continued more boldly, breaking into the tense silence with sudden urgency. "Could you contact these Elietimm? Could you find out more about them? Could you see if they might help us, teach us, maybe even make common cause with us? If they were to attack the lowlanders in the east, while we came down from the mountains, we could reclaim our lands, regain our pride!"

Aritane pulled her hands free to hug herself, shivering despite the sunshine. "You do not know what you are asking," she murmured. "I have heard of these Elietimm, of course I have. We have been forbidden to seek them."

"I am asking you to help your people," Jeirran said softly. "Sheltya took you away from your own that you might serve all those of the mountains. Is there anything else but such service in what I am asking? Do you want to go back to solving squabbles between silly women, arbitrating rows over grazing, dealing with death and foulness when some traveler brings pestilence to a remote valley, while all the time our people are made poorer and meaner by lowland greed?"

"You are a curious choice to be arguing for the greater good and selfless risk-taking," said Aritane dryly. "What's in this for you, Jeirran?"

"Power, what do you think?" He spread his hands wide. "The power to hunt Eirys' lands without fear of losing the best pelts to some lowlander's snares. I want to see her brothers able to sell the ores they labor to dig for a fair price. Power. I want to be rich, Ari, I want to keep Eirys in all the luxuries her little head can imagine and to stop the mouth of that mother of hers with an endless diet of honey and cakes, if that's what it takes to silence the hag. I want to hand my sons a handsome patrimony and to see my daughters set up to claim every right over and under the land that their blood allows. I want to be a power in the mountains, Ari, one to make the lowlanders look to the hills and fear my wrath more than the cold winter wind." He grinned at her. "I want to be a brother once again to the new leader of Sheltya. I want to have the ear of the woman who restores true magic to its rightful place of honor and influence."

Aritane shook her head but she was smiling now, a thin, heartless smile with a spark growing behind her eyes. "I'm not surprised that silly child Eirys fell for your blandishments, Jeirran. You always did have a tongue quicker than a mountain stream and more slippery than the rocks beneath it."

"Will you do it?" Jeirran persisted.

"I shouldn't even waste a moment's thought on it." Aritane pursed her lips. "I could find myself turned out on the bare mountainside with my mind as empty as a midwinter barrel. If anyone found out—"

"Who's to know?" demanded Jeirran. "I'm hardly likely to go gossiping to any passing Sheltya, am I? I'm as deep in this as you are, more so. You are the one with the power over me, you said so yourself. Your word alone could have me shunned across the breadth of the mountains, no reason given or asked."

"I can use my skills to try and get a response but with scarcely more certainty than setting a signal fire in the mountains and hoping someone will see the smoke. The trick will be reaching far enough away before raising the cry to escape notice closer at hand." Aritane was talking to herself more than to Jeirran. "If I do find these Elietimm, what then?" she challenged him abruptly.

"Then we have something to tell those who feel as we do," Jeirran said confidently. "There are plenty of us fed up with being bilked and cheated by the lowlanders. Deny

there are Sheltya chafing under the constraints of custom
and the Elders? We tell them that there are men and women
of our blood beyond the ocean who do not bow and scrape
and ever retreat in the face of lowlander aggression."

Aritane tilted her head to one side. "You always were
shrewd enough, I'll grant you that much." She moved with
sudden decisiveness, shaking out her unadorned skirts.
Looking toward the mountains to the north, she checked the
position of the sun overhead, moving this way and that to
assess the shadows before crossing to one side of the roof
and squinting at the misty shapes of higher ground. Nodding at some inner conclusion, she turned to Jeirran, her
face animated with daring and defiance for an instant before
resuming the mask of her earlier indifference.

"Sit with your back to the chimney, facing north." He
hurried to comply.

"You do not interrupt me, you do not touch me, you do
not move or say anything," Aritane ordered in a tone of absolute authority. She sat cross-legged, heedless of her dress
on the dusty roof. Elbows resting on her knees, she laid her
face in her upturned hands and began to breathe deeply, reg-
ularly, in through her nose and then forcing the air out of
her mouth in an ever lengthening exhalation, pushed deep
from within her.

Jeirran jumped, startled, when the low sound halted and
clenched his fists against the urge to go to her. Sweat began
to bead on his forehead. He moved a hand as if about to
wipe it away but stilled himself. His lips moved in what
might have been a muttered curse, had he dared to speak.
His eyes were unblinking, bright sapphire as he fixed his
gaze on Aritane, who was now taking shallow breaths,
pauses between each. Jeirran found himself following the
same ragged pattern, the color beneath his beard fading to
an unhealthy pallor until he lifted his chin with an explosive
intake of breath, panting uncontrollably for a few moments
before a natural rhythm was restored to his lungs.

High above, a hawk's thin cry was wheeled away on the

wind, serving only to emphasize the vast silence of the empty valley. A flurry of dust and nameless debris skittered across the roof as a fugitive gust swirled around Aritane's motionless figure. Jeirran blinked and spat out some fragment, shaking his head a fraction before forcing himself to immobility once more. The breeze vanished and the sun pressed down on his head, striking up from the stones and laying black shadows across the white surface of the roof. The chimney at his back was solid and reassuring but cold and silent where once it had been the warm heart of the rekin. A trickle of perspiration rolled down the side of Jeirran's face to vanish into his beard. Another followed, this one moving sideways to sting the corner of his eye.

A great crash reverberated around the circular wall of the compound, echoing back and forth with a sound like a hot rock shattered by the shock of cold water. Terror leaped in Jeirran's eyes for an instant, fear naked as the mask of arrogance and confidence was torn from his face. The noise came again, the rap of wood on stone and Jeirran took a long, trembling breath. It was the gate, wasn't it? Set swinging by a wind rising up from the valley bottom, that was it, surely?

He looked at Aritane, who was motionless as stone.

Was it the gate? Had someone else come here, Jeirran wondered suddenly. Would Sheltya be using their powers to watch over Aritane? Could some distant gray-bearded Elder have been listening in on their conversation? Was the sound the first warning they had been discovered, that Sheltya were come? One always seemed to be on hand when needed, but were they here now, to frustrate their plot?

Jeirran's breath came faster. He was sweating copiously, even when a new breeze cooled him. Hands clenched by his sides were shaking, tremors running up his arms to jar the stiffness in his neck and shoulders. The heat and the silence pressed down unforgiving, as if they would pound the rocks to dust.

Aritane lifted her face, dropping her hands in the lap of

her dress. Livid spots blossomed on her forehead where her fingertips had been digging into the skin. Jeirran pressed against the stone at his back as she turned her eyes to him. They were featureless pits of blackness, no white, no color, no life within them. He scrambled to his knees, a whimper of nameless terror escaping him.

Aritane blinked and her eyes were normal again. A warm rose softened her cheeks, and elation set her face alight. She drew a deep, shuddering breath. "Oh, Jeirran," she whispered in tones of wonder. "I found them!"

"I—" He coughed to quell the shaking in his voice. "I knew you could," he answered more boldly. "So what—"

Aritane shook her head. "Wait, let me compose myself." She stood, moving stiffly, brushing awkwardly at the dirt on her gown. Hugging her arms to her, she turned to stare out eastward. "They are out there, Jeirran, out beyond the Easterlings, beyond the ocean." She laughed with pure delight. "They didn't know me, of course, but they acknowledged my power, my right to come seeking them. They congratulated me on my daring, praised my skills. I can't recall the last time anyone did that here!"

"So what did you say? What did you tell them? Will they help us?" demanded Jeirran, striding over to stand at her shoulder.

"What?" Aritane's eyes were distant again.

Jeirran moved to block her view of the valley and the east. "What are they going to do for us?" He laid a hand on her, a breath away from shaking her.

"Oh, Jeirran, you always want everything all at once, don't you?" Irritation replaced the exhilaration in Aritane's expression. "I have told them I wish to discuss matters of grave importance and that I will contact them when I am next at leisure."

"Ari!" Anger roughened Jeirran's words. "Why the delay, why not simply—"

"Do not question my methods, Jeirran," she warned him. "This is my task and I know best how to go about it. Believe me, I have no desire to find myself answering to Sheltya before I have allies with the means to back me and defend me."

"So how long is it likely to be before you have the necessary leisure?" snapped Jeirran crossly.

Consideration furrowed Aritane's brow. "I think I had better come to visit your wife. I will let those to whom I answer think that she is concerned about her lack of a child. As long as you keep from her bed for a while, that should satisfy any curiosity. If I can have privacy, a decent room and a few comforts for a change, I should be able to concentrate all my energies on discussions with our new friends." She smiled with a predatory satisfaction.

"Eirys' mother will not be pleased," Jeirran scowled. "She'll start poking her long nose where it's not wanted."

"Then you will get your wife to assert herself as mistress of her own hearth," said Aritane crisply. "It's about time that girl showed a little backbone."

"That's hardly likely," Jeirran scoffed. "I wasn't looking for spirit when I wooed her!"

"It's up to you." Aritane turned to the steps down into the rekin. "You need me, if you want to pursue this further. Persuade Eirys to start fretting over her barrenness, and then no one will wonder at my visit. I know that you've been having words on that subject, haven't you? And doing your best to swell her belly, whether she's agreeable or not." This last remark was tossed casually over her shoulder as she descended.

"How do you know that?" demanded Jeirran, a furious blush staining his cheeks scarlet. He cursed under his breath and rubbed his hands roughly over his face before pursuing his sister. Running down the stairs, he skidded to a halt at the bottom, nailed boot soles grating on the stones. Aritane was nowhere to be seen.

"A pox on your games for the witless, woman," he shouted into the empty room, dust thick upon the flagstones, unmoved, unmarked save for Jeirran's footprints.

"Drown you!" He ran out into the center of the fess. "Aritane!" He stormed over to the workshops, but they were as desolate as before. "What do you think you are playing at? Aritane!"

The echoes of his wrathful bellow mocked him as they came bounding back from the impassive walls. As the noise faded, the silence pressed down even more heavily than before.

Jeirran shivered involuntarily before marching down to the gateway. He paused on the threshold to wedge the open door again but halted with a stone in his hand. Muttering under his breath, he moved instead to clear the stones from the base of the other, pulling the two together. With their weight and some trick of construction working to hold them closed, Jeirran turned his back on the gates, untied his pony and beat the reluctant beast into a weary canter.

The Chamber of Planir the Black,
Archmage of Hadrumal,
1st of For-Summer

A hesitant rap on the outside of the door was followed by a more confident knock.

"Enter." The single occupant of the room was relaxing in a leather-upholstered chair by one of the tall lancets of the window. He did not look up from the closely written letter he was reading. Sunlight brightened the dark wood-paneled room with sparkling fingers playing on the expensive mossy carpet, the polished furniture and the orderly rows of books and scrolls on the numerous shelves. The heavy black oak opened noiselessly on well-tended hinges.

"Archmage." The newcomer bowed. He was a tall, long-boned man with straight black hair cut off at jaw length, a sallow complexion and circumspect eyes. He cleared his throat. "So we are expecting to hear from 'Sar this morning?"

"Shiv, take a seat." The Archmage did not lift his eyes from his document. "Larissa will be here in a moment or so."

Shiv sat at a satiny table where a steel mirror stood on a mahogany pedestal. A silver candlestick stood in front of it, the creamy beeswax with its snowy tuft of wick as yet unmarred by flame. He opened his mouth to speak but cleared his throat instead.

"Take some water if you have a cough." Planir looked up briefly, gray eyes stern.

Shiv looked at his hands for a moment then poured himself a glassful. He set the carafe carefully on a nearby sideboard whose rich brown frontage was inlaid with garlands of flowers and sprays of leaves in all the shades that wood could offer the joiner.

"Is this really something Larissa should be privy to?" he said abruptly. "She's barely out of her apprenticeship and while I know you favor her, as a pupil I mean—"

"She has a double affinity, Shivvalan," interrupted Planir in a quelling tone. "That automatically makes her the Archmage's pupil. As my pupil, I deem it fit to involve her in my concerns. To do otherwise would seriously hamper me at present, since Usara has gone and Otrick is still insensible. Her affinities also mean that we can use her talents to weave a full nexus, rather than have to draw two other people into the circle. I am surprised you see fit to question my judgment on this."

Shiv set his jaw and gazed out of the window. "Is 'Sar having much trouble getting Livak to do as he wants? When I was traveling with her, well, she could certainly be very headstrong. Perhaps I should have gone with them. Better yet, you could be using 'Sar's talents here instead of mine." He fell silent as the Archmage folded his letter precisely, securing the creases with deft hands and using a touch of magic to soften the wax and reseal it.

"Usara is not having any trouble directing Livak's actions because he is under explicit instructions to let her do just as she wishes and, moreover, to keep his own presence as inconspicuous as possible," Planir stated firmly.

Shiv reluctantly turned his face to the Archmage. The senior wizard looked Shiv straight in the eye. Shiv dropped his gaze and frowned at the carpet. "Isn't this all a little too important to let Livak run loose after her own game? I'd have thought—"

"Would you, Shiv?" interrupted Planir. "Would you have thought, or would you have simply gone headlong after the first scent, let the consequences go hang?"

The glass of water slopped as Shiv's hand tightened around it. "Elietimm magic has left the Cloud-Master of Hadrumal comatose and unrousable, a double handful besides him in the same situation. I personally feel that finding a means to remedy the situation warrants rather more effort than letting Livak go off on some random search for any debased knowledge the ancient races might still possess."

"I'm used to that kind of pomposity from Kalion, Shiv, but that's only to be expected from our revered Hearth-Master, after all," observed Planir, a cutting edge to his voice. "It really doesn't become you, nor will it further the aspirations Troanna tells me you currently have to claiming a seat on the Council."

Shiv's lips narrowed but he made no reply. Planir laid his letter aside and crossed to a table where a row of decanters stood behind a rank of crystal goblets. "Wine?" he invited in a more friendly tone.

"No, thank you," said Shiv stiffly.

Planir smiled to himself and resumed his seat, a full goblet of rich plum-colored wine in one hand, the glass ornamented with precisely incised diamonds. "I confess I hadn't expected to have to lay it all out for you, like some first-season apprentice unsure of conjuring a candle flame, but I am happy to do so." He waved aside Shiv's inarticulate protest as he sipped from his drink. "Why did Trydek the first Archmage bring wizardry to the sanctuary of an island?" the Archmage asked, his air mock didactic.

Shiv looked irritated. "What—"

"Why?" demanded Planir with a sharp glare from beneath his fine black brows.

"Because of the fear and superstition the powers of the mage-born provoked among the mundane populace." Shiv rattled off his reply in a sarcastic singsong.

"What makes you think that so much has changed? How many apprentices do we get here who have been sent away from home so fast they've barely had time to pack a change of linen? How many ships that call send their sailors ashore for leave or recreation?" Planir leaned forward in his chair. "Enough of the former that no one even remarks on it and so few of the latter that one dockside tavern barely sustains itself on their custom. Don't be a fool, man; you know it as well as I. Why else have generations of Archmages hidden Hadrumal in mists of enchantment and legend?"

"Legends that you have told the Council only foster suspicion and mistrust of wizardry," retorted Shiv.

"Quite true," Planir nodded. "And wizards out and about on the mainland seeking out any records of ancient magic would soon be noticed, wouldn't they? Wouldn't that foster unease and misgiving, especially at a time when we are doing our best to bring wizardry to a more active role in the world? Alternatively, of course, the notion that mages need to go out and seek knowledge, that we lack something apparently vital, might lead others to think that we are sadly reduced in influence these days, powerless even. In which case we can bid a fond farewell to the courtesies, the respect and, most importantly in this case, the cooperation that mages are still able to command, as long as they don't appear any kind of threat, that is. In either case, we're looking at a losing hand of bones, aren't we?"

"But Kalion—" Shiv began hesitantly.

Planir waved a dismissive hand. "Forget Kalion for the moment."

"You have mages searching the archives at Col and the histories at Vanam for any hint of ancient enchantments," insisted Shiv. "How does that differ?"

"Firstly, those I have sent have had the need for discretion most forcibly impressed upon them." The Archmage smiled. "Secondly, I am relying on the resident scholars at both of those universities finding the single-minded pursuit of arcane knowledge so entirely reasonable as to let it pass unremarked, should any of them lift their heads out of their own studies long enough to notice, of course."

Shiv could not restrain an answering grin at Planir's dry tone but his face soon became serious again. "But what about Livak? I know Casuel didn't think so but this song book sounds like a promising lead. She's no mage, no scholar. What if she misses something? Come to that, what if she discovers something that 'Sar doesn't get to hear about? She is working for D'Olbriot's coin this time. That's another thing—"

"I think you might show a little more confidence in 'Sar, you know," chided Planir. "As for Livak, as I understand it, she sees ferreting out knowledge for D'Olbriot as her best hope of a blessing from his strong room or whatever else it might be that she's seeking. From what I have seen of that girl, I'd say her own self-interest will be a more effective goad than any we might devise."

"But what if she hands something vital to D'Olbriot and we don't get to hear of it until later? Otrick—" Shiv's voice rose in exasperation.

"I am as concerned about Otrick as you are, Shiv," Planir said sharply, "but I have a great many pieces on this board, and if I fail the result won't just be a White Raven ending up back in the game box. You were in Toremal over the Solstice with the rest of us; use your wits, man! What have the events of the past year told the princes of the Empire? That their ancient dominion was based on magic and the failure of that magic brought the whole edifice crashing down around their ears! Now they are threatened with magic from beyond the ocean. How many do you think will bother to distinguish between our magic of matter and its disciplines and the Elietimm magic of mind and illusion? Stand in their shoes and it's all one, a threat." Planir set his goblet aside, unemptied and unheeded. "D'Olbriot has the wit to realize he needs to fight fire with fire but he's not about to just set his house alight and make a dash for safety. He needs to feel that he has the upper hand, that we are doing his bidding, if he is to have any dealings with Hadrumal. Equally important, nothing short of his clear control will satisfy the other princes that he has not run mad and deserves to forfeit his preeminent influence in consequence."

"But Kalion—" frowned Shiv.

"Forget Kalion. Consider where this play is leading the game," stated the Archmage crisply, ticking off his points on long fingers. "I have Livak, a girl of no little resource and determination to shame a stag-hound searching out translations for this song book of hers. It came from D'Olbriot's library, his badge is around her neck, plain to see for anyone who might get wind of her activities, be they Elietimm spy or suspicious local ruler. Whatever she finds out, this new allegiance gets her recompensed by D'Olbriot, not a charge on my purse this time, by Raeponin's grace! D'Olbriot then has the information and can tell himself and any other Tormalin noble that this buys him our services, in defense of his lands and property. A clearly defined and entirely respectable deal, which is no threat to the Emperor's sovereignty or any prince's power." Planir's voice roughened with emotion for the first time. "This saves me the humiliation of going on bended knee to the Emperor, offering him all the gold Misaen ever made, imploring him to let me send my mages to counter these bastard Elietimm, since whatever threat they might be to Tormalin, they will be death to Hadrumal, if they find us out before we have a means to counter their enchantments. What price the mystery and might of wizardry then?"

Shiv could not restrain a shudder. "It's just that I wanted—"

"You wanted to go too," Planir completed the sentence for him in a softer tone. "You wanted some revenge for the suffering you endured at the hands of the Elietimm. You wanted to find some way of saving Otrick from that deathless sleep he's trapped in. You wanted to be a hero."

Shiv bit his lip and laced his hands together in his lap, knuckles white.

"That many do see you as quite some hero already is one of the reasons I have kept you here," continued the Archmage in a conversational tone, picking up his wine glass. "You have fought the Elietimm twice now, once on their own ground and once in Kel Ar'Ayen. Your defense of the colonists was a tale vivid in the telling around the winter salons of Tormalin. Didn't you hear? If you travel, there will be plenty of eyes and ears turned your way. 'Sar on the other hand," he shrugged, "he's a nonentity, Planir's cloak carrier, always two steps behind his master. It's a wonder to see him let out on his own."

Shiv laughed reluctantly. "That's hardly fair."

"It suits us all that people see him so, doesn't it?" Planir shook his head with a grin.

"Have we any idea whether or not Livak is following a true scent?" persisted Shiv after a moment's silence, broken only by purposeful steps in the courtyard below.

"Nothing definitive either way so far," Planir shrugged. "All the more reason to use our resources in more conventional researches. This quest is Livak's gamble; if it fails, the loss is hers. If she wins, we collect without risking any of our own credit. She will fail or she will succeed and unless you have some means of foretelling you are not telling me about, we have no way to know if our involvement would help or hinder. I'm going to let the runes fall as they may and play the spread as it lies." The Archmage's expression brightened with mischief. "Besides, had I sent you off on some new commission, I'd have had Pered to reckon with and I confess I didn't relish the notion of a row with your beloved in the middle of the quadrangle."

Shiv colored vividly. "He wouldn't have—"

"No?" Planir queried. "I rather think he would have, you know."

Shiv coughed and took a drink of water, looking around the room in all directions save the Archmage's. The timepiece on the mantelshelf chimed softly as the pointed indicator clicked a notch along its scale. A knock came instantly, a quick double tap on the oak. The door opened immediately, no summons expected. A strong-faced young woman entered, hazel eyes only for the Archmage as she brushed a wisp of nut-brown hair from her forehead and settled her cerise shawl decorously over her elbows.

"Larissa." Pleasure colored Planir's voice and softened the planes of his lean face, a smile deepening the fine lines around his keen eyes. He ran a hand over his close-cropped black hair. "Wine?"

Larissa nodded. "That would be very welcome, thank you."

Planir rose and poured her a measure of the deep ruby wine in a goblet. He refilled his own glass, raising it in a salute to the girl before returning to his seat.

Larissa took a chair next to Shiv. She smiled at both mages, smoothing her sky blue skirts as she sat and sweeping her long glossy plait back over one shoulder in a negligent gesture. "Good day to you, Shivvalan," she said.

He nodded an acknowledgment, avoiding her eye but unable to help noticing the little blue flowers embroidered on the sides of her stockings, the Ensaimin fashion for shorter hems exposing her shapely ankles and the swell of her calf. He cleared his throat. "Archmage, are you bespeaking 'Sar or do we wait for him to contact us?" he asked.

" 'Sar is bespeaking us." Planir looked thoughtful as he sipped his wine. He joined them at the table. "It should be any time now. Are you both ready to make a nexus?"

Shiv flexed his hands thoughtfully. "I think I would like a glass of wine, Planir."

"Help yourself," the Archmage nodded. "Larissa?"

"I'm still drinking this one," she answered a little awkwardly. "I'm ready, though."

Planir caught her gaze and held it until she smiled at him, a faint blush highlighting her broad cheekbones.

Shiv was lifting his goblet to his lips when a glow appeared, hovering in the air above the center of the table. It grew and spread, spinning outward from its center, impossibly thin and edged with amber brilliance.

"Planir?" A voice came thinly from the center of the shining disc.

"Usara, good to hear you." Planir snapped his fingers and the candle sprang into life with a spit of scarlet magic, the flame turning yellow in an instant, rising up tall and steady despite the open window. "Link hands, Shiv," commanded the Archmage curtly. "Larissa's too new at this to do it without."

The girl jumped a little as the two men gripped her hands and a desperate frown of concentration furrowed her brow. The metal of the mirror began to glow with an inner light of its own, scarlet, azure, amber and aquamarine rising and fading, coiling around each other, finally merging into a diamond radiance that reached out to draw the glowing disc into itself, a golden brilliance burning for an instant before fading into the mirror. A nimbus of coppery magic now fringed the metal and Planir turned it so that the three could all see the image within it. "Good," he said with satisfaction, dropping Larissa's hand, the last remnants of magelight fading unheeded from his fingers.

"Have you anything to tell me about these Sheltya?" demanded Usara without ceremony, his voice sounding unnaturally high and tinny. The mirror showed him sitting on a plainly made bed in a small plastered room. The whole image was overlaid with an amber tint that subtly changed hue as circles of power spread from the center of the magic.

"Nothing of any real use or substance, I'm afraid," Planir spoke frankly to the mirror. "Casuel has been able to find nothing in the Tormalin archives and all that the scholars of Vanam or Col can offer are half-remembered snatches of Mountain sagas."

"Most of the references give no clue as to their role." Larissa was rubbing at her fingers, deeply scored by the bite of the Archmage's ring. "A few seem to suggest they are arbiters or lawgivers." She looked at Planir for confirmation.

Shiv leaned back in his chair, mouth thinning as he sat in silence.

"What have these Mountain Men you're traveling with been able to tell you?" asked Planir.

"That it's best to let the Sheltya explain themselves." Exasperation was giving Usara's words an increasingly sharp edge.

Curiosity knotted Shiv's brows. "And Livak's accepting that?"

"For the present," said Usara tightly, "because pressing the point would mean she'd have to back me against her friends."

"But you said the sagas do suggest they have aetheric lore, now you've had them translated." Larissa won a smile from the Archmage for that encouragement.

"Their so-called wonders could still all turn out to be mere accident of nature and timing." The little image in the mirror grimaced.

"Whereabouts are you now, 'Sar?" Planir interrupted.

"The lower reaches of what they call the Pasfall Valley," the mage replied. "Where the river runs through the hills, rather than out on the plain."

"There will be men and women of part Mountain blood in the villages, won't there?" Shiv looked thoughtful.

"Those whose parents married out, like in Gidesta? Could you ask them the significance of these Sheltya?"

"I've already tried," answered Usara with a shake of his head. "Either they genuinely don't know or they're just not telling."

Planir, Shiv and Larissa shared a look made up in equal measure of dashed expectation and impatience. A silence fell as all four mages looked down at their hands, faces united in disappointment for all the countless leagues separating them.

"Perhaps the Solurans might know more." Shiv rubbed his upper arm. "We know their healers are very effective, and by every indication their cures are wrought by Artifice. I'd be a hand short of tying my own laces if they hadn't worked for me."

"Don't let this business sidetrack you from your other errands, 'Sar." Planir looked faintly concerned. "Keep track of the season."

"I haven't forgotten." Usara smiled wanly. "I think I can spare the time to amuse myself with a trip to take the Mountain air."

"You certainly look somewhat overtired." Planir looked at the image critically. "Go on your rest cure and let us beat our heads against the walls for a while. We'd better break this link before you exhaust yourself any further."

"The nexus is supporting me," insisted Usara. "It's just rather early in the day here and we were traveling until late yesterday. Has anyone bespoken Naldeth recently?"

Larissa nodded absently. "I was talking to him a few nights ago. Everything seems fine in Kellarin."

"And Guinalle?" persisted Usara.

"She said to pass on her regards, last time I was bespeaking Nal." Shiv looked up from his thoughts a little guiltily.

Usara's smile was plain in the image before them. Larissa looked from Planir to Shiv, a faint question in her face as the two other mages shared a conspiratorial look.

"I have other calls on my time, 'Sar," Planir said abruptly. "We'll speak again in five days, at noon by your reckoning, all right?"

Usara nodded, the reflection in the mirror fading rapidly as the magic unraveled, leaving the metal surface gleaming dully in the sunlit room.

"What's between Usara and Guinalle?" demanded Larissa.

"Could be something, could be nothing," Shiv said a little enigmatically. "I rather think he's like to make it something, but she's a lady who takes her responsibilities seriously."

"That he be the one to find a key to unlock the mysteries of Artifice is important to Usara in more ways than the obvious," agreed Planir. The Archmage's eyes slid over to Larissa and warmed. "Don't let me keep you, Shiv." The dismissal was unmistakable.

"I'd like to discuss this further." Shiv looked a little put out.

Planir rubbed a hand over his mouth. "Later." His eyes stayed with Larissa and a faint smile hovered around his lips.

Shiv hesitated on the threshold. "Larissa?"

"I'll be along in a moment or so." She lifted her chin but a faint blush colored her cheeks. "Don't let me keep you."

Shiv arched a sardonic eyebrow at Planir but the Archmage's face held impassive so the younger wizard left to walk noisily down the stairs. Shiv paused for a moment as he heard the lock secure itself behind him and his expression hardened. Emerging from the darkness of the stairwell, he blinked in the bright sunlight of the courtyard.

"Good afternoon," a passing apprentice called out, crossing the well-worn flagstones from the arch of the gateway to one of the numerous doorways flanking the quadrangle. Shiv nodded an acknowledgment and took an apparently idle seat on the rim of the little fountain playing a cheerful pattern of air and water in the center of the court. He glanced around, as if waiting for someone, checking the position of the sun and looking toward the great bell tower that dominated the four courtyards that made up this Hall of wizardry. A maid went past with arms full of linen for the laundry.

Shiv dabbled a hand in the fountain's spray and studied the basin intently. A shimmering image lay on the surface of the water. Planir was embracing Larissa, lips locked in a passionate kiss. The Archmage's fingers deftly unfastened the buttons down the back of her dress. She released him for a moment to push the gown off her hips, dropping the garment disregarded on the floor. Planir's hand around her waist drew her close, the other unlacing the top of her shift. Shiv could see little blue flowers embroidered on cotton so fine the rosy nipple showed hard and dark beneath it. The Archmage pulled away to strip off his own shirt and a certain regret mingled with the irritation on Shiv's face as he gazed down into the water. Larissa caught up the hem of her shift, revealing lacy garters, and Planir unbuckled his belt.

"Halcarion's tits, what is he thinking of?" Shiv shattered the image with an angry sweep of his hand, myriad glittering fragments dissolving beneath the patter of the fountain. "Other calls on your time, O revered Archmage? Yes, and we've all heard just what those might be." He stamped out through the archway into the busy high road of Hadrumal.

Othilsoke,
3rd of For-Summer

"Keis!" Jeirran's hail was blown away unheeded as he picked his way over tussocks of coarse grass. He left the track worn between the meager, wind-stunted bushes crouching among the rocks and entered a narrow gorge cutting in the broad sweep of the valley side. The breeze was baffled but the noise of metal on rock rang loud in the confined space. Jeirran stood and watched. Teiriol raised a pick high over his head, and then plunged it into the rocky soil with an explosive shout, ripping it back. He was at the uppermost narrow of the defile, digging waist deep below an outcrop of stark gray rock. A second man was shoveling the rubble with its blue-green streaks into a stream channeled on one side. A third raked and stirred, peering through water clouded with sand and soil. At his nod, another man shoveled stone into a long wooden trough where Keisyl was wet to his elbows, sorting through rocky fragments washed a second time in water brought down in a series of wooden pipes. All were dirty, sweating and grim-faced with concentration.

"Keisyl!" Jeirran picked his way uphill over the cording of rock and mud that marked the annual progression of the digging up the little cutting.

"What do you want?" Keisyl's displeasure was uncompromising. He dumped a handful of tinstone in a sack and knuckled the small of his back. Swinging a dripping shovelful around to the pile of debris behind him, he splashed Jeirran's polished boots.

"I brought some baking from my wife." Jeirran opened the lid of his basket, unfolding the layers of cloth within, thick wool surrounding snowy linen.

"Food," Keisyl bellowed, hands cupped around his mouth.

"Shut off the leat!" An answering wave beyond a rise in the ground was followed by the rattle of a sluice and the stream slowed to a trickle barely deep enough to dampen Teiriol's mud-caked boots.

"It's Theilyn should be ferrying the food. You should be working here," Keisyl growled. "That would be one less share in the season leaving the soke."

"It was your mother made the deal to bring in her kin," Jeirran said curtly. He beckoned to the hastening diggers with a smile.

"If we hadn't wasted so much time on your idiotic schemes, she'd have had no call to do so." Keisyl bit crossly into a pasty.

Jeirran peered critically up the pitted and ravaged hillside. "This cut is just about worked out. You and Teir between you would have cleared it by the last half of summer. The stupid crone has given away half the paltry pickings."

"She wanted this working finished before we started a deep mine," hissed Keisyl. "The shaft paid for with the riches you were going to bring back from Selerima?"

"The old busybody had no business making any deal for labor." Jeirran was intent on his own grievance. "That should have been Eirys' decision."

"Eirys wasn't here, was she?" Keisyl's sarcasm was unmuted by his mouthful. "You insisted on dragging her all that way and she hasn't even got a belly on her to show for it."

"Is everything all right?" Teiriol was the first to reach them, looking uncertainly between Jeirran's appearance of good humor and his brother's scowl.

"The women have been baking." Jeirran gave the basket over into eager, dirt-speckled hands. "My wife said you deserved better than waxed cheese and twice-cooked bread. Caw, Fytch, Cailean, good to see you."

"How do, Jeirran." The rake man, wet to mid-thigh, nodded a greeting. "You look mighty prosperous for a man who wasted half his season being gulled by the lowlanders."

Jeirran shot a hard look at Teiriol, who returned it with a defiant shrug. "Cailean asked. I wasn't about to lie to him."

Jeirran forced a smile. "We made a profit over what we'd have got in the valley bottom but I'll admit it wasn't as handsome as I'd been led to hope."

Keisyl's contemptuous bark of laughter was lost in a racking cough as a crumb caught at the back of his throat.

"Well, at least you tried, didn't you?" The one who'd been filling Keisyl's sorting trough looked around uncertainly. "Can't hardly blame you if the lowlanders all turned out dishonest dogs, can we?"

Jeirran passed the man a folded pastry with a rich golden glaze. "I thought I could find a fair deal, Fytch, but in the end we were little better than robbed and that's the truth of it."

"All thieves, lowlanders," grunted the man who'd been tending the sluice at the upper level. "We should keep to our own."

"We may want no dealings with them, but they're determined to have dealings with us." Jeirran shook his head. "Did you hear about the Teyvasoke?"

All the men nodded grimly. Teiriol's workmate took a second pastry. "Breed like rats in a midden, don't they?"

"I've a cousin with kin the far side of the Gap," volunteered Cailean. "He was saying that when they had to fight for their diggings, they'd lost before a sword was swung. Every one lowlander they sent back bleeding to his mother whistled ten more up and ready inside a day and a half. There's no use you looking at me like that, Elzer, it's the truth. Why do you think Kernial and his sons came west to herd goats for the summer, begging work from any fess that they can?"

"That's no work for a man in his prime," growled Elzer in disgust. "Kernial's a waterman nearly as good as me, knows streams and flow better than any mother-poxed lowlander, deep mines as well as surface work."

"The problem is we're so spread out," mused Jeirran. "By the time a messenger bird has flown from one fess to another, the damage is done and the ruffians fled."

"There's no helping that in this country," shrugged Fytch.

"Every soke keeps to its own," stated Elzer firmly. "That's the way it's been from generations back."

"Generations back didn't have greedy lowlanders carving up their land like mutton," retorted Jeirran. "Generations back, Sheltya kept the sokes in touch with each other, passed on news for ordinary folk, didn't just keep their powers for themselves."

A wary stillness touched the other men sitting on the heaps of broken stone.

"Just think about the old tales," Jeirran continued. "Kell the Weaver wouldn't have stood for lowlanders cutting his snares and stealing his pelts! No more than Morn stood by while thieves drove Isarel's daughters off their land. True magic defended the sokes in those days."

"That's me done." Keisyl flung a crust onto the coarse turf and wiped the grease from his fingers on the tail of his mud-stained shirt. "I'll walk down to the path with you, Jeir." Keisyl picked up the sack of ore and hefted it over one shoulder.

"Yes, I've a few things to say to you." Jeirran followed him out of the gully to a stack of sacks. Teiriol and the others exchanged glances of mingled apprehension and anticipation.

"There's a flask of dew in there as well," Jeirran called back, "but don't mix it too strong or all you'll be fit for this afternoon is sleeping!"

Laughter echoed around the defile and Jeirran grinned. When he turned back to Keisyl, his smile vanished. "I need you back at the fess."

Keisyl sat on the dusty sack of ore, scarred leather trews coated with muck. "You can go on needing. I've work here."

"And I've work at home," snapped Jeirran, "with Aritane."

"I told you I want nothing to do with your schemes," Keisyl retorted. "I don't like your sister either, tormenting Eirys. I found her crying her heart out in the scullery, worrying she was barren!"

"Blame your mother. What of all her talk about Ilgar's problems breeding those red cattle?" demanded Jeirran. "Wondering if the bull or the heifer was at fault? If I'm going to have some Sheltya asking questions about my tool or technique, I'll have one of my own kindred do it."

"But she's no kin of yours, not now, not since Sheltya took her," Keisyl challenged him. "You're an idiot, Jeirran. That woman gets wind of your schemes, we'll all be neck deep and drowning! Her first loyalty is to Sheltya."

"Aritane is loyal to her powers and to her people," said Jeirran confidently. "She's as eager as me to see glory and liberty restored to the mountains."

Keisyl snorted. "She'd better have something more impressive up her sleeves than those lily-white arms."

"Oh, she has," chuckled Jeirran. "And now that your mother has done enough cooking to ensure none of us starve in the next four days, she's taking Eirys and Theilyn off to visit their uncle over the crag. That's what I came up here to tell you. Ari can finally get things moving."

"What things?" demanded Keisyl suspiciously.

"We need allies against the lowlanders, don't we? Like Noral said, there are just too many of the rat-spawn." Jeirran's face was alive with zeal. "Aritane's found them— powerful allies, Keis, willing to help us."

A flurry of little brown birds squabbled over pastry crumbs among the tussocks. "Alyatimm?" Keisyl's voice dropped to a whisper.

Jeirran shrugged. "Their forefathers were, perhaps, generations since. That's not important. What matters is they are kin, with no more love of the lowlanders than us."

"Why should they help us?" frowned Keisyl.

"Why not? They share our blood and have been attacked by Tormalin themselves. It's only the lowlanders who won't act unless there's something in it for them!" Jeirran's words hung in the air. "This isn't just about me, Keis!" Jeirran gestured toward the diggers. "Half the sokes this side of the Gap are being bled, truth or lie?"

"I won't be involved in anything that goes against Sheltya." Keisyl's tone was uncompromising, but his face betrayed a hint of curiosity.

"All I want is your presence." Jeirran's hands were placating. "You don't even have to speak. But Ari will receive a visitor tonight and I want us both there to show she has men to back her. Someone born to this soke should be present."

"Where's this stranger from?" Keisyl gazed down the valley.

"Ari didn't tell me." Jeirran waved to Teiriol and the others still watching intently, horn cups in hand.

"What if Sheltya meet him, ask his business?" asked Keisyl. "Have you run mad?"

"Sheltya are no longer the power they would have you believe." Jeirran shook his head. "Ask Aritane! That's one reason we're in this parlous state. Lowlanders have their wizards' trickery while Sheltya Elders hoard away true magic and take it to their graves unspent!"

Keisyl kicked at the sack with one heel. "I suppose we've enough tinstone to get the ore mill ready. The wheel will need checking and I know the stamps want resetting." He stood. "I'll come and play Aritane's bully boy for this visitor but then you can get the mules up here and pack this lot down while I open up the mill. If you'd had the wit Misaen made for a mouse, you'd have brought a mule now rather than wearing out your boot soles!"

"Your mother took the mules, Keisyl."

"Then you find someone to lend you another, otherwise you carry this ore down on your back."

Jeirran's beard bristled as Keisyl went back up the gully, shouting to Teiriol, "You're in charge until I get back, but take heed of the others. They've been at this work longer than you have!"

After brief consultation with Cailean and Fytch, Keisyl rejoined Jeirran. "I've said I'm going to do an assay. That'll make some use of the time."

Jeirran set off in silence. A little way down the track, Keisyl turned off for a hollow where the ashes of a campfire were being stirred by an idle breeze. He fished in his pocket for a ring of keys. "It won't do the lad any harm to learn that being in charge isn't all picking the easiest job and counting coin." Keisyl pulled a bag and a blanket roll from a low stone-built shelter and snapped the lock shut again with a decisive snick. "And at least I'll get a bath."

Jeirran laughed but fell silent at an uncompromising look from Keisyl. They walked down the trail in long silence, reaching the sheltering walls of the fess as the sun slid behind the snow-capped peaks. Keisyl rapped on the main gate with an exasperated oath. "Where's Fithian?"

The gate swung open. "I was wondering how much longer you were going to be," said Aritane critically.

"Where's Fithian?" demanded Keisyl.

"I sent him to check on the goats." Aritane walked toward the rekin past dark and shuttered buildings lining the compound.

Keisyl's lips thinned. "You insult my father's brother by ordering him around like some herd-boy?"

Aritane paused where warm firelight spilled out over the threshold. "I wanted him out of the way."

Keisyl did not enter the house. "What gives you such a right?"

Aritane raised one disdainful eyebrow as she negligently brushed a hand over the breast of her plain gray gown. "A man of his age with no patrimony or marriage to recommend him can hardly expect anyone to polish up his dignity."

"Fithian chose to stay and support my mother after our father's death. He made over his portion to Teiriol and me." Keisyl's words were clipped with anger. "You know nothing of our history."

Aritane turned her attention to Jeirran. "You had better eat. You need a bath," she added to Keisyl.

"I'll bathe when I'm ready." He took the basket of ore from Jeirran. "I want a quick look at the mill and I may even do an assay."

Aritane turned on her heel, leaving the two men at the door.

"Do it tomorrow," Jeirran urged him. "You'll have the

daylight and I'll help. Once we've finished this business tonight, you can sleep in a real bed and be fresh for the morning."

Aritane was stirring a pot hung over the fire and Keisyl's stomach growled unbidden at the savory scent.

Jeirran shrugged. "Sheltya are used to everyone running at their command."

"That's the closest I've ever heard you come to an apology," sneered Keisyl. "This must be important."

"It's important to Eirys and her children," Jeirran snapped. "Weigh that in your scales against your assaying."

Keisyl swung the basket of ore in one hand and walked away without a word. The reddish light cast shadows on Jeirran's face that deepened as he scowled. He slammed the door behind him but Aritane tended the fire in the center of the room unperturbed. "Eat," she commanded.

Jeirran took a steaming bowl with grunted acknowledgment. Hunched on the long bench, he ate gracelessly, shoveling down stew thick with vegetables and herbs. The slate top of the wide table was marked with a few notes made next to a clutter of leatherwork and sewing was heaped on the far seat.

Aritane peered up into the beaten metal of the hood that hung above the fire. "There's something wrong with the draw on this."

"There's something wrong in every room of this windblasted fess," Jeirran said sourly. "The roof of the rekin leaks, every shutter is warped, most of the upstairs hearths smoke."

"No wonder Ismenia was so keen to let Eirys take a husband so glib with his promises and free with his patrimony," Aritane smiled without affection.

"You're going to help me make good on those promises though," Jeirran countered in similar vein.

The door opened and both turned, momentarily disconcerted. "I'll eat then bathe," Keisyl said slowly. "Wait for the daylight, as you say." He emptied the pockets of his trews onto the top of a dresser standing against the off-hand wall of the room. There were four such, shelves above packed with oddments, and cupboards below locked shut. Hanging his cloak on a hook, Keisyl took a bowl of stew. "Is there enough hot water?" he asked.

"I lit the copper earlier," Aritane replied with a certain aloofness. "I'll go and stoke it." The two men watched her leave for the scullery.

"Did she always have the charm of a bag of nails?" asked Keisyl through a mouthful of meat. "Or is that something Sheltya teach?" He ate in silence then followed Aritane.

Jeirran rose from his seat and made a circuit of the broad room. He checked that each window was locked and then barred the door. Returning a moment later, he unbarred it. Peering up the dark stairwell, he closed and locked that door, fumbling the keys as he shoved them in a pocket, bending to retrieve them with a muffled oath. He crossed to the fire and swung a kettle across the flames.

"I'm going to contact Eresken," announced Aritane as she reappeared. She moved the kettle off the heat. "I'm not wasting any more time on Keisyl's convenience!"

"Very well," said Jeirran slowly. "What am I to do?"

Aritane crossed to a half circle of chairs set around a rag-woven rug on the near-hand side of the room. "Just wait." She set an embroidered cushion at her back with nervous hands. "He said he would come when I called. He'd be here soon after."

"Like Sheltya?" Jeirran sat on one end of the long bench. "How is it you people are always where you are wanted, just as you're needed?"

"That is none of your concern," retorted Aritane with her habitual iciness. "Be silent and let me work."

Jeirran cleared his throat but subsided at Aritane's glare. She settled into the pattern of altered breathing and hid her face in her hands. The crackle of the fire was the only sound in the room. Jeirran watched intently until a sudden shiver forced him from his seat. Lighting a spill at the hearth, he prowled around the room, lighting lamps in the center of the table, on the dresser by the stairs, two set on stands either side of the door. He started as the scullery door swung open, but it was only Keisyl looking surprised at the flood of light as he toweled his hair.

"Hush." Jeirran's voice was tight with tension. "Don't disturb her."

Keisyl looked nervously at Aritane and both men froze as she drew a long shuddering breath. She held it for a moment before a long exhalation of satisfaction and pleasure opened her eyes, heavy-lidded, pupils huge and dark.

"Well?" demanded Jeirran eagerly.

Aritane seemed oblivious to Keisyl's dubious gaze and Jeirran's question alike.

The latch of the door lifted with a sudden snap.

"May I enter your home?" The figure on the threshold was hidden in a long dark cloak, hood drawn up and face shadowed. His words were harshly accented but fluent in the Mountain tongue.

Aritane sprang to her feet. "You are most welcome," she said hastily, smoothing the front of her gown.

The stranger entered and lifted his hood back to reveal a long, angular face, at once similar to those facing him and yet outlandish, dominated by eyes green as grass and penetrating in their intensity. His hair was barely light enough to be called blond, more brown than golden, but it framed his face with the same line as Keisyl's and had much the wiry texture of Jeirran's. "Aritane!" Her name was a caress on his lips. He caught up her hands, dropping a light kiss on one palm.

She caught her breath, momentarily at a loss.

"My sister is mistress of this house," Keisyl's words sounded harsh and he coughed. "I am here to welcome you in her stead," he concluded with a forced smile and milder tones.

The newcomer bowed low. "I am honored to be received here."

Jeirran rubbed his hands briskly together. "Have you traveled far? Let me take your cloak. Can I offer you some refreshment?"

A faint smile lit the stranger's eyes. "It has been a long journey, all in all. I would welcome a drink." He unpinned the brooch securing his voluminous cloak, black as the shadows outside. Keisyl stepped forward to take it, eyes wary. Beneath the cloak, the visitor was dressed in black leather, ornamented with silver studs on the outer seams of close-cut trews and patterned around the shoulders of a buckled jerkin. A gold gorget protected his throat, and from the tight stiffness of the leather Keisyl guessed metal plates lay beneath the forearms and breast of the garment. The cloak, dark as it was, would have passed anywhere between the mountains and the sea but this bellicose livery was like nothing he had ever seen.

Aritane was busy at a cupboard by the half-circle of chairs. She turned with a tray bearing a crystal flask and small gilded glasses brilliant in the lamplight. As she saw her visitor uncloaked her hands shook for an instant, the glasses ringing like tiny bells. "Please, sit and take your ease." She poured tiny measures of clear spirit, her hands steady now as a sharp scent of fruit filled the air. "Eresken, this is Jeirran, and Keisyl, the brother of his wife."

Eresken lifted his glass to all in mute salute before sipping at it. "This is very fine," he said admiringly.

"The women make it." Jeirran was recovering his bullishness. "My Eirys flavors hers with cloudberries."

"I must compliment her on her skills," Eresken said smoothly.

Keisyl did not sit. "What is it that you offer in return for her hospitality?"

"I admire a man protective of his household's interests," nodded Eresken. He looked at Jeirran, green eyes unblinking. "I came to assist in whatever way I might. How best can I serve you?"

"We are still discussing how to proceed." Jeirran chewed at his beard.

"The Solstice sun will shed light on the question, when it stirs the bones of the soke," added Aritane.

"And we will abide by that counsel." Keisyl looked to the others for agreement, mollified to see them nod.

The newcomer stared steadily at Jeirran. "We are both threatened by those sprung from Tormalin. We both wish to hold those lands we have right to, without fear or threat. We have shared blood to bind us to each other."

"Where exactly have you come from?" Keisyl asked, unnerved by the trusting way Aritane gazed at the man and the fatuous look of satisfaction driving the scowl from Jeirran's brow.

Eresken turned his full attention to Keisyl. "From islands in the far ocean, many days' sail from the farthest east. My people left these shores many generations past. We have bided our time against the day of our return for countless years."

"Then you are indeed Alyatimm?" Keisyl swallowed hard.

"We call ourselves Elietimm," Eresken smiled. "Many generations since, perhaps our forefathers said Alyatimm, but what does that signify?"

Keisyl felt there was something important eluding him. He shook his head as Aritane proffered the dew flask. Alcohol after a weary day and a hot bath must be blunting his wits.

"We can raise a good-sized band from the sokes hereabouts." Jeirran was circling the hearth, all eagerness. "Why wait? We can clear out those stinking huts and hovels from the valley bottom. That will bring more men to our standard. Working together, we can take back the mines the muddy-feet have stolen, let every man who joins us claim a share to add to his patrimony!"

"And the lowlanders will send up a double militia company to fight us for them before spit can dry." A massive yawn interrupted Keisyl, tiredness pressing down on him.

"So we send their horses back with corpses strapped to the saddle bow!" Jeirran poured himself another drink.

"There are advantages to letting your enemy set events in motion and pacing your moves to his," said Eresken thoughtfully. "We must go through the detail of your plans, to see where I can assist."

Keisyl struggled with another yawn. "Just what assistance are you offering?"

"I have commanded troops, I have fought to defend my lands and my family," Eresken replied with a smile.

Keisyl opened his mouth to ask against whom, but profound disinterest flooded through him. "I'm going to bed," he said thickly.

Eresken stood to bow to him. Keisyl shook his head, bemused as he unlocked the door, and then trudged wearily up the stairs.

"You can get the lay of the land while I gather men together." Jeirran was pacing around the room again. "And you can contact your people in the east. Yes, a double-pronged attack would be best. We'll raise a beacon here to carry light the length of the mountains, all the way to the ocean! That'll give every thieving lowlander notice to quit our lands!"

Eresken resumed his seat and took Aritane's hands. "Have you spoken to those friends of yours? Did you use the incantation I taught you?"

"I contacted Cleris and Bryn," Aritane smiled shyly. "I taught Bryn the charm and Cleris tried to eavesdrop as I sought him. She couldn't find either of us."

"I told you it would work." Eresken tightened his grip. "Do they see the wisdom of claiming rights in their own skills?"

"Oh yes," Aritane nodded vehemently. "And there will be others. Cleris knows several Sheltya in the Middle Ranges treated with courtesy scant enough to be insult. As for Bryn," Aritane floundered a little, "he has friends who have been rebuked for affection and removed from such intimacy, just as—"

"Just as he had you stolen away from him." Eresken picked up her trailing words with a fond smile. "I will try not to be too jealous of him, my prize." He lifted Aritane's hand to kiss her palm once again. She colored fiercely and glanced at Jeirran but he was still circling the fire, debating the best prospects for battle with himself.

"We must curb his enthusiasm for bloodshed until we have enough men to make a real army." Eresken gazed intently at Aritane, his eyes unblinking as a hawk. "We need Sheltya as perceptive as you. Once we have power to back physical force, I will make you queen of this land, my heart's delight. None of your kin need walk in fear of the lowlanders ever again!"

"And what of your kin, your home?" Aritane struggled for words, her voice little more than a whisper.

"Home is where the heart is." Eresken brushed a kiss against Aritane's cheek as he stood up. She looked up at him, mouth half open.

"What do you say to that?" Jeirran halted, bold confidence in his stance and expression.

"The lowlanders won't know what has hit them!" Eresken gripped Jeirran by the shoulders. "Great destiny lies ahead for you, my friend. I am fortunate to share in it!"

"It's late. Let me set a warmer in your bed." Aritane took a stone from the edge of the hearth, fussing with a length of flannel.

"I didn't secure the gate when I came in." Eresken released Jeirran. "I wasn't sure if others needed entry."

"What?" Jeirran looked bemused for a moment. "I'll see to it, don't worry."

As he closed the main door behind him, Aritane disappeared up the stairs. The sudden crossdraft sent the fire flaring, sparks spitting up the hanging hood. Eresken moved to the center of the room and both doors slammed themselves at his harshly accented command. After three rapid breaths, he shut his eyes. When they opened, the vivid green was gone, replaced with calculating brown, and when Eresken opened his mouth, another voice sounded in the silence, an older voice, with a curious hollow quality to it, as if it came from far, far away. "Are they open to you?"

"Both vacant as newborn babes." Eresken's tone was coldly jubilant. "Whatever skills the Sheltya teach these days, defense is not one they value."

"So nothing has changed." The other voice rang with contempt. "Are they fit for our purpose?"

"With the right encouragement," said Eresken confidently.

"Is the brother likely to make trouble?"

"He stinks of mistrust for Jeirran and all his works. Simplest just to discourage him."

"What of the rest of the household? Will you leave before they return?" the distant voice inquired.

"I think not, now I am here. From what I read in the woman, they are few enough and easily dominated with a little skill."

"Then you have your base. Get to work," commanded the unnatural voice.

Eresken blinked and the green of his own eyes was restored, a smile curving his thin lips as the doors released themselves at his word.

Six

Dragons were not nearly the danger I had feared in
Gidesta, but we would see them flying over in the spring and
sometimes raiding down into the valleys in the autumn. This
is one of the many Mountain myths in which they figure.

Maewelin made a dale
Of green and sheltered calm.
She set a tree girt lake
About with pretty blooms.
The jealous wyrms looked on
And gnawed the rocks below.
They rose up from the depths
And ravaged all the peace.
Maewelin saw the wreck
Of beauty she had loved.
She begged Misaen's aid,
He left his forge to cool.
Misaen fought the wyrms,
His hammer broke their fangs.
They fled into the dark,
But vengeance chased them still.
One wyrm called down the rocks
To crush Misaen's bones.
He shattered them to dust,
That choked the wyrm to death.

The next spewed forth dead air,
A breathless, stifling trap.
Misaen called a gale,
That ripped the wyrm in rags.
The weak wyrm wept a stream,
The waters drowning deep.
Misaen froze the flood.
The wyrm died in the ice.
The last wyrm, vicious, cruel,
Spat fire to scorch the sky.
Misaen quenched its ire
With dust, dead air and ice.
He chained the gasping wyrm
And dragged it to his forge.
Its fire relit his hearth
And thus he forged the sun.

Upper Reaches of the Pasfal Valley,
13th of For-Summer

"Come on, wizard! Any slower and your lice'll get off and walk!" For all his cheerful words, I noted 'Gren was leaning on a large boulder as he taunted Usara.

"It wouldn't hurt for you to take it a little easier," I retorted. "The air up here's thinner than a beggar's dog!" That was an exaggeration but I was finding the steady incline a long haul. At least there was a breeze to cool the early summer sun. A hopeful butterfly went past in a lazy pattern of pale blue that mimicked the bleached sky above us.

Sorgrad, some way ahead, sat down on the rough turf fringing the narrow scar of the path. "We might as well stop and eat before we go any farther."

Usara's pack hit the ground with a thud. "How much

farther is it to the next village?" he asked, narrow chest heaving.

Sorgrad shook his head. "There'll be no more villages, not this high. This is Anyatimm territory now. Westerlings keep to the old ways, more than anyone."

"So if there are no villages hereabouts, where do these Westerlings live? Where are we likely to get shelter, come to that?" I looked up from unpacking the calico bag of provisions I'd wheedled out of the last hamlet, from women short and stocky, light of hair and eye.

"We stop at the next fess, the next compound," replied 'Gren with a touch of scorn. "Any traveler has the right to ask for fire, food and shelter."

"Which is freely given because everyone knows they're in the same situation when they travel," added Sorgrad. "This is a hard land and the only way to survive is to cooperate."

I nodded, seeing the bleakness underlying the thin soil and short-lived blooms so bright with the sun's gloss. I wouldn't want to be up here much beyond the turn of For-Autumn. "So who were those people in the valley bottom?"

"Lowlanders." 'Gren held out his hand to me and I filled it with a wedge of creamy sheep cheese and some coarse bread.

"They looked mountain-born." Usara had got his breath back.

"Some Anyatimm men marry lowland women," explained Sorgrad, "but they're no longer counted as blood."

I chewed thoughtfully on my bread, not the finest I'd ever tasted but at least it was light with leaven and baked in a proper oven. "Is that important?" I picked a husk from between my teeth.

"Yes, to the Westerlings certainly. Once a man leaves the mountains, it's hard for him to come back. If he's married a lowland woman, it's nigh on impossible." Sorgrad unhooked a waterskin from his belt and drank.

Something chirruping in a stand of long grass was the

only sound to break the silence. I wondered how far we were from Selerima. We'd walked right out of Aft-Spring and on into For-Summer, nearly a whole half-season by my reckoning. The comfortable little towns of Solura growing fat in the lush river valley had dwindled to smaller villages carefully tending stock and crops in less generous lands and these had finally given up to close-shuttered knots of stout stone houses resolute in the hollows of the rising hills.

I looked around as I ate. My wonder at this country was slow to fade. Rolling hills of lush green grass had sharpened to stark fells, purpled with ling and berry bushes, striped with screes and waterfalls. Our pace had slowed and there were days when I'd wondered if we were getting any nearer at all to the great folded mountains that rucked the land up to the sky. Now we were into that land I realized the distances had deceived me. What had looked like a mere shrubby cloak draping the bones of the land was revealed as forest to rival the land of the Folk. Unfamiliar firs mingled with tall straight birches cascading down steep hillsides in endless billows of trees. There were no roads worth the name and precious few tracks. It was a vast country, daunting, and it made me feel very small and insignificant.

On the far side of this valley, I could see a blackened scar of wildfire softened with a bloom of new green. Beyond, a jutting jag of stone burst from a jumble of grass and saplings, a stream fell to its fate over the angular edges, splitting and plaiting to plunge into a rainbow haze. Behind, a rampart of flat-topped rocks marked the far side of another valley hidden in the folded land, no way of guessing how far, how deep or how long it might be. The striped and dappled face of a cliff shifted and changed as a cloud passed between it and the sun. Still farther away, a saw-edged peak pied with snow and rock was merely the nearest of the massive mountains drawing clouds close around their shoulders.

"Are those the high peaks?" I asked Sorgrad.

"No, just the southern ranges. The land falls away again

beyond there, into a wilderness of lake and plain. The highest peaks are a season's journey farther north again." He looked up at the sky, face unreadable.

"So where exactly are we?" asked Usara with a frown.

"Hachalsoke." 'Gren waved an expansive arm. "Home to the Hachalkin."

"One family owns all this tract of land?" Usara's confusion was hardly surprising. You could fit Hadrumal and all its wizards into the wide valley whose sides we'd been toiling up.

"You have to understand that things are very different up here," said Sorgrad slowly.

"Tell us," I encouraged. "We don't want to get someone's hackles up by saying the wrong thing."

"You need to watch what you say, both of you." Sorgrad was deadly earnest. "This isn't the Forest, everyone used to new faces and new ideas. Things move slowly up here and change comes seldom. The sokes have good reason to be wary of incomers; whole kindreds have been wiped out by pestilence brought by travelers."

I couldn't see any sign that hand or boot had ever touched this place. "Do you know where the closest compound is?"

Sorgrad pointed to the middle distance. "That spur valley where the river runs down toward the lake. A fess needs water, shelter, and timber to hand. It'll be set halfway between summer and winter grazing, close enough to the heights for hunting and mining, not too far from the main valley for taking the metals and pelts down for trade and exchange."

"So what makes this compound different from a village?" Usara's face was unenthusiastic as he assessed the terrain we'd have to cover.

"Each fess is just one kindred," replied Sorgrad. "Maybe fifty or more people in a big soke, not counting the children, but all just the one family."

"How in Drianon's name does that work?" I spoke before I could help myself. All family ties meant to me was the heavy disapproval laid on my head by my mother's bevy of superior sisters and my grandmother's constant scorn for my Forest blood. "What if you can't stand each other?"

Sorgrad paused before speaking. "You have to understand that the family is everything in the mountains. The soke is more than valleys and dales. Anyatimm belong to the land more than it belongs to them. That's been so since Maewelin raised the mountains and Misaen forged the people. A soke is bloodline as well as territory and both are the women's privilege; they are its guardians."

"Eldest daughter inherits?" I prompted as he fell silent. I'd shielded him from Usara's prying questions all the way up here but now it was time for him to lay out the runes for all to see.

"It's not like Tormalin land, which can be owned, bought or sold," he said finally, eyes acknowledging my silent demand. "Each daughter gets a share in the resources of the soke: the animals that can be caught or pastured there, the metals or gems that can be dug. The rights are tied to the blood. If a woman has no daughters to follow her, the rights are passed back up the line, mother to mother and down to another branch, sister or niece."

"And the men do all the work," grunted 'Gren. I passed him a honeycake to stop his mouth.

"The men do the physical work," Sorgrad echoed, "away in the hills for half a season at a time. But that's their half of the compact sealed on the hearth of the rekin. A stone is set there when a boy reaches his ninth summer and leaves his mother, when a couple marry, when an elder steps aside to yield precedence to son or daughter. The hearth is the heart of the rekin, the stronghold, I suppose you would call it. The rekin is the heart of the fess and the fess is the heart of the soke.

"Those elders fit enough and younger boys herd the goats while the men in their prime go trapping in the winter, work the mines in the summer. A son's labor is owed to his father until he's of age in his twenty-seventh year, you see. Up here a man works to bequeath coin and valuables to his sons, who will take that patrimony to a different soke when they marry. That's their contribution, the means to trade for whatever a soke may lack. The women work in the rekin and the fess, cooking, weaving, spinning, curing hides, rearing the children."

"Curious." Usara's color was better for some food.

"No more so than paying someone to take a daughter off your hands with a dowry and eldest son grabbing everything at the deathbed," Sorgrad laughed. "Lowlands customs amazed us at first, didn't they, Sorgren?"

"It was those enormous black cows I couldn't stop staring at," shrugged his brother. "I'd only ever seen goats."

I shared out the rest of the cakes and chose my next words with care. "So what brought you both down to the lowlands?"

The brothers exchanged a strangely reluctant look.

"It's not only the Forest Folk think it's ill omened to be born at the dark of both moons," admitted 'Gren. "It wasn't so bad when I was still at my mother's heel but once I was out in the diggings, every accident or piece of ill luck was laid at my door." He shrugged. "I got sick of it and decided to leave."

"And I came too." Sorgrad's blue eyes were as distant as the sky beyond the farthest peaks. "Middle sons of a long family, no one missed us."

"Did you live in these mountains?"

"No, the far side of the Gap, what would be called the Middle Ranges."

"So it had nothing to do with you being mage-born?"

It took a breath for my ears to convince my wits I'd heard right. "What did you say?"

Usara was looking intently at Sorgrad. "I asked if your decision to leave the mountains was related to the fact that you're mage-born."

"You're mistaken, wizard! The air's too thin for your wits

up here!" But as I spoke, I saw 'Gren look at Sorgrad and knew it for truth. "Why didn't you ever tell me?"

"I'm telling you now, aren't I?" Sorgrad gave a careless shake of his head but his eyes were angry. "When's it ever been relevant? You've always said magic is trouble and I agree. That's all it's ever been to me. They said 'Gren was unlucky, but no one wanted to be within arm's length of me after tinder started lighting itself in my empty hand! No one would go in a shaft with me, in case firedamp blew everyone clean down to the plains. My first winter hunting, I was lost for three days in a blizzard and everyone said the wind was trying to claim me for its own."

"I thought your affinity was for fire," interrupted Usara eagerly. "I should have realized you were helping to warm Zenela. It was the flood confused me; the more I thought about it, the more certain I was some elemental disturbance provoked it. What exactly were you feeling when—"

"Shut up," I told the wizard abruptly. "Did you choose to leave or were you sent?"

"I was banished," Sorgrad told me, pain fleeting in his voice, ignoring Usara utterly. "Still, it could have been worse. The Middle Ranges haven't fallen completely away from the old ways like the Easterlings above Gidesta, but on this side of the Gap the Westerlings probably still kill anyone marked for Misaen." His smile was thin and humorless.

"Is there anything more to eat?" 'Gren took the calico bag from my numb hands.

"But where did you get your training?" demanded Usara testily. "I've been watching you every step up this valley and your control's had me uncertain all the way. That discipline has to be taught and by an advanced practitioner. What wizard gave you instruction, without either sending you to Hadrumal or at least contacting the Archmage—"

"We've never had anything to do with wizards." 'Gren's words were muffled with dried fruit. "Not before our girl

here got us mixed up with you." He clearly had no high
opinion of that turn of events.

"I've been taught by no one." Sorgrad shook his head.
"All magic means to me is trouble."

"I cannot accept that." Usara flushed. "Unguided affinity
manifests itself, come what may. There is simply no way
you can restrain it as you do without expert direction—"

"If you're calling me a liar, mage, you'd better have a
knife in your hand," said Sorgrad softly.

I had to divert this before blood started flowing. I
snapped my fingers. "Was ill-omened runes what you
meant about being born to be hanged?" I demanded incoherently of 'Gren.

He stopped looking at Usara with an air of anticipation.
"That's right. That's what Sheltya said."

"So just who are these Sheltya? A ruling clan, the reign-
ing bloodline?" I hazarded.

"You're still thinking like a lowlander," Sorgrad chided
me. "No one rules the Anyatimm. Each soke has charge of
its own affairs."

"That's all very well if whoever's in charge is committed
to fair dealing," I said cautiously.

Sorgrad nodded. "Which is where Sheltya come in." He
was looking thoughtful again. "They are outside the blood,
still of the people, but free of ties and bias. If a dispute cannot be settled, they arbitrate. There were appalling feuds in
the ancient days, a quarrel would spread right through kith
and kin."

"A feud lasts three years for theft," 'Gren supplied. "Nine
for violence or twenty-seven if a death's involved."

"That must keep everyone busy," I commented.

"Sheltya mostly keep the sokes from outright bloodshed.
They're healers as well, for when they can't stop the fighting." Sorgrad grinned. "They are teachers, philosophers.
They hold the old sagas and, by custom, should be consulted about any proposed match, in case two sokes are
breeding too close. That's the theory anyway. I don't recall

seeing one more than a handful of times as a child before some strange old man turned up at the mines and announced I had to leave."

"What gave him that authority?" Usara wrapped his arms around skinny knees, intent on this new puzzle.

Sorgrad ignored him. "Once he had spoken, that was that. Even my father wasn't going to gainsay him and I'd seen him stand up to a bear spring-roused from winter sleep without flinching. I was packed off before sunset."

"And I went as well," 'Gren chipped in. "This old fool kept going on about my birth omens."

"So their word is law?" I saw Usara's impatience out of the corner of my eye but dared not look away from Sorgrad.

He shook his head. "Sheltya were losing their influence in the Middle Ranges even then. My father couldn't gainsay the banishment but he forbade my death, which is what the old bastard first called for. My uncles all agreed that custom was the only thing they were going to throw off a mountaintop. My grandmother insisted on Sheltya being summoned if a match was proposed, but after she died my mother and the other women usually debated marriages between themselves."

"But you think they will still be around these mountains?" I asked Sorgrad.

"If they are anywhere." He nodded. "And if any Anyatimm know any aetheric magic, I'd say it'll be Sheltya. They're certainly the ones you need to talk to about that book of yours."

"If they exiled you for magebirth, what do they reckon to wizards?" I wondered aloud. "Will they be able to tell what Usara is?"

"I can't say." He shot Usara a piercing glance. "Don't do anything to give yourself away."

I retrieved the calico bag from 'Gren and shook out the few remaining crumbs. "We'd best move if we're to make that fess before sundown."

Usara rose wearily to his feet and looked at his pack with distaste. "We should have kept the donkey."

"And fed it on what? Fresh air and sweet words?" Sorgrad's composure was iron hard as ever.

"There's plenty of grass," objected the wizard.

"This is winter grazing for the goats of the soke." Sorgrad shook a mocking head. "You don't trespass your animals on someone else's forage up here."

Usara sniffed crossly as he shouldered his pack with a stagger and set off up the narrow path. 'Gren sauntered along behind him and I walked more slowly still with Sorgrad. "So that's why you sold off your finery and trinkets along the way?"

He adjusted the strap of his single satchel where it was catching on the scrip at his belt. "That, and I wanted an impressive purse of coin to jingle in case anyone wonders why we're traveling up here. I think I'll be a younger son of good blood who's made himself a fat patrimony in dealings with the lowlands and is looking to settle on a nicely schooled bride in a comfortable rekin."

I laughed. "They'll welcome you, will they? Good breeding stock?"

Sorgrad shrugged. "Perhaps. We all know the dangers of breeding too close up here but strangers bring their own dangers. It's a fact that Mountain women marrying lowlanders suffer far more losses and dead births."

I grimaced. "And what about 'Gren?"

"No one with any sense travels the uplands on their own," said Sorgrad. "Even the best weather can turn to storm and fog inside less than a chime."

"So I'm a balladeer, keen to learn more about my song book? What's Usara doing? You've heard him sing; no one's ever going to believe he's a minstrel."

"He'd best be a scholar of history again. Sheltya hold the sagas after all." Sorgrad hissed slow breath between his teeth. "With luck we'll be able to just rely on travel truce."

"On what?" I shifted the tie of my own kit bag where it was digging into my shoulder.

"Travel truce; it's good for three days and three nights. If you claim formal right of fire, food and shelter, no one can pursue a feud or demand any information you don't wish to give, not even your name."

"That's worth knowing." Looking up the path, I could see Usara slow his first obstinate pace. "You could have warned him you were going to sell the donkey."

"I can't help it if he's unobservant," Sorgrad grinned.

"He has his uses," I protested. "Don't forget the flood!"

"Living on some magical island is precious little schooling for country like this," said Sorgrad bluntly. "I'll shed no tears if his stupidity gets him killed but I'll come back from the Otherworld to haunt you if I end up dead because of it."

We walked on in companionable silence, a few birds rustling about in the grass and one soaring high above, the liquid delight of its song poured out in profligate ecstasy.

"Now I understand why you wanted to go to the Forest first of all," I remarked some while later.

"If we'd found what we needed in the wildwood, there would have been no need to raise all this." Sorgrad's eyes were fixed on the still distant glen. "But I have it tamed, whatever our noble mage may think."

"Is that hard?" I wondered how so close a friend could hide so huge a secret.

"Not these days." He gave me a familiar wicked grin. "More so when I was younger. Remember that apothecary's shop? I'm afraid that was me."

"From what I heard, the foul-mouthed old skinflint deserved it." The years of trust between us outweighed this one deception, now I was over the first shock. "It's of no consequence to me."

"But claiming a debt from this Messire is, isn't it?" Sorgrad looked at me. "And if that's important to you, it's important to me."

"I don't doubt it but you've more reasons for being here than that, haven't you?" He still owed me some answers.

"I wasn't that sad to leave, truth be told," he said after a while. "Me and 'Gren were already talking about heading into Gidesta, where the Easterlings are more tolerant of marrying out and working with the lowlanders. As middle sons, our patrimony would have been thin enough, and anyway neither of us particularly relished marrying girls we'd known all our lives. I'd rather have left of my own choice but lowland life has suited us well enough, you know that."

"So why go back, why now?" I pressed him.

"Why not now? This landed in front of me and I thought I'd play the runes as they fell." We walked on a little farther. "It's your man who'll be doing the asking, after all, and he has magic of his own if they decide to take offense. I'd like to know what powers Sheltya hold, beyond the weight of fear and custom," he admitted. "I'd like to know why some trick of birth brought their hatred down on me. When I was a youth, I just accepted that it was so. Now I'll see some justification, if they can offer it."

"Curiosity got Amit hanged," I reminded him.

"Not in that song book," he countered with a mischievous smile. "I'll take the risk."

I felt uncomfortably responsible now that the stakes were so much higher. "Whatever deal I make with D'Olbriot, getting Draximal to call off his hounds will be non-negotiable. Fair recompense?"

'Gren was getting bored, casting off to either side of the path, looking for entertainment. He scrambled down a rocky crag in front of us. "I saw bear tracks up there," he announced, bright-eyed.

"Let's have a look." Sorgrad climbed after his brother and I picked up my pace to join Usara.

A dew of sweat beaded the wizard's forehead, sticking the sparse tendrils of his hair to his sun-reddened scalp. "You need to be wearing a hat," I said.

He hoisted his pack higher in a vain attempt to ease the

burden. "Life in a lofty tower doesn't really fit you for expeditions like this."

So he and Sorgrad could agree on something. "No one expects scholars to have much stamina." I passed him my water flask.

"So I'm hoping to study these sagas?" puffed Usara. The wizard groaned as we saw the path coil away downward to a ford at the bottom of the valley hiding the fess. "These people can have a good laugh at the idiot academician carrying such a weight, and then they can have the pick of what I don't need. That should earn us some good will?"

Sorgrad and Sorgren arrived as we started down the hillside. "There is a bear," said 'Gren eagerly. "We can kill it if it attacks us, that's not poaching."

"Is that likely?" I asked Sorgrad.

"Only if 'Gren pokes a stick up its arse to rile it." He shook his head. "No, they're fat and happy eating in the summer seasons."

We walked down to the ford without further diversion and picked our way over the slippery stones. The shadows were lengthening as I looked up the valley. Close to the stream, a sparse crop of grain whispered in the breeze, green but already yellowing at the tips. Goats were being driven into sturdy stone-built pens while a handful of mules on long tethers still grazed. I studied the fess. The massive perimeter wall was pierced only by a double gate to the front and a water gate to the off side where the little stream had been taken under the protection of the walls, regaining its freedom through close-worked metal bars.

"There's a sally-gate on the far side?" I queried 'Gren.

"Even a rabbit knows a one-entry burrow is a death-trap," he confirmed.

I looked up at the central keep; the rekin, I reminded myself. Foursquare and forbidding, built of solid gray stone, at least one sentry was keeping an efficient vigil from its watchful windows. The main gates opened as we made our way up the valley and a handful of men moved between us and the goats, another taking an uncompromising stance on the path.

"Good day to you and yours." Sorgrad stopped some paces from the man. I found it strange to hear him speaking his mother tongue like this.

The man said something in a thickly clotted Mountain accent but he smiled and his hand stayed away from the sword at his belt. He was about the same height as 'Gren, white hair fringing a bald pate and deeply wrinkled face. His face was pitted with tiny scars and an ugly wound, long healed, marred one cheek. Age was tightening his hands with joint evil but hadn't yet wasted impressive muscles.

"Hachalfess are pleased to offer you shelter in your journey," he said to me and Usara, his Tormalin nigh on impenetrable.

I smiled warmly. "We are honored by your hospitality."

The man nodded but I had the distinct impression he hadn't understood a word. I turned the friendly smile on the lad tending the mules and two younger boys who had driven their goats almost to the gate in their eagerness to see who had fetched up. Their huge brindled dog, thick coat ruffed around its neck, came closer, sharp face questing for our scent and ears pricked with curiosity. The men who had backed up the speaker shooed the lads away, helping pen the goats and leading the valuable mules inside the protection of the walls for the night. The dog barked loudly, answered by more hounds giving tongue from within the fess.

"I don't see us troubled by too many curious questions here." Usara was nodding and grinning like a marionette.

"How do we find anything out if we can't talk to them?" My own face was starting to ache.

We went through the lofty gate and I dropped the smirk. We emerged from a virtual tunnel made by the thickness of the wall into a broad open yard. The regular rasp of grinding spoke of grain milled by the stream and hammering rang from a smithy close by the gate, someone laying into stubborn iron with a heavy hammer. A man at a bench beside an open hearth was working sparkling gold with fine tools while another was intent on white metals, a young lad at his elbow studying the techniques.

The rekin dominated the compound, tall, square and adamant. The windows at ground level were little more than arrow slits and the ones above scarcely wider. The main entrance was a door that looked built to withstand a battering ram and now that we were within the walls I could see a second entrance on one side, where a wooden stair ran up to a door on the first of the upper levels. I looked a question at Sorgrad.

"So you can retreat to the higher floors and then cut away the steps," he supplied. "Then attackers have to take the main door while you're dropping things on their heads from above. Once they're inside, they can still only come at you one at a time up the inner stairs."

"I thought you said these Sheltya kept quarrels from ending up in fights?" I frowned.

Sorgrad shrugged. "We've always built that way. After all, you never know, do you?"

The air was heavy with sweet fermentation and a woman emerged from a door opening on the wide tuns of a brewhouse. A younger woman came out of the rekin, wiping her hands on a stained apron, and consulted briefly with the brewer. Both wore round-necked linen blouses belted over undyed woolen skirts reaching to mid-shin, boots laced to the knee beneath. They were unmistakably mother and daughter, pale hair braided close and gleaming in the sunshine.

The old man led the way. "His name is Taegan," Sorgrad told us. "His eldest daughter's husband is away in the hills at the moment, so Taegan holds his authority in trust."

"That's the daughter?" I queried.

"Damaris," confirmed Sorgrad, "and the mother is Leusia."

'Gren and Sorgrad both swept low bows and Usara managed a creditable attempt. I wasn't about to try curtseying in breeches so hoped another smile would suffice.

"You are welcome to our home," the daughter said. Her Tormalin, while heavily accented, was fluent enough to suggest we might actually be able to hold a conversation. Her mother continued smiling, a sideways glance of pride at her daughter.

"Thank you for taking us in," I said, for want of anything more inspired.

There was an awkward pause and then the younger woman, Damaris, ushered us all inside. The central hearth of the large room was hemmed in with firedogs, iron tripods for cook pots and a complicated arrangement of arms and hooks where several small kettles and a griddle hung. Two women of about my own age were busy cooking while a bevy of children sat around a long table where lamps cast a golden glow on their painstaking efforts. The unmistakable scritch of slate pencils set my teeth on edge. All the youngsters looked up until the old woman at the head of the table recalled them to their lessons with a few soft words.

An old man chuckled to himself. He could have been Taegan's older brother, age spotting a head bald as an egg and the backs of his withered hands. He was deftly working bone with knife, file and fine chisels to make a comb patterned with diamond panels. As I watched, he fitted copper studs to hold the teeth secure.

"This is my aunt's husband, Garven," Damaris introduced him with a wave of her hand. I noticed that half of the room was subtly divided with stools and low chairs, clutter on the shelved wall behind separated with regular spaces. Sorgrad and 'Gren stepped forward and greeted the old man, who replied eagerly. Usara stood a pace behind them, looking a little uncertain.

Damaris laid a gentle hand on my arm. "You will sit with us, on the women's side." Two middle-aged women on the far side of the hearth looked up with bright curiosity, distaffs laid aside, baskets of brown wool at their feet. I hoped I wasn't expected to join in their work; I've no more idea of how to spin than fly. I took a seat on a high-backed bench, a blanket of fleecy weave softening the whole, expertly embroidered cushions resting on top. These women must learn needlework in their cradles.

One of the spinners said something and Damaris turned to me. "These are my aunts, Kethrain and Doratie." I fixed the names in my mind; Kethrain had a wider forehead and little gold drops hanging from her ears while Doratie was missing a tooth in her lower jaw. "Kethrain says you have pretty hair."

"There are women in the lowlands would walk barefoot over hot coals to be as golden-fair as you ladies." Flattery is always easier when it's the truth.

Damaris translated and all three laughed. I folded my hands in my lap and hoped no one thought it friendly to offer me needle or thread. These women might admire my hair but they'd be appalled at my sewing. I felt my smile becoming a little fixed, so I looked around again.

A tow-headed little girl peeped around her shoulder at me, unruly curls falling over her eyes. I winked at her and she whipped her head back around, hunching over her work and whispering to her neighbor. The old dame supervising was about to speak when Damaris clapped her hands together. My two new friends immediately stowed their work away while the children hastened to clear the table of slate pencils and counting frames. One fetched a cloth to wipe it down while others began setting places with polished pewter plates, cups and jugs.

The old craftsman, Garven, made his way slowly to the door, his back twisted with more than age. He pulled on a bell rope to send light brazen clangor ringing out across the valley. Approaching voices grew louder and soon the room was full of sturdy men and women in creamy linen, tan leather and brown wool, all with a similar cast to their features. There seemed to be no fixed seating pattern at th table; one girl swapped places with another and two little boys were forcibly separated by Damaris when they began messing about with their spoons. The only exception was a high-backed chair with solid arms set at one end of the table. A few moments behind everyone else the whitesmith and his lad appeared carrying the gold-worker, whose legs were wasted and useless. He was set on his seat, cushions wedged around him without fuss.

I hurried to sit between Sorgrad and Usara. "Accident or disease?"

"Cave-in down a mine," Sorgrad replied. "Garven said he was lucky to survive it."

I wouldn't have called it luck myself but at least a cripple here looked better placed than a lowlander begging in the gutters. A couple of girls were ferrying plates to the women at the hearth. "I'd like chicken," I told Sorgrad, seeing some go past.

"You are welcome," one girl said in passable Tormalin, taking my plate.

"We teach them the lowland tongues since last year," one of Damaris' sisters said across the table. "Else the boys cannot trade and the girls not deal with travelers. More come every year, even to the uplands."

One of the older men, flour dusting his shirt, spoke patent disapproval. Doratie rebuked him and I looked at Sorgrad. "It's an old complaint," he told me, "that lowlanders always expect us to speak their tongue but never learn ours."

"You'd better give me some lessons," I said ruefully.

Everyone was eating heartily and conversation swelled around us. One of the half-grown girls was casting longing eyes at the whitesmith's lad and he was preening himself with that realization as he talked to the goldsmith. Two of the old men were having a heated discussion about something or other, punctuated every so often with a pointed interjection from Kethrain. I applied myself to an excellent meal of pot-cooked fowl.

Usara reached past me for some black bread. "You and I stand out like poppies in a cornfield here, don't we?"

"Yes, but we knew that would be the case, didn't we?" A girl appeared at my elbow with a foaming jug and I held up a bright pewter tankard. I felt easier to be an outsider here than being taken for kin in the Forest by folk superficially similar yet so strange. I sipped at the curious brew. Darker than any ale I'd come across, it had a resinous taste and an odd, oily quality. I realized I was being watched with amusement from all sides.

"What am I drinking?" I murmured to Sorgrad, the rim of the vessel hiding my lips.

"Fir beer." He drained his own measure. "But there's malted barley brew, if you prefer."

I finished my drink, deciding that much was a point of honor, but laid a hand over my tankard when the lass went to refill it. "I think I'll stick to what I'm used to."

Damaris' sister passed a jug giving off a reassuring scent of hops. "I'm Merial," she introduced herself.

"I'm Livak, and this is Sorgrad," I turned to my near hand, "and Usara." 'Gren was some way down the table between two children with others all craning to see him rolling a coin down the back of one hand. He made it disappear, only to pluck it from behind the ear of a wide-eyed toddler sitting on his knee. "And that is Sorgren."

"Middle Range names?" Merial was studying Sorgrad with a frank interest.

"True, but we left our homes long ago," he said easily. "We have been traveling and dealing in the lowlands."

"And your present business?" These Westerlings shared 'Gren's directness. This truce clearly didn't stop questions, even if it entitled us to refuse answers.

"My brother and I are thinking of returning to the uplands." There was a hint of encouragement in Sorgrad's pleasant smile. "We find ourselves traveling with this scholar," he nodded to Usara, who was mopping the last of the gravy from his platter with yet more bread. The mage swallowed hastily. "I am an antiquarian of sorts and eager to learn the sagas told in the Mountains."

Merial raised one fine golden eyebrow. "It's seldom a lowlander thinks we of the heights might have worthwhile knowledge."

"A true scholar respects all learning," said Usara earnestly. "There is no single path to an enlightened understanding of this world and our place within it." There was no mistaking his sincerity. If I could learn how to fake that, I'd have a fortune made inside a year."

The old man barked some query, nodding at me. "I am a singer, a traveler," I said readily enough. "I bought an ancient book with songs in the old tongues of Plain, Forest and Mountain. I want to learn their meaning."

Merial smiled. "You must talk to Garven and to Doratie's mother."

"When I was a boy, such tales were told by Sheltya," remarked Sorgrad casually.

Conversation around us faltered as that word fell on everyone's ears. "Yes," Merial said slowly. "That is so here."

"I've only heard half-tales from those Easterlings who dwell in Gidesta," Usara said with honest eagerness. "I would dearly love the chance to talk to your Sheltya. Are they not keepers of important knowledge?"

Merial looked at Sorgrad, who spoke to her in rapid Mountain speech, manner courteous and reassuring.

"That might be possible." Merial turned to attract the attention of the old man sitting by Doratie. He shot a suspicious glance at Usara but as she continued his face grew more open and even a little smug. He nodded finally and Doratie added what sounded like approval.

"My uncle sees no harm in Sheltya judging you for themselves," she told Usara, her eyes flicking to Sorgrad.

"How do we contact them?" asked Usara. "Forgive my ignorance."

Merial shrugged. "When they are wanted, they will come. That's always been the way of it."

That sounded promising, I thought. From the little I'd learned from Guinalle, being able to hear thoughts from afar was a fundamental part of what she called Artifice.

A bowl of summer fruit mixed with toasted nuts and grain was set between us and my plate was swapped for a fresh one. A platter of flat oatcakes was added, with some rounds of bright white cheese. That had to be made of goats' milk, even if I hadn't smelled it coming. I opted for the fruit and grain.

Merial turned to talk to Doratie, drawing Sorgrad into their conversation. It was no hardship to sit quietly with my thoughts for a change. I let my mind idle through imagining what Ryshad was doing, wondering how Halice was finding life on the far side of the ocean as she captained the mercenaries defending the unlikely colonists of Kellarin. Unlocking the secrets of aetheric magic would give her increased protection against Elietimm greedy to seize that fertile land and kill any who disputed their claim. She was another friend depending on my success, so this scent had better lead to something.

The meal drew to a close and children were shepherded through a far door to sounds of protest and washing. The aged men and older women drew chairs up around the hearth, now clear of cooking pots. A few had needle and thread or some small craft in their hands, but work was desultory at best. Doratie fetched a flask of clear liquor from a cabinet high on one wall and Kethrain followed with tiny crystal goblets. The atmosphere was warm with good humour and tolerance.

Merial passed me a stack of plates. "The scullery is through there." Sorgrad shared a smirk with Usara, which Merial soon wiped away. "You two can help with the firewood."

As I headed for the scullery, I saw 'Gren disappearing up

the stairs with an adoring covey of children, clamoring for more entertainment. I wondered if Damaris knew what she was letting herself in for.

⨭

Othilfess,
14th of For-Summer

Teiriol yanked at the recalcitrant mule's bridle. "I'll stake your hide out for the fork-tails to peck at," he told the black and tan face. The mule set its ears back and lifted its gray muzzle sharply, nearly banging Teiriol on the nose.

"Get on!" Cailean cut at the animal's hocks with a switch and it jumped forward. Teiriol hauled on the reins, giving the beast no chance to dig its hooves in. With three others jostling behind it, the mule yielded, ears pricking at the prospect of water and fodder as it recognized its stable.

Teiriol gaped at the activity all around the compound. Both forges, the small one he'd always considered his own and the larger one cold since his uncle's death, were red hot and blazing, molten scale flying in brilliant sparks as hammers pounded iron into submission. One smith quenched his handiwork in a hiss of steam and, as he raised the tongs, Teiriol recognized a spearhead. Satisfied, the man laid it beside a line of others and stood for a moment to watch his colleague deftly shape the tang of a sword blade.

The mules all balked at the commotion and Teiriol's charge threatened to buck as a lad chased a frantic goose past them, a cleaver in his hand showing the bird its fate only too clearly. Jeers came from an open workshop, a drift of bark and shavings blowing all around as a gang of men turned rough poles and narrow wands into shafts for spears and arrows.

"Catch it, Nol," urged one, laying his knife aside with an

air of finality. "That's a quiver's worth of flights and a good roast dinner getting away from you!"

"He couldn't get work as a whorehouse handyman, that one," sneered another, cursing as his blade snagged in the wood he was shaping.

A dull, repetitive thud penetrated Teiriol's bemusement; the ore mill was working. "You see to the animals. I'm going to talk to Keis."

Cailean's indignant protest went unheard in the general hubbub. Teiriol hurried to a long building set against the far wall beyond the rekin. The steady beat was being driven by a weary mule pacing a circular track and harnessed to a pole that turned a pillar driving a shaft running through the wall of the building. Teiriol looked in vain for anyone tending the sweating animal and shoved open the door.

The rhythmic noise was redoubled inside the stone shed. Iron-shod timbers lifted in sequence as lugs on the rotating shaft caught matching spurs in their sides. Released as the shaft turned, they dropped to crush tinstone against a granite mortar. Keisyl was sorting unhammered ore, his concentration complete. Fine sandy dust hung in the air, coating Keisyl, the mill and a large tub of water with pale scum.

Keisyl coughed and noticed Teiriol. "Outside. Can't hear myself think in here!" Wiping his face clean of muck and sweat, he pulled the door to behind them. "When did you get back?" Keisyl took a deep breath of fresh air.

"Just now." Teiriol pointed to Cailean who was unloading bulky sacks of ore from the mules with mumbled complaint.

Keisyl knuckled his red-rimmed eyes. "I'll start crushing that lot tomorrow. We've plenty stamped fine enough for dressing. You and Cailean can make a start on that. The assay looks good and rich. When are the others due back?"

"Tomorrow but—"

"I'll boil his arse for axle grease!" Keisyl hurried over to the mill mule and brought it to a halt, no great task since the animal was fit to drop. "Get some water, Teir."

Teiriol hesitated, mouth half open, but took a bucket from beside the door. Going down a passage built into the thickness of the massive wall, he filled it from a rock-cut cistern, working in the darkness with the ease of familiarity. He counted the stairs down to the water out of old habit and frowned as he registered how far down the level had fallen. So many questions clamored to be asked that he could not frame a single one.

"Will you just look at this?" Keisyl raged, carefully easing harness from a bloody gall. "I told him I needed the boy out here. Have you seen Nol, that beggar boy from the valley bottom?"

"What's going on, Keis?" demanded Teiriol, perplexity threatening to turn to anger.

"It's nothing to do with us," snapped Keisyl. "I'm keeping well clear and you'll do the same."

"Clear of what?" Teiriol asked, exasperated.

"Jeirran reckons he's going to take on the lowlanders," spat Keisyl, voice thick with contempt and dust. "Drive them out, reclaim the land, get reparation for ten generations of loss!"

Teiriol looked at the purposeful activity on all sides. The lad had managed to corner the goose and was now inexpertly stripping the twitching corpse, fluff clinging to his hair and face. An elderly fletcher was busy with the long feathers, oblivious to the banter all around.

"It might be time to make a stand," said Teiriol slowly. "Remember Teyvasoke."

Keisyl snorted. "You think Jeirran's the man to do it? His brave words are the same as his promises of riches in Selerima. Follow him and you'll end up worse off than just empty in the pocket! No, when he runs himself over whatever precipice he's headed for, we have to be here to take care of Eirys and Theilyn."

Keisyl led the mule out of the jinny-ring and into the stable. Cailean was busy bedding the other beasts down with old straw, clicking his tongue over the poor hay left in the racks. "Who's had all the forage?"

"Who do you suppose?" snarled Keisyl.

Cailean began to groom the mule he was tending. Teiriol took a stiff-bristled brush to the next and they worked in tense silence, broken only by the whickers of the mules and the occasional scrape of a hoof on the cobbles of the floor.

"So, what does Eirys think of all Jeirran's plans?" Teiriol asked at length.

"She thinks he's run mad. Her home is filled with strangers eating the table bare without so much as a by your leave." Keisyl's savage tone was at odds with his gentle fingers salving the jinny-mule's galls with unguent from a small green-glazed pot. "They're halfway to drinking the cellar dry and Theilyn's already been offered more insult than I have time to settle if I fight a man a day from now until Solstice. I tell Jeirran to get his sorry crew of scavengers in hand and he just says he has weightier matters in hand."

Teiriol frowned. "Perhaps we should talk to Eirys about repudiating him, if he's fallen that far short of the marriage compact—"

"She won't." Bafflement outweighed scorn in Keisyl's reply. "She says she loves him. Whether that's the truth or she's just plain scared of him, I couldn't say, but all she does is make excuse after excuse for him."

"Perhaps we should act for her," suggested Teiriol dubiously. "I mean, Sheltya—"

Keisyl's laugh was a hollow bark. "Sheltya are already here, my lad, and dug in as deep as any." He wiped his fingers clean on the mule's woolly back and stoppered the jar with a sigh. "They're taking their lead from that whey-faced bitch Aritane. I'd say she's planning her own little campaign among the keepers of wisdom." He looked sharply over to Cailean. "And you keep that to yourself, do you hear? In fact, you keep clear of the whole mire, if you've got any sense."

"I'll be back to the diggings as soon as may be, don't fret," Cailean replied readily.

Keisyl's eyes were preoccupied again. "Teir, you'd better come and see Mother, but we'll not eat at the hearth tonight. Cai, I'll get Theilyn to bring us some food upstairs and we can discuss how best to organize the smelting."

Teiriol gave Cailean a half-hearted wave of farewell and apology as he followed his brother. Keisyl's lips moved in silent calculation, points ticked off on his fingers as he ran through some list. Queasiness undermined Teiriol's happiness at being home; strangers infesting the familiar surroundings brought some indefinable sense of menace. Why was Keisyl distancing himself from everyone and everything? Always being told what to do by an elder brother was bad enough, Teiriol decided, but being left without guide or instruction could be infinitely worse.

"Hi there, you!" The curt hail startled both brothers out of their preoccupations. A gray-haired man riding a dappled jennet with silver-mounted harness had ridden unchallenged through the open gate. He was surveying the courtyard, hooked nose lifted with an arrogant air. "Tell Jeirran I've got all the ironstone he wanted, wet-dressed and ready. Show me where the furnace house is." Teiriol saw a mule's head poking inquisitively over the threshold. "I'll see to the melt tomorrow," the man continued. "It's too late in the day to start now."

Scarlet fury suffused Keisyl's face. "The furnace house here is mine, from bellows to float stone, and I'll thank you to remember that."

"Jeirran's paying me to smelt for him." The newcomer shrugged. "You'd better take that up with him. Where do we stable our beasts around here?"

Keisyl was already crossing to the rekin, angry strides eating up the distance. Teiriol hurried after, the ground seeming more uncertain beneath every step. Keisyl kicked the door open with such violence it crashed back on its hinges with an audible crack of splintering wood.

"There are certainly advantages to letting an enemy set things in motion and then pacing your moves to his," Jeirran was saying with an air of grave consideration. He barely missed a breath at Keisyl's precipitous entrance. "But equally there are benefits to seizing the initiative. One can catch a foe off guard by doing the unexpected, leaving them unable to see where your strategy is leading." Jeirran lounged in a high-backed chair set by the hearth while four other men on stools leaned eagerly forward.

Keisyl marched to stand in front of Jeirran, thumbs tucked into his belt and cold rage in his face. "Why's some Middle Ranges hireling saying he's here to run a smelt in my furnace?"

"Wernil? So soon? Then we're ahead of ourselves already!" Jeirran preened himself in the admiring nods of his companions.

"I've tin to work and no one smelts on my floor without my say-so," glowered Keisyl.

"You work the diggings on Theilyn's behalf," Jeirran corrected him with silky courtesy. "I think she'll allow Wernil a turn with the bellows, given how hard I am working for the future of this soke."

"You conniving—"

"Keisy, Teiro, can I speak with you for a moment?" The scullery door opened to reveal a thin woman pleating her apron with nervous hands. Her hair was faded and colorless, her eyes washed-out blue. Years of worry and toil had carved deep lines into her face, but her back was straight with resolve and the determined set of her countenance was echoed in her sons' features.

"If anyone sets a brand to my furnace without my permission, I'll ram his head in after it," Keisyl growled in a vicious undertone. He pushed past and left the room. Teiriol followed, eyeing the clutter of leatherwork and horn shavings all around the room, the long slate table covered in debris. He found his way blocked by the women's chairs, drawn back from the hearth and tight in a circle. He looked, dismayed, at the grubby fingermarks on the embroidered linen cushions, at a torn edge to the rug hemmed in by the seats.

"Mother." He went to embrace her but she retreated, shutting the scullery door before laying her forehead on his shoulder with a silent sigh. In the next breath, she pulled away to brush the hair from his forehead with a fond smile. "What's going on, Mama?"

"Jeirran's got some Middle Ranger—" began Keisyl hotly.

"Yes, dear, I heard." Ismenia laid a finger on his lips to silence him. "But let him work his ore. The sooner he's done, the sooner he's out of our home."

"Mama!" protested Keisyl.

"Will your tinstone go rotten in the next few days?" A shadow of a smile flickered briefly across Ismenia's face. "Is it too much to ask for peace in the household?"

"There'll be precious little peace if Jeirran arms every malcontent west of the Gap and marches on the lowlands." Keisyl's voice rose in frustration and anger.

"If letting him make his weapons means he marches this rabble out of here, then that'll do much for the peace of the soke," retorted Ismenia. "Keep your voice down. I don't want Eirys disturbed." Worry creased her forehead.

"Where is she?" Teiriol looked around the scullery. The usual racks of plates and pots were joined by a couple of workboxes, cloth stuck with threaded needles and two distaffs propped in the corner. The normally bare and scrubbed table had three rough stools set around a clutter of pewter beakers.

"Upstairs, resting." Ismenia looked as if she needed to sleep from sundown to sundown herself. She glanced briefly at a sink where leafy vegetables awaited attention, but with a shrug took a seat.

"Resting?" Keisyl looked sharply at his mother.

"We think so. Misaen make it so," she added in fervent prayer.

"Eirys is with child?" Teiriol tried to catch up with the conversation.

Ismenia nodded. "We think so, which is why I want you both to bite your lips till they bleed if need be. Let Jeirran play the lead-ganger all he wants. This early on, if Eirys is worried or—well you know as well as I that if Jeirran loses his temper, she'll be the first one he takes it out on."

"If he's mistreating her, why doesn't she stand up to him?" demanded Keisyl. "She knows we'll back her! If she gives me leave, I'll beat the piss out of him willingly. Perhaps we should go to Sheltya ourselves if that cold bitch Aritane is cowing her."

"Eirys is as likely to turn against Jeirran as she is to fly." Despair tainted Ismenia's voice for the first time. "She won't hear a word against him. Bad-mouthing him just makes her cry, so keep your opinions to yourself. Maewelin grant it's early days with the child making her so sensitive."

"We can't go on like this, Mama," protested Keisyl.

"No, not forever." Ismenia rubbed a water-wrinkled hand over her face. "Until the babe is born and that's why I don't want anything to risk Eirys letting slip, do you hear?"

"And when the babe is come?" Teiriol watched his mother closely.

"Then Eirys will have something to love above that glossy little cock," replied Ismenia, a steely look in her faded eyes. "Since he's not about to make a fond father, she might just see him for what he is. He's too used to being the hand-fed kidling to take kindly to anyone usurping his place."

"We could get her to repudiate him?" asked Teiriol hopefully.

"And what if her next choice is as bad?" Keisyl muttered. "She's always had more hair than sense, has Eirys. Come to that, Theilyn could land us with someone just as useless."

Ismenia looked at him sharply. "You thought well enough of him when they were courting, don't deny it. We all did, not seeing fine clothes and fancier words was dressing up fools' gold. Now, about Theilyn—that stuck-up sister Jeirran's claimed back from Sheltya has taken her under her wing. Don't tell her anything that you don't want Jeirran to know, especially not the chance of a baby. Did you see her in the yard at all?"

Teiriol frowned. "Isn't she up with Eirys?"

"No." Ismenia rose wearily from her seat and poured water from a heavy ewer into the sink. "She'll be trailing after Aritane or skirting around the ne'er-do-wells in the workshops."

"Mother!" objected Keisyl.

"Don't raise your voice to me, Keisy." She lifted a warning finger. "If she's so keen to be considered grown, she can behave herself or face the consequences."

"But what if—" Teiriol hesitated, reddening.

"What if she comes in with her petticoats soiled and swearing she found the bracelet?" The pair of them gaped at their mother's coarseness.

"Then we'll get another birth to the soke, and if Misaen wields any justice it'll be a girl." Ismenia set her lips in a bloodless line. "And if no man after will overlook her dishonor for the sake of fathering his own children, it'll serve Theilyn right. You two will be assured of the diggings for as long as there's ore to be dug, won't you?"

"That's hardly just—" began Keisyl with some heat.

"I told you not to raise your voice to me," snapped Ismenia. "It's no harder a truth than all the others I've faced since your father died. I've kept this soke safe for my children thus far and I'm not about to give up now."

Teiriol looked uncertainly from his bitter-tongued mother to his grim-faced brother. "I'll go and see if I can find Theilyn."

Ismenia turned to the sink with a snort and began sluicing through green leaves. Keisyl rolled up the sleeves of his shirt. "So do you want these chopped or stripped?"

Teiriol left the scullery hurriedly rather than see Keisyl

doing woman's work and then wondered where under the sun he should go.

"Ho, Teir, come over here." Jeirran called him to the far side of the fire.

Teiriol reluctantly crossed the room. "Good day to you." He studied Jeirran's companions. The two older men, one graying, one bald, each had mining calluses on their hands, the bald one missing two fingers on one of his. Both were looking at Jeirran as if he could offer them a fresh-faced bride with her own gold seams. The younger men shifted in their seats, glancing from the door to Jeirran, restlessly shuffling boots on the flagstones. One had been richly dressed but was now travel-stained and ragged. When he reached for a cup, the sleeve of his shirt pulled back to reveal flogging scars on his arm. The other was neat enough but had a sly cast to his muddy gray eyes. Both were more sandy-haired than blond, faces soft.

"Take a seat, Teir." Jeirran shoved a stool with a foot and proffered a beaker of mead, pewter dull with countless fingermarks. "Listen to what Ikarel has to tell us."

The sly-faced man shrugged. "I can't say if it's truth or not but I heard the same tale in two different villages. There's wizardry afoot in the Great Forest. Some great mage has been rallying the Folk, using sorcery to defeat any who stand against him and claiming the wildwood for his own."

Teiriol felt distaste curl his lip.

"False magic," spat the man with the missing fingers.

"Eresken should be told." Jeirran frowned. "Where is he?"

"Find Aritane, you'll find him," sniggered the youth with the whip scars. He subsided at Jeirran's glare.

"I'll go." Teiriol hastily set aside his untouched cup.

"No, wait, I want—"

He ignored Jeirran's indignant words, cutting them off short with a slam of the door. Circling the rekin, pushing past a gang of strangers half-heartedly urging two yapping dogs into a full-blown fight, he saw his quarry. "Aritane, a moment."

Aritane turned haughtily. She unbent a little when she recognized Teiriol. "I didn't realize you were due back. You are welcome."

"And good day to you." What right had she to welcome him to his own home? "Theilyn." He made his sister a curt bow and was pleased to see uncertainty at war with defiance in her smoky blue eyes. He was less impressed to see her hair curling loosely around her shoulders and the way her cross-tied shawl accentuated the curves of her developing figure.

"And I am Eresken." The man between the two women offered his hand. Teiriol took a firm grip on the smooth palm unmarred by toil or injury. He closed his fingers tight, eyes expressionless as he looked for the other man's reaction.

"I am very pleased to meet you." Eresken's smile remained unchanged and after a moment Teiriol dropped both the stranger's hand and his own gaze. "Mother needs your help in the scullery, Theilyn," he said without preamble. "Whatever else is going on—" he shot Aritane a hostile glance— "you should not forget your duties or your responsibilities."

Theilyn colored, lifting her chin arrogantly. Aritane forestalled her reply. "He's right, my dear. I am keeping you from your work." She favored the girl with a private smile. "Run along and we can tell Teiriol just why we have filled his home with strangers. He'll see how a little sacrifice now will lead to so much greater reward in the future."

Teiriol folded his arms a touch defensively and studied Eresken critically. Who was this man of obviously mixed blood, for all his local clothing? "Jeirran wants you. Someone's brought news about wizards in the lowlands."

Aritane frowned. "What has that to do with us?"

"Jeirran keeps himself fully apprised of anything that might affect his plans." Eresken rested his hand briefly on hers. He smiled at Teiriol. "It is something, is it not, that a man has finally emerged to voice all our dissatisfactions and urge us to stand up to the lowlanders?"

Teiriol felt uncomfortable as Eresken's green eyes bored into him. Memories of past outrages, witnessed, reported and spoken of over long winter evenings down the years echoed in the back of his mind. Whatever he might think of Jeirran personally, it was true that the man was displaying a courage no one else had shown in recent times. Disloyal irritation with Keisyl's aloofness pricked him.

"Come on, Theilyn." Taking her hand, he hurried back to the shelter of the rekin.

"Do you think he will join us?" Aritane asked dubiously as she watched him go.

"I think so," nodded Eresken. "There's much anger inside him, and an outward-looking mind. As long as we can focus that where we want it, he'll be unable to hold out for long." Eresken pointed to Theilyn hanging on her brother's arm and talking intently, half skipping in her urgency to match his pace. "Theilyn will convince him." In the shelter of gathering shadow, he lifted Aritane's hand to kiss it swiftly.

"I wish I could read people as well as you." Aritane's cold poise was melted now, humility mixed with a hint of envy.

"You will, one day," Eresken promised her with warm affection. "When we have peace in the uplands, I can teach you everything I know. When you share that learning, you will raise the Sheltya to the honor rightfully theirs—and yours."

Aritane's mouth opened on an intake of breath. "Then you will be staying? Truly?" Hope strangled her words.

"I will need my father's blessing, but I cannot see him refusing, not once he has met your mind in the honesty of true magic." Eresken ran a self-conscious hand over his hair, dark against her fairness. "I cannot see him rebuking me for falling in love with a woman of Tren Ar'Dryen, just as he did."

Aritane was at once distracted. "What did you say?"

"My mother was of the Plains to the east and south of here," said Eresken with a shrug. "My father crossed the ocean long years since and where he made landfall her people took him and his voyagers in. They were of the ancient blood of the Plains; a few still hide from imperious Tormalin steel." He smiled. "Not all have passed into lowland myth as Eldritch-men living in the shadows of the chimney corner. When the ship sailed in the spring, she was aboard and I within her." His face fell a little. "I have heard some disparage my blood. I suppose I am a lowlander mongrel but—"

"The ancient race of the Plains shared in true magic, the sagas confirm it," interrupted Aritane hotly. "Such a lineage is no disgrace."

"Perhaps we might circulate the truth among our immediate circle," suggested Eresken diffidently. "I had better see what Jeirran needs. Until later, my beloved."

He turned from Aritane and within a few strides the modesty that had so touched her was replaced with a well-disguised look of satisfaction. Aritane twisted her hands together before walking toward a knot of gray-clad figures sitting around a glowing brazier.

"Ari! Hold up there!" Another man in the dusky wool and long tunic that marked out the Sheltya hailed her. He was tall for their race, narrow shoulders hunched, wringing large hands in an absent gesture. A few curious heads rose around the compound and immediately ducked back to their work when they caught Aritane's commanding glare.

"Bryn," she inclined her head in reserved welcome. "I hadn't expected to see you so soon. Didn't we agree you would best serve the cause by continuing to travel with Cullam?" There was a faint sneer in her tone as she mentioned the name.

"Cullam has gone over the heights, summoned to the Hachalfess," Bryn replied, confidence in his tone belying the diffidence of his manner.

"Sheltya at the beck and call of every goatherder as usual,"

Aritane commented sarcastically. "You didn't fancy the trip?"

"I made excuse to stay behind," Bryn told her a little hesitantly. "I didn't think it wise to go so far that I would only be able to contact you with far-speech and risk being overheard by the Elders."

"If you don't have the skill to shield yourself, perhaps that was wise." Aritane looked at Bryn a touch contemptuously. "But why come here? I wanted you to stay within the fold for the moment, to warn us if suspicions are aroused."

"The Elders will have more important things to concern them," retorted Bryn with spirit. "Cullam has asked me to relay a message to the high peaks. A scholar has come to Hachalfess, seeking old sagas and asking about ancient lore. Cullam senses he is searching for true magic and wants to know what to tell him."

"That stupid old man?" gasped Aritane. "He must tell this fool nothing, not a word. How else will our skills baffle the enemy? Surprise is our greatest advantage!"

"So what do we do?" demanded Bryn. "I've not yet passed on the message but I'm already going to be rebuked for delay. I cannot hold it much longer without arousing suspicions. The bones at Solstice telling every Sheltya and every soke to follow Jeirran to war will do me no good if I'm stripped of all knowledge before you act!"

"Come with me." Aritane hurried Bryn toward the rekin, a forceful hand behind his elbow. "We must talk to Eresken at once."

Hachalfess,
15th of For-Summer

"What do you suppose he's telling him?" 'Gren shifted in his chair, as he had been doing constantly all evening. "Perhaps—"

"Perhaps you should be patient?" I waited for Halcarion to drop a star on my head. Usara and Sorgrad were deep in conversation with an old man in gray but the genial hum of the room made it impossible to hear what they were saying. I was no less keen than 'Gren to be involved but Sorgrad had told us very firmly that we were not wanted. Reluctantly I had to agree that introducing Usara as a scholar with Sorgrad to translate was as much as we could risk, given the aged visitor's obvious caution in dealing with lowlanders. The men and women of the soke were keeping very strictly to their separate roles and duties around the old man so I'd dug out skirt and bodice from the bottom of my bag.

I studied the old man covertly. About the age of Garven, small-boned and hungry-looking, his loose gray tunic and cloak looked to have been made for a bigger man. With thin white hair and watery gray eyes set deep in a wrinkled face, he sat hunched in a fine-carved chair listening intently to Sorgrad. One disregarded hand shook with a faint palsy and I'd seen the same tremor in his head earlier. There was no way such a frail and ancient man had come up the trail we'd followed, not without help or a beast of burden.

"You were going to ask Doratie about Cullam," I reminded 'Gren. The old women had been the first to welcome him when he arrived with no pack, no water and no support beyond the prop of a staff.

"She says he's from the eastern reaches," 'Gren shrugged.

"The valleys leading down to the Gap?" I wanted to be quite clear on this. "Across the higher ground to the west? He got here from there since yesterday?"

'Gren nodded. "Sheltya do that kind of thing."

Which was either a lie to impress the people of the soke, or it was the truth. What was gained by a lie? Pretense to impress bites back when the falsehood's revealed and these things always come out. What if it were truth? Then these Sheltya, whoever they were, had the same means to shift themselves

from place to place that made Elietimm such a frustrating and
dangerous foe. Which meant aetheric magic. Hope warmed
me more than the dancing flames of the hearth.

'Gren fidgeted again. "I could go and see if they want a
drink." We were sitting as close as we could without attracting comment, which meant we could talk as long as we
didn't mind other people overhearing. The goldsmith's assistant and one of the younger girls were doing the same at
the opposite end of the room. From the affronted glares another lass was giving me, we'd taken the place of some
other couple keen to get to know each other under the be-
nign restrictions of family and custom.

"No," I said a trifle curtly. "So, what have you been up to
today?"

"Helping dose mules for worm, playing with the children, chopping firewood, the usual. I told the children an
old story about wyrms burrowing under the mountains, eating up the rocks until Misaen captured them and locked
them away!" He smiled with happy recollection. "You want
to learn that one."

"And are you going to be the one getting up past midnight when the little ones are all wetting their beds with
nightmares?" Damaris wasn't going to thank him for that.

"They won't wake up. How did you get on with these
lovely ladies?" he asked with a touch of malice.

"I had a very nice time polishing the pewter." It might
have been more productive if any of the women had spoken
enough Tormalin to gossip properly but at least I hadn't lost
the touch. I picked some sand and wood ash from beneath
my scuffed fingernails.

"Good evening." Merial came to sit beside me, nodding
politely at 'Gren. His eyes brightened at her small tray bearing gold-rimmed goblets and a small green glass bottle of
colorless liquor. "We call it mountain dew. We make it
from . . ." she frowned a little as she poured, "varsi? I don't
know the lowlander word."

"Rye," supplied 'Gren with pleasure.

I sniffed at my thimbleful and rolled it around the glass, noting the sluggish lines clinging to the sides. I was pleasantly surprised by the smoothness of the spirit and the tang of herbs on my tongue.

"My mother used to flavor hers with rowan berries," 'Gren was saying, "but I think this has more character."

"It's very fine," I agreed. "Do you distill it yourself?" If I couldn't listen in on Sorgrad's conversation, I could at least make myself agreeable with some of my own.

Merial busied herself with her spinning basket. "If there's grain enough to spare."

"Every soke has its different ways of finishing and flavoring it," volunteered 'Gren, pausing to raise an inquiring brow at Merial before reaching for the flask at her nod. "One of my uncles always said if he got storm-lost in the heights, all he had to do was find a fess, taste the dew and he'd know where he was."

Merial laughed. "A fair few men could claim the same." She was deftly spinning woolly animal hair into a fine, even yarn.

"I've never come across goats that you could pluck before," I commented. "Lowland goats are only good for milk and hide. It's sheep that are sheared for spinning."

"Damaris said stripping the nannies made you sneeze?" Merial managed not to laugh.

"Yes, I'm afraid it's obviously not a task for me." I'd been forced to resurrect my housemaid skills in order to salvage some pride.

Merial continued her work with unconscious ease. "Sheep don't do so well in the heights but sometimes we trade for fleeces. They're much messier to spin." She reached over to brush an unnoticed fragment of fluff from my sleeve. "Still, it can be worth it for the chance of colors. The goat yarn doesn't take dye very well. We breed for different shades of coat—"

She broke off, spindle whorl slowing unheeded. The

main door to the room swung open slowly, the cold draft
setting lamps flickering in their niches all around the walls.
Four shadowy figures stood on the steps behind the gate
ward. Everyone in the room rose to their feet, me and 'Gren
the same as the rest.

Taegen barked a sharp demand. Uncertainty colored the
gatekeeper's reply.

"What is it?" I mouthed at 'Gren.

"Sheltya," he murmured between motionless lips.

I looked at Merial and saw that all the blood had drained
from her face. Damaris beyond her looked fit to faint.

"Why the reaction?" I shifted half a pace closer to 'Gren,
not about to risk anything louder than a voiceless whisper in
the tense silence.

"Four of them—pestilence or capital crime," he breathed.

Somewhere off toward the scullery, someone's knees
gave way. The scrape of the chair as she sat caught everyone's attention. I used the moment to edge behind Merial,
wishing fruitlessly for some way of covering my hair. This
was not a good time to be a poppy in a cornfield; they get
yanked out good and quick.

The gatekeeper had moved to stand behind Taegen's
shoulder. The old man was deathly pale, the ribbed scar on
his cheek livid in contrast but his voice sounded calm and
polite. I seethed silently with frustration. Drianon be my
witness, I was going to make a Solstice vow to learn every
tongue spoken from the wilds west of Solura to the eastern
ocean and down to the southern archipelago.

The Sheltya entered the room, four of them, gray-
cloaked, gray-hooded. The leader put back her hood, revealing a long face with deep-set, arrogant eyes and
satisfied superiority curving her smile. Her cut-close hair
was a blond almost white and her skin was so pale that
veins showed blue at temple and neck. An ice maiden. No,
that mouth was anything but frigid, and worse, those
opaque eyes were lit with a dark intelligence.

She waited, perhaps a sign of respect or more likely calculating to put the onus on the aged Cullam. The old man leaned heavily on his stick, palsy shaking him. Sorgrad beside him looked apprehensive and awe-struck all at once, just like any other son or nephew of the house. Cullam spoke; his voice was firm and authoritative, for all the uncontrollable shudder in his hands. Whatever he was saying, he was displeased. The man next to the woman in charge put back his hood with reluctant hands, his tone defensive as he answered Cullam's accusations.

The woman cut across them both, her voice sharp. I watched the figures behind her, both anonymous beneath gray cloth and thought I caught a glance in my direction, a glimpse of eyes neither blue nor brown. A faint chill fingered my shoulder blades and I fought an impulse to shudder. I slid my feet silently on the flagstones to put Merial fully between me and whoever lurked beneath that hood.

As the Sheltya raised voices on both sides, I noticed uncertain looks passing across the hearth and around the room. Taegan was frowning now, anger rising above his apprehension, keen to start asking his own questions.

"You say you are a scholar?" The woman's clipped accents notwithstanding, her Tormalin was precise and clear. She took a few paces forward and fixed Usara with a disdainful stare.

"That is correct, my lady." Usara bowed with exquisite courtesy. "Of Col, and I am most eager to learn the history of your mountains and of your people—"

She cut him off with a contemptuous laugh. "Why do you lie when we can see right through your pretense? You are a deceiver and a sham."

"I assure you, my lady—forgive me, I know neither your name nor title—but—" Usara's high cheekbones were colored with temper.

"You are a mage, a dealer of false magic." She raised her voice to drown his soft politeness. "Tergeva!" She stabbed one long white finger at him. Whatever this meant, it was unwelcome news to these hospitable people. Everyone close to Usara took a hasty step away. Sorgrad did the same, face mirroring the shock around him, but the woman turned her accusing finger on him.

"Tergeva na tures," she spat. "Misaen en shel tures."

Sorgrad answered her back robustly. I missed his words as Merial turned toward 'Gren, sadness in her eyes. 'Gren nodded regretfully. I'd never seen such mortification in his face.

"You there, woodswoman! You are with them!"

I tried to look innocent, silently cursing Merial for stepping aside. "I am just traveling with them—"

"That is no excuse. Nor do I believe you. There is word of the mages of Hadrumal suborning the Folk of the Forest. I see your presence as proof of such a plot!"

Didn't this bitch let anyone finish a sentence? I kept my face bemused as the woman spoke on in the Mountain tongue. Halcarion knows what she told them; Damaris looked utterly betrayed and Kethrain began weeping silently into a handkerchief.

Who was this arrogant shrew, coming in to play judge and jury without so much as a by your leave? That her accusations were in some sense true was beside the point. I stood expressionless under her harangue, soon as isolated as Sorgrad as everyone edged away. She was someone with enough power, both by magic and custom, to do exactly what she wanted. That made her extremely dangerous. Not that that was going to bother 'Gren. He came sauntering around the hearth to stand beside me, a mocking smile on his face as he bowed to the woman. He said something that halted her in mid-tirade and brought all her lackeys up short. Again, I caught a disquieting glimpse of that rearmost hood turned toward me.

"Don't make them mad, 'Gren," I warned. We needed to get something besides our necks out of this unwelcome turn of events. I began searching my mind for options.

"You will quit this place now, at once." The bitch was back to Tormalin, her sweeping gaze encompassing us all.

She pointed dramatically to the doorway, still open to the night. "No fess will give shelter to such deceivers!" She had a flair for the dramatic to rival Niello, I thought contemptuously. She also had a fine-braided leather belt around her trim waist, a little purse, a knife and a few other oddments tied to it, hanging against her unadorned gray gown. Someone must be raising that color of goat exclusively for Sheltya use.

"Kovar en ria—" one of the younger girls spoke up without thinking, blushed scarlet and hid her face in her hands. The Sheltya woman stared incredulously around to see who had dared to voice an objection. She took a deep breath, a withering look in her eyes.

Before she could speak, Taegan stepped forward. "Kovar al tures," he said firmly to Sorgrad. "Ilk marist en firath." His voice cracked a little and he looked beseechingly at Cullam.

"Sikkar," the old man confirmed. This time it was his turn to drown the woman's protests, shouting her down with an unexpected authority. Disquiet ran rife around the room.

"What are they saying?" I demanded of 'Gren.

"The bitch wants to put us out into the night," he said, eyes bright. "Taegan is claiming right of travel truce and old Cullam's backing him."

"May I say something?" Usara's mild request was so unexpected it silenced everyone. "Please will you translate for me, Sorgrad? First, if Cullam is in any way able to vouch for the truth of my words, I would be very grateful for him to do so." The mage folded his hands together, looking about as dangerous as a milk-fed pup but with unmistakable authority in his bearing. "It is true that I am a wizard as well as a student of history. I have the ring of a scholar of Col, though I do not wear it at present. Yes, I am a mage of Hadrumal, but I did not believe that would be an offense of itself against your customs, as long as I wielded no magic within your territory. Nor did I believe it was wrong for

Sorgrad to come here. As I understood the tale, he was banished from his home, not from the whole of the mountains in perpetuity."

He paused for breath and Sorgrad rapidly translated for those unable to follow the wizard's own speech. When Sorgrad finished, there was a tense moment until Cullam nodded.

"Sikkarl turat en tergeva," the old Sheltya said curtly.

Usara nodded as one equal to another. "I came to learn what I could of your history and your wisdom. The misunderstandings between lowlands and mountains are longstanding and many arise from ignorance. Knowledge can salve that ignorance and perhaps enable us all to live and work in harmony. As for magic—"

"Silence!" the woman shouted harshly. "You will not speak of such things on pain of death!"

That grabbed everyone's attention and I slid a hand inside my sleeve to check the knife I kept sheathed there. All my other weapons were up in the room where I had been sleeping, so if I only had one throw it had better be a good one.

Usara's unruffled calm made a mockery of the woman's flushed and angry face. He looked briefly at Cullam, at Sorgrad and then turned to Taegan. "I apologize that we have inadvertently trespassed on your hospitality and your good will. We meant no offense. Rather than bring further discord to your house, we will collect our belongings and leave at once. Please accept my most sincere regrets."

He bowed and made for the stairs. Sorgrad was relaying Usara's words to Taegan loud enough for everyone to hear, and from the time he was taking about it adding some amends of his own. Taegen's reply was understandably curt but not outright hostile. Sorgrad bowed deeply and followed Usara.

"Come on," I said to 'Gren. "Let's get our kit and clear out. Time to cut our losses and draw again."

He followed me to the stairwell door where I looked over my shoulder before going up. The Sheltya woman was in the midst of a nervous knot of women and girls, composure restored as she played the gracious lady answering their hesitant questions. Her male companion stood a little awkwardly by the younger men, none of whom seemed to have much to say for themselves. Cullam stayed next to Taegan, exchanging remarks in low voices and directing carefully neutral glances at the woman. The remaining Sheltya were still standing by the door, motionless apart from the breeze plucking at the hems of their cloaks. The one at the back turned a hooded head toward me again and this time I caught a flash of green eyes from within the shadow.

An inexplicable disquiet gnawed at me. These eyes were not the clear green of the Folk, echoing summer leaves, but had the cold pallor of the winter ocean. Why did that worry me so much? Sudden fear sent me fleeing up the stairs like a child seeking the sanctuary of blankets to shut out the night's terrors. I stumbled on the uneven risers of the steps.

"Slow down!" 'Gren exclaimed, his own boots scraping on the stairs as they spiraled up through the thickness of the wall. "What's the hurry?"

I paused, breathing heavily. "I—" I found I had no answer. "Why can't you cursed people build an even flight of steps!"

"Because uneven stairs trip up anyone trying to attack in the dark, why do you think?" 'Gren's literal-minded approach to life didn't miss a breath.

"What?" I stared at him.

"Different pattern in every rekin," he explained readily. "Go up and down them every day, and you never notice. Try being a stranger sneaking up in the dark and you'll go flat on your nose!"

"And I thought it was just you two who were paranoid." The thrill of dread had evaporated, leaving me feeling small and foolish. "I'll meet you back here."

Going up the next set of stairs, I reached the female floor of the rekin and passed through the smaller rooms set aside for married women until I reached the broad dormitory for girls and guests. I unlocked the little chest set at the end of my allocated bed and took out my kit-bag with a little regret. I'd been looking forward to finding out more about the finely worked Mountain Man locks that were traded the length and breadth of old Empire.

I shed my skirts without any compunction. Since we were already as welcome as a mangy dog, the household could be scandalized by me in my breeches. I wasn't about to go out into the dusk with only thin wool between the biting insects and me. I also swapped soft shoes for my usual boots, checking the daggers sheathed in the seams and the darts in my belt-pouch. I didn't trust that loud-mouthed virago down there not to try something to finish us off once we were beyond the shelter of the fess. I wasn't done with her either, I decided, loosening the dagger beneath my shirt sleeve and unbuttoning the cuff so I could palm the blade in an instant.

'Gren's double knock on the outer door set me stuffing the rest of my belongings anyhow into my bag. I hurried back to the stairway and found all three of them waiting for me.

"We will make our departure with dignity and courtesy," Usara said firmly. "I do not wish to cause any more upset."

"It's her can't keep her tongue behind her teeth," I objected. "What about—"

"We are leaving," said Usara, cutting me short just as ruthlessly as the woman.

"As long as Cullam is on their side, those other Sheltya can't make too much trouble for the soke." Sorgrad laid a hand on my arm, expression somber. "If we do anything to turn the old man against us, these people could find themselves without the help of any Sheltya when they really need it."

I studied him for a moment. "All right." I moved to let Usara lead the way down the curving stair, Sorgrad at his heel. As I walked down, I rubbed at my elbow as if I had inadvertently knocked it on the wall. I could feel 'Gren's eyes on the back of my neck but forced myself not to look at him.

Conversation more normal in pitch and tone was filling the downstairs room now, but everyone still fell silent when the four of us entered. A pathway cleared to the far door in an instant. Usara walked slowly, smiling to either side, for all the world like Messire D'Olbriot gracious to his tenants at a festival supper. Sorgrad followed him, expressionless but uncowed. I did the same, but as we drew level with the Sheltya woman, 'Gren halted.

"Mer dalta enres?" he inquired genially. "Dalrist maires reman ilkreal girast nor surel."

The woman blinked with startled outrage. The older women looked bemused, some of the girls giggled, and 'Gren took a pace closer to the Sheltya female, mischief in his smile. She stepped back as I moved forward, ostensibly reaching out for 'Gren's arm. We collided, I apologized profusely and hustled 'Gren past her, hurrying for the door where Usara was waiting, irritation in his eyes, faint suspicion in Sorgrad's. I kept my head down, hands thrust deep into my breeches pockets, not daring to look at the hooded figures standing to one side.

"Let's go," Usara said grimly as we walked through the compound beneath the unseen eyes of sentries. The kenneled dogs had been roused by the disturbance and barked inquisitively, a lantern bobbing through the gloom as someone went to them. We were passed out through the main gate without a word and took the track leading down to the river in continued silence. It was a pale blemish in the dark of the grass, everything colorless in the deep twilight, but with care there was enough light to be sure of our footing, with the brilliant stars and the lesser moon waning to its half in a clear sky. The air was cool but not unpleasantly so, fragrant with the moistness of dew refreshing the sun-parched grasses. We trudged on, the glen featureless in the darkness until the chatter of water over stones told us we were nearing the river. I looked in vain for any paling of the sky but Halcarion's Crown was still bright on the western horizon.

"Can we cross this without light?" Usara peered forward. "I don't think this is quite the time for me to raise magefire to show us the way."

I laughed dutifully at the feeble attempt at a pleasantry but the others stayed silent as we slowly picked our way across the stepping stones, luckily without mishap. I paused to fill my waterskin and the river was as cold as a mother's curse as I hurriedly rinsed the handkerchief I'd been clutching.

"We'll keep moving until daybreak," said Sorgrad suddenly. "We want to get clear of the soke and down to the villages as soon as we can."

"Then we can plan our next move," I agreed. I sucked at the shallow cut on the ball of my thumb, tasting the bitterness of the dried blood. Full-time cutpurses carry a sliver of horn to protect themselves from their own blades.

"Then we head down into Solura," Usara corrected me.

"I think you can lose the lordly tone now that you've finished impressing the girls back there." I was going to have my say now. "What's the point of going back to Solura? We know they've got the knowledge we want up here now. What we need is to set about planning a way to get it!"

The wizard halted, faint light reflecting off his balding head, his face in shadow. "Knowledge isn't some silver cup you can go about stealing, Livak!"

"Where's that written, O wise one?" I retorted.

"You can't say something's impossible until you've tried it, wizard." 'Gren's smile was a gleam of white in the darkness.

"Do you have a better plan?" inquired Sorgrad, a creak of leather suggesting he was putting his hands through his belt.

"Curse it, Usara; you were the one complaining about wasting time in the Forest. Now that we know where to look, why delay?"

The wizard ignored me, much to my irritation. "What exactly did that woman say? Did she give any reason for her hatred of our magic?"

Sorgrad's tone was both light and bitter at the same time. "We are apparently abominations in Misaen's eyes, a foul betrayal of Maewelin's goodness, polluting whatever we touch."

"Oh," said Usara blankly. He sighed. "If she had a rational argument, no matter how flawed, we might have some chance of pointing out the error in her logic. If it's a matter of entrenched belief, no amount of reason will prevail."

"So why bother arguing with her?" I demanded.

Usara peered upward to check the sky. "We should see the first arc of the greater moon tomorrow, shouldn't we? If we can make it back to Pastamar by the end of For-Summer and as long as certain people have remembered the Soluran calendar doesn't march quite in step with the Tormalin one, there's someone I need to meet."

"What are you talking about?"

"Spit it out, Sandy!"

"What's in Pastamar?"

Usara shook his head at all our questions. "Given we know Artificers can eavesdrop on conversations from quite some distance, I would prefer to get away from that unpleasant female before I discuss it further."

That silenced us all. We began the long and weary trudge up the side of the main valley and I struggled to contain my irritation. As soon as Usara was prepared to talk again, my first question would be what did he have planned to make up for having to spend the Summer Solstice in some benighted Soluran backwater. The next was how were we going about getting our hands on the undoubted knowledge of the Sheltya. Usara could give up if he liked, but I wasn't about to. I owed the bitch that much.

Seven

When our children were young, we moved to the milder lands of Dalasor. Their nurse would sing them to sleep with this song and its words of caution proved most effective in curbing their irresistible urge to wander the boundless plains that surrounded our steading.

> The rainbow offers many ways,
> To pass beyond the humdrum days,
> But so you may be lost.
> You cannot see your fate's disguise,
> When jewel colors blind your eyes,
> And you will rue the cost.
>
> The shadows open many portals.
> Twilight mazes foolish mortals.
> Do you dare step inside?
> If darkness swallows moon and star,
> If no sun shows you where you are,
> What then will be your guide?
>
> So keep your feet within the path,
> And do not wander from the hearth,
> And heed your mother's charm.
> Let well alone the broken light,

The gloom that mimics honest night,
And you'll bide safe from harm.

✦

Pastamar Town, Solura,
41st of For-Summer (Tormalin Calendar),
27th of Lytelar (Soluran Calendar)

"These people really know how to enjoy themselves." I
didn't bother muting my sarcasm.

"I'll bet it's harder than it looks," 'Gren protested.

We were watching a lad balancing one shaft of wood upright on the end of another. Given both pieces were about as
long as my arm but barely thicker than the circle of my finger and thumb, I suppose it wasn't that easy. The lad got the
balance right and the circle of admiring youths around him
rapidly broke away. The lad thrust upward, the top shaft
soared high, fell back, and he hit it smack in the middle with
the piece he still held, a full-blooded blow that sent it away
in a soaring arc. A cheer went up and a little boy went scam-
pering down the grassy strip that divided vegetable gardens
from the wide muddy flow of the Pasfal. He retrieved the
billet of wood and marked where it fell with a piece of stick.
The youths were taking advantage of their noon break to
practice for the forthcoming Solstice celebrations.

A gate opened in one fence and a woman looked out to
see the cause of the commotion. She shouted, and after a
few defiant responses the lads drifted away through the alleys that led up to the market square and the high road. A
few yelled mocking insults, but only after the woman's gate
was safely closed. The sweet scent of roses floated on the
breeze. Most of the fences were covered in pink-edged yellow blooms and we had left our landlady debating when
would be the best time to cut hers for the mid-summer door

garland. Early enough to steal a march on her neighbors, late enough that the blooms would not drop too soon, that was her dilemma.

"When is the Solstice?" I asked 'Gren as we continued to wander aimlessly upstream, chewing on rough bread and sharp yellow cheese. "I can't recall when I last saw an almanac."

"Yours or theirs?" He offered me a bite of his cold bacon.

I gave him a look. "Solstice is Solstice wherever you are, 'Gren. That's the whole point of us being here."

"Four days from now," he told me after a moment's thought, "and they get two days' holiday."

"We'd get five in Ensaimin," I grumbled, "as well as a lot more exciting sport than peasants beating the sap out of defenseless bits of firewood."

"There's going to be bonfires," 'Gren volunteered. "And a venison roast. Lord Pastiss gives the town some stags for the festival."

As well he might, given he was so keen for them to break their backs earning their days of leisure. I looked up at the massive bulk of Castle Pastamar, the great keep distant and unassailable inside the ring of its walls. Tall towers were spaced to give warning of any assault and in particular to keep watch on the great span of the bridge. The stone arches rose above us as we wandered along the bank, marching away across the river low in the summer heat. Lord Pastiss's device, the silver boar's head on a blue ground, was on a carved and painted stone shield above the central span, on the pennants that fluttered from the guard posts at either end of the bridge and flying from just about every vantage point on the great gray fortress. It had to make him feel important to see his emblem everywhere, something to make up for his fiefdom being mostly made up of peasants grubbing a living from scrubby pasture, untamed woodland and rank marsh.

Wagons rattled across the bridge, halted to pay their dues

and voices drifted down to us, arguing the rights and
wrongs of Soluran duties levied by the wheel rather than by
the axle. Understanding them was some reward for spending the endless walk back down the length of the Pasfal
badgering Sorgrad to teach me what he knew of the Soluran
tongue and extending my knowledge of the Mountain
speech. It had given me something to concentrate on when
my impatience with Usara threatened to boil clear over into
rage.

'Gren looked at the muddy path beneath the nearest arch
of the bridge with disfavor. We'd kept reminding each other
to look to the long game but I wasn't going to do that for
much longer and nor was he. "So when did Usara say this
mysterious person was due?"

In unspoken agreement we turned back up into the little
town and I remembered again I needed to find someone
hereabouts to resole my boots. "He said the Solstice holiday." I paused at the edge of the street, hard-packed earth
without so much as a cobblestone. That was no particular
problem with the summer sun keeping it dry, but come the
autumn rains it would be axle-deep in mud. Well,
whichever way the runes fell, I would be long gone by then.
Frustration surged up within me; this was like a bad dream
I'd once had, being stuck in a game where for every winning throw I lost twice the coin on the next hand, but for
some reason I'd never quite grasped I couldn't just throw in
the runes and walk away from the table. No, it was more
like being stuck in one of those pointless mazes that were
currently all the rage for the Tormalin nobility. Or had that
fad passed? Fashions could change a great deal in the quarter-year I'd been on the road, couldn't they? I suddenly
found myself missing Ryshad horribly.

"This friend of your boy had better bring something useful to the party," muttered 'Gren. "We've come a long way
from the uplands for nothing, if he hasn't."

"He says this person will know how to contact Anyatimm
in the mountains south of Mandarkin and make inquiries of

the Sheltya up there." My calm reply was a notable achievement given I'd argued the point with Usara all the way from the uppermost tributaries of the Pasfal down to this broad and barge-laden waterway.

"Who's to say that Sheltya woman hasn't warned every rekin, fess and soke against us from the Gap to the Wildlands?" retorted 'Gren.

"You go and convince Sorgrad then," I snapped. "As long as he's backing the wizard, we either go along with him or strike out on our own." Sorgrad had been adamant with all the authority of an elder brother that we retreat long enough for the echoes of our precipitous expulsion to die away.

I felt an odd qualm of fear, and not for the first time, as I contemplated going back to the mountains. Was I turning coward? Was it the lurking realization that if I found myself facing Saedrin's questions at the door to the Otherworld Ryshad would be left on this side, grieving for me?

'Gren was muttering, hands shoved crossly in his pockets.

"Come on, maybe it won't be so bad spending the festival here." I turned down the broad street, the gables of cruck-framed and thickly thatched houses on either side. Shops and workrooms were set nearest the roadway, households living in the next room back, kitchens and the like beyond. A few of the long low buildings had clouded glass in their windows, but most simply had wooden shutters and none looked very secure; I doubted if anyone had anything worth stealing though. We skirted around a noisome heap of plaster being mixed with dung where some keen peasant was mending his mud and wicker walls.

Soluran notions haven't progressed as far as inns. Anyone with money or influence stopping here stayed in the castle; the more important, the closer they lodged to the keep where Lord Pastiss and his family held court. Everyone else had their choice of the various houses that sold ale, offered food or let out rooms. Solurans patch together a living in many and varied ways.

I pushed open the door to our lodging. The stale and sweaty odor of the dim interior told me our hostess had acquired another lot of discarded clothing from somewhere. She made most of her coin begging worn-out garments from her neighbors, washing and mending them and then selling the shoddy goods back again. For all that, she reckoned herself comfortably off. She had proudly explained to me that what I had taken for oddly shaped cobbles underfoot were in fact the joint ends of cattle bones, split and driven into the earth. It was a hardwearing surface apparently, warmer to the touch than stone and for these parts reckoned luxury.

There was no sign of Sorgrad or Usara so I shut the door and looked at 'Gren. "Where do you suppose they are?"

"Getting some food?" he suggested hopefully.

"Livak!"

To be hailed by name so far from home instantly turned my head. A heavily built man rode up on a stubborn-nosed black horse. The man's close cropped hair and full beard were much the same color as his steed's and his neck about as thick. He wore a scarlet cloak over a chainmail hauberk, shoulders massive with the padding of his arming tunic, but the size of his hands on the reins showed most of his bulk was honest muscle. A few peasants glanced incuriously at him; men in mail, long swords at their belt were a common enough sight in and around the castle.

"No wonder Usara wasn't telling." And I'd just thought the wizard was enjoying having the whip hand for a change.

"So who's the dancing bear?" 'Gren was ready for any amusement this new turn of events might offer.

"His name's Darni." I laughed at the notion of the burly warrior with a ring through his nose, capering to the goad of a stick. "But you don't get inside the reach of a bear's chain, do you? This one's just as dangerous."

"Livak," Darni greeted me with a curt nod, as if we'd spoken no more than a few days since. "Or are you going by something else? Terilla, wasn't it?" His slab of a face was as hard to read as ever beneath the obdurate beard but this was as close as he was going to get to a joke.

I smiled back thinly. "Livak will do." Terilla was the name I'd given this charmless bastard when I'd been pretending the valuable tankard I was selling was my own and he'd been pretending to be an honest merchant buying it. " 'Gren, this is Darni, agent to the Archmage. He's the one who gave me the choice of working for Planir or being chained up and handed over to the Watch."

'Gren grinned up at Darni. "Looks like you owe our girl then, pal."

Darni looked down at him. "Besides saving her life?"

"You and half the wizards of Hadrumal," I scoffed. "Anyway, we'd already escaped from the Elietimm before you turned up." As I spoke, something teased at my memory but fled before I could grasp it.

"So where's 'Sar?" Darni turned in his saddle and I realized he had a companion. The second man urged his horse forward. He was of common height and build with middling brown hair and the pale skin of someone used to an indoor life. His eyes were large, liquid brown, a shade darker than his hair and wide-set beneath high, arching brows. His undistinguished face was adorned with luxuriant mustaches, chin clean-shaven apart from a tuft of beard.

"So who's your friend?" I countered.

"My name is Gilmarten Forn," the stranger replied obligingly, a Soluran lilt to his words. He swept off his lavishly plumed hat and made a creditable bow for a man on horseback. "I am of the fifth order of Eade and professed to Lord Astrad of Castle Stradar."

"Good for you," murmured 'Gren.

"A pleasure to meet you." I was about to say I had no idea where Usara was when I saw the mage hurrying toward us, Sorgrad walking more slowly behind him. "There's your wizard."

Darni dismounted and accosted a rather vacant-looking boy, giving him a couple of coins. "Here, you, take these horses up to the guard stables at the castle. Tell the commander to stable them on Lord Astrad's authority." The boy gaped. "Just do it." Darni unhooked his saddlebags and glared at the lad. "What are you waiting for?"

The man Gilmarten slid from his own horse, face alight with curiosity as he studied Usara. The lad decided he'd rather brave the known evil of the Guard commander than risk further words with this dangerous-looking stranger and hauled the animals off hastily.

"Darni, good to see you," Usara said a little breathlessly. "I wasn't expecting you for another couple of days."

"Planir said it was important," replied Darni. "So, where can we talk?"

I pointed to a house with a besom nailed up over the door, Solurans not going in for real tavern signs. "Over a drink?" The midday thirsty had already gone back to their labors. The place was nearly empty when we went in and, under Darni's hard-nosed glare, those still idling over their tankards decided they had better places to be.

We sat on low stools and were served with palatable ale, 'Gren and Sorgrad studying Darni, Gilmarten watching Usara, and the wizard glancing at everyone in turn. I caught his eye and held it. "So now that I know we're to have the pleasure of Darni's company, what next? How soon can we be back in the uplands?"

Usara looked shifty. "I think we have learned as much as we are likely to on this trip, Livak. Darni is on his way back to Hadrumal and we should travel with him. He's all the escort we'll need through the Great Forest, and once we're back in Ensaimin we can get a coach to Col and pick up a ship there—"

"You just rein it in, wizard!" I sat, open-mouthed. "You're quitting?"

"I'm acknowledging we have come to the end of our

journey." He cleared his throat. "We have determined that there is aetheric lore in the traditions of these Sheltya and that is valuable information. Planir can decide how best to pursue it."

"What we want to pursue is that cold-faced piece of work who threw us out!" I retorted.

"When she can turn every single mountain dweller against us, needing no more than her unsupported word?" demanded Usara.

"You never had any intention of going back, did you?" I cursed myself for a trusting fool.

"I thought it possible that Gilmarten might be able to help," replied Usara, trying to sound affronted. "That turns out not to be the case, so I'd say that has to be the end of the matter for the moment."

"Hold hard." I raised a finger. "How do you know that, if the pair of you have only just met?" I swung around on my stool to give the newcomer a searching look.

"It is true that we have only just met," he said politely, "but we have been in contact for some days now."

"You're another—" I managed to stop myself from punctuating my words with obscenities—"wizard?"

"Of course," Gilmarten nodded, faintly puzzled.

"You've been in contact for some days?" I rounded on Usara who had the grace to redden. "What's going on?"

"I've been looking into the ways Solurans train their wizards." Darni replied for the mage with the arrogance I'd so disliked before. "Gilmarten is coming to Hadrumal to meet Planir. Once it looked increasingly likely your scheme would come to nothing, Planir told me to meet 'Sar here and escort him home."

Darni would be taking goods home to the Archmage while I was left empty-handed? Not if I could help it.

"So you've been in touch with Planir as well, Usara? You didn't think to mention it? Have you had any interest in our search or was I just saving Planir the cost of hiring you a wet-nurse for your journey?" I wasn't about to give him the satisfaction of losing my temper but rage was scalding my throat and boiling behind my eyes.

"I think that I have made best use of so much traveling by handling several commissions at once," replied the mage pompously.

"Most folk reckon a fool chasing two hares is going to end up with neither," I snapped.

"If he doesn't want to see the task through, we're better off without him." Sorgrad spoke up from the corner where he had been sitting silently watching. "We'll just take the road east and do it that way."

"Which puts us halfway back to Messire as well," 'Gren chipped in, never slow to take a hint.

I nodded and nailed on a broad smile. "It always was an even bet Gidesta would pay off better, wasn't it?"

Sorgrad was unconcerned. "It was worth testing the water here, since we were coming to the Forest anyway."

"I'm sorry?" Usara was baffled by this rapid change in mood.

I waved a dismissive hand. "Don't worry about it. You just do as Planir tells you. Messire will pass on what he thinks you need to know."

"In due course," added Sorgrad.

"So, you are a mage as well?" I turned to Gilmarten, who was looking frankly bemused. "But here in Solura, you aren't under Hadrumal's thumb?" I was all polite curiosity, like the Tormalin noble ladies who'd patronized me to screaming point over the Winter Solstice.

"No, we follow a rather different tradition," he replied slowly. "If a child proves to have magic in his nature, it is required by royal law that a mage tests his potential. If it is strong enough to train, the child must be apprenticed to an established wizard or be branded and confined." With me, 'Gren and Sorgrad all looking expectant, Usara preoccupied with the implications of Sorgrad's words and Darni, aloof as ever, slowly drinking his ale, Gilmarten was drawn into filling the silence.

"The kings of Solura have been rightly concerned at the potential dangers of rogue magic. No mage may have more than one apprentice of less than four years' standing at any one time and he remains responsible for the conduct of all apprentices for life, whether they stay with him or look for advowson elsewhere."

"Advowson?" Sorgrad was listening with more than a pretense of interest.

Gilmarten leaned his elbows on the table. "The most proficient of mages are retained by a Lord to work for the good of his fiefdom. Though, of course, a Lord is subject to severe penalties under royal law, if he misuses his wizard's skills. Every other mage within the offender's order can be set against him if need be."

Usara looked up. "What is the significance of an order?"

"An order denotes the lineage of apprenticeship," explained Gilmarten readily. "I am of the fifth order of Eade. Eade was a noted wizard admired by many. His apprentices were therefore styled the first order, those that they taught the second, their pupils in turn the third, and so forth."

I had no interest in this and stepped in when the Soluran took a breath. "You and Usara will have plenty to talk about on the way to Hadrumal then. We'll travel through the Great Forest with you, Darni, but after that you'll have to manage on your own. The roads down to Col should be safe enough once the harvest's underway. No bandit with any sense works the roads when they're choked with wagons, even if he does see pullets ripe for plucking going by." I smiled sweetly at Usara.

"You'll be heading east, I think you said?" Darni wasn't about to rise to my bait. "You'd better take care in Dalasor. There'll be mercenaries raiding north out of Lescar at this season."

"If they're any good, we'll probably know them." 'Gren was unconcerned. "If not, it'll be easy enough to leave them grinning up at the thistle roots."

Darni turned his attention from the middle distance. "You've spent time in Lescar? Who with?"

"Wynald's war band, the Brewer's Boys, Arkady the Red . . ." Sorgrad ticked them off on one hand and frowned.

"Strong-arm's Corps and the Ast Maulers," supplied 'Gren with an air of happy recollection.

"When were you with Arkady?" inquired Darni suspiciously.

"We were at Seye Bridge, if that's what you're asking." Sorgrad sat upright in his corner.

"On what side?" Darni similarly braced for action.

I looked for my quickest route to an exit; there was no room in here for bystanders as well as a brawl.

"Both," grinned Sorgrad.

Darni's sudden laugh was deafening in the low-ceilinged room. "I'd better pay for the ale then."

With a free drink in his hand, 'Gren would rather swap tales of mayhem and booty than see if he could punch Darni's teeth out through the back of his neck, so I relaxed on that score. Darni began explaining his own circuits of the endless circles of Lescar's civil wars so I caught Sorgrad's eye and jerked my head minutely toward the door. We needed to talk and since Usara had pointedly shifted his stool around to exclude me from his conversation with Gilmarten, this looked like the ideal time.

I drained my ale and stood up. "Time for the necessary." Once outside I sat on a bench in the sunshine and closed my eyes. A shadow fell across me and I squinted up to see Sorgrad silhouetted against the bright sky. "So are you serious about going east or did you just want to knock Sandy onto the back foot?"

"Now that we know Sheltya really do have the knowledge we want, I'd say we try Gidesta." He sat beside me.

"That woman throwing her weight about in Hachalfess won't bother sending word that far." Sorgrad looked grim.

"You really think she'll be doing that this side of the Gap?" I was still not convinced.

"Oh, most certainly," Sorgrad assured me. "That's why we had no choice but to come back down to the lowlands. We'd have got no more help, not even shelter, once the word had gone around that we were to be shunned." He smiled. "You didn't think I was just doing it on Sandy's say-so, did you?"

"Hah!" I vented my irritation loudly. "He's been playing a double game all along. Do you suppose a wizard ever deals honestly? I was hoping he'd be able to make use of this for me." I held out a little knife, the kind for paring nails or cutting string. Its scabbard was worn and tattered, the loop of leather at its top stretched and torn. You would have to look closely to even see that it had been cut through.

"That's what you got off the Sheltya woman?" Sorgrad took it and studied it. "It's been a while since you and 'Gren worked jostle and cut but you haven't lost your touch, have you?"

"What was it he said to her anyway?"

Sorgrad chuckled. "He asked if she had any sisters. Said a woman with her kind of spirit gives a man more horn than a billy goat in rut." He handed me back the knife. "So what did you think Sandy would do with it?"

"Listen in on her conversations, track her to some other Sheltya, I don't know." I shrugged. "It seemed like a good idea at the time."

"Mages and magic are nothing but trouble," Sorgrad reminded me. "Let's roll for a new start in Gidesta. We can hand over what we find to this Messire of yours and he can have the pleasure of haggling with Planir."

I sighed. "Do you think we will find anything back east? I feel I've wasted half a year chasing Eldritch-men in the shadows and got nothing to show for it."

"It's long odds but those pay off best." But Sorgrad's face betrayed his own doubts now that it was just the two of us alone. "If we can track down anyone who knows anything of Sheltya or their lore, I'll do anything short of selling my arse to pin them down. I owe them a bad turn. I've lived with being driven from my home as a boy but Maewelin can drown me before I let them forbid me the whole of the mountains like that."

I looked around at his grim tone but he startled me with a smile. "More importantly, I'd forgotten how tedious the Soluran borders can be." He gestured at the sleepy little town, drowsing in the midday heat as it nestled beneath the overbearing walls of the castle. "Once he's spent a few days reminiscing with that Darni, 'Gren's going to be all fired up to get back to Lescar and some real action. We can't do that without your Messire settling accounts with Draximal for us, can we?"

"No, that's true enough." The reminder that more people than me needed a decent pay-off from this game stiffened my wavering resolve. I groaned loudly with frustration all the same. "I would say this feels like slipping back two paces for every one you take, but given how far we've walked it's more like a hundred leagues against ten!"

Sorgrad put an encouraging arm around my shoulders. "It's only good-looking princelings in ballads who trot off down the nearest track and find gold waiting in a heap at the end of it. There'd be no fun if the game was all that easy."

"I could stand a little less fun just at the moment," I said dryly.

"If you want boredom, then you're in the right place," he replied critically. "Solura's known for it, like its wool."

"And its horses." I sat up straighter. "If we're taking the high road back, we'll wear out some iron shoes rather than anymore boot leather. Usara should still have plenty of Planir's coin and I'll bet Darni isn't traveling on copper and good will. The Archmage can buy us some horses, don't you agree?"

"I'd say it's the least he can do," agreed Sorgrad. "How about we go and talk to this Guard commander and find out who does Lord Pastiss' horse-trading? I don't see any need to worry Sandy with anything more than the bill."

Which would also needle Darni, who fancied himself a judge of horseflesh. I got to my feet and turned my face determinedly to the next stage of this seemingly endless chase.

The Great West Road,
2nd of Aft-Summer

Eresken moved cautiously through the sun-dappled woodlands. The spicy fragrance of spruce and fir in the heights gave way down here to a damper, earthy aroma, rich in the warm, motionless air beneath trees thickly cloaked in summer greenery. Distaste distracted him. The evergreens hadn't been so bad; similar trees grew in the more sheltered valleys of home, even if to scarcely a fifth the height. The lowland forests had looked truly beautiful from a distance, clothed in their delicate swathes of fragile green. Close to the trees were positively ugly, each one grown randomly in all directions, marked by vine and damaged by weather, new growth warped by the scarring. Eresken lowered himself slowly to kneel behind the thick bole of a misshapen tree, the nubby bark moist with moss.

Teiriol joined him, taking pains not to stir the leaf litter of countless autumns beneath his heavy boots. "What do you see?" The younger man's face was set with anticipation.

Eresken pointed, the pale skin of his hand now tanned and scratched. "This is where we will hit them, my friend."

Teiriol frowned. "On the open highway?"

Eresken laid a hand on Teiriol's mailed shoulder, part reassurance, part mute warning. "I will make sure there are no witnesses. If anyone comes upon us, I will use Sheltya skills to simply wipe the recollection from their minds."

"When do you think they will be here?" Teiriol looked up in vain for the sun, hidden by the dense canopy of leaves. There was an unhappy note in his voice.

"Very soon," promised Eresken. "And it is imperative that these all die, you do understand that?"

Teiriol nodded but gnawed at his lip. "Some of the men have been worrying about violating travelers, the truce is sacred—"

"Sacred to us, yes, but since when have lowlanders and wizards observed such honor?" Eresken's smile was warm though his hand rested more heavily on Teiriol's shoulder. "And now we know that the villains of Hadrumal are not only using their false magic to plant their power within the Forest, they are allying themselves with the mages of Solura. Remember what the bones of the sokes told Sheltya at Solstice?"

"The Solurans have always shown us good faith." The doubts in Teiriol's voice were strengthening. "They trust us to keep eastern passes closed to Mandarkin. What if they close the lower valleys to us, cut off our trade?"

Eresken gripped Teiriol's shoulder until the pressure made him turn his head. "I don't understand these wizards' plots but we all heard how they are using sorcery to beguile the Suratimm, didn't we? We must deal with this threat first, to keep the Forest dwellers out of our fight with the lowlanders in the Gap. Didn't Jeirran explain?" Eresken's green eyes stared unblinking into innocent blue.

"Yes, he did, of course." Teiriol's bemused expression cleared to reveal new determination. "And killing these wizards will warn off the rest. This way we keep our quarrel with the lowlanders a fair fight. Misaen will either prove the justice of our cause with victory or condemn us to the beaks of the ravens." He sounded like a child reciting its letters by rote.

"This way, the fewest possible need die." Eresken released his gaze and his grip, satisfaction smoothing his brow. It was time these mages learned a little humility. Their cursed ability to defile the elements had been murderous when they'd had a boat full of wizards to call on, but this would be different. "Get yourself and your men in position. You'll know when to move."

Teiriol made his stealthy way back up the hill and soft chinking noises betrayed the armored force easing themselves closer to the road. Eresken moved to a vantage point above a large boulder tangled with undergrowth in a thicket of smaller trees. He closed his eyes with a cruel smile. "Right, you redheaded bitch, a little humiliation before the death you owe me and mine."

The clatter of hooves on the hard surface of the road struck echoes from the tree-lined sides of the defile. Eresken began to breathe deeply, words of enchantment a slowing rhythm on his lips. His eyes fluttered, rolling up in his head as the trance took him. That part of him that stayed aware hovered expectant in the back of his mind. Birdsong floated overhead, the sun was hot on his neck and the breeze stirred a fugitive scent of flowers. The peace was ripped apart by the terrified neighs of a horse, a scream was cut short and a cacophony of male curses came from several directions at once.

Eresken blinked and looked down at the chaos on the road where one man had been instantly thrown from his terrified horse. A feathered hat was trampled in the dust as the panicked animal believed itself assailed on all sides. That was the Soluran mage, Eresken noted with satisfaction. The wizard who'd come so foolishly spying in the uplands gave up the unequal struggle to calm his steed and kicked his feet free of the stirrups. Eresken bared his teeth and the animal shrieked, twisting away from unseen tormentors. Eresken cursed as the Soluran dragged the fallen mage from among thrashing, iron-edged hooves, saving his balding head at the cost of a deep gash to one thigh.

Where were Teiriol and his men? The only blond heads

he could see were the two who had sold themselves to the false magicians. Both had abandoned their horses at the first hint of trouble and stood back to back in the center of the road, hands drawing the swords from their belts. Eresken hissed with disgust. They had not been so armed in the uplands. No matter, neither wore mail or breastplates to save their skins.

Where was the redheaded slut? He moved for a better view and nodded with cruel glee. She was struggling to stay in her saddle, fingers twisted in reins and mane as her maddened mount writhed and plunged, driven to madness by the terror raking its mind. The big man forced his own horse beside hers, mastering the animal with main force and sheer brutality. Bloody foam from the beast's mouth spattered its chest and legs, eyes rolling white edged in its head.

"Vengeance later, whore," Eresken promised silently before reciting the precepts of trance once more. Where was Teiriol?

Teiriol was hesitating in the gully beside the road while the horses shied and balked at unseen terrors. The doubts that seemed so foolish when he was with Eresken assailed him with redoubled force. Yes, he'd heard the arguments for a strike against the Forest. Jeirran had carried everyone along on the flood of his eloquence. Why was he no longer so certain? Teiriol felt suddenly wretched at the prospect of explaining himself to Keisyl. What would his mother say? How had he fallen for Jeirran's blandishments?

But it wasn't just Jeirran, was it? Aritane had summoned other Sheltya and all had brought the same tale from the dark mysteries of the ossuaries of the different sokes. He shivered at the thought of those hidden bones, silent until the Solstice sun linked Misaen's realm to Maewelin's not five days since. The wisdom of ancient blood could not be denied. After thrice ten days of waiting and preparing, it decreed now was the time to carry battle into the lowlands.

"Do we go?" Ikarel's sly face was eager, the man licking

his lips with an unpleasant relish. His mail was already rust-ing and smeared with dirt, but his sword was bright and keen.

Another uncontrollable shudder rippled through Teiriol. "We go!" Sword before him, he scrambled out of the gully, Ikarel at one shoulder, the beggar boy Nol at the other. Un-reasoning fury spurred Teiriol irresistibly on. These lowland-ers would die beneath his blade to recompense him for being born to such a straitened bloodline. Their blood would requite that snowfall that robbed his father of fingers and feet. These spoils would make amends for the pitying glances from girls guessing his miserable patrimony down to the last pennyweight. The lowlanders were responsible for everything, with their greed and deceit, the foul magic of their wizards! His confused grievances dissolved into a killing rage.

Teiriol swung at the traitor before him. He spat a curse as his blow was turned aside and hastily blocked a scything stroke that tried to hack the jaw from his chin. Nol was jab-bing ineffectively, hampered by unfamiliar armor and more hindrance than defense on that side. Ikarel was trying to get a thrust in, but was vacillating with fear. The traitor's eyes flicked from side to side, face fixed. A searing pain clawed down the back of Teiriol's hand, blood fouled his grip, the sword slipping in his hand.

He hesitated and in that moment the traitor's low stroke shattered Nol's knee. The child fell, whimpering in agony amidst the rioting voices of men and horses. The spurting wound gushed scarlet until scant breaths later, he died on a choking sob, life's blood soaked away into the thirsty soil.

Horror almost betrayed Teiriol to the same fate. A rush of men he did not know, recruited by Jeirran's eloquence on the journey down from the heights, saved him. The boy's body was kicked aside by urgent feet and the traitor was driven back, all his energies taken up with staying alive be-neath the hail of hate-filled blows. Blades flashed bright in the sun beneath streaks of blood and muck as they rose and fell with the weight of untold years of grievance. Teiriol hacked at the man's guard, the sticky wetness of Nol's blood on his hands goading him to ever fiercer fury. He brought his sword around and down, again and again. The foe stumbled, hard-baked ruts in the road treacherous beneath his feet. Ikarel, still hovering, saw his moment and sunlight flashed on steel thrust in hard and direct.

In the instant Teiriol expected the razor-sharp point to cleave the traitor's neck, Ikarel was thrown backward, clean off his feet. Ripped from the mêlée and flung away, he hit a mighty tree with an audible crack. Branches splintered and, falling helplessly, Ikarel landed broken beneath them.

Two more died for a moment's lapse as the unseen assault startled them. The traitors were fighting with the coward's backing of false magic, Teiriol raged. He lifted his sword but something unseen was tying his arms to his sides, threatening to strangle him. Faint blue radiance crackled in the air, the snares of sorcery and terror choked him. As the men around him broke and fled, Teiriol stumbled backward, but the soil beneath his boots was splitting, crumbling, and betraying him with every step. He fell heavily, unable to save himself with arms pinioned, mired to the knee in broken clods of earth.

Eresken abandoned the youth's confusion and cursed at the scene below. The mages and the woman had taken cover behind a fallen tree, cowering behind the fat and bearded man who was swinging his massive sword two-handed to deadly effect. Five gory bodies lay in motionless testimony to the folly of getting within his arc.

A mage stood up and flung a handful of fire. It flew, straight as an arrow, at the foremost attacker. Clinging to his chest, it ate through mail and leather, devouring the man's clothing, his skin, his hair. The corpse collapsed in a shower of sparks, the metal of his useless armor glowing white hot. The sparks glowed against the dark earth and then began moving of their own volition, spreading and searching out another victim. One man looked down with horror as his boots ignited and the all-consuming flames seized him.

"Innat ar rial, nar fedrian rek!" Eresken concentrated on the balding mage with every fiber of his being. Satisfaction warmed his malice as he felt that mind, so focused, so disciplined, but so pitifully undefended. Working swiftly, Eresken wrapped it around with myriad images of the Forest, spiking the illusion with a terror of being lost in trackless woods that was inadequately concealed in the back of the mage's mind. Eresken felt how order and learning were so highly valued, and sowed seeds of whimpering fear in a distrust of the unknown. Rising panic at feeling abandoned and alone blurred the wizard's concentration and the ground beneath Teiriol's feet stabilized.

Howling wind came up from nowhere, from all directions and none, dust and leaves swirling around the attackers, the heavy gusts restraining them bodily as they sought to advance. The traitors were unaffected though, Eresken saw with anger, seizing their chance to take a stance either side of the big man, backs to the dubious protection of the fallen tree.

Eresken snatched at the second mage's mind. This was harder than the first, thoughts flicking rapidly from one notion to another. The Soluran's terror at the prospect of a violent death sparked frantic desire to do as much damage as possible. This impulse warred with fear of the consequences, constraints of law and an inborn reluctance to kill. Eresken thrust his own will deep into the man's mind, stirring up a maelstrom of long-forgotten events, unsought remembrance, distorting anything where uncertainty of recall offered his malice a fingerhold. As the man's recollection spiraled into chaos, Eresken started picking at the reason he could sense frantically groping for control.

A sharp pain at the back of his neck startled Eresken into an oath. He slapped a hand to his collar, as if at a biting insect, bemused to see a smear of blood on his palm. A sec-

ond sharp pain caught him just below the jawbone and a
dart fell to the ground with a cold gleam of steel. As he spun
around, Eresken's arcane senses, so long honed by harsh
discipline, easily pierced the tangle of undergrowth.

There she was, the redheaded whore, believing herself
safe as she crouched motionless, white-faced, lips bloodless. Eresken glanced back to the road where the three
swordsmen were now hard pressed, Teiriol and his follow-
ers now free from assault by the stricken wizards. Rage
threatened to curdle Eresken's concentration; the woman he
saw there was an image woven of false magic to cover the
bitch's folly as she tried to take him with her petty pinpricks. He lashed out to rip into the vulnerabilities he had
sensed in the wizards but now found those minds barred
against him. He battered harder, but could find no way in
through desperate focus on some archaic ward.

No matter. He would have his vengeance on the woman
and then deal with the rest. Eresken took a pace toward the
slut's hiding place but the ground seemed to shift beneath
him. This was no treachery of earth or water but his own
body was betraying him, he realized, as confusion between
eyes and ears threatened to make him nauseous. Eresken
felt his control slipping away like water running out between his frantically grasping fingers. A mad euphoria
soared within him; what did it matter? Freedom beckoned,
tempting, sensual, release from all care, duty and fear. He
had been drugged, Eresken realized dimly.

Scalding anger clearing his head just long enough for
him to seize on the first principle of mind over body, fundamental lore beaten into his memory. He drew breaths of
deepest trance, focusing within himself for the taint of poison and bending his will to burning it out. The confusion
still swirling around his consciousness began to recede and
Eresken reached for the nearest source of power to bolster
his own, drawing pitilessly on the frail resources of the
Mountain Men. They were only here to serve him, after all.

A single blow to the pit of his stomach sent him crashing

backward into the thicket. The breath was knocked out of him and, before he could gasp for more, knees crushed his ribs, hands gripping his throat sought to squeeze the very life out of him. Blood thundered in his temples. Eresken opened his eyes to see the woman above him, hatred burning in her green eyes. She knew him, he realized and, in that instant, he was glad of it. She would know who killed her. He dug nails into her hands, tearing at her skin, twisting to bite at her wrists. She would know that he had finally repaid her for the humiliation of being captured by her and her fellow spies. With a convulsive heave, he threw the bitch off, her fury no match for his greater weight. She would die at his hands as her lover had died at his father's. Eresken sprang to his feet, reaching for his sword.

Hot agony rippled through his gut. Wetness oozed down his belly and into his groin, warm slickness turning cold. Eresken groped beneath the heavy links of his hauberk to feel the hilt of a dagger driven up into his belly in the harlot's first assault. He fell to his knees as sickening pain flooded him, every pulse of his heart striking fresh torment from the wound.

"Save me!" Eresken poured every scrap of heart and will into a despairing appeal, reaching up and out and beyond the woods, past the gray crags of the stony heights, beyond the windswept expanse of the plains and out across the vast, trackless ocean. With a suddenness that made him gasp more than any shock of pain, another mind seized his. As he was lifted bodily away, consciousness crushed beneath a pitiless grip, Eresken welcomed oblivion rather than face his father's wrath.

He came to himself in a leafy hollow, so similar to the one he had left that he jumped to his feet, looking in all directions for the murderous trollop with her assassin's daggers. The knife that had stabbed him rattled to the ground.

"Calm yourself." The voice within his head rang with contempt, a stinging slap behind his eyes an added rebuke.

Eresken clutched at his belly. His trews and shirt were

torn and damp with blood but the skin beneath was whole. His fingers traced the cicatrices of a new scar with dismay.

"You can carry those marks as a reminder of your folly," the voice told him curtly. "Be grateful I was minded to let you off so lightly."

"You are indeed merciful," replied Eresken wordlessly with a sinking dread. "Where am I?" He snatched up the dagger.

"Just far enough away to keep you from being gutted like a seal pup." There was amusement in the voice now. Eresken breathed more easily; better to be the target of mockery than rage. "Get down to the road and head east," ordered the voice.

"Yes, Father." Eresken obeyed hastily, slipping and adding fresh scratches to hands and face. Reaching the road, he ran, armor heavy on his shoulders and rattling with every step. Sweating freely, his pace did not falter until he rounded a bend to see bodies strewn across the blood-stained track.

He skidded to a halt, clutching at his head with clumsy hands. Dark brown eyes looked out at the carnage and grim satisfaction curved Eresken's mouth in a smile not his own.

"Not what we hoped for but something can be made of it." The lips shaped words echoing and far distant. "Use this and if you impress me your earlier failure may be overlooked." The voice turned cold. "Disappoint and it will go hard with you."

Eresken staggered beneath a blow to the very center of his being, senses reeling. Then the presence in his mind was gone, leaving only an echoing memory of helpless blindness. To be used as another's eyes was bad enough when it was expected, he raged silently; to be taken like that unheralded was infinitely worse. Hastily stifling disloyal anger, Eresken took a deep breath and brought his hands together in front of him, palm to palm and fingers matched and spread. In a soft voice, he recited the incantations to center his mind afresh. That should satisfy any spies lurking to steal his thoughts, he thought in that one secret part of his mind he hoped was still inviolate.

Teiriol's troop lay all around, some hacked with swords but more struck down by magic. Three were burned beyond recognition by foul, creeping fire. Others lay unmarked but abnormal angles showed bones broken by the hammer blow of unnatural winds. One corpse was still smoking, a black score traced down from head to the shattered ruin of a foot, white bones stark in the charred flesh. Another lay with jaw shattered and hanging limp, the bones of the face broken like an eggshell with fragments driven deep into the brain, which showed gray and gelid in the depths of the wounds.

"How do they do this?" muttered Eresken aloud.

A feeble croak sought to answer him. Eresken looked around, startled. The sound came again and he followed it to the ditch beside the road. Distraught blue eyes looked up from a mire of leaves and blood. "Teiriol?"

"I ran away," sobbed the younger man. "I ran away. I was trying to bring them all back, trying to get them to rally, but once the lightning started, once I saw Seja hit—" He broke off with a cry of pain and Eresken saw his sword hand was useless, naked spikes of shattered bone sticking out of the wrist, the fingers hanging bloodless and limp, thumb all but severed. Teiriol cradled the ruin of his arm helplessly, weeping like a child.

"What happened?" Eresken shook him furiously but Teiriol was incoherent with pain and distress. Eresken seized his chin and forced it up; Teiriol's eyes widened at the shock of the sudden assault.

So that was the way of it, Eresken thought grimly as he stripped out memories, heedless of the pain he was inflicting. The mages had hit Teiriol's men with foulest sorcery, the swordsmen going on to hack down remaining resistance. The Mountain Men had died unable to defend themselves against double assault of spell and blade. The Soluran mage had sprung the woman from the empty air and they had run, the black-haired man slinging the wounded wizard over one shoulder, the traitors to the ancient blood on either side.

Eresken let go his grip on Teiriol and the younger man collapsed. Eresken walked rapidly down the length of road, checking every body, even those unrecognizable lumps of charred flesh. Some lingered, clinging desperately to life despite their injuries. Eresken ruthlessly snuffed any vital spark he found; there were wounds enough to explain the deaths. No one would suspect his hand in so thorough a slaughter and most would have died anyway, without rapid aid at least.

But he still needed Teiriol, for the present. Eresken walked back to the weeping man hunched over his agony. "I must summon help," he said breathlessly. "I must call Aritane, to bring Sheltya to save those not yet dead."

"Not yet—" Teiriol lifted his face, incredulous hope shining through the muck and blood. Eresken seized the boy's surge of longing, seeing Aritane pictured within his mind. He wove that pitiable yearning for home and healing into his own tight-focused appeal, masking his intent with Teiriol's piercing need.

"You must come, my love. Come to me. We have been betrayed, murdered, slaughtered. You must come."

Eresken tore himself away from Aritane's frantic appeals for explanation and direction. Her talents were notable for her race, he thought, but no match for any of his clan. Still, he didn't have much time. "What is that?" Eresken looked down the road, mouth open.

Teiriol turned his head and Eresken plunged the bitch assassin's dagger into the base of his skull, twisting the blade to leave the young man twitching helplessly, blindly for an instant of horror before death.

Pursing his lips for a moment, Eresken released the hilt of the dagger. It could stay in the wound for someone else to remark on, another pennyweight in the scales demanding vengeance. He scrambled rapidly up the hillside to the dell where he had been attacked. That whore would pay with her own blood for the shedding of his, he promised grimly. Eresken rummaged among the crisp leaves, peering at the dart he retrieved. There was still a faint smear glistening on it, rainbow mockery as he tilted it to the sunlight. Good enough.

Eresken drove the point into the back of his hand and let himself fall gracelessly to the ground. He seized the dizziness of the drug and nurtured it, forbidding the instinct to drive it from his blood. He heard movement on the road beneath but forced himself to stay motionless. If it were passers-by, no matter. They could hardly remove the bodies before Aritane arrived and no one was going to know any truth beyond what he chose to tell them.

He relaxed into the insidious charm of the poison, mind drifting idly around a hidden tether of inmost consciousness. Aritane's desperate thoughts brushed past, nearly missing him before horrified realization struck her. Eresken opened the surface of his thoughts to her, seemingly half insensible, coloring the sight of the corpses in his mind's eye with Teiriol's shame and anguish. "Beloved . . ." He infused that one despairing word with all the frustrated passion he sensed in Aritane, with the memory of their discreet kisses, her nervous delight at his exploration of her body, never yet satisfying her cravings, calculated to leave her always longing for more.

Now her hands were beneath his head, cradling him to the soft swell of her bosom, the galloping beat of her blood drumming in his ear, her breath rapid and ragged, hysteria threatening. Eresken warded himself discreetly from that mental turmoil but did nothing to soothe it. Opening his eyes, he let them roll upward before fixing with visible effort on her face.

"What happened?" Aritane was pale as milk, a vein throbbing at her temple.

"We came to parley, as we discussed—" Eresken coughed and tried to rise but collapsed as if the effort were beyond him. "The wizards, all we wanted was their under-taking to leave us to settle our disputes—"

"They attacked you? Under parley?" Aritane was trembling now, fury and shock rippling through her arms as she held Eresken close to her heart.

"We did not expect it." He allowed himself to feel bemused. "Even if they did not agree, we did not expect to be assaulted."

"What happened—"

He felt the first confusion clearing from her mind. She was wondering how he was spared when the rest were so bloodily slaughtered. Eresken thrust the image of the red-headed whore at her, no need to dissimulate as he struck her with his disbelief and outrage and the memory of poisoned darts.

"Then she was truly a spy?" cried Aritane in horror.

"Worse, she knew me." Eresken let Aritane feel the echo of the slut's hatred. "She was one of those who came to rob my father's house, at the bidding of the Archmage. They kidnapped me—I feared for my life . . ." He let her see the little boat driven through the ocean on the glow of false magic, he let her hear the cruel jests about eating him if his captors should go hungry on the voyage. "They came for me again!" Eresken flooded Aritane's mind with dread of retribution, hiding the fact that it was his father's wrath he feared. The terror was real enough to make shedding a few stifled tears easy. "I could not help them, I could hear them being killed, but I could not help them." He thrust image after image of the dying and the dead at Aritane, tainted with the dizzying seduction of the drug. She gasped and clutched him ever tighter.

Eresken could hear other voices down on the road. "Is that Bryn?"

"And Ceris," Aritane replied. "Rest easy, my love."

"No," Eresken forced himself up out of her embrace. "I must help, I must see what has happened." He got to his feet, careful to lean heavily on Aritane. This series of shocks left her ready to accept any offer of leadership, Eresken realized. Good. Now he must ensure that the rest of these half-trained hopefuls saw events as he wished. With Aritane struggling to support him, Eresken saw Bryn and Ceris walking slowly from corpse to corpse. Farther down the road were a couple more of the gray-clad fools whose names he had not bothered with.

Ceris stopped for a moment beside Teiriol's corpse, hands going to her face as she saw the dagger in the back of his head. "Treachery! Murder! Stabbed as he tried to flee or sue for mercy!" Her thoughts may as well have been shouted aloud, weak-chinned face bloodless beneath her head of golden curls.

"We met the wizards to ask for a parley," Eresken told them, barring his mind to their questing thoughts with a pretense of grief and pain. "We appealed to them to allow the Men of the Mountains to redress their grievances against the lowlanders in fair combat. They seemed to be listening courteously enough, so we relaxed our guard. We didn't wish to insult them with any suggestion of mistrust. Then they attacked us; the mages turned nature itself to wreak evil upon us." He ripped a few holes in his facade, giving them glimpses of apparent memories within.

"Tell us everything, from the beginning." Bryn strode toward them, intent darkening his eyes.

Eresken felt the force of the man's determination to wrest the truth from him and allowed his knees to buckle. Letting his arm slide from Aritane's shoulder, he slumped to the ground, the woman unable to support the burden of his dead weight. "Let him be," she snapped. "Can't you tell? They poisoned him!"

As she pillowed his head on a bundle of her cloak and straightened his limbs with gentle hands, Eresken wrapped himself in a cocoon of deception and lurked within, listening intently. Aritane's voice was as hard as diamond, he noted with satisfaction. The vulnerability he was exploiting remained unseen by anyone else, schooled as she was in the unflinching mask of the Sheltya.

"Look carefully, mark every death and the manner of it," she commanded coldly. "We will let every soke know how their sons spent their lives."

"To kill from afar and with such violence . . ." words failed one of the younger Sheltya, Remet. Eresken picked his name out of Aritane's mind unnoticed, matching the voice to a face still waiting for the strength of manhood, full of youthful appeal but without substance to either wit or convictions.

"That's what these mages do," spat Bryn. "Why do you suppose the lowlanders drove them into the sea so many generations ago?"

"What of Jeirran and his men?" the other woman gasped. Krelia, that was her name. Eresken recalled a nervous face and hands with nails chewed to their quick, a mind worn thin by endless demands, never taking time for herself.

"Who will tell Jeirran that his sister's brother was so foully slain?" asked Ceris of no one in particular, a sob in her voice.

"We must keep the Suratimm out of the battle," said Bryn with grim determination. "If they are truly working with the mages of Hadrumal."

"Of course they are! One of their spies struck down Eresken!" Aritane slapped all four with a sudden vision of the redhaired slut. "She was up in the Hachalfess trying to cozen Cullam, along with that wizard. How much more evidence do you need?"

Well-concealed satisfaction warmed Eresken. Aritane would do his work for him without need for further prompting.

"Then it is war?" Realization strengthened Remet's voice.

"We didn't want it and we didn't start it but we cannot let an outrage like this go unchallenged," Bryn answered him dubiously. "If we do, this slaughter could be visited on innocents in every soke, if lowlanders seize land with false magic at their back."

"We should fight," declared Aritane. "This is not just a struggle for the men of the sokes, not just a fight of swords and axes. We must support them against the false magic with every power at our command."

So the seeds he had planted and nurtured were finally coming into bloom, Eresken thought with relief.

"Sheltya are sworn to be impartial," Krelia whispered.

"In conflict between soke and soke, between fess and fess," agreed Aritane. "Where is the oath binding our hands when our people are to be driven naked into the snow?"

"The Elders—" Remet choked on a strangled objection.

"I will answer to the Elders," said Aritane defiantly. "As Sheltya loyal to no single bloodline, I must be sworn to the service of all or to none. I will either die in defense of my people, of all my people, or I will stand proud at my brother's shoulder when he has led us to victory and I will claim him once more as kin. Let the Elders judge me then. If they condemn me, then I will go north into the ice as the Alyatimm once did and face Misaen's judgment."

Inarticulate protest from Bryn escaped Eresken.

"You think they did justly?" Aritane was scathing. "To exile those who would use true magic in defense of their rights? What price Misaen's judgment now? The Alyatimm did not freeze and die, I can tell you that now. Eresken is of their blood, of their lineage. He brings word from far islands where his people live free and unchallenged. They are not afraid to use the true magic they have kept pure and strong. Even as we speak, they are defying the wizards and the Tormalins who stretch their greedy hands out over the ocean to seize yet more land."

Curse the woman, why couldn't she keep her foolish mouth shut? Eresken waved a feeble hand, instantly diverting Aritane.

She knelt beside him. "Are you with us?"

"Some water?" he asked breathlessly.

Bryn held a bottle to Eresken's lips as Aritane raised his head. "So you are of Alyatimm blood?" Mistrust hovered around the edges of his mind.

Eresken gazed deep into the man's eyes. "My forefathers' forefathers followed the men who called themselves such and went into the ice to face the judgment of Misaen. We call ourselves Elietimm and use the powers of true magic to survive in the cold islands of the northern ocean. We are assailed by Tormalin greed backed with the false magic of Hadrumal. I came looking for allies to help save my people and I found brothers in blood whose plight echoed our own."

Bryn nodded slowly and Eresken let fresh blood flow from his wounds to stain Aritane's dress and hands. "We have to get him back," she insisted.

Eresken relaxed in her embrace as the five wove power of mind over matter to carry them back to safety. Once this story was told and retold, reinforced with appropriate nudges from him, these pitiful Anyatimm would howl down from their mountains as if their forefathers had never been the cowards of legend. War in the Forest would spill out to crush the farmers of the lowlands after a few judicious incidents managed by himself. With all Tormalin eyes and arms drawn westward before the summer was out, his father could choose his moment to strike. Eresken relished reward and adulation to come, to be savored just as intensely as wrath and punishment were dreaded.

◢◤

The Great West Road,
2nd of Aft-Summer

"Slow down!" I was so out of breath my desperate appeal was barely a hoarse gasp. Stopping dead, I bent to ease the

catch in my side, drawing warm, sweet air deep into my
lungs. Blood pounded in my head. Sorgrad realized I was
no longer at his shoulder inside a few paces and halted,
'Gren doing the same. Darni slowed, red-faced and sweating like a pig. He let Usara slide from his shoulder, the wizard leaning heavily on his arm. "Saedrin's stones but you're
heavier than you look, 'Sar!"

Usara looked pale and queasy and my stomach was still
revolting from being moved about like a bird on a Raven
board by Gilmarten's magic. Never mind, we could empty
our guts when we had leisure to spare. Were we pursued?

Sorgrad must have heard my thoughts; he peered back
down the road. "No sign. I think we can take it a little
slower."

"Bless you," Gilmarten struggled, chest heaving, "for
that."

I wasn't so sure. "What about their enchanter? He could
be here inside a heartbeat—they come out of the shadows
like Eldritch-men!"

"He can do that wherever we are," pointed out Sorgrad
with irritating logic. "Let's clean our blades and get our
breath before the next bout." As he spoke, he led us to a hollow where we could see the road before being seen ourselves. Sorgrad stationed himself at the edge and indicated
a faint trail heading into the deeper woods. "We run that
way if need be and then swing back to the road." He began
wiping the streaks of blood from his blade, emerald flies
soon gathering around the enticing scent.

"I only run away from men with swords who are bigger
and nastier than me," grunted 'Gren, looking at his gory
gloves with distaste.

"And only if there are more than we can comfortably
kill," grinned Darni. His look of complicity with both
brothers gave me a serious qualm. Two of them was bad
enough, Drianon save me from a trio of eager brawlers.

"Won't your poisons have done for the enchanter?" Usara was limping heavily, a slow ooze of blood trickling from

the ragged tear in his breeches. He dabbed distastefully at it with the hem of his gown, brushing inquisitive flies away.

"Unlikely." I pulled my sweat-soaked shirt away from my neck. "It was tahn ointment."

"Not bluesalt?" 'Gren looked profoundly disappointed.

"There was no time," I apologized. "Poldrion willing, the tahn will keep him out long enough to bleed to death."

Gilmarten's eyes were bulging so wide he risked them falling clean out of his head and dropping into the dirt. I gave him a bright smile. "You're not wounded?"

"Thank you, no, my lady." He swept me a ragged bow. "A little shaken, I'll confess, but otherwise unharmed."

"They started it." 'Gren looked crossly at a shallow slice in his forearm. "Those shitty-tailed horses must be halfway back to Pastamar by now. What can I clean this with?"

"Here." Darni poured spirits on a rag ripped from his shirt and passed over the bottle. He dabbed at grazes on his own knuckles, hissing absently through his teeth. "You'd better be next," he nodded to me.

I looked at the gouges the Elietimm bastard had left in my hands but I had more to worry about than cuts and scrapes. "That enchanter, I knew him."

"I suspected as much," commented Usara, "when you started cursing his sexual practices."

"Firsthand knowledge?" joked 'Gren.

"No jokes, not now." I shot him a hard look. "Firsthand knowledge of his people, of the way they go ripping into your mind to pull out whatever they want." My voice shook and I held onto my hot anger, warmth against the chill of recollection. "That man—me and Shiv and Ryshad, we captured him when we were trying to get away from those accursed Ice Islands. He had some measure of authority and we aimed to trade his life for ours, if we were taken." I shook my head. "But he used his pox-ridden, whore-sucking magic to get away, vanished clean out of the boat." I took the cloth and scrubbed at my hands, welcoming the sharp sting ridding me of the foulness of his touch.

Usara looked up. "That he escaped, even under attack—"

"—and with my dagger in his guts," I interjected.

"—suggests he is powerful, which would argue we don't assume he's dead until we've seen the body," concluded the mage thoughtfully.

"Until we've seen the body, cut off his head, stuck it on a stick for the ravens to play with and burned the rest to ashes," corrected 'Gren. "You can do that last bit, wizard," he said to Gilmarten generously.

The Soluran mage mumbled something noncommittal.

"An Elietimm enchanter backing an attack by Mountain Men?" Darni looked sharply at me. "You're certain it was the same man?"

"We all look alike?" Sorgrad smiled at him without humor. "If our girl here says it was the same man, it was the same man, friend."

I nearly told Sorgrad I could fight my own battles against Darni but decided I was content to have the arrogant bully outnumbered for the moment. Darni reached for his bottle of cleansing spirits. "Drop your breeches, 'Sar. That needs cleaning and stitching or you'll have maggots in it before the day's out."

Usara unlaced himself without protest and we all winced at the ragged gash ripped through a massive purpled bruise on his thigh. I was amazed he had managed to walk at all. Darni sloshed spirits into the cut and Usara went as pale as old bone, mouth gaping on a silent scream.

"Just try to keep still," murmured Darni as he sacrificed the rest of his shirt for dressings. 'Gren caught my eye and mouthed something at me. I shook my head, mystified, but got it on the second attempt. *Dancing bear.*

I could see what he meant; Darni stripped to the waist showed impressive muscles beneath a pelt of black curly hair that would probably fetch him an arrow from a careless hunter. I wondered if his wife took a hearthrug to bed when he was away making mischief for the Archmage.

Usara sat down heavily, gray around the mouth and eyes. "Let me find the tahn ointment," I rummaged through my own scrip. "Dab it on, to numb the skin."

"And my wits along with it?" Usara managed a thin smile. "I don't think we'd better risk it."

"Your choice," Darni grunted, threading a curved needle.

"A moment." Gilmarten leaned forward to proffer a small flame dancing on his bare palm. "Heat the metal in this, to prevent corruption getting into the wound."

Usara went paler still as he watched the needle tip glow red and then white. I cast about for something to distract him. "So, Usara, we have an Elietimm enchanter hereabouts that we last saw working for that Ice Islander bastard who was so keen to kill us all the year before last. What do you make of it?"

"We also know that Ice Islander was hoping to claim Kellarin for his own." Usara spoke through gritted teeth as Darni set to work. "Toremal and Hadrumal between them put paid to that ambition."

I held the wizard's gaze with my own. "So what's this enchanter doing here?"

"The people of the mountains do have justified grievances. If they were to be roused—" Usara broke off with a stifled curse, beads of sweat trickling into his eyes that had nothing to do with the heat.

"Sorry," muttered Darni in a perfunctory tone. "It's a diversion, has to be. Stir up trouble on a different flank and your opponent has to spread his forces."

"The lords of northern Solura would be most perturbed at unrest hereabouts," chipped in Gilmarten, looking worried. "We rely on the Men of the Mountains to secure our border with Mandarkin. If the passes are not guarded, Mandarkin will take advantage soon enough."

"Even more chaos in the west," I nodded. "Wouldn't that be nice for the Elietimm?"

"Everyone looking the wrong way when Ice Islander ships land in Tormalin on the spring tides?" Darni glanced up from his work.

Whatever his other faults, the man was not stupid, I reminded myself. "Or Kellarin."

Darni grunted and continued his careful needlework. "We need to know exactly what this enchanter is doing before we can counter him."

"Whatever they are planning, they didn't want to risk us getting wind of it," observed Sorgrad. "Bet you a penny to a pack-load that's why we got thrown out of Hachalfess."

"And he had Sheltya doing his dirty work there." 'Gren stripped off his jerkin and folded it around the soiled front. "That tall piece with the haughty manner at very least."

"So what are they up to?" All I met were blank looks, even from Usara, though that changed back to clench-jawed endurance in the next instant.

"That'll do," said Darni with satisfaction, snipping off his thread. "Now we have to tell Planir what is going on." He stuck his sword into damp leaf mold to clean it, scraping out a hollow in the black earth where he buried the stained remnants of his shirt. "We don't have much of a tale though." He sucked his teeth in an unattractive manner.

"We've more than you think." I hesitated; this was hard to put into words. "When the woman threw us out of Hachalfess, do you recall the others with her, who didn't show their faces? One of them was that selfsame enchanter I just tried to gut, I'm sure of it." I clasped my hands together to stop them shaking.

"You didn't say anything at the time," said Sorgrad cautiously.

"I only realized when I saw him today." I looked at my hands, pleased to see them steady again. "There was something nagging at the back of my mind about what happened at Hachalfess, but every time I tried to think about it I got jittery, worrying about going back up into the heights, about having aetheric magic used against me. You know I'm not given to fretting, and anyway, it all stopped as soon as I knocked that bastard off the board with the tahn. He was messing with my mind somehow, I'll bet any purse." Anger outweighed any other considerations now.

"You're sure of this?" Darni's skepticism was ill hidden behind his thick beard.

"Guinalle told me the easiest way to manipulate a mind is to enhance fears or desires already present," said Usara thoughtfully. "Which is strictly forbidden," he added hastily.

"Sheltya do it," said Sorgrad, grim-faced. "When they are punishing someone."

"So you can place this enchanter with the woman. What's the significance?" Darni was sticking to the original scent with characteristic tenacity. "What we need to know is whether or not we've still got them on our tail!"

"I can scry for them," Usara said slowly. "I'd prefer it if we can find a different medium to use. I don't fancy working in a handful of my own blood again."

"You know, that was brilliant." Gilmarten looked up from studying the laces on his boots. "I would never have thought of that, and if you hadn't been able to find that man we could have been utterly lost."

Usara smiled deprecatingly. "After you have run into aetheric magic a few times, you become more used to the notion that your senses may betray you under its influence. When it seemed I could not see any of you, I knew I had to turn to more certain means of sight."

"You couldn't have done it without the shielding chant Ryshad taught you," I pointed out.

"It was a little more than that," said Usara with an irritating superiority. "Guinalle and I have made considerable study of the ways we can ward ourselves against Artifice."

"Magic only gets you so far." Sorgrad was unimpressed. "Livak stuck the knife in him."

"Only because Gilmarten put her next to him," countered

Darni, mage's man speaking up in defense of his paymasters.

"I think Gilmarten's simulacrum of her was equally crucial," Usara winced as he foolishly tried to flex his leg.

"Yes, you're all very clever," interrupted 'Gren impatiently. "So, work your magic, Sandy, and find out if they're coming after us!"

Usara heaved a sigh and knuckled his eyes before sweeping meager strands of hair off his face. "Do we have something that will hold water with enough surface for scrying? Does anyone have any ink?"

Gilmarten wordlessly offered a little silver mounted and stoppered horn from the capacious bag at his belt. Darni stood up, frowning. "I had any number of things in my pack," he muttered crossly. "Cursed useless horses, no training worth their oats."

Sorgrad began turning out pockets in the breast of his jerkin. "There's no rim to this but if I can find a decent stone—" He held out a metal mirror the size of my hand.

"He always likes to know he's looking his best, my brother," mocked 'Gren.

"And to have means to send a signal, dazzle a pursuer, see around a corner in case the Watch are waiting," Sorgrad nodded in similar vein. "And to make sure I look good for the ladies, obviously."

Darni was unamused. "That's never going to hold water."

"If I might assist." Gilmarten reached for the mirror. The Soluran mage studied it carefully from both sides and then held it between his palms. A faint smile curved his lips as he concentrated and then he handed the metal back to Usara, now dished like a spoon. I half expected the water to steam or bubble as Usara poured it carefully in, but rather disappointingly it didn't. Usara lifted the little bowl to study the underside, peering closely.

"You can swap notes later," I pointed out. "The scrying?"

Usara peered into the shallow water, face dappled with

greenish lights striking up from the silver. "No sign of pursuit," he said finally. "The road is clear, as far as I can see." He frowned. "But I can't find the place where we were attacked. I know I broke up the surface of the road and Gilmarten's air spells would surely have left some sign."

"Aetheric enchantment," I said grimly. Wizard's magic was going to be a lot less useful if Artifice could help people hide from it.

Usara ignored me, leaning ever closer over the bowl, but his hands suddenly shook and emerald radiance slopped over the side, falling to vanish into the ground.

"That's enough." Darni leaned forward and took the little dish from the unresisting mage and tipped out the inky water. "We can try again later when 'Sar's had some rest."

"You give it a go." 'Gren shook Gilmarten's shoulder with brisk encouragement.

"I'm afraid I don't have much facility with the arts of water," the Soluran mage said hesitantly. "In Soluran tradition we keep far closer to working our natural element."

I could see frustration building in 'Gren's face. "Come on, let's see if we can find anything to eat around here." I pulled him away down the game trail.

"Those wizards may burn hot and bright when they get started but they're soon down to ash," he grumbled, kicking at some inoffensive bush.

"Be fair," I told him firmly. "The kind of magic they were flinging around earlier takes a lot out of them. They can faint dead away if they overdo it and I don't think we want that."

"I'm here to take on any Elietimm fancying his luck," 'Gren said aggressively.

"Yes, but that's because you don't have the sense to know when you're killed, let alone exhausted," I pointed out.

He grinned at me. "It's the way Misaen made me."

"Well, be grateful he made mages the way he did." I looked around in vain for some plant I might recognize as edible. I should have paid more attention to the foraging women of the Forest Folk. "Otherwise they'd be ruling the world by now." My words struck an echo somewhere in my memory. "Otrick on why wizards don't rule the world."

'Gren looked quizzically at me. "What?"

"Never mind." I pointed to a bush dotted with scarlet fruit. "Do you suppose we can eat those?"

'Gren picked one and ate it before I could stop him. "Tastes like a driftberry."

I sniffed cautiously at one. Smaller and darker but it did smell like a driftberry. I set about gathering them in a fold of my shirt. Perhaps one of the wizards would be able to tell for sure. 'Gren helped, eating plenty as he did so. I didn't bother suggesting caution to him.

Otrick. As I picked my way between the spines of the bush I thought about the old wizard. I had liked him, he wasn't some cloak carrier for Planir, polishing up his Council seat with a well-padded rump. When Otrick wanted to learn about the winds and currents of the ocean, he'd taken up with a pirate ship. Elietimm enchantment had him in a deathless, lifeless sleep now, struck down as he'd used his powers to stop the bastards slaughtering the hapless colonists of Kellarin. So there was someone else depending on us finding out the secrets of aetheric magic.

We foraged for a while longer but discovered nothing more than the fact that the height of summer is a bad time to try living off the land. This side of the turn of autumn, flowers and bitter green berries were just a mocking promise of fruitfulness to come. In glum accord, we headed back to the others.

"This is all we could find." I divided up the spoils into waiting hands, giving Usara the prince's portion. We all ate hungrily, but the berries did little to fill our bellies. I wondered crossly where those cursed horses had gone. I didn't relish the prospect of a journey through the Forest without sustaining food, water we could trust or ideally a change of linen. Wishing to no avail for something more to eat, I wiped my hands on my stained shirt and looked around the dejected circle. "So, what now?"

"We get instructions from Planir," said Usara glumly.

"We need to scry more widely, find out just how many are arming," mused Darni. "If it's just a single kindred with an itch to scratch, that's one thing. If it's every valley this side of the heights, we're in for a bloody autumn."

"You do as you see fit," I told the pair of them. "I came on this trip to find aetheric lore and I'm not quitting on that."

"That game's finished, Livak," snapped Usara, "all the runes rolled and done. We're as empty in the pocket as we were when we started."

"Then it's time to gather the bones for another hand," I told him. "Losses only count if you have to walk away from the table bearing them. As long as you're playing, you can set about winning your coin back." And if necessary, you set about making your own luck, if the run of the runes is against you. Especially if the other player is already scraping the odds.

"And how do you propose to set about that?" Darni's tone quite plainly anticipated that I had no real idea.

"Has Planir got anywhere closer to finding a means of waking Otrick?" I demanded of Usara.

"No," he sighed heavily. "We tried everything Guinalle could suggest over the winter. We failed and unless Planir's forgotten to tell me, no one has unearthed any scholarship that might help since."

"I bet that Elietimm enchanter knows how," I said. "Knowledge may not be a silver cup to steal, but we could try stealing the head it's held in, couldn't we?"

Usara looked at me with mingled disbelief and irritation but Darni's dark eyes were lit with interest.

"Well, we could, couldn't we?" I insisted. "And we could probably find out just what the Mountain Men are up to. And what pots that Elietimm bastard is stirring. And we could probably find answers to most of the questions about aetheric magic that Guinalle can't answer. We know these warding incantations of Guinalle's work now. As long as we get the drop on the Ice Islander, he won't have a chance to try his tricks." And I could prove to myself once and for all that Elietimm enchantments need not be feared with the nausea that bastard had planted in the back of my mind. "We had him once before and we can get him again. Tied up and knocked out, he'll be no more trouble than any other sack of shit."

"I forbid it, absolutely!" Usara made the mistake of trying to stand up and gasped at the pain.

"Saedrin grant he's already through the door to the Otherworld," said Darni slowly.

"If Raeponin's doing his job," I agreed fervently. "But what if he's not?"

"How do we find out?" demanded Darni.

"This." I dug in my belt-pouch and held up the little knife. "It belonged to the Sheltya woman. She's been with him before; she'll be with him again. Usara can find her and we find him."

"The one who dismissed us from the uplands?" Usara was aghast. "You stole from her?"

"You don't think she realized it was you?" Darni glowered in the bullying manner I remembered all too well. "You don't think that's what brought them down on us?"

"Five fives of men, all armed to the teeth and out for blood, just for a pocket blade and after waiting right around the greater moon and start again?" I raised an eyebrow at him. "I hardly think so. I doubt she's even missed it, and if she does she'll think she just lost it when the leather snapped." I waved the tattered end at him and grinned at Gilmarten, who was looking quite nonplussed.

"If Livak cuts your purse after lunch, you won't know about it till you try to pay the reckoning for your supper," Sorgrad told Darni firmly.

"I'm here on the authority of the Archmage and I simply will not countenance this!" Usara protested. "I certainly won't assist you with scrying."

"We don't work for you, pal," said 'Gren sunnily.

"Or your Archmage," added Sorgrad with a hint of menace. "And if you won't work the magic for us, maybe I should have a try."

"I told you before I'm the dog with the brass collar on this hunt," I reminded the mage. "We're going to do what we want, with or without your help."

"I'd like to see you try," scoffed Darni. "Impossible."

'Gren smiled. "No such thing as impossible—"

"Just long odds." Sorgrad stood next to his brother.

"And those are the kind that pay off best." I joined them. "We're on our way. Are you coming?"

"We should stick together through the Forest," Darni glowered. "For safety in numbers."

The wizards exchanged looks of impatience and uncertainty but each had the sense to realize that with Usara in such a state they needed swords and darts at least as much as spells to protect them.

We started to walk and I began racking my brains; without Usara's cooperation, I was short of a few key runes. I wondered how to get them, but I was determined to play this hand. Gambling may be all about winning but that doesn't mean it can't be about getting even too.

Eight

The wind is a constant feature of life in Dalasor and this song sums up all its various moods—the chill wind of winter, the warm breath of summer, the violent storms that rage above the open grasslands and those oh so rare moments of stillness when it takes one a moment to realize what is missing.

Power so mighty that moves stealthy, never seen
Stream that is ceaseless yet water has never been,
Always it passes yet will remain last of all.
Weakest will bend and live, strongest will broken fall,
Searching and scouring and merciless stripping bare,
Yet both concealing and blowing away all care.
A howl in the darkness with no tongue to make the sound,
Yet biting the bone and the dry flesh split all round,
The cold and the cruel drives sunshine far from the
*   heights*
Till moons bring their pity to soften the shrinking nights,
Moist kindly kisses and healing touch to all ills,
Bringing the glory of flower crowned rolling hills.
Storm raging fury and rain lashing naked back,
Twisting and turning and washing out every track,
Senses bemused and all courage fled long ago,
Calm bringing wisdom and bidding the heart to slow.

Respite from fear and true knowledge of self alone,
Peace for reflection and innermost secrets known.

Othilfess,
4th of Aft Summer

The long slate table was bare, a body laid out on the cold stone, wrapped to the neck in white linen. A cowl of the same cloth hid the hair but a few wisps escaped, dull with smears of rusty blood. An insidious hint of decay hovered in the air like an unwelcome truth. The lonely flames of candles set at head and foot held back the darkness as evening fell outside, leaving the rest of the room in disregarded gloom as the fire sank to a sullen red heap of cinders.

Aritane watched the three women weeping as they began stitching the corpse into a shaped shroud of stiff leather. "I see no reason for salting the body," she remarked coldly. "I could perform the charnel rites at once, if you would only let me."

Ismenia bent to kiss the marble white brow before closing the folds over Teiriol's face, hands deft and gentle; Eirys and Theilyn were barely able to hold their needles, let alone sew, their fingers shook so much. The old woman looked up. "I'll have Sheltya who remain true to their oaths lay my son under the sky for Misaen to judge and the ravens to reclaim," she said calmly. "Get out."

The girls both froze, trickling tears their only movement. Aritane's chin came up on an indignant intake of breath. "You owe me the courtesy of my calling and I'll thank you for it. You would not have his bones at all, were it not for Sheltya bringing him home."

Ismenia's eyes flickered to her daughters. "Please leave us to mourn our dead," she said in more temperate tones.

"Mourning is all well and good." Aritane looked around

at the disordered furniture and unswept floor with disdain. "Taken to excess, it becomes self-indulgence." She moved briskly to the hearth and piled fresh wood on the remains of the fire.

Eirys was fumbling as she attempted to thread a needle in the uncertain light. "If my child is a son, I'll name him for Teiro, Mama."

"You are truly with child this time?" Aritane's slaty eyes bored into the girl. "So it would seem. Have you told Jeirran yet?"

"I've had no chance." Eirys' face crumpled with distress. "I've seen so little of him—"

"Do not tell him," commanded Aritane coldly. "You may well yet slip and he needs neither to be distracted by the prospect of a child nor by the blow of its loss."

Ismenia's lips narrowed to a bloodless line as Eirys ducked her head to hide fresh weeping. "Leave my daughter's care to me, if you please."

"Pander to her endless hysterics like this and she will surely lose the brat," snapped Aritane. She did not sound displeased by the notion.

Theilyn's mouth fell open, puzzlement coloring the pain in her eyes. A dead silence fell, the circle of light around the women of the soke excluding the Sheltya in her severe gray robe.

"There are more besides Teiriol have spent their blood in defense of their beliefs," Aritane said pointedly after some moments' silence. "I will ensure their bones are in Maewelin's embrace as soon as may be." She strode out of the rekin, back stiff with indignation.

"Why not let her do it, Mother?" whispered Eirys. Her fair skin was blotched from weeping, her eyes red and swollen. "We owe her much, you know that." She rested a hand briefly on her full skirts.

"Don't credit her with your blessing," said Ismenia icily. "She won't welcome anything that might distract Jeirran from the mark she's setting up for him. All I owe her is the death of my child. Don't doubt that I will repay her some-how."

Theilyn looked from mother to sister, her eyes deeply shadowed in her pale face. "You should not say such things. Don't even think them."

Ismenia looked at her sharply. "You'll be running with tales again, will you?"

Theilyn's mouth trembled, her lips chapped and bitten. "They can hear such things unspoken," she said hoarsely. "Sheltya and the man from the east."

"Do not grace them with the name of Sheltya," hissed Ismenia. "They do not deserve it."

"But how will we get the rites said for Teiro?" wailed Eirys, fresh tears running through the smudges dried on her face.

Theilyn wasn't proof against this renewed assault of grief and wept bitterly in her turn. "It's all my fault," she choked. "If I hadn't told him what Eresken wanted, if I hadn't listened to Aritane. I don't know why I did, I don't know what I was thinking of."

"You were flattered by their attentions, you saw their favor promising you a good match, a rich husband and whatever else it is you want but you're not prepared to work for," Ismenia told her curtly. "I need no Sheltya powers to know just what you've been thinking, my girl. Don't ask my forgiveness."

Theilyn burst into noisy sobs and fled up the stairs, stumbling as she went. Ismenia sighed and rested her head in her wrinkled hands. Eirys sat in mute misery, absently winding a thread in and around her fingers, finally pulling it so tight she drew blood. She looked at the welling red with bemusement.

Heavy boots sounded reluctant on the steps outside and the door to the rekin opened slowly on the summer twilight. Fithian looked around the heavy oak and sidled in, twisting a rag between his hands. "I brought him," he said simply, his lined face deeply graven with weariness and grief.

He pushed the door wider and ushered Keisyl in. The younger man was thick with dust from the trail, unshaven and filthy from the diggings. Horror haunted his eyes as he looked at the shrouded body on the bare table and he hesitated on the threshold.

Ismenia looked up and managed a watery smile. "Oh my boy, come here."

Keisyl stumbled toward her, scowling as he fought tears of his own. "I'm sorry, I'm so sorry. I should have stopped him, I should have stayed—"

Ismenia held him tight. "It's no one's fault," she said hoarsely.

Keisyl hid his face in her embrace for a moment before forcing himself upright. He wheeled around and stared at the central hearth where flames suddenly burned bright and heedlessly cheerful as the wood laid on it caught fire. Face contorted with rage, Keisyl grabbed a massive poker and swept aside the logs, sending sparks showering in all directions. Raking embers all over the broad stone plinth, he smashed the iron down on the glowing heart of the fire, strewing the coals to scorch the floor, burn holes in the rugs and cushions and to die, first to red and then to ashy gray, all warmth spent on the cold stone. He stamped furiously on the scattered clinker, reducing the fragments to powder. Ismenia and Fithian watched in silence, faces solemn yet sympathetic. Eirys clutched a scrap of linen, bleeding finger forgotten in her mouth as she looked on aghast.

When the fire was a ruin of cooling ash, Keisyl stood, shaking, head bowed. He dropped the poker with a clang that rang around the room like a death knell. He drew a deep, shuddering breath and raised his head but before he could speak, the door was flung open to reveal Jeirran silhouetted against the colorless sky.

"Keisyl! I saw you arrive," he said with restrained enthusiasm. "I wish you were returning under better circumstances." His voice trailed off as he saw the smoldering destruction within. "What do you think you are doing?"

"No fire will burn here," Keisyl snarled, face haggard. "Not while my brother's body lies waiting for due ceremony."

"The fess is full and the men have to be fed," objected Jeirran with rising irritation. "We're all upset but life has to go on. What of dinner?"

"Cook yourselves eggs over skillets in the forge," spat Keisyl. "This is a house of mourning."

"This is a time of war," Jeirran retorted. "We are up in arms to avenge Teiriol and those who died with him. We will claim double payment in blood from those lowlanders responsible." He marched into the room and looked around for agreement.

"It's you who are responsible," said Keisyl softly. "It's you who tempted Teiro with your false promises, your fool's ambitions, your faithless Sheltya. You owe this soke a life, Jeirran!"

"You cannot see beyond the walls of your fess, can you?" sneered Jeirran. "Teiriol believed in what I am doing. He knew the time had come to set the record right. He wanted—"

"Teiriol wanted to please." Keisyl shook his head in abrupt denial. "That's the only reason he ever paid heed to you. He just wanted to please, to live a quiet life, someday with a contented wife and children, trusting to a modest patrimony under the hearth. You robbed him of that, Jeirran, just as surely as you robbed your children of their birthright to buy yourself out of prison down in Selerima!"

Jeirran paled and could not stop himself glancing at Eirys, whose shock was absolute. "What is he saying, Jeir?" she asked in a wretched voice.

Jeirran lashed out to punch Keisyl, taking him completely by surprise. He stumbled backward, split lip bleeding. Jeirran looked defiantly around at Eirys but before he could speak Keisyl surged forward, an upper cut shutting Jeirran's mouth for him with a teeth-rattling snap. Keisyl's other fist drove into Jeirran's gut, doubling him over, but

Jeirran recovered fast enough to bring his head up into Keisyl's face, butting him but just missing his nose. Keisyl's sweeping blow landed on Jeirran's ear, forcing an exclamation of pain from him. As Keisyl hesitated, shocked at his own actions, Jeirran backhanded him across the face, a ring scoring an angry line across Keisyl's cheek.

Cursing, Keisyl grabbed both of Jeirran's shoulders and forced him backward, running him into the stone wall of the rekin, lifting him forward to smash him back again and again. Jeirran brought his forearms up hard to break Keisyl's grip and tried to butt him again, but Keisyl's fury was too strong. He stamped down hard on Jeirran's feet, raking his own metal-capped boots down the man's shins. Jeirran struggled, spitting in Keisyl's face, trying to bring up his knee but only managing to reach Keisyl's thigh. He managed to wrestle himself away from the wall and tried to snatch up a stool, but Keisyl pulled him away with an oath.

"Stop it, stop it, the pair of you!" Ismenia sprang to her feet and seized the poker, hammering on the hearth with it, halting them both with the shock of the noise. She tried to no avail to shift the corner of the grimy plinth. Fithian came to her aid, working a fire iron to lever aside the stone. "Eirys! This is for you to do."

"Just leave it, Eirys. Don't believe what they are saying." Jeirran tried to get free but Keisyl would not release him. "It's about time she saw you for what you are, you slime," he growled through the muck and spittle disfiguring his face.

Eirys reached into the hollow beneath the stone to take out an iron-bound casket. Her hands were trembling so much she couldn't get the key in the lock but her face was a frozen mask of disbelief. Ismenia stood beside her but did not offer to help, expressionless as Eirys finally opened the box.

"There was gold in here at Solstice," She looked at Jeirran, incredulous. "I saw it, we all did. Where has it gone? What have you done?"

"Was there gold at Solstice?" demanded Ismenia. "Was it gold or deception woven by that sister of yours? Where's your good faith now, Jeirran?"

"You're worthless!" Keisyl threw Jeirran back against the wall, hands flung wide in a gesture of utter contempt.

Jeirran rubbed a hand over his beard. "There are more important things—"

"Not to me." Keisyl stepped forward. "Not to me and not to my blood. One of our own is dead and we will honor him." He stopped on the threshold, nose to nose with Jeirran. "You are not of his blood. There is no child to link you to this soke. You have forfeited your oath to my sister. Neither you nor any of your band of misbegots will set foot inside this rekin while my brother's body lies here, do you understand me?" His voice was menacing.

Jeirran's chin jutted forward. "You have no right to bar me from this place, nor keep me from my wife," he said haughtily.

Keisyl raised a fist but lowered it again. Just as smug satisfaction rose in Jeirran's face, Keisyl seized him by the collar. The shorter man's struggles were no match for Keisyl's fury and contempt. Pulling open the door, he flung Jeirran down the steps. Jeirran stumbled and fell, scrambling upright, indignant and red faced. A few onlookers exchanged curious glances and remarks. Jeirran brushed the dust from his trews and straightened his shirt collar but could do nothing about his furious color as he turned his back on the rekin and marched toward the gate-house of the fess.

Keisyl watched him go then closed the great door softly. He leaned back against it and closed his eyes, groaning. "Eirys, my dearest, I'm so sorry. I never meant to say it."

Eirys was still staring dumbly into the empty coffer that had once held her fondest hopes. "How could he?"

"Because his ambition and his greed have finally outstripped his principles," said Ismenia with resignation. "Set it aside, my dear."

Eirys closed the casket with a soft click and laid it carefully on the stone. "I think I'll go to my room," she said with brittle calm. "Please don't disturb me before morning." She made her way slowly up the stairs, moving like a woman in a walking dream.

Keisyl thumped his fist into the wood of the door. "I couldn't imagine how this situation could get any worse. Now I know better and that's all my fault as well."

"The sooner everyone stops blaming themselves for the lad's death, the sooner this soke will start healing," said Fithian unexpectedly. He shoved the hearthstone back with a grunt, raising a cloud of fine ash that hung in the air in a mockery of smoke. "Teiro was the best part grown and knew his own mind. He made his choices and he lived and died by them. We all do that, boy, it's the way of things. You take this route or that and only Maewelin knows if you're choosing to step into the path of an avalanche. Two men walk on a frozen lake and Misaen rolls the runes. One man freezes to death when he falls through the ice while another catches the fish that's the meal to save his life. Teiro could have died in a rock fall and he'd be just as dead, just as young."

Ismenia nodded in mute agreement, eyes dark with remembered sorrows.

"This is nothing like the same!" Keisyl shook his head obstinately. "This is all Jeirran's doing. He's the one stirring up the trouble with all his fine words and promises. He's the one making war on the lowlanders!"

"Not on his own, he isn't." Ismenia looked up from her thoughts. "Look out of the door and see just how many he has following him."

Keisyl moved instead to one of the narrow windows on one side and peered out at the compound. Knots of men, threes and fives, were staring up at the closed door, heads close in discreet speculation. "He wouldn't set them on us, would he?" he asked despairingly.

Ismenia came to stand with him, raising herself on her toes to see out. "I'd believe that fool capable of anything," she said grimly.

Both of them turned at a sudden sound but it was only Fithian unlocking his private chest. He took out a flask and glasses and wordlessly brought each a drink of fine, straw-colored spirit.

Keisyl laid a hand on the heavy latch of the door. "Where are the keys, Mother?"

"Here." She lifted a bunch hanging from a chain at her waist. "For all the good it would do us."

Keisyl caught his breath as sudden movement down by the gate turned heads all around the courtyard. Jeirran strode forward, head held high, arms swinging confidently. He marched to the steps of the rekin and looked up at the closed door for a long moment. Even though he knew the darkness within hid him, Keisyl felt as if the man's eyes were locked on his own. Jeirran turned on his heel, boot nails scraping the stone.

"You all know what has happened," began Jeirran. He did not shout but spoke with a calm authority that rapidly silenced the speculation all around. "This rekin mourns," he lifted a hand to the blank stone face, "the soke mourns and so do thrice three more, as Sheltya return their dead sons. We are not unused to grief; Misaen made us a hard land and Maewelin is unforgiving in her trials. But this is more than a fate we must bear as our due. This is not life claimed and paid in return for the gifts of wood and mountain. These lives were stolen. Our parley was dishonored. The bodies of those that offered up their good faith were left discarded like so much rubbish."

Angry murmurs swelled for a moment and Jeirran fell silent until the noise subsided. The air was ripe with expectation.

"Are we to suffer this insult? Is this to be yet one more abuse of our land and our people that goes unchallenged? Are the lowlanders and their Forest allies going to bar us from roads and trade now that we've been bold enough to mark our boundaries?" His voice was unexpectedly calm. "Isn't it time to tell them enough is enough? Mustn't they learn we will not stand to be so disparaged and denied?" He shook his head. "I've been breaking my heart and testing your patience with questions long enough. You must decide what to do. All I know is I have a murder to avenge. I will not cross my wife's threshold until I have claimed a life to repay the soke for its loss. I will not take food from her hearth until I have lit a pyre to break the bones of that murderer to splinters. I will not return until I can swear to my sons and daughters yet unborn that I have defended their birthright. Misaen and Maewelin both may judge me if I do not spend every last drop of blood in my veins before I abandon this pledge."

Jeirran did not look back as he walked away from the rekin. He strode forward but eager men shouting their support, reaching forward to shake his hand or slap his shoulder, soon blocked his path. Those who could not get close raised clenched fists in noisy approval, more soon raising weapons in their hands. The crowd moved awkwardly toward the gate, shifting and seething until it emptied through the narrow stone tunnel. Men in twos and threes ran hastily between the workshops and storehouses of the compound, emerging with sacks, bundles, swords and quivers. They halted for a moment as a great cheer boiled up outside the walls, the sound echoing from the cliffs all around, startling birds from their roosts.

"Do you suppose Eirys heard all that?" asked Keisyl despairingly. "She'll be opening her arms to him soon enough if she did."

"I don't care if she was listening," said Ismenia grimly. "That's an oath that won't go unheard where it matters."

"You don't believe he means what he's saying?" Keisyl demanded. "That's just his way of excusing himself to his rabble, avoiding explanations when they see this door is barred to him."

"Whether or not he means it doesn't matter," said Ismenia with cold satisfaction.

"Misaen and Maewelin will answer when their names are invoked, even in vain," nodded Fithian.

"He just realized that there were no fancy words he could use to get men to force their way into the rekin." Keisyl sighed. "When he has them eating out of his hand by boasting he's their champion for ancient rights, he's hardly going to risk all by asking them to break down the door and defile custom along with the threshold."

"None of them would go that far," nodded Fithian slowly.

"Jeirran's not got the wit for that," said Ismenia scornfully. "It'll be that harlot he's reclaimed as sister."

"Aritane may be many things and some of them foolish, but harlot she is not."

The unexpected voice was rough with emotion and male.

Ismenia whirled around, hugging her arms to her, face ashen. Fithian reversed his grip on his flask and raised it menacingly. Keisyl stepped in front of his mother, fists clenched and scowling. "Theilyn! What do you think you are doing?"

The girl stepped down from the stairwell door and the gray-cloaked figure behind her put down his hood. "I went to find Bryn," Theilyn said in a shaking voice. "Even if you'll never forgive me, I wanted to make some amends to Teiro." She glanced at the corpse and bit her lip but she had shed all her tears for now.

Bryn twisted his large hands around each other. "She has good cause to be concerned," he began apologetically. "In this season, even salting the body—there is very real danger of corruption."

"I'll have no Sheltya dancing to Aritane's tune saying the rites for my son," Ismenia told him with simple truth. "I'll risk the stain on his bones and answer for it if need be."

"We could argue the rights and wrongs of what Aritane is doing from Solstice to Equinox but that will be of no use to

Teiriol. I cannot leave matters like this." Bryn colored and shifted uncomfortably. "It looks as if we will be leaving within the day. Once we are gone, I can ensure some Sheltya unconnected with all this will come to you, if you wish it. But I would need to have your word that you will not speak of Jeirran's army or of any Sheltya presence here."

Keisyl couldn't ever recall hearing fear in a Sheltya voice before.

"I would not lie to Sheltya, even if I could." Ismenia shook her head, more puzzled than defiant.

"Do not say how Teiriol died," pleaded Bryn. "Or rather, just say that he was attacked in the lowlands, not that he was part of a parley or anything to do with Jeirran's ambitions. Sheltya will respect your grief, you know that."

"That would surely suffice, Mama. The important thing is to get the rites for Teiro," said Theilyn. "If we say anything more, then Sheltya will put us all to the test and Eirys will never be able to stand it."

Ismenia scrubbed her hands over her face, looking up with hollow cheeks and disordered hair. "I will not lie but I will not volunteer what I know," she said finally.

"We don't know that much as it is." Keisyl looked unsmiling at Bryn. "We've done our best to keep ourselves out of this folly." He moved to open the door. "It's up to you how you answer for your part in all this."

"No, I'll leave by the side steps," said Bryn hastily. "It's better that I am not seen."

He patted Theilyn clumsily on the shoulder as he turned and hurried up the stairs. She nodded absently and moved to the long table, picking up her needle and resuming her task with even stitches. After a moment, Ismenia moved to look over her daughter's shoulder. With a grunt of approval, she pulled up a stool to the great slate slab and began working an awl through the stubborn leather, marking a line of holes for Theilyn's sewing to follow. Keisyl collapsed on a stool between them, laid his head in his arms and wept, ceaseless tears falling on the indifferent stone. Fithian sat in a corner and drank from his flask with single-minded intent.

The Great West Road, 6th of Aft-Summer

I wasn't really paying attention when the arrows came raining in; since murderous Mountain Men hadn't caught up with us so far, my main worry was our empty bellies and the thirst that was closing my throat. The road was deserted and I was some way ahead of the others, having no wish to take a turn supporting Usara any sooner than need be. The mage was doing his best with a rough crutch, though his leg must have been ablaze with agony.

The arrows sprang from dense thickets low beneath mighty trees, cleaving the air with their spiteful swish. I had barely time to register their flight before all burst into flames. Bright gouts of fire flared in the shadows striping the road and a stink of charred feather hovered on the slow-moving air as scorched arrowheads clattered down. A rustle of consternation in the bushes betrayed at least one assailant. I backed rapidly to join the others, where Gilmarten was looking justifiably pleased with himself.

Darni stepped forward, one hand on his sword-hilt. "We have no wish to fight anyone. Can we parley?"

"You have been fighting, we see your wounded." The shouting voice sounded young, nervous and angry, a bad combination. A second voice told us we had enemies in the branches of the trees. That's all it told us, since this one spoke the Forest tongue. We exchanged looks of incomprehension.

"You, there, you of the blood," it yelled in exasperated Tormalin. "Are you prisoner or traitor?"

"My father was of the blood, but I was born and raised an outdweller," I called out cautiously. "These men are friends and companions of many years. They have attacked no one."

There was a puzzled silence. "What of your wounded one?" The question came from another direction and I wondered how many we were facing. From the timbre of the halting Tormalin this was an older man and one whose life had been rudely shaken. With luck he'd be keen to avoid any more fighting.

"We were attacked three days ago," I shouted. "We lost our horses and our gear and only wish to pass through the Forest as fast as we may."

"Who attacked you?" demanded the first voice, more uncertain but less angry. It was a young man's voice, easier to persuade but more inclined to impulsive decisions.

"Men of the Mountains," replied Sorgrad clearly. "Westerlings. My brother and I were born to the Middle Ranges but we've lived in the lowlands for many years. We were looking to trade but were driven out."

"Why do you block the road like this?" Darni's face darkened. "Have you been attacked?"

"Attacked, burned out, harried and hunted," raged the first voice. "By men as fair as your friends there and with magic at their backs."

Usara jerked upright on his prop. "Magic? Of what nature?"

"Has this been magic of fire and water, of strange winds and broken earth?" I stepped forward and scanned the bushes again. "Or has it been terror in the mind, delusion baffling the senses?"

"What do you know of such things?" This was a new voice, a stronger, more measured tone.

"It was trying to understand this magic of the mind that took me to the uplands." I could feel furious glares from Darni and Usara scorching the back of my neck.

A fluting whistle was passed down the highway from

quite some distance ahead. A man of the Forest Folk stepped out of a low thicket, belly spreading in his middle years, dark auburn hair sprinkled with white, square-jawed face quite grim enough to be a match for Darni. "Riders are approaching. Get off the road and we can discuss this further." This was the last speaker, who looked at us with a measuring copper eye. "We can offer you food and water."

Darni and the wizards immediately stepped forward, or limped, in Usara's case. 'Gren looked at me and I looked to Sorgrad; the three of us followed more slowly. More Folk than I expected emerged from the trees above us and out of the undergrowth. Leggings and tunics of dun and leather were newly splashed with mud and irregular splotches of fresh dye while rags of green and brown cloth were tied around arms and legs, covering hair and faces. These people were actively seeking to avoid being seen. All were armed with bows and sufficient quivers that Gilmarten would have spent his magic long before they ran out of arrows.

A rattle of hooves behind us turned my head back to the road. I caught a glimpse of heads and backs, yeomen by their clothing, solid chestnut horses trotting stolidly along. I could get back fast enough to hail them, to shout for help and say whatever might induce unimaginative farmers to take me to safety. My hesitation brought Sorgrad's head around, piercing blue eyes unblinking.

"Go if you want to," he said softly, "but I'm going on. I want payback as well as a pay-off now. Exiling us is one thing, trying to kill us raises the stakes."

I still felt a shadow of the qualm that Elietimm bastard had planted in my mind but anger burned it away, hot and urgent beneath my breastbone. Sorgrad held out a hand and squeezed my fingers for a moment; I nodded wordlessly and followed. North of the road, the land was more broken, rising in odd abrupt slopes. Trees clustered densely for a stretch and then left stony ground bare but for hummocks of moss and dips filled with drifts of leaves. Evergreens stood sullen and dusty in the summer heat and dense tangles of bramble and gorse were claiming ever more ground with each season. The Folk walking grim-faced to either side of us looked much the same as those farther south, ancient blood seasoned with a cast of the eyes or a tilt of the nose brought in from both east and west of the wildwood.

We rounded a hillock of gravelly ground and found ourselves on the edge of a wide hollow backed by a rocky crag. The scars of a score or more fires were black on the swept earth and each was surrounded by a close-gathered ring of Folk, a couple of hundreds all told, huddled together with scant bundles of possessions and food. Many were flat-faced with shock; others were hunched in distress or sharpening weapons already gleaming in the sunlight with futile rage. Grim depression twisted an old woman's face in contrast to the blank disbelief of the child folded in her arms. I wondered where its mother was.

"Men of the Mountains," said the man who had brought us here. "They have been coming down from the heights, driving us back, killing and burning where they may."

"We must speak with your leader." Worry was plain on Gilmarten's face.

"They have no leader, not in the sense you mean," I told him. "Where are the men who manage the hunts for you? What about healers?"

Darni was scowling. " 'Sar needs a healer, if we do nothing else here."

"Yes, I know." I stifled my irritation. "Healers or trackers might be able to tell us where the Mountain Men are attacking. Does anyone have a map?"

Both wizards shook their heads but Sorgrad looked up from making a rough head count. "I know the lay of the land around here pretty well."

"Where would we find a healer?" I asked the man.

"Yonder." He pointed to the outcrop overhanging a wide,

shallow cave. We picked our way through the dense gathering, unease rippling outward as 'Gren and Sorgrad were noticed, blond heads in stark contrast to the varied shades of red and brown all around. The tenor of the murmurs was distinctly unfriendly. The Folk who had arrived with us dropped away to their own people, the sharp tone of questions rising here and there. I smiled reassuringly at Sorgrad but he remained grim-faced. The air grew thick with tension rather than heavy with the apathy of defeat; these Folk might lack any formal leadership but they could still find common cause in lynching Sorgrad and 'Gren quick enough.

A daunting number of people were wrapped in soiled blankets on the broad shelf of rock beneath the crag. Green poultices and oddly stained dressings covered wounds to arms, hands and heads. A double handful of men and women were busy among the prostrate figures, lifting heads to give sips from wooden cups or pellets of closely wrapped leaves for chewing. One of the healers was kneeling beside a gray-haired woman whose eyes were hidden beneath a swathe of linen.

"More work for us, Bera?" he asked with a shadow of a smile. Old blood was black on the front of his tunic and caked around his fingernails.

"This is Harile," our guide nodded. "A leg wound for you and a puzzle for the rest of us," he told the healer.

Usara limped forward and Harile's attention immediately focused on the mage's stained dressing. "Let me see."

Usara leaned on his crutch, unlacing his breeches awkwardly. He gritted his teeth as Harile gently eased the foul linen away. The bruising was now a nauseous greenish purple covering most of the wizard's skinny thigh and the wound looked ominously swollen and angry, seeping with yellow pus. I'd thought Usara had been lucky to catch a glancing blow; after all, if the bone had been broken, we would have been in a great deal more trouble. Now I wasn't so sure. He might well lose the leg anyway and that infection could kill him regardless.

Harile spoke rapidly to a woman of easily twice my heft, round-faced with a solid bulk to her. She poured water from a kettle hung over a small and smokeless fire and added a judicious selection of herbs from a bag at her belt to the bowl. As she approached, I realized she was singing Orial's healing song under her breath. Harile picked up the refrain in an absent whistle, using the warm and fragrant liquid to wash away the crusted mess. "The bruising makes it look worse than it is."

Usara's shoulders sagged and he scrubbed a trembling hand over his face, a pathetic figure with his breeches around his knees, shirt grubby beneath the soiled front of his gown. Testing one's magic against the wider world is all very well, I thought, but that's a wizard who's going to be mighty glad to be safe on his hidden island again. I wondered if he'd make it with one leg or two.

"There are herbs we can poultice to promote healing," continued Harile. "We can dull the discomfort and you must rest for your body to mend itself."

"You'll be fine, 'Sar," said Darni briskly as the mage eased his breeches up painfully. "Now, where were you attacked and by what numbers?"

An older man with wiry white hair fringing a bald pate above a lean, keen face pushed past Bera. "What do you know of the storm that has burst over us?"

"This is Apak," said Bera hastily. "The eldest of trackers." He was backed by a double handful of people looking just as hard for answers.

Darni looked down with unconscious arrogance. "I am an agent of the Archmage of Hadrumal, Planir the Black. Usara is a mage deep in his confidence and Gilmarten is a wizard of Solura, traveling with us." His tone forbade further inquiry but Gilmarten bowed hastily.

"Are mages to blame for this calamity?" Apak returned

Darni's haughtiness in full measure, thumbs tucked in his belt. "We know the Men of the Mountains are backed by magic, make no mistake."

"I can assure you their enchantments are none of our doing."

I was relieved to hear a more moderate tone in the big man's words but Apak snorted, unimpressed. "And what of you three?" His eyes and those at his back were hard and distrustful. I felt 'Gren stir beside me, reacting badly to the palpable hostility coming from all sides.

"We were looking to trade in the Western Ranges," said Sorgrad soberly, accents of Col resonant in his words. "We were summarily expelled from the heights and we have been pursued with murderous intent." He indicated Usara and the rest of us still spotted with blood in our stale clothing, his expression neutral in the face of accusing stares.

"What do the Men of the Mountains want with us?" demanded Apak, pent-up frustration finding a target in us. "Why are we fugitives in the wildwood that should shelter us?" He was spitting and stumbling over his words, Forest accents distorting his fluent Tormalin. "Me and mine were grazing our donkeys in the upper margins while the grass was good, the women harvesting herbs, the rest hunting hare or fox. We set our sura in the customary places; the Mountain people have turned their flocks to the upper pastures by now and are busy at their diggings, but some always travel down to trade metal goods and pottery for herbs and woodwork." The anger in Apak's face faded to perplexity. "When we saw some men coming, we thought nothing of it, but they carried swords and spears and outnumbered us two for every one. They called us thieves and parasites, cursing us for hunting their lands, saying we stole their pelts. They burned our sura, broke whatever they could lay hands on or cast it into the flames. The women were taken against their will, those who resisted whipped raw." Burning rage surged in his voice. "We hunt those slopes both sides of Solstice but leave them willingly when the season turns. Mountain Men come down from the heights and we move south before the snows." His voice trailed off as he gazed into some evil memory. "We fled, what else could we do?"

We were the center of attention, Folk moving closer, abandoning their low-voiced conversations.

"And then?" prompted Darni with more gentleness than I expected.

"Not enough for them to drive us from the margins," spat Apak. "They followed us deep into the greenwood. Every time we halted, we were attacked, no matter how we sought to hide or evade them. Those standing firm were cut down and those who fled were trapped with magic." The word was a curse on his lips, echoed in murmurs from those ringing us. I was looking for the fastest way to get clear. Sorgrad and 'Gren could take care of themselves and Darni and his mages would just have to take their chances.

"What was the nature of the sorcery?" demanded Usara.

"What do I know of magic?" Apak glowered at Usara before turning his wrathful gaze on Sorgrad, who was doing his best to look wholly inoffensive, and 'Gren, who was fidgeting with growing defiance.

"Just tell us what happened," I requested politely.

"People ran mad." Apak's voice shook. "Men who know every bend of branch between here and the southern seas were utterly lost. Some ran in terror from sister or brother, straight onto the blades of the uplanders. Others turned on their own, striking them down with hand, knife, fire irons, cook pots." His perplexity and trepidation was mirrored on faces all around. "The Men of the Mountains laughed to see it and then they killed them."

"Our beasts turned crazed as well." Bera picked up the tale somberly. "We were by the streams above the marsh where the Forest narrows, cutting rush and reed, waiting for the moons to bring the mickelfish to spawning. They came down from the heights, called us foul names and killed all they could catch. But Mountain Men never come to the marshes, never once, not in all the years I have traveled that way!" He remembered what he had started to say. "We might have fled through the mosses, but our animals turned against us. They went wild, kicking and biting anyone who dared approach. It was worse than the cursed thirst." Bera shook his head, bemused. "Some died where they stood, hearts burst with the terror."

"That's what happened to our horses," I told him, "when we were attacked."

"That is no magic I could work," Usara spoke earnestly. "My powers are over the elements that make up the world that you see, the air, the earth, fire and water. Had I wished to attack your Folk as they worked in a marsh," he turned to Bera, all fervent honesty, "I would have raised the water against them, turned the mud to liquid beneath their feet to trap them, woven a fog to baffle—"

"That's not exactly reassuring them, Usara," I interrupted. Apak was fingering a dagger at his belt and an unease encircled us like the cold wind presaging a storm.

"Wizardly magic has no power to reach into the mind," Gilmarten spoke up suddenly, his Soluran lilt turning heads. "This is a new and evil enchantment."

"Or an ancient one in the hands of evil men," I corrected him. Guinalle and her scholars might be using their Artifice this side of the ocean someday.

"If you are wizards, can your magic help us?" demanded a voice from somewhere. Ominous expectation hovered like a threat of thunder.

"My vows to Lord Astrad, that is, we are forbidden—and I don't think I would be able to argue that the Forest is without the King's laws—" Gilmarten looked stricken.

Usara's pallor wasn't only due to his wound. "I could not act without sanction from Planir."

"Not to attack these Mountain Men," continued Darni smoothly. "Clearly, any mage may act in defense of himself or the helpless." He nodded politely to Usara but the smile that curled his lip looked more like the warning snarl of a mastiff to me.

I wouldn't have thought it possible for Usara to go any paler but he managed it. Harile leaned forward to bruise a pungent leaf under the mage's nose. The wizard coughed with irritation but it struck a spark of color from his angular cheekbones.

"Scrying can tell us where the Mountain Men are camped," Darni spoke on with barely a pause. "Their movements will hint at their plans and we can certainly make sure we keep out of their path. But isn't it time we started taking this fight to them?"

Bera and Apak exchanged uncertain looks but a fair few of the rest looked at Darni with new hope rising above their despondency. He could play this hand if he wanted, I decided. At least it should keep people from measuring Sorgrad and 'Gren for a shallow grave.

"We?" queried Bera.

"These same Mountain Men attacked me and mine." Darni folded shirtless arms over his broad chest, emphasizing the muscles in limbs thicker than my thigh. He looked nigh on a giant among these Folk, coarse black hair curling in the neck of his jerkin. "I'd say we have a common foe, don't you?"

"You're going nowhere until you've all had some rest." Harile blocked Darni's path, pinching his forearm. The skin held the imprint of the Forest man's fingers, slow to sink. "You're too big to go so long without drinking. Get yourselves fed and watered and then your wits will be all the sharper."

The ring of Folk around us immediately broke up, but now the dead silence of the sheltered basin was lively with low-voiced conversations, even laughter, albeit hurriedly suppressed.

"I hope you know what you're doing," I murmured to Darni as I sat on the hard dry lip of the rock ledge.

"Once 'Sar scries them out, we can plan our attack." He nodded with satisfaction.

"These folk'll be slaughtered going up against chainmail and broadswords with no more than leather and skinning knives," I objected with some heat.

Sorgrad leaned forward past me. "Skirmishers?"

"The usual." Darni's expression had all the savage glee of a feral cat. "Harry them, draw them out, bleed them dry."

Sorgrad smiled broadly. "He knows what he's doing."

"Care to share the secret?" I asked with a touch of sarcasm.

"We can harry the enemy, cut down stragglers, and maybe make a few night attacks on their camps." Darni's voice was matter of fact. "We can't deny them the ground, so we make it as costly to take as possible and then raise the price of holding it too high for them to bear." He looked at the assembled Folk in the broad dell, expression thoughtful.

"That's a long game to play." I accepted a wooden bowl of thick and savory soup from the fat woman and ate hungrily. Even the flatbread was welcome, soaking up the last of the hot liquid as I scooped up shreds of meat and greenery with a battered spoon that Sorgrad produced from one of his pockets. A lad went past with what looked suspiciously like squirrels strung on a stick but I put the notion firmly from my mind. It was probably deer meat in the soup.

"That's better." Darni drained the last drops from his own bowl, wiping his matted beard with the back of one hand. I felt as filthy as he looked, my shirt sticky with sweat.

"We need to find the closest threat," said Usara, talking more to himself than anyone else. "The ones that attacked Apak."

"There must be at least three elements working their way in from the north," 'Gren pointed out, face intense as he turned his thoughts to strategy and tactics.

"I'll wager any money the assaults are being coordinated using Elietimm enchantment," scowled Darni.

"That's what I'd do," nodded Sorgrad.

"So we need to come up with a plan to stop that," I noted innocently.

"What kind of force do you reckon we can stitch together out of these people?" 'Gren looked around the basin, a predatory eagerness in his tone.

"Think how close Apak's people were to Grynth when they were attacked. Bera's were on the edge of the Lakeland." Darni's jaw jutted forward. "We have to do something or the whole of the Ferring Gap will be dragged into this. Come to that, they'll have set the entire Forest alight before the end of the season. How's Brakeswell going to react if the Great West Road is closed? What about Pastamar?"

"We mustn't be hasty," said Usara desperately. "First things first. I must bespeak the Archmage. Planir will know what to do."

I sat silently and drank from a flagon of water. I wasn't particularly concerned whether or not Planir knew what to do. I had plenty of ideas.

The Chamber of Planir the Black, Archmage of Hadrumal, 6th of Aft-Summer

"So, you see, you must send help and quickly. If we do nothing, there will quite simply be chaos." The urgency in Usara's words rang through the shining mirror to strike faint echo from the goblet in Planir's hand.

The Archmage took a reflective sip of his emerald green cordial. "I think you need to widen your focus here, 'Sar."

"Is there a problem with the spell?" Usara frowned.

"Think through the consequences of what you are suggesting," said Planir patiently. "For you and the Soluran to help these Forest Folk is one thing. For the wizards and Archmage of Hadrumal to engage in the fight would be quite another."

"But these Mountain Men are backed by at least one enchanter from the Ice Islands," protested Usara hotly. "They seem to have suborned these Sheltya. There's no telling how powerful they might be!"

"You can counter their enchantments with your own sorcery," Planir reassured him. "This is a dire threat and you must do everything in your power to halt this enchanter's ambitions. But I am not prepared to raise the stakes in the greater game by having the mages of Hadrumal take on Elietimm enchanters who have set this landslide in motion."

"They have stirred up the mountains with Misaen only knows what lies!" cried Usara. "Surely we must show them that we simply will not tolerate such deliberate malice?"

"What would the King of Solura feel, seeing mages waging war on behalf of the Forest Folk?" Planir demanded, face stern. "What would he think of the wildwood becoming the province of wizards with no ties or loyalty to his laws, rather than his realm's age-old safeguard against Tormalin ambition?"

"We would leave once the situation was resolved," objected Usara.

"And when would that be?" Planir queried with polite interest. "How long before we could be confident the Mountain Men would not simply storm down from their heights the instant the last mage returned to Hadrumal? How would you reassure the Forest Folk that they would be safe from further attack? Don't you think they would want at least a few mages, if only to summon help if they are invaded again? Are we going to commit ourselves to supporting the Forest Folk, when they have proved to have no learning of any real worth? Do we want to make enemies of the Mountain peoples, when they have aetheric learning that we so desperately need?"

"I'm sure we could come to some compromise." Usara sounded less certain.

"What would the great guilds of Selerima and Vanam have to say, the good burghers of Wrede or even of Grynth?" Planir set his glass aside and laced his fingers together, elbows resting on the arms of his chair. "Remember how fiercely these cities and lordlings prize their independence. It may be twenty generations or more since they threw off Tormalin domination, but the memory of the struggle lingers. How would they react to wizards in the Forest dominating the road to all the lucrative markets of Solura? We could have them expelling every mage within their boundaries, forbidding the cities to any wizard, reinstating the penalties for wielding magic that forced Trydek to bring his motley band of apprentices to Hadrumal in the first place."

Usara made no reply, merely looking increasingly dejected.

"That's on the one hand. On the other," Planir suited gesture to his words, "we would find ourselves besieged with requests for help. What of the Ferring Gap? We'd have guild masters hot-footing it to the nearest philtre seller, demanding immediate aid on all manner of spurious grounds."

"They'd be disappointed then," said Usara tartly. "All parties in the Gap have given just as much offense as they have received injury."

"How do you propose refusing help when you have just overturned generations of tradition by fighting in support of the Forest Folk?" inquired Planir.

"This isn't mere competition for profit," Usara objected. "These people are being slaughtered!"

"So it's a matter of principle?" Planir raised a finger. "It's principles that have kept the Lescari at each other's throats for ten generations, isn't it? The rights of a ruler to bequeath his sovereignty to his own blood as opposed to the rights of whoever feels strong enough to make a grab for the crown. If we use our powers to halt one slaughter of the blameless, how can we let that chaos go unchallenged?"

"That's completely different!"

"How, exactly?" Planir's calm words were in increasing contrast to Usara's heated tone.

"We are facing a decisive encounter with a rival magic!" snapped the younger mage.

"Only if we so choose," Planir waved that away. "All right, I'll grant you it's a dangerous situation. Suppose we draw our line in the sand and challenge these enchanters to a pissing contest. How do you propose to explain it to the good people of Ensaimin and anywhere else dragged in? Just what principle is so important that we have the right to bring their world crashing down around their ears?"

"Mages are not answerable to the mundane populace!" retorted Usara.

"No," agreed the Archmage. "We are not answerable to anyone. We can fight these sorcerers with all the power over air, earth, fire and water that we can summon, and no one can gainsay us." He paused. "How will that affect our current negotiations with the princes of Tormalin? Don't you think they might decide that facing the Elietimm on their own, with whatever aid Guinalle and her Adepts can offer, is preferable to allying with mages who take heed of no authority?"

"But that would be simple foolishness," Usara replied angrily.

The gleaming surface of the mirror pulsed faintly with ripples of magic sliding across its surface. The candle burned fiercely, unnatural flame devouring the wax, hot drips sliding down the silver stick to threaten the polish of the table.

"If I say we should just ignore the princes of Tormalin and everyone else, you're going to tell me I'm sounding like Kalion, aren't you?" said Usara at length, with the shadow of a rueful smile.

"I would never be so impolite." Planir's grin gave the lie to his words as he leaned forward. "But I could spend all day finding arguments why the Council of Hadrumal cannot be seen to involve itself in what is, to all appearances, a fight for land and its attendant wealth. Here's another one for you. We support the Forest Folk in this one conflict, but we deny our aid to anyone else who comes seeking it as a matter of principle—"

"You're mocking me now," Usara protested.

"Oh yes, 'Sar," said Planir earnestly. "Where was I? These men of Wrede or the Duke of Draximal's representatives, they go away empty-handed. There are a great many wizards out in the wider world, 'Sar. Who's to say one might not be tempted, could not be bought, to use his powers in what could be argued was a good cause?"

"Every mage knows they are answerable to Hadrumal." Usara wasn't smiling.

"True enough, but how well could I impose the authority of this office if it came to it?" Planir lifted the heavy gold ring of the Archmage, its massive central diamond set between sapphire, amber, ruby and emerald. "When I have my Council split between defending the Forest in the west, fighting Elietimm in the east and beyond the ocean, while I spend what little remains of my time trying to convince everyone else we do not aim to recreate the Old Empire with me at its head?"

"There's no reason to suppose anything like this will come to pass," said Usara crossly.

"No reason to say it won't," countered Planir. "Sorry, I'm wrong. I can say with fair certainty that none of this will happen if I don't allow the Council of Hadrumal and the Office of Archmage to be dragged into your fight in the first place. I grew up in the mining country of Gidesta and one of the first things every child is taught is never disturb a scree. Taking one stone from the wrong place can bring down half a hillside on your head."

"And that's your final word?" Defeat faded Usara's voice.

"That is *my* final word," Planir replied with deliberate emphasis. "You on the other hand are a free agent. You are at liberty to use any and every means at your disposal. You will have to answer to Council, but I can assure you of my absolute trust in your judgment and complete support."

"Thank you for your confidence," said Usara dryly. "But I don't see quite what I can hope to achieve on my own. Other than Gilmarten, there isn't another mage within leagues of here."

"Why are you so sure of that?" Planir snuffed out the candle between two fingers, the image dissolving around Usara's puzzled expression.

Candle smoke rose in a fragile blue spiral twisting and braiding itself in the shafts of the evening sun slanting in through the windows. Planir rose from his seat and moved to look out over the long roofs of Hadrumal. The gray stone of the halls was warming to gold in the last light, the courts and alleyways thronged with people as wizards and scholars turned their minds to food, drink, conversation and relaxation. The Archmage gazed down, following individuals here and there until the little figures disappeared through gate or doorway.

He wheeled around, eyes keen and dangerous. Hanging wisps of smoke shook and dissipated as Planir swept past to stand in front of the empty fireplace. "So what was it you wished to discuss with me, Shiv?"

Shiv had been sitting on the far side of the room, deep in the shadows of a winged chair. "I have had news of Kalion, Archmage," he said diffidently.

"Should I be concerned?" Planir sounded surprised.

"Given what you've just been saying about Toremal worrying over mages with unbridled ambition, I should say so!" Shiv's initial hesitation was rapidly evaporating.

"Tell me what you've heard," invited Planir.

"That Kalion spent his time in Relshaz meeting all the most powerful men in that most influential of cities. Supposedly he was promising all manner of profit and advantage when 'wizardry takes its proper place in the upper levels of decision-making.'" Shiv's mockery was bitter. "At the turn of Aft-Winter he moved on to Toremal. He was invited to all the best parties, from what I hear, met all the well-connected nobles. Now I believe he is traveling between the Dukes of Marlier and Parnilesse in Lescar, offering his services as an honest broker in their negotiations."

"What makes you think I'm unaware of the way Kalion has been amusing himself?" the Archmage inquired politely.

"You've been very busy lately, Archmage." Shiv struggled for words. "But if you say—I am satisfied . . ." He got hastily to his feet.

"I don't think you are," Planir crossed the room to light a branch of candles with a snap of his fingers, incidentally blocking Shiv's path to the door. "And I don't think I am. Do sit down."

Shiv's knees buckled beneath him, color rising under his sallow skin.

Planir took a chair on the far side of the fireplace. He studied Shiv for a moment. "You say I have been busy? Yes, granted, my duties keep my days full, but of late no more than usual."

Shiv coughed awkwardly. "You've been a little preoccupied."

"Indeed?" Planir leaned back and crossed one elegantly booted foot over his knee. "By what?"

Shiv stood up again. "Obviously I was mistaken. I'm sorry to have taken up your time."

"Or did you think that I had myself tangled in a pretty girl's garters?" asked Planir genially.

Shiv's jaw dropped. "I wouldn't say—" His mouth snapped shut as the Archmage began to chuckle. "Since you put it like that, most revered Archmage, yes. Chimney-corner gossips all over Hadrumal say you've been head down and tail up after a wet scent since Larissa first flirted her petticoats at you!"

Planir's laugh at this was a full-throated guffaw that startled a roosting pigeon from the window ledge. "Oh, sit down, Shiv, and let's have a drink." He went to the sideboard, collecting a wine bottle and clinking two glasses negligently together. "I seem to be doing this earlier and earlier each day at present," he remarked, glancing at the timepiece on the mantel. "Now that would be something you really would have to concern yourself with. You weren't here when Gelake was Flood-Master, were you? That man drunk was an absolute menace."

Defiance and apprehension warring in Shiv's face fled, replaced by simple confusion. He drained his glass in one swallow.

Planir sat back in his chair. "I'm touched by your concern, but it really is unnecessary."

"Is it?" retorted Shiv. "That's not how it looks to me or to anyone else. We see Kalion, whom we all know to be blindly ambitious, waving the potential assistance of Hadrumal in the faces of anyone with the least power or influence. He's a joke here, where there are plenty of people to keep him in check, but out there, with all his fine clothes and his lordly manners, people are taking him very seriously! Why aren't you doing something about it? Because all your time is taken up squiring your pretty new apprentice around parties and dances and giving her late-night tuition that lasts until breakfast at least three times a week! Troanna doesn't approve and as Flood-Mistress, as long as you keep refusing to appoint a Cloud-Master to replace Otrick—if Kalion were to mount a serious challenge to you in Council—" Shiv stopped speaking abruptly and peered into the depths of his goblet.

"You've made your point." Planir refilled Shiv's glass with the crimson wine. "Let me offer you a different perspective. I am fully aware Kalion is letting his mouth write notes his purse cannot hope to honor. He can make all the promises he wants, but he cannot make good on any of them. However long he pulls out his leash, I still have hold of the end and can yank him back whenever I choose. For the moment, I'm content to let him take all the slack he wants and get himself thoroughly tangled up. Then I will naturally come to his aid and with all his fine words proved worthless he will look extremely foolish. Believe me, that will do more to discredit him than any rebuke or penalty I could impose. Kalion will doubtless continue to do all he can to rouse the Council in his support, but I do not propose to give him solid grounds for enmity by express action against him. I won't make an enemy of Kalion, Shiv, because ultimately he truly wants the best for wizardry and, beyond that, to put the wider world to rights. I have no quarrel with that ambition; we just differ rather radically in our approach."

"You're sure you have the Council?" Shiv asked.

Planir smiled. "Kalion's supporters have become both bold and careless, assuming I am far too busy with the delights of the flesh to pay attention. I've been noting just who is feeding Ely and Galen gossip. With Larissa's help, I've laid out some very tempting morsels for those scavenging around the inner circles of the halls. They've taken the bait, but it's Kalion who'll find it so horribly indigestible. He doesn't have nearly the support he imagines, not least because whenever I see Ely and Galen charming someone I later make my own discreet appeal to that individual's common sense."

"Yes, Archmage," Shiv looked sheepish.

The Archmage's genial expression hardened. "Troanna does not approve of my dealings with Larissa, that is very true, but being both old and wise she knows that sensual pleasures are entirely separate from the business of magecraft. Do not make the mistake of confusing the two, Shiv, on my account or on your own. Troanna will judge me as

Archmage on my discharge of my duties, not on how I
choose to spend my time inside my bed-curtains. You of all
people should appreciate that."

Shiv colored and shifted uneasily in his chair. "Yes,
Archmage."

"I have my own contacts in Relshaz and Toremal. You remember Mellitha? When Kalion is promising both moons
and the stars in between to one of the Magistracy, the first
thing he does is talk with her. Kalion cuts a fine figure in his
tailored gowns, talking loud and long about the infinite resources of wizardry. What he doesn't see is that the non-
mage-born find the idea of magic rather worrying,
especially in the hands of a brash and forceful man. Kalion
says he can do all manner of things, but he never stops to
ask if anyone actually wants him to; arrogance raises hackles, Shiv.

"So they go and talk to Mellitha, whom they know to be
a mage, granted, but far more importantly, has lived in their
city for nigh on a generation and everyone agrees is a fair
and honest tax contractor. She tells them not to worry, that
Kalion is all gong and no dinner and the person they need to
look to is the Archmage." Planir grinned. "A mage even
more daunting than this unstoppable enthusiast? No, not at
all, Mellitha tells them. He's a man just like you, enjoys
pretty girls, a dance and a drink and a dubious joke. Everyone knows that to be true, in Hadrumal or anywhere else."
The Archmage's eyes glinted steely gray in the candlelight.
"Reassurance the princes of Tormalin may cling to, if I am
ultimately forced to drive these Elietimm into the ocean
with fire and lightning, flood and earthquake. I will loose all
the might of Hadrumal against these enchanters if need be,
Shiv. What I won't do is waste time and energy in dealing
with petty pinpricks when the real danger is us all having
our throats cut if I misstep."

"Yes, Archmage," the younger man mumbled.

Planir sighed heavily. "As for Otrick, well, I'm not prepared to give up on the old pirate just yet."

"It's been seven seasons out of the eight," Shiv pointed out, face sorrowful.

"While he is still breathing, as long as we can tend his bodily needs," Planir's voice tailed off. "If nothing comes of 'Sar's trip, then yes, I will take the matter to Council, but even then I will be advising against any hasty decision. Otrick is not suffering, after all."

Glum silence hung heavily in the air.

"I know you couldn't sanction Council involvement, but can I go?" Shiv looked up eagerly. "If this Gilmarten's element is air, with my water talents and Usara holding the earth we'd only need a fire mage to have a nexus."

"Where would you find this fire mage?" Planir smiled at Shiv's expression. "I'll make a deal with you; if you square the circle before 'Sar does, I'll send you to give him the answer."

He opened the door and ushered the younger man out, Shiv's brow now knotted in thought. Planir swung the heavy black oak shut and leaned his forehead against it for an instant. Forcing a smile, he crossed the room and opened a second door, skillfully made to remain unnoticed in the lines and folds of the carved paneling. The Archmage entered a small room dominated by an elegant bedstead whose curtains of yellow silk were embroidered with bright vines and flowers. Larissa sat in a chair upholstered in the same style, hands folded neatly in her lap and ankles crossed. She stared out of the window at the sunset, face set like the snowy stone of the marble washstand beside her. A gown of azure satin overlaid with gauze expertly flattered her figure while her chestnut hair was caught up in combs and curls, discreet cosmetics enhancing eyes, cheeks and lips.

"And now you are, what, angry or upset?" Planir sat on the edge of the bed and took off his boots. "Or both?"

Larissa glared at him. "You tell Shiv I'm simply here to serve as a means of spreading your own particular rumors? After all, everyone's going to believe what I tell them, aren't they? If you can't trust a woman to spread pillow talk, who can you trust!" Rising color clashed with the softer blush of her rouge.

"You've always been fully in my confidence when it comes to seasoning the gossip with a few judicious tidbits, my dearest." Planir dropped his shirt on the floor. "As I recall, you've played the game willingly and with considerable skill." He grinned at her.

"What if I did?" she said crossly. "Doesn't it bother you, what everyone is saying? And now I hear I can expect sniggers and innuendo anywhere from Col to the Cape of Winds! My role is just to reassure all and sundry that you are a man with manly appetites?"

"I don't deny people thinking that is something I can turn to my advantage, but I can't do anything about gossip. I'm very sorry if you find it humiliating; frankly, I could do without it myself," Planir shrugged. "The office of Archmage has many and varied powers, but stopping people thinking what they want is beyond me."

"But you use the prattle, turn it against the tattlers." Larissa's voice was losing the certainty of affront in the face of Planir's calm.

"True enough," he agreed. "I use all and every means to discharge my duties; I told you that from the outset. But I haven't done anything to create gossip. I have neither flaunted you nor hidden you away as if we had anything to be ashamed of. That's the other side of the coin after all, if I were to let myself be influenced by the whispers and snide remarks." Planir unlaced his plain broadcloth breeches, stepping out of them and crossing to a wardrobe where he found a clean shirt of soft silk. "I told you from the start that there would be talk and that it would be for you to judge if it ever weighed too heavily in the scales against me."

Larissa looked down at her hands and the room was silent but for the rustle of silk as the Archmage dressed.

"All I ask, my dearest, is that you weigh my words before anyone else's," Planir said gently. "Have I ever lied to you? Have I ever deceived you? Do you believe me when I tell you that your wit and your company, your charm and your passion, are the greatest gifts ever bestowed on me? With you at my side, I would count myself the most fortunate man in the world, were I the meanest miner in Gidesta, never mind the Archmage of Hadrumal."

"But you are the Archmage of Hadrumal," said Larissa with a catch in her voice.

"I am," Planir nodded. "And I have to bear all that comes with it. You do not, unless you choose to, my darling. You know that."

Another silence threatened to lengthen interminably until bells all over the many-towered city began to strike their chimes. Planir looked at a small timepiece on the nightstand beside the bed. "For the moment, we have to decide if we are going to the dance at the Scaward Hall. There will be grist for the rumor mill in every set we dance together, but then again if we do not go that will spark a whole new round of speculation and rumor. Has his eye lighted on some other maiden? Has she got the advancement she sought, whatever that might be? Is he moving on now he's got another notch on his bedpost, or has she tired of being an old man's folly?" His voice was gently teasing. "But that won't alter the fact that if you prefer not to go, that is good enough for me. If we go, that's of no significance beyond the fact that I like to dance, that I particularly love to dance with you, and that I feel like shedding the cares of my office for an evening and reveling with the most beautiful girl in Hadrumal." He moved to the door, an elegant figure in understated black silk, tailoring impeccable.

Larissa stood up, twitching aside the skirts of her gown. "Find your dancing slippers, O revered Archmage." She was smiling with a combative light in her eye. "Let them talk. Though, as for reveling," she linked her arm through his as they departed, "that will depend on whether or not you tire yourself out on the dance floor, won't it?"

The Great Forest, 6th of Aft-Summer

While Usara was fussing around with his mirror and a spill from the fire, I followed one of the healers out of the hollow and down a farther slope in the forest floor to a long narrow lakelet. Trickles of water ran down the fern-draped face of rock laid in layers of gray and ocher pierced with damp blackness here and there. Cool struck up from the slowly rippling water; groups of men and women were bathing, washing clothing and picking their way carefully along a slippery green ledge to fill pans from the clean water of the spring. I washed thoroughly, gasping at the chill on my hot body but relishing being clean again. Draping my jerkin around me, I went in search of what passed for clean linen.

The man Harile was busy with bowls of steeping herbs in the mouth of the cave and nodded at me as I rummaged in my bag. "You are of the Folk?" He sounded doubtful.

"No," I shook my head. "My father was, but I am an outdweller." I had that much clear by now. My parents' past was theirs and my future was my own. I lifted the precious book out of the bottom of my satchel and checked that the wrappings were intact. I looked at Harile. "That song you were singing earlier, it was 'Mazir's Healing Hands,' wasn't it?"

He glanced up from his work. "What of it?"

"Did you know there is power in the song, in the jalquezan?" I smiled at him.

Polite mystification creased Harile's forehead. "What kind of power?"

"A form of enchantment." I laid every pennyweight of sincerity within me on my words. "I came east at the behest of Tormalin scholars, to learn the hidden lore of the ancient races. I found the jalquezan."

Interest was beginning to replace the doubt in Harile's expression. "But how can it be enchantment? It's just nonsense."

"It's far more than that," I assured him with utter conviction. "No question of it."

"If jalquezan is a means of enchantment, what can it do against the Mountain Men?" He seized on this notion as I'd hoped he would.

"You find a song to suit your needs. If you wish to hide, you sing of Viyenne and the Does; if you are lost, sing of Mazir and the Storm and you'll find your path again." I made it sound as easy as shelling peas. "The jalquezan ties enchantment to the song. It's all in this book." I hugged it tight and hoped he wouldn't ask to see it.

"You can work enchantment just by singing?" I kept a curse behind my teeth as I heard doubt faltering in Harile's voice.

"I've been traveling with these wizards for the best part of the year. They've been trying to solve this puzzle for a generation and jalquezan proved the best piece to fit!" I felt I was bluffing with an empty hand to win a king's ransom.

"We just have to sing?" Harile looked toward a group of little children. All were tear-stained and one kept looking over her shoulder, her puzzled demand for "Mamamam" understandable in any tongue.

"You sing and you trust in the power of the jalquezan." If I could match this depth of earnestness, I could persuade the Emperor of Tormalin to pay me for the right to his own throne.

"Do we all have to sing?"

Saedrin save me, what had the scholars' theories been about Artifice? Belief was the key and the more minds focused on something, the more power that belief could draw

on? Just trying to make sense of it made my head hurt and I
closed my eyes. Why try to make sense of it? Why not just
do it and trust to luck? I opened my eyes to see Harile looking at me expectantly.

"Try to get as many people singing as possible," I said,
all calm confidence. "Just tell them to concentrate on the
words and their wish to have your people safe and well. The
jalquezan will do the rest."

Harile's brow cleared and he shrugged. "If it does no
good, it can do no harm," he smiled wearily. "And singing
will certainly put some spirit in people."

I'd have preferred a more whole-hearted endorsement
but I'd take what was offered. "If you'll excuse me, I'll go
and see how my friends are getting on." That was one rune
laid, time for some more.

I saw the others clustered around Usara, who was settled
on the ground, legs outstretched either side of a broad shallow bowl. I stood next to Gilmarten. 'Gren sat cross-legged
opposite and Darni looked down over Usara's head. Sorgrad
sat a few paces away eating something, face neutral.

Dim green light began to gather and swirl in the bottom
of the bowl, coalescing into a reflection that sparkled with
the sharp uncluttered sunlight of the mountains, odd contrast to the muted light filtering through the woods where
we sat. The image swooped and took flight, plunging down
a stony track that coiled down the parched turf. Dry earth
and broken rock filled the image, sliding past with a speed
that baffled vision. I closed my eyes as my stomach
protested.

"Where's someone to fight?" demanded 'Gren.

Usara flexed his hands, tongue between his teeth as he
concentrated. "I can't find anyone close at hand, that's
something at least."

"Just find the main bulk of their forces," ordered Darni.

Usara looked up over his shoulder. "This would be a
great deal easier without you breathing down my neck. I'll
manage my scrying as I see fit, thank you all the same." He

scowled. "I can't be sure if their cursed aetheric magic is baffling my scrying."

"Try it with this." I dangled the Sheltya bitch's paring knife over the bowl and smiled sweetly at Usara. "Isn't your scrying much more certain with someone's possessions?"

Usara narrowed his eyes at me but took the knife and dropped it into the water with an expressive flick of his fingers. I grinned at Sorgrad and 'Gren.

"Here we are," said Usara suddenly. We all moved to look over his shoulder, jostling each other but careful not to jog the mage.

Green light rose from the water, soft and fragile in the sun. The silver of the knife blade glittered for a moment before disappearing as a little image floated on the surface of the water. It was the woman, in a rekin somewhere.

"I wouldn't say all you Mountain Men look the same but your homes sure as curses do!" I murmured to Sorgrad. The woman was standing by a long slate table that could have been cut from the same slab as the one in the Hachalfess. As I spoke, the Sheltya woman crossed the cluttered living hall of the rekin. She went outside; Gilmarten caught his breath while the rest of us swore.

The compound was thronged with men and activity. Sheaves of arrows were being handed out from a workshop, swords strapped over mail-shirts and helms buckled beneath determined chins. The woman went from group to group, leaving each man grim-faced with hatred or bright-eyed with a hot rage that only vengeance would quench.

"You should have used the bluesalt, my girl," said 'Gren without pleasure. He pointed out a head darker than the rest, gray Sheltya robes over workday leathers. It was the Elietimm enchanter and I cursed vilely.

"We'll get him next time," Sorgrad murmured. "See how he copes with a sword through his guts."

I managed a thin smile. Usara's spell drifted above the compound and we watched as the crowd ebbed and flowed, people spilling out onto the hillside below the great gates.

Mules laden with nameless bundles were tracking up the long haul, unidentifiable people trailing up after them. The broad valley was cut by myriad workings, old and new scored into the land around like the gouges of giant claws. Stone mills and limekilns sat huge and squat, the fess and the rekin almost insignificant, huddled among sprawling heaps of spoil. The mountains dwarfed everything, reaching upward into the blue sky, the color mirrored in Sorgrad's eyes as he studied their summits and scarps.

"Someone's planning a war," Darni said with grim satisfaction.

"Show me the peaks," asked Sorgrad abruptly.

Usara's breath was laboring now, thin shoulders hunched, but he wheeled the image around and lifted it to the mountains high above the fess. A sharp-edged ridge of bare rock ran up to a snowy field of white, ice defying the summer sun in the hollow breast of the mountain. The ridge split into two, one spine running up to a ragged summit of tumbled rock, the other to a higher crest, notched and dished like a well-worn knife. Two mighty peaks dominated the head of the valley, one a thrusting spearhead clad in ice, riven down one face with deep clefts, the other dark and brooding, tolerating no snow on sides that the summer sun struck with the sheen of a raven's wing.

"Teyvasoke," said Sorgrad with utter certainty.

"You're sure?" demanded Darni.

Sorgrad looked at him, face impassive. "I'm sure. You were taught the streets and houses of your hometown as a child? We are taught the peaks of all the ranges, east, west and middle."

"Teyvasoke." Darni tried the unfamiliar name on his tongue. "Where are we in relation to it?"

"About twelve days or so from here, traveling fast and light. I'll draw you a map," murmured Sorgrad. "If they don't get here first."

We looked down on a sizeable number, all intent on their various tasks. Tents were being set up, some in circles, others in neat rows, a few on their own. People were bringing in arms of brushwood and stubborn thorn, stacking the fuel by fire pits while others ferried water and slops. Chainmail gleamed in the sunlight and a few people hurrying to and fro without the burden of armor were dressed in the anonymous gray of the Sheltya. I stifled a faint shudder.

We watched for a while and nothing much happened but then the gates of the fess swung open and a small group emerged, catching up the curious as they headed for an open space in the valley. Everyone sat in a half-circle on the dry ground while the man who'd come out of the fess stood up to address them. He was stocky in build but with a face Niello would have paid good coin to model for an actor's mask. Wiry golden hair was swept back from a broad forehead above a proud nose. The man's jaw was square beneath a close-trimmed beard and, given his gestures, his mouth was as eloquent as it was handsome. He turned from side to side, hands expressive as they were spread in appeal, clenched in determined oration and finally raised to the skies in impassioned exhortation. The crowd stirred, soon nodding and echoing his movements as his words spurred them on. When he finished whatever it was he was saying with a flourish of his sword, his audience sprang to their feet, waving and visibly cheering, eagerness bright on every face. My frustration at not being able to hear this charismatic leader's words was mirrored on everyone else's expression as they gazed down at the face framed in the bowl while Usara bent all the spell's attention on the man.

"We'd need ten times the men we've got here to stop them," growled 'Gren.

"Who's to defend these, if we take everyone who can stand and hold a weapon?" Darni glowered at the children, the elderly and the infirm.

"That would be a legitimate use of wizardry," offered Gilmarten.

"Wouldn't you be more use fighting?" Sorgrad countered. "A lightning bolt in the right place could do more damage than half a Tormalin cohort."

"We're going to have to be very careful where and how we fight." Darni was ignoring this byplay. "Picking the right ground is going to be crucial."

'Gren was watching the tiny figures drifting away from the speaker. "I don't think he's managed to rouse any complete soke. If this was a true host, like the old sagas, every fess would have its own fire, its own standard."

"So who's behind him?" I looked closer, trying to discern any difference worth the name in the multitude.

"Exiles, those driven out for some crime, real or imagined," suggested Sorgrad with a thin smile.

"Younger sons from hungry lands," offered 'Gren. "Sons of those that married out and lost their blood claim?"

" 'Sar, I need you to scry all the closest valleys," decided Darni. "See if they are all taking up arms or whether this is a limited rising, stirred up by Blondie there."

"I don't know what difference that makes," muttered Usara rather testily. "There are scores of them, all with swords, and they're heading this way."

"Not necessarily," Sorgrad shook his head. "They could head out into the Gap just as easily as swing south toward us."

"All the more reason to try and put a stop to this good and fast." Darni looked at Usara with ill-disguised impatience. "Look beyond the reach of your own hands, man!"

This was soldiers' talk. But I'm not a soldier, never have been, never want to be. On the other hand, on a very few, desperate occasions in my early years on the road, hunger had forced me into lurking in alleys, cudgel in one hand and heart in my mouth. I'd always looked for some man careless in his drink with a well-filled pouch that I could follow and relieve of both senses and purse. At a head shorter than any potential mark and half the heft, I wasn't about to take on anyone in an equal fight. A footpad goes for the head, not the arms.

"What if you kill off their leaders?" I asked. "The Ice Islanders fighting in Kellarin last summer gave up at once when their commanders died."

"Then Elietimm have less in common with the Men of the Mountains than they claim," responded Sorgrad with contempt. "Anyatimm are trained to take over any task if another man's injured, be it in the diggings, on the trap line or fighting lowlanders in the Gap."

"They're paying a lot of heed to Pretty Boy though," mused 'Gren. "I bet him catching an arrow in the throat would give them pause for thought. A mob's only as strong as whoever's holding it together, 'Grad, you know that."

"What about the Sheltya?" I suggested. "Especially if they're using aetheric magic to keep everyone together."

Sorgrad grimaced. "You'd be swapping silver for copper, my girl. Killing Sheltya gets you staked out on a mountainside alive for as long as it takes the ravens to find you and peck out your eyes and liver. Kill Sheltya and that army will be out to avenge a blood feud."

"What about this Ice Islander?" Nervousness gnawed at the pit of my belly.

Darni looked at Sorgrad. "Would blood loyalty extend to him? I'll bet half the wealth of Hadrumal he's at the bottom of this mischief."

"Even if he's claiming to be Sheltya, he's not born to any soke this side of the ocean, let alone the Gap," replied Sorgrad slowly. "Everyone can see that from his face and hair. They'd probably look to avenge his death, but I can't see it ranking as blood insult."

"Family's everything in the mountains," 'Gren nodded. "The knife cuts both ways; if you're not family, you're nothing."

"So what if we take the Elietimm enchanter out of the balance?" I persisted. "The Sheltya stay neutral normally, we know that." I felt my way cautiously through this. "For them to get involved, something must have stirred them up. Given what we saw at the Hachalfess, the Sheltya reckon to be cock of the dunghill, so it would have to be someone out of the ordinary run of the runes. It has to be the enchanter, doesn't it?"

"He could well be a key link holding a lot of this together," Sorgrad looked more cheerful. "It's got to be worth seeing what happens if we snap it."

"So the three of us go up into the heights and deal with him," suggested 'Gren. "You lick these Folk into shape, Darni, and stop Pretty Boy's little army getting any deeper into trouble in the meantime."

"I'd certainly take any road that offered a short cut through this," muttered Darni. "I've no troops for a pitched battle."

"I'm sorry but I really cannot agree to this." We all looked at Usara and the wizard's fair coloring betrayed him. "I need Sorgrad here," he said, getting defiantly to his feet and letting his spell fade unheeded. "Planir told me I was to use my powers together with Gilmarten and any other mage I could find locally."

"I'm no mage and neither you nor your Archmage has any claim on me," replied Sorgrad in a level tone.

"I understand you could never explore the potential of your wizardry, given your birth and upbringing," Usara continued as if Sorgrad had not spoken, "but even untrained as you are we can drill you in some simple spells."

"No," said Sorgrad.

Usara stared at him. "What do you mean?"

"I didn't make myself clear?" Sorgrad's eyes were cold and hard. "No."

"This is no time to be stubborn, man. You are mageborn!" Usara's puzzlement soured toward anger. "You have a duty to use that wizardry and I cannot imagine a more crucial time for you to accept your responsibilities!"

"I have no duty to an accident of birth," replied Sorgrad with contempt. "I bear no more responsibility for it than you do for losing your hair. My loyalty is to my blood and my friends."

"Even if your attitude leaves these people dead on the Forest floor?" demanded Usara hotly. "When your cooperation could have saved them?"

'Gren stirred and I gave him a warning glare; I had another rune to turn this hand. "What exactly did Planir say?" The wizard was momentarily disconcerted as I claimed his attention by standing between him and Sorgrad. It wasn't the most sensible place to be but someone had to stop this from turning into a fistfight.

"I asked what I was supposed to do, given there wasn't another mage hereabouts beyond Gilmarten—and me," Usara replied crossly. "Planir said not to be so sure of that and then he broke the link. He must have meant Sorgrad, that's all there is to it."

"Says who?" demanded 'Gren belligerently. "How's he ever even heard of my brother?"

"I told my Archmage that I had discovered magebirth was not unknown among the Mountain Men, as we have always supposed." Usara lifted his chin defiantly. "That you seem unaccountably able to suppress your elemental affinity—" he shot Sorgrad a look of annoyance and suspicion—"is something better left until we return to Hadrumal. We can explore that peculiarity there."

"You can forget that, mage," said Sorgrad disdainfully. "I'm not going to Hadrumal as long as I've got a hole in my arse."

Usara squared up to Sorgrad like a bantam taking on a fighting cock. "Planir said—"

"Why do you say magebirth is unknown among the people of the mountains?" Gilmarten's courteous question in his soft Soluran lilt cut through Usara's ire like a knife through cheese. The mage was still looking relatively dapper after our rough couple of days, though the loss of his hat meant he was a little sun-scorched around the face.

"Because it is, I mean, they don't." Usara looked bemused.

"They do in Solura." Gilmarten looked a little self-conscious. "At least, I have met mages of both half- and quarter-Mountain blood and heard tell of at least one pure-blooded."

"Something else you lot in Hadrumal got wrong?" 'Gren taunted.

"What about Forest blood?" Usara's question was half a heartbeat behind my own.

"Something else you don't know, Sandy?" asked 'Gren silkily.

The Soluran wizard nodded. "It's the same as far as I know; uncommon, but not unheard of."

"There's your answer then." I spoke hurriedly to stop 'Gren stirring the fire any higher. "If you want to get yourself a new apprentice, we see if there's someone here with the . . ." I couldn't think how to phrase it. "Somebody mage-born."

"We have methods of teaching by rote in my tradition that could certainly offer these people some means of protection," offered Gilmarten with a nervous smile. Usara looked obstinate but also unsure, aware that the ground had somehow shifted under him.

"Let's get a grip on the reins here. Squabbling among ourselves is just handing advantage to the enemy," said Darni firmly. "We need to know who we are fighting, so 'Sar, scry out the closest valleys. See which are mustering for a fight. You two, you know the mountains and you know fighting; the hunters here know the woods. We need to draw up a map tying everything together. We'll want at least one trained mage in any fight but if we can find mage-born folk hereabouts who can defend their own, that'll free up more fighting men and women. Gilmarten and Livak, go and see what you can find out."

Darni's bull-headed assumption of command at least broke the deadlock. The big fighter headed for Bera and 'Gren followed, Sorgrad walking more slowly, expression unreadable. Usara sniffed crossly as he bent over his scrying bowl but the irritation in his face gradually waned as he wrought his magic.

I turned to Gilmarten, who smiled uncertainly at me. "Let's start with Harile," I suggested. "He'll probably have some ideas about who might be mage-born."

We went into the gray gloom of the cave mouth. "Harile?"

"Over here." He picked his way through the pallets and blankets wrapping tightly packed bodies. "What can I do for you?"

"Usara's scrying out your enemies," I pointed out the mage hunched over his bowl. "If you've something to dull pain without addling his wits, it would help."

"I can make a tisane to give him a lift," Harile suggested.

"Many thanks." I felt Gilmarten stir beside me. "I was wondering, do you ever have mage-born among the Folk?" I asked casually. "It shows itself about the age Drianon bloods a girl, among the outdwellers at least."

We followed Harile to a fire where he swung a battered kettle over the hottest flames. "We tend to notice it hereabouts when Trimon breaks a boy's voice. With girls it's any time after Larasion brings them into bloom."

"What do you notice? What exactly signifies magebirth to you?" Gilmarten tugged absently on his tuft of beard.

"Some are an utter nuisance anywhere near a hearth until it passes. Fire either burns through half a night's fuel inside a few moments or just dies away and refuses to be relit." Harile paused in mixing pinches of herbs in a beaker. "You get some who don't leave a footprint for half a year, and there's always the story of one lass who got rained on from Solstice to Solstice, just her, you understand, no one else." He laughed. "But I've heard that tale from a handful of folk between here and the southern sea, all saying it happened to a friend of a friend, so I think that's just wind in the long grass."

"Let me take that to Usara." I reached for the cup and Gilmarten walked with me. He scratched his head, perplexed. "I've never heard of sympathy with an element just going away."

"Can you tell if someone is mage-born? Is there some test?" I set the cup down next to Usara and we went back to Harile, who was mulching some leaves into a poultice.

"There are methods of determining where the principal sympathy lies," Gilmarten answered, "when the effects are first manifesting themselves." He looked concerned. "Is it possible that if a sympathy is not trained it is lost?"

"Not if Sorgrad's any guide," I said with determination. "Harile, do you know of anyone here who once showed signs of magebirth? They might be able to help our wizards defend your sick and elderly."

Harile set his bowl of pulpy mess down at once. "Come with me." He led us to a fire no more than a few embers smoldering in a nest of feathery ash. Those sitting around it were somewhere between youth and adulthood, with little more than a blanket and a few salvaged possessions to cling to. None had anything like blithe confidence I had come to expect from Forest Folk.

"This is Sarachi." Harile indicated a youth with Forest red hair over a face that should have been following a plow in Caladhria. "He showed magebirth, as far as we could judge."

"What of it?" The lad had a hint of spirit left.

"This wizard thinks you could help him." Harile indicated Gilmarten.

Sarachi started to get to his feet but Gilmarten waved him to sit again. I perched on a stump and watched quietly. Gilmarten lit a twig from the last glow of the fire.

"Concentrate on the flame." He handed it to Sarachi. "See if you can make it smaller." To my eyes, the feeble yellow flicker didn't vary in the slightest until the flame threatened his fingers and Sarachi dropped the spill.

"I need a cup of water." Gilmarten looked around as if he expected to see a potman. One of the girls wordlessly handed him a carved wooden beaker. "Cup your hands." Gilmarten poured a little water into Sarachi's hollowed palms. "Keep it there as long as you can." Disappointment

was audible all around as the water trickled out from between Sarachi's fingers, despite the effort whitening his
knuckles.

"No matter." Gilmarten sounded as if he meant it. If he
didn't I'd finally met a wizard to challenge to a game of
Raven. The Soluran scraped up a handful of earth, picking
out fragments of long rotted leaf and then dusting it lightly
with ash from the fire. He pressed this into Sarachi's open
palm. "See if you can lift the ash out of the earth. Concentrate, visualize the gray moving out of the brown and being
carried away on the wind."

Sarachi frowned with effort and in the next instant the
whole handful spiraled upward into the air. We all looked
up and then cursed as specks of dirt fell in our open mouths
and wide eyes.

"An air sympathy," said Gilmarten happily, "or affinity as
they would call it in Hadrumal."

"But you told me to concentrate on the earth," objected
Sarachi.

"Bluffing, wizard?" I teased.

"Something like that. An untrained sympathy can hamper itself; combined trials get around the problem."
Gilmarten looked around. "Does anyone know someone
else who showed signs of magebirth?"

A thin girl with lank brown hair raised a bruised and dirty
hand. "Castan did."

We found this Castan at a hearth on the far side of the
hollow, a no-nonsense woman with red-rimmed eyes. The
notion that her previously disregarded magebirth might
help protect her three young offspring set the fire raging beneath her cook pot. Gilmarten explained, we doused the
conflagration and moved rapidly on to the next potential
wizard.

By the time we returned to Usara, we had seven in tow.
Sarachi was joined by a lad whose fuzz of a beard only
showed where it caught the light and a tired-faced man in
his middle years. Castan was leading three younger women,

all smiling nervously and variously encouraged or teased by their friends. We left behind five others, some disgruntled, some relieved, when Gilmarten had pronounced them either never mage-born or with a sympathy so faint it could not be trained.

"Darni is one of those, an affinity too weak to work with," I told the Soluran quietly as we left one disappointed man crossly poking his recalcitrant fire with a vindictive stick.

"I didn't know that." Gilmarten looked thoughtful. "Still, that means we can bespeak him with fire and metal if he's elsewhere."

"He doesn't have to be an actual wizard for that? Just mage-born?" The next step was an obvious one.

Gilmarten made it. "No, and that means we could contact your friend Sorgrad, if he is willing to acknowledge his sympathy to that extent."

"I'll see if I can talk him into it." Sorgrad might not want to be a mage on Hadrumal's terms, but if he didn't see advantages in having wizards keeping us informed about what they could scry out, he wasn't the man I knew. Of course, there would be disadvantages as well, but we'd find ways around those.

Usara looked up from his bowl as we reached him. He eased his stiff shoulders, each giving a crack that made me wince. "Well?"

"Seven," Gilmarten's excitement was understandable. "One each with earth and air, three with fire, which is most unusual, and two with water."

Usara's tense face lightened considerably. "That's two full nexus groups!"

Gilmarten tugged at his beard. "That's not a way we are accustomed to work in Solura, but perhaps we can manage."

"We could do without all this noise."

Darni came over, parchments in hand, 'Gren and Sorgrad behind, heads close in conversation. The gentle song of a lute was blending with a pipe somewhere the far side of the dell, underscored with voices here and there. The melody swelled as everyone united in the same measure for a few moments and ebbed with descant and counterpoint floating in from different directions.

"I like it," said 'Gren with simple honesty. A single clear voice lifted a new tune, others repeating it a few measures later, doubling and redoubling into a round song.

"If your countrymen have an ear for a tune, it'll lead them straight to us," pointed out Darni. I held my breath and my tongue.

"I can use air to cap it?" Gilmarten offered. "I'd be loath to forbid it since they do seem to find some healing in the music."

Usara shot me a suspicious glance that I returned with a bland look of innocence. I wasn't about to admit to a hand in this outbreak of singing, not until I had some way of judging whether my speculation was paying off.

Darni grunted. "So what have you found for us?" He smiled at the nervous would-be wizards with all the charm of a man-trap.

I moved to talk to Sorgrad and 'Gren as Gilmarten told his tale. "How've you been faring?"

"We've got some sound maps drawn up," Sorgrad said neutrally.

"You agree we should make a play for this Ice Islander? Knock him off the board?" If Sorgrad reckoned this was folly, I'd have to abandon the idea.

"If we can find the bastard." Sorgrad nodded. "It's got to be the quickest way to put the mockers on this fighting. These Forest Folk might be getting hit with the shitty end of the privy stick for the present, but if the lowlanders get involved penny to a pack weight the Anyatimm will lose in the end."

"That's good enough for me," said 'Gren, looking dangerous.

"Since when did you need an excuse?" Sorgrad gave his brother a genial shove.

I looked up, but Darni and Usara were still deep in conversation with Gilmarten. "This Ice Islander, he's going to know plenty about this aetheric magic. That's what we've been looking for, to turn into coin since we started this game. I've been thinking he might be worth more to us alive."

"You're still aiming to kidnap him?" Sorgrad looked at me sharply. "That's a high-stakes game, my girl."

"Long odds pay best," I told him. "We don't have a lot to show for half a year on the road so far, do we?"

"But Sandy said you mustn't!" gasped 'Gren, wide-eyed in mockery.

"Since when did I answer to him?" I retorted with a grin.

"It'll be cursed dangerous," commented Sorgrad thoughtfully. "We'd have to make sure he can't use any enchantments on us."

"If we can't work out a way to do it safely, then we just kill him," I promised.

"Knock him hard enough on the head and he won't be any trouble," suggested 'Gren.

"Knock him too hard and he won't be any use," I countered.

"Sandy and the Bear won't like it," pointed out 'Gren with ill-concealed glee.

"By the time they work out what we're up to, it'll be too late." I smiled. "They agreed we could take him out of the balance. I never said exactly how."

"According to Darni, those mages will be able to bespeak me," Sorgrad said dourly. "Whether I like it or not."

"Couldn't you suffer having Usara scry out our escape route and telling us if the way is clear? What are they going to do even if they see things they don't like? They're not going to be able to stop us." I waved a dismissive hand.

"Over here!" We all turned our heads at Darni's peremptory summons.

"He really does think he's biggest toad in the pond," murmured 'Gren.

"Let him play king of the log if he wants," I advised. "We're in this for ourselves. Yes, Darni, what now?"

Darni looking determined was an awesome sight. "Now I start drilling anyone and everyone capable of fighting. 'Sar and Gilmarten teach their new apprentices enough to keep the tail end here safe from harm. You three try to take this Ice Islander out of the game. The good news is this uprising looks limited to just three valleys. We need to nip it in the bud before it spreads, and the loss of their enchanter might just be enough to do it."

"Fair enough." Anticipation warred with misgivings inside me. But this time I'd have Sorgrad and 'Gren with me to tilt the odds my way, I reminded myself.

"If we're going to tackle him, we need to know where he is," Sorgrad said to Usara.

"He's been sticking closer to her ladyship than her shift," the mage replied. "In the Tcyvafess."

"Can you get these Folk to hold the line long enough for us to get there?" I demanded.

"Can't Sandy do some magic to send us?" protested 'Gren. "It's a cursed long walk."

"A mage can only do that kind of thing to somewhere he's already been," I explained.

"One of you mages will have to bespeak me if she goes anywhere else." Sorgrad looked at Darni. "You'll have to spare us some bowmen, preferably ones who can handle a sword. It'll just be the three of us going in, but we have to expect pursuit. They can wait half a day back, closer if the ground favors concealment."

"I'm coming with you," said Usara abruptly; his face was pale and set. "I cannot let you risk Elietimm enchantments without some real magic backing you up. We've all seen what these people are capable of and I am not going to be the one telling Planir I let you go without all the support I could offer." He managed a strained smile. "Worrying as I find these Ice Islanders and their enchantments, I'm rather more afraid of our revered Archmage."

"But you can barely walk, man! And you wizards are horribly vulnerable when you set your minds on your own spells," I pointed out. "That's how they got at Otrick."

"This enchanter would have to know I was there in order to go hunting me," Usara said stiffly. "With Guinalle's help over the last few seasons, we have been finding ways of working magic to evade aetheric notice."

That was all very well as long as it was only his own sanity he was risking, but if the Elietimm got him they'd be halfway to getting me. Unfortunately, I couldn't see how I was going to stop him coming short of stabbing him in the other leg, which I couldn't see going down well with Darni or Gilmarten.

"There's no chance of you coming into the fess itself; Sheltya clearly have some way of telling mages. You stay with the bowmen and you sit on your hands until after we've made our move." Sorgrad's decision startled me but his tone made it clear it was final. "I want your word on that, Usara, by everything you hold holy."

"If he can't come in and he can't use his magic, why do we want him along?" objected 'Gren. "And he'll have to hop all the way there and back."

"He can learn to use crutches or he'll just have to follow on behind." Sorgrad smiled at Usara. "We're likely to come out of there with every hound in the soke on our trail. Then you can use all the magic you want, Sandy, raise fire to scour our scent clean off the rocks."

'Gren and I exchanged a look of understanding. Getting in to steal something is only ever half the task. It's getting out again with the spoils that marks the successful thief.

Nine

In this Mountain tale of how the world was made, we find both familiar and strange ideas. Only the gods know the truth and perhaps they have shared it among the peoples, so that we may only learn by sharing our knowledge.

> Maewelin made the world,
> Carved it with rivers deep.
> She folded hill and vale,
> And raised the saw-edged heights.
> She looked and yet she wept.
> Her beauteous work so fair,
> Had no one to delight,
> Unseen, untouched, unheard.
> So to Misaen's forge,
> She went and bade him make
> A people and all beasts
> Of water, land and air.
> Misaen took the clouds,
> And folded feathered fowl.
> He plaited fish from rain,
> He shaped the beasts of earth.
> He took the finest clay
> And sought to make a man.
> It slipped beneath his hands
> And stubborn would not yield.

433

"Maewelin! Give me gold,
The sinews of the rock,
The mountain's jeweled heart,
That I may forge true worth."
"The power you would use
Could hold my world in thrall,
Could seize the very moons.
I can but lend such might."
Maewelin made a pact.
Misaen set his seal.
So life that could not die,
Would pass to deathless sleep.
Misaen took her gifts
And blended them with fire.
His greatest work was made
To burn full bright then fail.

Teyvasoke,
18th of Aft-Summer

"Just walk slowly, keep your hood up and avoid catching anyone's eye," 'Gren murmured out of the side of his mouth. He spoke slowly to ensure I understood. Neither brother had talked anything but the Mountain tongue since we had left Apak's camp, which had done wonders for my understanding of the language. It had been worse for my temper; some days I'd been so frustrated I'd have cheerfully punched them both on the nose. My accent was reasonably convincing by now—having a good ear for a tune helps there—but there were still too many things I just didn't know the words for.

I ran a hand over my hair, damp with sweat in the noon heat. The short crop still felt strange, the hair strawlike after Harile's foul-smelling concoction had leached out most of

the color. Sorgrad was confident passing eyes would slide
incuriously over a light-eyed, sandy blond in the company
of two undeniably pure-blooded Mountain Men. Still, I was
taking no chances, concealing myself in a sacklike garment
'Gren had acquired. Some woodcutter had learned the hard
way not to leave his linen drying on the broom bushes
fringing his little steading.

"So where have this lot been?" wondered 'Gren aloud.
We'd waited and watched and finally come in on the tail
end of a straggle of returning troops.

"Raiding the lowlands," Sorgrad nodded at the dust
kicked up by protesting flocks of abducted sheep in the
grassy expanses farther down the valley.

I looked around at the new arrivals competing for
cramped space to spread their blankets and set up cook
pots. "No one's going to be surprised to see faces they don't
know hereabouts, are they?"

We walked slowly up the broad floor of the wide valley,
which was crowded with tents and rough shelters. On either
side ramparts of rock marched down from the heights to en-
fold the soke with their protection, pierced with the dark entrances of mines. Ahead the land rose in a shallow sweep,
past broken ground pocked with workings up to a gentle
rise still dotted with a few remaining trees, then it changed
abruptly, folded into deep, forested gullies. The twin mountains, light and dark, reared up beyond, clouds streaming
like banners from their summits.

I brought my wits back from that distant beauty to considerations closer at hand. They might be a motley crowd
but this was more than the ragtag collection of raiding parties that Lescari dukes dignify with the title of army. In the
time it had taken us to reach here, a sizable host had gathered. I only hoped they'd disperse as rapidly if we could get
rid of the Ice Islander's enchantments. I looked sideways
from beneath my hood at a gang of youths sitting around an
unlit fire pit. One with dark eyes startling below corn-silk
yellow hair was brushing his mail-shirt free of specks of

rust, another with the rounder features of mixed blood was
using a whetstone on a sword with a notch in the metal
jagged as a freshly broken tooth. A third bent over a dusty
boot that looked to have covered more leagues than my
own. The ring of hammer and metal punctuated conversation on all sides.

"If we'd bleached what was left of his hair, Sandy could
have passed among these mongrels," 'Gren said cheerfully.

"I think he's better off where he is. That limp and those
crutches are just too noticeable." We'd left the exhausted
wizard with a handful of determined Forest hunters in a disregarded hollow beyond the knife-edged ridge on the sunrise side. He was under strict instructions not to use any
magic lest he draw attention of the Sheltya or the Elietimm.
Usara might be confident Hadrumal's tricks would hide him
from an enchanter's notice, but we weren't prepared to let
the mage risk it. Not until we had our quarry. I hoped he'd
stay unscathed. I'd left my precious song book with him,
for one thing—a mage being the nearest I could find to
safekeeping for the present.

But once we had the bastard, I'd welcome Forest arrows
or spears of lightning or anything else to cover our flight.
Sudden shouts behind me froze the hot trickles of sweat between my shoulder blades, cold fingers of fear running
down my spine.

"Wrestling," Sorgrad grinned, seeing my expression.

I wished I knew a Mountain equivalent of that finger flick
Caladhrians use to convey rebuke.

"Everyone's bored." 'Gren's expression grew animated.
"Same as when snow keeps you all to camp or stormy
weather makes the mines too wet to work."

"You're not to get involved, you hear me?" Sorgrad's
face was serious. "Get overexcited and kill someone again
and ten men will be dragging you up before Sheltya who'll
empty your head to your bottom teeth."

"I thought the whole point was to get ourselves Sheltya?

Oh, all right, I'm only yanking your hood," 'Gren grumbled.

"We'd best steer clear," I said noncommittally. "We don't want to be noticed and you flattening all comers would start talk."

The path took us up beyond a jagged spike of rock and away from the ranks of tents where tense men eyed each other like hounds chained too close in a kennel yard. We stopped to take our bearings.

This ridge of rock marked a deliberate division. There were women up here, some in voluminous drapes like the ones hampering my knees, others in long skirts dusty around the hems and blouses loose-necked in the heat. I looked back down the valley; there were no females of any age in the tents below the little waterfall valiantly making the most of its meager reserves as it tumbled glittering over the rock. A handful of women were lingering by the side of the stream, water pots in hand, idly chatting. One lass was paddling her naked feet in the frothing water.

"She's trouble going begging for business," remarked 'Gren with a certain relish. A burly man stripped to the waist as he laundered his linen was on the other side of the stream, watching with interest. He tossed a stone into the water, splashing the young woman's skirts. She shook her head at whatever it was he said to her but her smile and the flirt of her skirts gave the lie to any denial. A second man, not overtall but with shoulders massive from years of breaking rocks, came up behind her. Catching the incautious wench unawares, he shook her hard enough to snap her head backward. The other women scattered back to the dubious sanctuary of their tents.

"Our pal had better get this lot fighting some enemy or he'll have them fighting each other," observed Sorgrad thoughtfully.

"They'll just knock the rough corners off." 'Gren was unconcerned. "Remember early season in a trapping camp or at a new digging."

"There aren't any women to fight over after a wasted day at the trap lines," countered Sorgrad.

"Would it be worth our while setting a spark to the tinder?" I wondered.

"I'm game," volunteered 'Gren.

"Perhaps if we need a diversion on the way out." Sorgrad turned to look at me. "You'd pass for a man better if you were wearing a hauberk."

"In this heat, I'd pass out," I retorted. "No one's going to tell me buck from doe as long as I'm wearing this sack."

Both 'Gren and Sorgrad were in sleeveless chainmail, burnished so bright by the sun it was painful to the eye. They bore the strength-sapping weight uncomplaining and with little enough sign of discomfort, but I hate wearing armor and wasn't about to slow myself down with it in this heat. I eased the clinging linen of my shapeless overtunic as it clung to my sweaty neck. The sun beat down relentlessly and I envied these people the stuffy shade of their tents. "Has anyone got any water?"

Sorgrad passed me his bottle and nodded to the thirsty arrivals jostling for water below the little waterfall. "We'll go higher upstream and get a refill."

A man with a massive hammer sloped over one solid shoulder went past with a self-important air, a lad behind him struggling with a hampering bag of tools clutched to his narrow chest. I drained the last tepid mouthfuls of leather-tainted water, musty but still preferable to the cloying sourness of my mouth. We strolled across the flat stones separating the scored turf from the summer-shrunken river bouncing and sparkling down its rocky bed.

"Let's take a seat over there for a while." Sorgrad pointed to a scatter of angular gray boulders, the sun striking rainbow fragments from faint white lines of crystal. We'd see any interest turning to us before it could arrive and by splashing through the shallow river we could lose ourselves in the throng on the far bank.

"So where next?" demanded 'Gren. "We came here to get ourselves an enchanter."

"So we need to know where he is." Sorgrad's eyes fixed on the gate to the fess. The broad sweep of the wall was enclosing a larger area than Hachalfess and the rekin within was both broader and taller. For all that, the whole still managed to look insignificant against the great heaps of broken stone on either side. The pitted face of the cliff behind was scarred with rock-cut stairs. Smeared across the yellow-streaked face of the gray mountain, inky stains glistened damply despite the heat as green-tainted water oozed from the pierced heart of the darkness.

But there was no sign of clean water channeled in beneath the walls of the fess from the stream or of foul drainage coming out to any kind of channel, so we wouldn't be going in that way. I looked at the main gate. The massive lattice of beams was faced with jointed planks and studded through with iron bolts, proof against determined assault once closed. But it was standing heedlessly ajar, people going in and out, sentry sitting idly on a stool, sword at his waist and armor discarded in the baking heat.

Sorgrad's gaze followed mine. "They're not expecting trouble in the heart of the soke."

My spirits rose. "He'll be in there, surely?"

"I think we can spare the time to be certain," Sorgrad said judiciously.

We sat and waited, idly kicking our legs, doing nothing that might attract notice, all our attention fixed on the fess. The sun slid slowly down from its scorching zenith and I waited in vain for the day to cool a little. In the meantime I studied the roof of the rekin, counting silently as the sentry made his regular circuit, trying to assess if I'd have time to climb from the top-most rank of windowsills to the parapet while he was still behind the massive bulk of the chimneystack. As long as this little adventure went according to plan, there was no reason why I should have to, but it never hurts to keep every alternative in mind.

"They definitely have Sheltya in there, look." 'Gren pointed to a gray-clad figure walking briskly out of the gate.

The anonymous hooded figure went to an organized group of tents, two equal ranks drawn up in precise parallel. Men were watching a lad wedging a pole in the dusty turf with shards of broken stone. A man at his elbow swung a goat's head idly by one curved horn. The rest of the beast was jointed and spitted some way beyond, a scarlet-faced woman sweating over a fire colorless in the bright sunlight.

"You said the Sheltya were healers?" I nodded toward the figure, now revealed as a woman with silvering hair and a thin, parched face, her hood pushed back as she bent to a young girl proffering a hand swathed in bloodstained rags.

"They are staying true to some part of their vows then." Sorgrad's eyes were cold in the heat of the day.

The men began throwing knives at the goat's head, cheers and groans raised for every strike or overthrow. Newcomers drifted over to take their place in an ever lengthening line. A particularly inept throw sparked rowdy joking, but the voices soon turned sour and two men had to be pulled apart by their respective friends. 'Gren watched with interest.

"Is it worth waiting to see if our man comes out?" murmured Sorgrad, leaning forward, elbows on thighs.

"I can't see him patching up a sliced finger, can you?" I shifted my seat on the unyielding rock, rough gray surface hot beneath my palms. "In any case, snatching him in plain view of half an army would be a fool's notion. We have to get him on his own." I resolutely ignored the fluttering of unease in the pit of my belly. We'd be three to one and we knew what we were going up against. If we played this right, he wouldn't know what had hit him.

"So when do we go in?" demanded 'Gren.

"Once the sun's going down?" Sorgrad squinted up, the heat and glare still merciless.

I nodded my agreement. "Before they eat or change the guard, so we catch that sentry tired and not paying attention."

"My arse is going numb." 'Gren was surveying the bustling campground. "Let's get a feel for what's going on down here."

Sorgrad and I exchanged a look; best to keep 'Gren amused. We began a leisurely circuit of the crowded valley. I kept behind the brothers, head down and shambling along.

"This is no time to play the village idiot," Sorgrad warned me as we passed rough huts newly lashed up from green wood and untanned skins.

"Who's going to take an interest if they think I'm simple-minded?" I objected.

I caught a sardonic sapphire glance. "They'll be curious to know what happened when you were driven into the soke at midwinter of your ninth year, to face Maewelin's judgment on whether you should live or die."

I pulled myself a little straighter.

In the upper reach around the fess, the women were busy baking on griddles over their fires, making the hard, pale biscuits you take on journeys, either to guarantee you food to eat, or better yet to smash and use in a sling to fell anything more tasty. Their men must have slaughtered every animal with meat on its bones within a day's travel. A gang of reluctant youths were spreading dust and gravel on a blood-soaked stretch of land to baffle iridescent flies and racks of meat were drying in the fierce sun.

A woman standing at the alert with her spray of green leaves offered us each a strip of dark, slightly sticky flesh. I tucked it in the broad pocket across the front of my smock. I could always use it to resole my boots if I wore this pair out.

'Gren chewed with appreciative noises. "There'll be plenty of rations on the march, then."

"Have you heard something?" The woman swatted at a few hopeful flies, the nails on her hand broken and chipped, dried blood stubbornly staining their edges. "Is there to be a real strike into the lowlands at last?"

"We don't know," Sorgrad shrugged apologetically. "We've only just arrived."

"My husband could always use more swords at his side." The woman's shale-gray eyes turned calculating. "Why don't you join up with us?"

"Shouldn't we get our orders from the rekin?" queried Sorgrad.

"What rights have they over you? Just tell them you're tying up with Yannal's men," she urged. "You're Middle Rangers, aren't you? We've not been at outs with any soke over the Gap since my foremother's time."

I could sympathize with her eagerness to put more swords between her husband and the enemy. That way she stood a better chance of not going back home a widow.

Sorgrad smiled at her. "I'll go and suggest it to the others."

We moved on down the valley. "This army's holding together about as well as a madwoman's knitting," I commented to Sorgrad.

"Let's hope yanking the enchanter out sets the whole thing unraveling."

We continued our apparently aimless circuit of the valley, pausing here and there to admire the new arrivals showing off their spoils. Wooden trinkets and some gold and silver jewelry suggested they'd cleared Folk out of a stretch of woodland but the bulk of the loot was barrels of flour, bales of blankets, household goods of little value. A whiff of smoke suggested fire as well as blades had been used to good effect. These returning heroes had just gone on a rampage through defenseless upland villages.

No, the brave warriors had been driving off armed intruders, greedy interlopers, according to the fragments of gossip the three of us picked up along with bits of bread, meat and fruit kindly offered. Their appetite for fighting was undimmed and all the talk was of carrying the battle down into the lowlands proper, even of reclaiming the entire Ferring Gap, reuniting Easterlings and Westerlings. What they couldn't understand was the reason for delay.

I found it increasingly hard to choke down the well-meant gifts as the day crawled sluggishly on. Apprehension was filling my belly and gnawing at my ribs. I just wanted to get things in play. I'd be able to name my own price to Messire, or Planir come to that, I reminded myself firmly. I could invite the other to match it and stand back while their rivalry made me rich. Coin gives choices the poor are denied and I wanted to explore my preferences with Ryshad. That did more to settle my stomach than any apothecary's remedy as we worked our way back to keep watch on the gate of the fess.

"Sun's sinking," 'Gren observed finally.

Sorgrad nodded. "Let's get you ready for your performance."

"We should have brought Niello," I joked feebly as we moved to a conveniently obscure hollow among the abandoned diggings.

Sorgrad lounged casually on the turf to keep watch and 'Gren and I started work. He opened his belt-pouch while I pulled seemingly endless folds of linen over my head, relishing the touch of the cooling air on my stifled skin. I bent and untied one garter, stuffing it in a pocket and letting my stocking droop.

"Let's be having you." 'Gren tipped a little water from his belt-bottle into a wooden dish. "Head back so I can make you beautiful." He was mixing a nauseating palette from cosmetics we had begged from the Forest women.

I tilted my face obediently as he rubbed black, purple and yellow into my cheek with gentle hands. "It's got to look a few days old," I reminded him, "and make sure that bastard isn't going to recognize me. If he sees me for who I am, it's all over." I swallowed hard to clear my throat of qualms.

"Your own mother wouldn't recognize you." 'Gren smeared a convincing fakery of old, dried blood around one eyebrow and temple, drawing painful cuts across the corner of my eye.

"She hasn't seen me for ten years or more," I pointed out. "That's no great achievement."

"A bit of green as well, I think." 'Gren applied judicious pigments to his fingers and laid them carefully around my neck to leave the prints of a strangle, grinning evilly at me. I stuck my tongue out and crossed my eyes.

My spirits were rising as I rolled back the sleeves of my shirt, warming my blood, as is generally the way, once a game's in hand. 'Gren seized my forearms, drawing me close for a moment. "We'll be right beside you, all the time."

"You'd better be, pal." I blew on the pigments to dry them before letting my cuffs fall loose and unlaced. "What do you think?" I turned to Sorgrad, who was gazing out over the valley, motionless as the mountains themselves. The long twilight was nearly upon us now and the peaks behind him were gilded by the sunset. Snowfields on one hand were fringed with lace against the buttery softness of the rock. The dark peak was warmed, severity muted by shadow, a fallacy of beauty in the deceptive light.

He drew his gaze back from distant illusions to the realities of the present. "Some dirt in your hair?"

I scooped up a handful of dust. 'Gren was about to stuff the grubby smock into his pack in place of the thin blanket Sorgrad pulled out. "Wait a moment." I took the crudely dried meat out of the pocket. "A trace of scent is always the final touch, isn't it?" I rubbed the sticky lump against the ripped neck of my blouse, the blackened residue of blood smelling both sweet and metallic at the same time. "Let's get this masquerade on the boards." I wrapped myself in the blanket, the bold pattern of blue chevrons against the yellow wool unmistakable and well worth the coin it had cost us down in the foothills. I wondered if that peaceable little village was just a burned-out ruin by now.

'Gren caught me up in his arms and I lolled boneless against his narrow shoulder. He made nothing of my weight, and I felt the haste in his steps as we headed for the rekin. An insane urge to giggle swelled in my throat as I recalled playing the wilting blossom like this one year at the Selerima races. The impulse died on my next breath; we weren't here gulling touts out of coin, busy crowds to hide us from bully boys with nailed boots and pickaxe helves.

I let my jaw slacken in despair, eyes blank and lifeless. I'd once seen a brutalized girl mercilessly used by Lescari mercenaries; I recalled her terror-filled screams, her agonized hysteria as she had clung to me and Halice, barely able to stand, once 'Gren and Sorgrad had raised a riot and fought through to rescue her. The memory helped me force a few sluggish tears, not so many as to risk runnels in the paints on my face but just enough to give my eyes a crystal sheen of grief to convince onlookers. Niello would have been proud of me. Beneath the facade of helpless victim, I steeled myself.

Sharper notes rose in the voices around us, horrified questions, hisses of outrage and pity. 'Gren's strong arms held me close and I hid my face in his chest. The metal links dug into my cheek at every step but I was willing to add a few real scrapes to the painted deceits. Sorgrad's forbidding presence stopped anyone getting too close, rebuffing offers of help with a curt explanation. We were going straight to the Sheltya, for healing and for justice. The cautious agreement I heard wasn't as wholehearted as I might have expected.

"Jeirran will already have avenged the insult, like as not." One voice sounded loud in the jumble of concerned voices. This assertion raised a full-blooded roar of approval. I pondered this as I was carried, limp as a discarded doll. Would taking the Elietimm out of the scales be enough to unbalance Mountain Men determined on war? My grimace of frustration could be one of pain for the onlookers. No, I'd worry about the fate of the uplands later, or preferably leave it to someone else. I just wanted the Elietimm enchanter.

"Let us pass!" Sorgrad's demand was nicely pitched between challenge and supplication, a break in his voice suggesting near intolerable anguish. "We need to see Sheltya!"

"What's your concern?" The guard's voice trailed away as Sorgrad stepped aside to reveal my pitiable form cradled in 'Gren's arms. I felt the beat of his heart picking up pace beneath his hauberk and smelled the sharpness of fresh sweat. My own pulse was rapid in the hollow of my throat, every sinew tense.

"I'll get one of the women to tend to her," said the gate ward hastily.

"We want to see Sheltya," demanded Sorgrad. "Not some wise woman. We've tended to her hurts as best we can but we don't know exactly what happened. We need Sheltya's care for her memory, to tell us just what those misbegotten lowlanders did to her!" The air of suppressed fury in his voice was most effective. I let tears spill over my lashes, shuddering faintly like an injured animal.

"I'll send for someone," offered the hapless guard.

"Maewelin freeze your seed!" spat Sorgrad. "Do you keep us on the threshold like lowland beggars, every curious eye to see her shame, every eager ear to hear her misery?"

"What's going on here?" A new voice, older, less easily swayed by his own emotion or anyone else's.

Sorgrad modified his tone accordingly, respectful and to the point. "Our sister was attacked as we traveled. We were told there were Sheltya who could ease her memory. We can wait but not here, where everyone can stare. The fewer who know . . ." He let his voice trail off.

"Traw, take them to the kitchen yard," the voice ordered briskly. "I'll send word to Sheltya—"

"Would that be Cullam?" asked Sorgrad eagerly.

"No, it'll be Aritane or one of her people." The voice did not like to be interrupted. "She'll send somebody as is convenient. There are more than your sister needing healing this day."

"My thanks," Sorgrad began but the voice was already turning away to deal with the new sentries.

I let my eyes wander around seemingly unfocused as we followed Traw the gate ward around to the back of the rekin. The court of the fess was thronged with people, some walking fast with an air of purpose, others slowing at the end of a long, hot day, weariness in gait and faces. Tension lay beneath the rumble of conversation, ripe with anticipation and antagonism. All seemed rapt in their own concerns.

The doors to the kitchen and scullery of the rekin stood open, lamplight spilling out into the slowly deepening dusk. A low wall bounded a paved yard where a sizable number of men and women sat with various degrees of patience. Most of the men bore obvious battle wounds, some with dressings tied tight around legs and feet, a couple with bandaged heads. One had the bruised eyes and dark stains behind his ears that always bode ill. The women made up for the silent men with animated conversation. Some were seeking lotions for burns from fire or sun; two others were looking for Sheltya support in some quarrel. A couple of young girls were going to and fro with bread and meat, beakers and bottles, and as we approached an elderly man emerged from the rekin, scratching his head in apparent confusion. He moved aside with a muttered apology as an agitated youth pushed past, one hand clasped tight around bloody linen swathing his remaining two fingers and thumb.

'Gren set me carefully down on the broad coping of the little wall, my face away from the revealing light. Sorgrad stepped over the notional barrier to sit facing the rekin, alert to every coming and going. I raised a cautious corner of my blanket to conceal my face and to dab away sweat that might set my bruises running.

"So what now?" 'Gren demanded.

Sorgrad leaned back so I could see his face. "No one seems overly interested in us."

"Any guards?" I picked off bits of the gritty stuff at the corner of my eye. This was no time to find myself blinded by tears.

"Not that I can see," murmured Sorgrad. "Plenty of people going in and out, but no one seems to be asking their business."

"We should get hunting, while we're sure they're not expecting us," I decided. "There's no point waiting for some Sheltya to come and look inside my head and call me a liar." I wasn't ever going to risk aetheric magic rummaging through my memories again.

"We go in through the side door, and if anyone comes asking we're looking for this Aritane?" 'Gren asked.

"Privies are that way," nodded Sorgrad.

In the privacy of the fetid little outhouse, I tied up my drooping stocking and checked my belt-pouch, making sure everything I was going to need was ready. I took a moment to look down at my hands. They were steady enough in the dim light filtering through the half-moon cut in the wooden door. It was time to draw the runes and see how they lay.

Teyvasoke,
18th of Aft-Summer

Eresken turned aside from the sturdy arch of pale stone that spanned the chuckling river. Crunching across gravel, he dipped a handful of water from the dimpled surface; he spat crossly—the taint of beasts was bitter in the water. Straightening up, he knuckled the small of his back and waited for the stubborn ache in the back of his legs to ease. He'd never walked so many leagues in his life!

Scorn soured his stomach. These fools had so much land and yet they used so little of it to good effect. Properly managed, even the parched desolation of Aritane's once beloved home would support a fertile clan breeding loyal sons eager to fight. No wonder Misaen had sent the best of his people to be refined in the howling crucible of the ocean islands.

At least these soft stay-at-homes had a proper attitude to encroachment on their territory. Eresken shook his head in renewed wonder. It was so easy to persuade these people their lands were under threat, that the loss of so much as an arm's length out of all this bounty would leave them destitute. His father would have no reason to criticize his efforts there. The Elietimm's spirits rose, the ache in his muscles fading.

He noted the number of fires across the river, busy cooking suppers made known on the fragrant breeze. Were these fresh fools flocking to the cause or had Jeirran arrived back before him? Exasperation darkened Eresken's mood; he'd meant to keep a closer eye on the bumptious fool, but what with keeping his own force toeing the line and making sure Aritane had this valley under her thumb, when had he had the time? Cold striking up from the water hit him like an omen of his father's disapproval. He'd better get some sleep, the better to take charge of this multifaceted task once more.

A hand shook him by the elbow. "What do you want?" he snapped, a vicious glare searing the man hesitating beside him.

Reflexive anger straightened the man and his face hardened in the failing light. "What's the delay? We've been marching since noon without a break."

"Of course." Eresken managed a conciliatory tone. He held the man's eyes for a moment, searching blunt features beneath a grubby bandage obscuring one brow. There was weariness in the man's mind, and an ominous shadow of doubt, both in the wisdom of taking on the lowlands and in the men and women supposedly leading this campaign, all because of a few reverses when the sheepherders turned defiant and some tree dwellers bolder than the rest had loosed their pinpricks on unwary stragglers. So much for the bold and mighty Anyatimm who had driven his forefathers away. Were these fair-weather warriors to be the guardians of the ancestral lands? The sooner true heirs of Misaen claimed these peaks, the better. Let worthy men see the real secrets revealed by Solstice suns.

Eresken curbed his contempt lest it seep into the man's unwitting perception. He reached through clouding tiredness and looming misgiving and dragged a memory of recent looting to the forefront of the man's mind. He struck an echo from the guilty delight in such easy spoils and the relish of violence let loose. The man's face lightened, all in no more time than it had taken Eresken to draw a long breath. The Elietimm considered thrusting deeper, but his own exhaustion and exasperation balked at further effort.

"Take the goods we recovered to the stores-master at the fess." Eresken laid a friendly hand on the man's shoulder. "When it's all been noted, tell him you've my authority to take back the ale. We've won some mighty victories and I think we're due a little celebration!"

"Misaen made you true gold!" The man shouted his extravagant approval to the bedraggled troops and Eresken muttered a complex chant beneath his breath. With that charm following him, the man's renewed enthusiasm would be carried along by his words into the minds of any he spoke with. That should keep the fools from brooding on recent minor setbacks.

The long column of laden men trudged across the bridge. Most were silent, many glum, faces set and shoulders bowed. They were just tired, Eresken decided; a good night's sleep, a few days' rest, Jeirran's undoubted eloquence with the whisper of Elietimm enchantment running beneath it and he would have them marching down again to grind the Forest Folk beneath an iron heel. His stomach growled low but insistent at a tempting savor of frying onion. When had he last eaten?

Men burdened with litters and supporting the ungainly struggles of walking wounded had reached the bridge now. "Go straight to the fess," Eresken told them, face concerned. "Sheltya will tend your hurts." And soothe away memories of pain along with disloyalty stirred by the shock of injury, Aritane's scruples be cursed.

Grazed and bruised faces lightened with gratitude. "Come on, I'll walk with you." Best to get these miserable failures out of sight. Bloodied stumps and gashed limbs would only spoil the goodwill mixed from a few looted barrels and some judicious manipulation of memory.

Crossing the bridge with the first of the litters, Eresken considered the simpletons gawking by their campfires. Could he enlist Aritane's help in turning the thoughts of the more fatigued back to the rage that had first spurred them on? Eresken warned himself against demanding too much of her too soon. Aritane's usefulness still depended on her cherishing the illusion that, though breaking her vows and defying her elders, she was still working for the greater good of her people.

Raucous cheering distracted him. A group of men were clustered around a figure whose beard and hair glowed golden in the light of the flames. So Jeirran and his men were back earlier than expected from the lowlands. Eresken's annoyance was tainted with jealousy. Had Jeirran won some great victory that had enabled him to return in triumph?

"You all go on up to the rekin." Eresken turned to the wounded men who had obediently halted to wait for him. "I must just speak with Jeirran." He forced a smile to answer the grins of admiration the men were turning to their leader. Jeirran's voice was loud, his gestures animated. "It sounds as if he has successes to report, doesn't it?" There would also be food he could commandeer to stifle his gnawing hunger.

Eresken began to force his way through the crowd gathering around Jeirran. Tiredness weighed him down like a physical burden but he managed a warm enough greeting. "Jeirran! Good to see you back so soon. How did you fare?"

"Eresken!" Jeirran pushed a man with a flagon of ale aside and dragged Eresken into a crushing embrace. Jeirran's breath was piercing with an unfamiliar, woody sweetness, eyes bright with the exuberance of alcohol.

Eresken detached himself with some difficulty and held Jeirran at arm's length for a moment in a passable imitation of affection. "So how did you fare?"

"We drove those mewling cowards of villagers clean out of the foothills, all the way down to the chase above the lakes." Jeirran laughed uproariously. "We thought about ducking them in the water but let them alone once they'd cleared our lands."

"For the present, anyway," quipped a bystander to ominous laughs.

"I thought you were to drive the Folk of the Forest south of the road?" Eresken managed a tight smile to cover his annoyance.

"Oh, we sent the squirrel fanciers scurrying up their trees, right enough. Took 'em on, man for man, fair fight and no quarter asked or given!" Jeirran took a swig from a crude glass bottle and sucked in air to cool the mellow burn of the spirits in his mouth. "We hit 'em first, burned 'em out, told 'em not to set foot on our lands again!"

Eresken steeled himself to look beyond the surface confusion of recollection and wishful thinking in Jeirran's mind. Teasing out the truth was no easy task; memory was curdled by drunkenness and complicated by deliberate refusal to acknowledge darker truths lurking in the depths.

Jeirran had heeded the agreed plan to begin with, Eresken saw, attacking a small group of Forest Folk already fallen foul of an earlier sortie from the uplands. Eresken listened to Jeirran's vainglorious boasting while seeing the truth of the events in his mind's eye. The Forest Folk's few possessions were dragged from their feeble grasp, the men hacked mercilessly down as they fought despairingly. Any woman who took up a weapon was cut to the ground by the fury of the Mountain Men. Those that sued for mercy were cruelly disappointed, used and discarded, bleeding and weeping.

Eresken nodded his approval; that much at least had been done properly. It had taken long enough to convince these fools to wage war as it should be done, unpicking their nicety and scruples, convincing them to use every terror as a tool.

He stumbled over a fearful recollection Jeirran had thrust deep into a recess of memory, cloaked in shame and confusion. So the heroic leader had joined his men in the wholesale rape? After all his high-flown words and claims to a lofty cause, he'd gone nosing in the dirt as eagerly as any beast, but this wasn't just something done in the heat of the moment, Eresken realized with interest. Jeirran had a taste for it, unmasked by the deceits of drunkenness. That would be worth letting slip to Aritane, if her loyalty to this fool ever threatened to draw her away.

Eresken's concentration wavered as anger shook him. The arrogant shit could take the western sweep next time, deal with the shoot-and-run tactics of the cowards with their bows and spears. Let Jeirran lose his best men to deadfalls and pit traps, find his nights poisoned as sentries were stabbed from the darkness by darts bringing death and madness.

Jeirran broke into a paroxysm of coughing, the spirits searing his throat as he tried to subdue unlooked-for memories with an unwary gulp from his bottle. Eresken blinked and saw the other man was ashen beneath his golden beard. He had to be more careful; if the sot mentioned such disturbance of thought and memory, Aritane would realize what he was doing, even if her idiot brother didn't. Not that Jeirran was likely to tell her though, admitting weakness, when all the dolt's own sense of worth depended on the admiration of others.

"So what took you out to the villages?" The Elietimm slackened his grip on Jeirran's mind.

"It was time to take the fight to the real villains," replied Jeirran robustly if hoarsely. His men had been squabbling over the inadequate spoils won from the Forest Folk; his unconscious mind told Eresken loudly. "Suratimm are like ticks on a goat, they drain its strength but can't do too much harm, not if you burn their arses with a hot ember every so often," Jeirran continued with an expansive gesture. "It's the lowlanders that are the real thieves, the ones who'll rob you blind and then steal what's left from under your nose." He paused, frowning a little as his own meaning escaped him. He need not worry, thought Eresken sardonically. The audience hanging on his every word were well on their way to being so drunk they'd cheer a quacking duck.

"So we took the fight to them," Jeirran repeated, nodding with satisfaction. "Fought 'em, drove 'em off, a boot up the arse so hard their teeth shook loose!"

Eresken tried to make sense of his jumbled recollections; thatch burning in the gray light of dawn, screaming women, howling children, the outraged roars of men dragged from sleep by sudden assault. He gave up the struggle with a silent curse of derision. Come the morning he'd determine if Jeirran's success was all the fool was claiming or just another ineffectual raid that would have to be gilded with enchantment to satisfy the men they had indeed won a mighty victory.

Eresken closed his eyes for a moment. Another task to remember, yet more demands on his time and energies. Well, he'd use more direct methods in the morning, no more tiptoeing around the edges of Jeirran's arrogance, stealing his memories unseen. He'd go in with the ruthlessness his father favored; Jeirran could put the subsequent headaches down to indulgence in looted lowland liquor and any evil memories down to the lash of conscience. Sudden desire seared Eresken, to drown all the myriad tasks clamoring for his attention in the seductive golden depths of a bottle.

The Elietimm turned his back on Jeirran. Such release was denied him but Aritane was up in the rekin. Perhaps this was the time to break down her idiotic scruples and make a true woman of her. Once she'd forsworn that final vow, she'd be unable to betray him. He could draw on her strength, force her to take some of the load. Eresken's step quickened as he headed for the fess. A brazier was smoking by the gate, white and red beneath a layer of fresh fuel. The Elietimm strode past without so much as a glance at the knot of men chatting casually around it.

Inside the fess, the noise confined within the massive stone circle buffeted him. Every building around the walls had windows lit and chimney smoking. Some doors were closed on work or sleep within, more were open to people coming and going, stepping around each other with scant apology. Two men stood unyielding as everyone else flowed around them, intent on comparing closely written slates. A shout made them both look up and one hurried over to a heap of sacks, spilled grain drifting at his feet. The main steps to the rekin were clogged with men deep in conversation, women exchanging news and opinion. The stone walls were dappled with shadows of torch and fire-light until they reached high enough to cut a hard black outline in the starlit sky.

Eresken fumed; once he and his kind held sway here, this would all stop. True magic was meant to rule. No Elietimm enchanter would be at the beck and call of every self-important buffoon puffed up over a few bare leagues of mountainside. Hunger nagged at him so he skirted the rekin. He clicked his tongue with annoyance at the miserable crowd in the kitchen yard. Pushing his way past importuning hands, he tapped one of the Sheltya briskly on the shoulder. "Where is Aritane? I must speak with her."

Krelia looked around, her face drawn with the anguish she took into herself with every healing touch laid on some needy body. "Did she go inside, for something to eat perhaps?"

The fool woman was going to lose herself completely soon, Eresken realized with a faint chill, seeing the vagueness in her eyes. He must watch Krelia more closely; if she was going to dissolve into madness, she wasn't going to hamper his plans when she did so. He'd smother her in her sleep first.

"You're looking for Aritane?" Remet halted, all manner of questions in his raised brows. "Bryn came; they went inside to talk in private." Remet's eyes were alert in the soft lines of his face, a newfound maturity in their focus. "He had news of Jeirran."

Eresken nodded and hid curses in the deepest hollow of his mind. Bryn's long friendship with Aritane made it so much harder to displace whatever doubts his news might fix in her head. What had Bryn heard from Jeirran? Did he know something Eresken didn't?

"Thank you." Eresken managed a friendly smile, man to man, overlaying it with a faint promise of confidences to come, of admission to an inner circle of knowledge. As he turned, he felt the youth's eyes on the back of his neck. Yet another thing to remember and to step wary around. This onslaught of incessant and varied demands had tested Remet's training in a way he'd never have faced in ten years of trailing up track and down vale after some ineffectual soothsayer. The boy was starting to think for himself and Bryn only needed someone to share his faltering loyalty to go running to his Elders, ruining everything.

Eresken's pace quickened. The side door was ajar, a few huddled figures cowering on the wooden steps. Eresken spared no glance to encourage some worthless request. He took the stairs two at a time and hurried to the door at the far end of the corridor.

He halted on the threshold, honeyed words dying on his lips. "What are you doing here? Where is Aritane?"

Ceris sprang to her feet, looking for guidance from the men flanking her. "She went with Bryn?" Her pathetic smile beseeched him not to be cross with her.

"Who is this?" Eresken scowled at the older man, whose gnarled hand clasped the girl's drooping shoulder. "You should work healing outside, not where we gather to meditate!" He took a seat behind the long table, forcing the others to rise from their chairs, stamping his authority on the situation.

The newcomer matched the Elietimm glare for glare. "I'm her father and this is her brother. We've come to see how she does, now that Jeirran tells us Sheltya need not be cut off from their blood no more."

Yet another cursed complication to deal with. Eresken heard hurrying steps in the corridor. "Then please take your reunion elsewhere." The Elietimm rose, expecting to see Bryn or, better yet, Aritane. Instead two unknown men charged into the room, faces alight with a hostility that hit him like a kick in the stomach. A woman followed, face obscured by some ghastly mask of paints but green eyes clear and bright with hatred.

It was the wizard's slut from the Forest. Pain searing along his jaw told Eresken the bitch was using her cursed darts again. He stumbled with the cold shock of the drug in his blood. Scrambling around the table, he swept maps, parchments, goblets to all sides, throwing the jug bodily at the burlier attacker.

Closest to the door, Ceris drew breath on a panicked scream but the woman silenced her with a slap. The frail blond crashed back into the stone wall to slump whimpering to the floorboards. Eresken goaded Ceris' startled father to attack, seizing on his impulse to protect his child. With an inarticulate roar, the man swung at the whore's back. The elder of the traitors with her stepped in to block the vengeful fist, equal violence bolstered by the energy of youth. Eresken took a moment's thought to weave the attacker's face into an image of Jeirran's foulest lust, with Ceris the weeping victim beneath the heaving body. He rammed this into her father's mind, burning it into his consciousness, heedless of the damage he did.

"See what they—" He had no time to reinforce the vision with words. The second man, the skinny one with savage eyes, was a scant pace away, knife in his grasp. Eresken seized Ceris' brother with hands and wits, throwing him bodily onto the gleaming blade. In the instant of agony distracting the boy, Eresken grabbed hold of his mind. He tied the lad's wits tight in a web of chaos, isolating him mercilessly from all conscious thought and memory. Working faster than ever before, Eresken denied him any perception of pain from the myriad blows and cuts the frustrated attacker inflicted. Ruthlessly ripping out any instinct for defense and protection, he set alight every unconscious fury and hatred the boy harbored, turning each involuntary movement into aggression, tying the whole into a storm of mindless violence.

Eresken snatched himself from the maelstrom of the boy's ruined mind just in time to see the shorter attacker go down under that insane rage. The father was laying into the other one with a chair leg, wood splintering as the agile man dodged and feinted and blows crashed into the wall behind him.

What of the whore? Eresken saw her biting her lip with vicious intent, halfway across the room with an upraised dagger. Eresken overturned the table, the stout oak board a futile defense, but it gave him long enough to drag Ceris' body to its feet. With a frantic reach of his mind, he crushed the girl's feeble volition with one explosive curse, leaving the girl's eyes vacant pools of darkness. Barely an instant before the Forest bitch reached him, Eresken flung Ceris onto the whore's back, uncoordinated limbs flailing, dead weight clinging, gray cloth hampering, dragging the murderous slut down.

Echoes of agony reverberated around Eresken's mind as the brother died. Illusion of invulnerability was no defense against being bodily broken into a bloody mess, joints shattered, sinews cut, throat cut with a savagery that all but severed the head. The traitor was already moving forward, teeth white in a rictus of savagery against a mask of gore, reddened knife thirsty for Eresken's blood. Kill or be killed, the simplicity of this one's mind rang louder than any other thought in the room. A simple mind and one with no defenses worth the name.

The Elietimm felt the hardness of stone at his back, floorboards slick beneath his feet, the reek of blood, ordure and hatred thick in the air. The drug was tainting his senses, colors distorting, sounds both deafening and distant in the same moment. Eresken gritted his teeth, forced the turmoil from him with a shouted incantation and plunged his razor-sharp intellect, honed over so many years, into the naked reason of his assailant.

That much was easy. The Elietimm exulted in the sudden success before a sense of wrongness undermined him. Where was the shock? What of the recoil from sudden invasion that Eresken had learned so painfully to resist and then to redouble, turning panic back against the assaulted mind? All sensation and sound faded from Eresken's consciousness as his world shrank to the confines of the mind he sought to capture. Why was he the one ripped from reality, when he had the chains of his iron will to bind this madman? Where was the flaw or weakness offering up the consciousness within? The Elietimm redoubled his efforts, but in a baffling reversal this domain, where he knew himself the master, turned itself inside out. Now Eresken found himself frantically seeking escape from a mental maze. How could this be? The man had no discipline, no training in the manipulation of mind and memory.

The enchanter found himself in the center of a nightmare world of blood and barbarism. The destruction of Ceris' brother whirled past him in a dizzying circle of images. Scarlet life blood foamed up into a mouth already broken from teeth ripping into ragged lips. Bluish cords of throat and gullet were laid bare with a sweeping downward stroke from a red-streaked silver blade. Dark loops of gut bulged from the belly, a deadly gash oozing unheeded filth. A pale gloss of bone was overlaid with a tracery of blood as an elbow was split, the merciless knife piercing linen, skin and sinew, a calculated move to cripple for life had the boy not already been dead, kept moving only by the will Eresken had sent into madness without limit. Horror surrounded the enchanter in a seamless sequence as each vision came again and again, ever more vivid, ever more threatening. There was nothing beneath his feet, no sound in his ears, just this endless parade of horror and he had no eyes to close to it.

But where was the fear? Where was the desperate seeking for justification, the noisy reasoning as the mind sought to excuse the inhumanity, to distance itself from responsibility and the freezing grip of guilt? There was none. With an intense effort, Eresken managed to force a small stillness for himself in the midst of that abominable array of consciousness. With a sinking horror, he realized he was hemmed in on every side by a hard, hot exultation, reveling in the intensity of physical perception, surging rapture in that unfettered release, overarching ecstasy at facing the ultimate challenge of mortal battle and winning through.

The memories stopped, frozen images fading into crimson darkness. The limits of the enchanter's refuge of sanity began to buckle and bend beneath an inexorable pressure.

"Who are you?" yelled Eresken into the blood-blackened silence oppressing him.

"My name's 'Gren, at least that's what my friends call me," a cheerful voice echoed all around the enchanter, incongruous against the deepening sense of menace. "But you don't really need to know that because I'm going to kill you." Now the threat was all in the voice, hard and bright as steel.

"Do you know who I am?" demanded Eresken, incredulous, forgetting in that instant the inexplicable burden constraining his powers.

"Not really," admitted the voice. "Livak and Halice both say you and your kind are scum-sucking bastards. Let's find out." With uncomplicated brutality, a single-minded curiosity ripped through every defense Eresken had ever learned beneath the blows of his father's cane and the lash of his scorn. Dragged helpless and unresisting to the furthest edge of memory, Eresken saw people and places he thought long forgotten. That mewling slave girl his father had brought back from one of his earliest forays across the ocean, once he had recovered the lost art of defying currents that swept ships to oblivion. Eresken scarcely recalled his mother, always turning her face from her child of rape, pulling long brown hair across her branded face. Her tears and thinness of unrelenting misery shifted, face swelling, blackening, tongue protruding and eyes bulging in the aftermath of hanging.

His father's harsh face loomed large in Eresken's mind's eye, eyes so brown as to be nigh on black, pale skin crowned with dead white hair. "She was weak, disloyal, of neither use nor ornament. What purpose did her life serve, when so many need food and warmth?"

Nor had she been the only one condemned to die in that harshest winter of his childhood, sacrifice to his father's wisdom. Fiefdoms ruled by lesser men had fallen to disease and dissension. There was no food to spare in that hungry season when the scant harvest had rotted green in the fields, when the seabirds had flown early and the sea-beasts had come late and few in number, bony and diseased when the hunters' harpoons had finally reeled them in. The grudging streams had frozen solid, the vital heat beneath the earth seemingly withdrawn for good, and people had murmured in corners that Misaen had finally forsaken them.

Not so Eresken's father. This was a sign, clear as the eruption bringing the contrary death of burning to so many starving at the icy turn of the year. He had the vision to see a testament to Misaen's will, that they had been proved by this bitterest trial. This was the signal that time had come to leave their barren fields, the few sheltered valleys where stunted trees clung to life, the pitiless reaches of gravel and broken rock that ran up into the snow fields and glaciers that cloaked the mysterious heights. Once he had knit the empty lands of those cursed by Maewelin into a power to rule the Elietimm, it would be time to reclaim the lands of western plenty. Why else had he been granted the powers over wind and sea so long lost?

No longer was Eresken an unregarded junior in the rigid hierarchy of the keep. Now he had all the attention he could have desired and fully understood the paradox of being careful what one wished for, lest it be granted. To be claimed as his father's son was to be schooled hard and long in the arts of true magic, to be trained in tactics and strategy, to be sent against rival clans when any opportunity offered itself or pretext could be claimed to cross a border, attack a stronghold, shed competing blood. Finally he had been set in the place that was rightfully his by birth, to defend his father's shield arm or die in the attempt.

"Strike my stones, but you're a boring lot, aren't you?" Memories were pulled out, examined, tossed aside, Eresken raging helpless and wretched as 'Gren went searching for something to interest him, his disdain loud in the silence of recollection.

"If we are to cross the ocean to fight for our rights there, we will leave none behind who might stab us in the back." His father's oft-repeated words rang in Eresken's mind, judgment on a neighboring fiefdom destroying it down to the last infant.

"Sound enough reasoning," 'Gren's voice sounded approving, a fleeting instant when his crushing grip relaxed.

"Who are you?" demanded Eresken, trying to drag him-

self free of the treacherous mire of recall. "How are you doing this?"

"Who knows? Who cares?" The looming threat all
around him returned, ever more ominous. "You're the one
came into my head uninvited and now you get to take the
consequences. I'm not going down without a fight!"

"But who are you?" raged Eresken, treacherous fear
gnawing at him.

"Someone who's had a shitload more fun out of life than
you have, pal." Scarlet fire shot through the darkness, as-
sailing Eresken on all sides with bright visions that both terrified and perplexed him. The traitor's brother was holding
out a hand, urging him on as the two children explored
every last nook and cranny of some remote fess. Memory
jumped outside the walls, a furtive foray into the woods,
following older brothers, uncles and father on a trapping
expedition, nearly fatally lost in a sudden blizzard, only returning half frozen in the dawn light to hysterical women
and a day's slow warming in an outhouse. That last bit had
been no fun, the two had concluded. They had to learn how
to beat the cold and the weather in order to go farther afield
the next time.

Recollection sprang down a dark cavern. Mines weren't
so cold and weather couldn't reach them underground. That
foolhardy premise died beneath the discovery that exhaustion was as insidious a potential killer as the cold, while
rain on the surface half a day away could leave a bold youth
exploring a cave up to his neck in water inside a few
breaths. Fear a hair's breadth from madness rang through
Eresken's mind, recollection of a dive through flooded tunnels, lungs aflame in the midst of icy water, the insane urge
to take that killing breath of drowning. In the next instant,
all terror was submerged in the maniacal laughter of the exultation of survival.

The pace of memory increased, intensity deepening as
experience built on experience. Growth, responsibilities
and a gathering realization of alienation. The first death, an

accident in a wrestling match, cause for mild regret, but an awesome revelation all the same that he had such power in his own two hands. Eresken grew sick with panic at the memory of the Sheltya attempting to discipline this mind and the way it had made this madman determined never to suffer such invasion again. This defiance was something entirely beyond Eresken's experience.

He flinched from vivid images of warfare, bloody set battles with army cutting army to pieces, smaller vicious skirmishes at night or from ambush. Comrades came and went, either to their deaths or getting out while still alive to spend their coin. All losses were regretted and none. In the mercenary life there were no restrictions, only freedoms. Orders were followed if agreeable, evaded if not. One brother relied on persuasive reasoning to avert disaster where possible, the other on physical resilience to get them both out of ever more hazardous situations.

Every death was held up to Eresken's appalled gaze, a chilling chuckle echoing around and around him. 'Gren was amused by his captive's reaction and piled horror on horror. Rivals were stabbed or beheaded in unexpected assault. Any enemy identified was murdered as soon as possible before they could launch their own attack. Gratifying deaths, these. Men were disemboweled in battle and bled out their life with unavailing curses and pleas; such deaths were not directly pleasurable, but welcome insofar as they brought loot and payment to spend on the parallel pleasures of women and gambling. Those fallen foul of the crude discipline of the battlefield were hanged from the nearest sturdy tree, bodies jerking in the throes of slow strangulation, deaths of no consequence.

Eresken felt his defenses crumbling beneath the unrelenting onslaught, sanctuary shrunk to a cramped desperation, vainly struggling to hold out against the contempt crushing him. He couldn't feel the floor beneath his feet, the stone beneath his fingers, no sensation of breath rasped in his throat, no pulse of terror rang its beat through his body.

There was nothing but this shattering ridicule breaking him apart.

"You're a coward, aren't you?" the hateful voice continued in a conversational tone. "There's nothing for you in the hand-to-hand, the kill-or-be-killed, the ultimate gamble. You fix the odds by messing with people's minds. You'll send folk to their deaths with your trickery but you don't like to do the killing yourself. Now you've made a mistake because you've gambled more than you're willing to lose, pal. You shouldn't ever do that. You're not really a killer, not truly, but I am, and that means you're the one who's going to die."

The Teyvarekin,
18th of Aft-Summer

"You can let go of me." I twisted vainly against Sorgrad's iron grip. My wrists would carry the mark of his fingers long after I'd washed off 'Gren's handprints.

"Drop the knife," he commanded. "If anyone kills him, it'll be me."

I complied with difficulty, bloodless fingers numb. The blade with its oily smear of tahn clattered to the floorboards.

We stood still as statues on a shrine, me and Sorgrad poised, the Elietimm frozen, eyes empty hollows into the blackness of his heart, 'Gren motionless beneath a mask of blood, face slack, gaze of sunlit blue glazed over.

"If his eyes go black, it means they have him," I warned Sorgrad, trying to watch both unmoving figures and find some weapon within reach all at the same time.

'Gren blinked sapphire eyes and I jumped as if I had been stuck with a brooch pin. "Are you all right?" The Elietimm slid down the wall. "Is he dead?" I demanded hoarsely.

"I reckon so." My heart rose at 'Gren's familiar cheeky grin.

"What did you do?" Sorgrad was checking the limp figure for breath or pulse of life.

"He got inside my head and I didn't like it." 'Gren shrugged. "What he didn't expect was me not letting him out."

"You're telling me you know Sheltya tricks?" I couldn't stop my voice from shaking.

"No." 'Gren sounded a little affronted. "But he came rummaging around in my mind, so that meant I could have a look around his. I decided he was a worthless piece of shit so I sort of squashed him. He didn't put up much of a fight."

"I don't suppose he'd expected one." And of course, 'Gren never believed he could be beaten, did he?

"You're sure he's dead?" Sorgrad kicked the Elietimm with all his strength and a metal-capped boot.

Recollection quenched my sudden optimism that we had finally found a weakness in the Elietimm.

"Artifice can separate mind and body," I said with a sinking feeling. That was how the colonists of Kellarin had passed countless generations untouched by the years, down in their hidden cave.

"So his mind could have fled somewhere safer?" Sorgrad looked down at the inert heap. I wondered how a man who'd wielded such fear in my imagination could be reduced to an insignificant figure, dirty blond hair falling over a nondescript face hollow with hunger and shadowed with weariness, clothes stained, boots thick with the dust of travel.

"We can make sure," 'Gren said obligingly. He grabbed a fistful of the enchanter's straggling locks and thrust his knife blade deep into the joint of neck and skull, twisting it around. I wrinkled my nose and coughed on the reek of blood. "I thought Halice was joking when she said you lot used to collect heads."

"We'd best—"

The opening door slammed into Sorgrad's words. A woman froze on the threshold, jaw dropping at the carnage within, slate-blue eyes white-rimmed in consternation.

Sorgrad and I had her before she drew breath. Leaping over the bodies, we seized the woman, dragging her into the room with irresistible hands. Kicking the door closed, Sorgrad spun around to force her backward into me in one fluid movement. I had tahn-soaked cloth ready in one palm. Cupping it over her mouth and nose, I twisted my other hand mercilessly in the hood of her long gray robe. Her hands clawed at mine, adding fresh blood to the mess of paint and bruises. She kicked like a mule but soft indoor shoes were no real weapon. Sorgrad caught her under the knees, her struggles weakening as the smothering drug and the strangling hood did their work. She went limp and heavy in my arms and we laid her hurriedly on the floor.

"It's that bitch that threw us out of the Hachalfess," observed 'Gren, abandoning his grisly attempts to claim a trophy.

"Then she's Sheltya and that means aetheric magic and that's what we came for," I said incoherently. "She'll do." Action took over from thought. Pads of soft linen for her eyes, tied tight with broad swathes of bandage. Plugs of wool for her ears, covered with more creamy bands. A kerchief folded around a dark lump of thassin for her mouth, to keep her quiet if the tahn wore off. More bandages tight around her jaw and lower face; let her try enchantment while unable to see or hear or speak.

"She may be unconscious but she does still have to breathe, my girl." Sorgrad reached down and tweaked a fold of cloth around the unrecognizable woman's nose.

"Aritane, wasn't that her name?" 'Gren looked at her with interest.

Tying off the last knot with deft hands, I sat back on my heels, heart drumming, breath fast and furious. My exultation faded at the sight of the younger man, broken like a butchered hog, and the older, unmarked save for the killing gash of Sorgrad's knife in his throat. "They must have been waiting for the lass, already here before we started watching the stair."

"I did try to stun her." Sorgrad looked regretfully at the dead girl, golden curls matted with blood leaking from the shattered bones of her skull puddled around the chair leg he'd used to fell her.

"I don't think you can, not when aetheric magic gets inside their heads. She had me all but strangled," I reminded him soberly. Another set of bruises that would linger after I'd washed away my disguise. "I need to clean myself up." I looked around for water.

"You and me both," chuckled 'Gren, waving sticky hands.

Sorgrad passed me his water bottle. "Get your mail off," he ordered his brother, stripping the woman Aritane of her long gray gown. With its wide sleeves and cowled neck, it covered 'Gren's blood-soaked linen and breeches entirely.

"Belt it up shorter or you'll go flat on your nose the first time you go up stairs," I advised. "You're not used to skirts and you'll trip on the hem." No one would notice his boots in the darkness and the blood was nigh on invisible against the oiled leather.

Aritane was pale and limp in her decorous linen shift and Sorgrad rapidly bundled her up in our bright blanket. He'd entered carrying an unconscious woman in it; he was going out with the same, wasn't he? No one was going to look too closely in this confusion. I smeared some of my painted bruises on her flawless arms and then scrubbed off as much of the rest as I could. I coughed at the sickly smell of blood overlaid with the foulness of voided bowels and bladders and swallowed hard. "Let's get clear of this charnel house and fast."

'Gren threw the linen smock at me as Sorgrad opened the door a cautious crack. "All clear. You go first, 'Gren. Hood up, head down, and don't talk to anyone. You're Sheltya, so that means cock of the walk."

"Cock-a-doodle-do," whispered 'Gren from his anonymous cowl.

"Head for the postern gate," I told Sorgrad. "I'll catch up."

As the others made their measured way down the stairs, I knelt by the door. I narrowed my thoughts to the task in hand; there'd be time enough later for nightmares and nausea. Taking picks from my pocket, I worked on the complex lock, closing my eyes the better to feel the stubborn tumblers beneath the metal fingers.

"What are you doing?" A tall man in Sheltya gray stood at the top of the stairs, coarse-cropped hair bristling like a brush. He twisted his hands around each other in an unconscious gesture.

"I were sent for my lady Aritane," I mumbled, palming my lock picks and dropping my chin to my chest. "Door's locked."

The man reached the door in a few strides. Moving to let him pass, I got myself halfway to the stair unnoticed. He rattled the latch impotently before looking back over his shoulder. "Get me some woman who holds keys."

I was down the worn stone stairs and into the busy fess like a cat with its tail on fire. People pushed past, I shoved back, and slipped through any gap that offered. There was a new urgency in the air, a harsh note of fear in the voices clamoring for attention. I ignored it, ducking and sidestepping. Sorgrad's armor gleamed in the torchlight ahead before the seething crowds closed between us. 'Gren's Sheltya gray was clearing a path toward the rear gate, Sorgrad close behind with the woman Aritane disguised in the gaudy blanket.

Some new commotion broke out over by the main gate. People halted, rising on their toes to try to see what was amiss; I seized my chance, weaving my way through the

hesitating crowd. We could find out what was happening
when we were clear of the fess. It wouldn't take that
Sheltya man long to get into the room and blood might already be seeping through the ceilings below.

I caught up with the others at the little postern. One man
was pulling the gate closed while another hefted the closing
bar, thick as his arm and bounded with iron like the bracers
ringing his wrists. A third was pacing to and fro with a torch
from a wall bracket. A flurry of horn signals struggled up
the valley against the breeze.

"Did you catch that?" asked the first, running a three-
fingered hand over grayish hair.

The torch-holder screwed up his eyes with effort. "I can't
make no sense of it."

"Then go ask. Ebrin will know." Bracers with the fastening bar rolled it between his hands.

Three Fingers turned to 'Gren. "What's the news?"

"Send your man to your commander," 'Gren said curtly,
face invisible beneath his hood. "Let us pass."

"They sent signal to secure the gate." The torch-holder
gestured to a distant flame swept urgently from side to side
on the top of the wall.

"Secure it behind us," 'Gren's voice was soft with benev-
olent menace. "Or do you claim some authority over the
gray?"

Even in the uncertain light of torch, brazier and starlight,
I saw the man blench. Bracers pushed the gate open at once.
'Gren strode through, back straight, head high, managing to
radiate subtle threat. Sorgrad was a few strides behind,
cradling Aritane, shielding her face with a protective fold of
blanket. I scuttled along at his heels, head down in my
grubby smock. 'Gren lifted one hand in a lordly wave once
we were through the irregular tunnel and the solid wood
slammed emphatically behind us, bar rasping home. Whatever dangers lay outside, we were safe from pursuit.

Deprived of firelight, it was a dark night. Glare above

the parapet only cast a deeper shadow at the foot of the wall where the path curled away down toward the looming mass of a spoil heap. I blinked and the night-sight my Forest blood favored me with gradually sharpened. Good night-vision was a trait shared by all the ancient races, which was one reason we'd waited for the darkest night Halcarion offered us.

"I could get used to this," Gren was chuckling to himself.

"Don't," advised Sorgrad. "Real Sheltya catches you in that gray, we're all for a flogging."

"Is she still off the board?" I peered at Aritane. "Maybe I should give her a few drops on the bandages, just so she gets the fumes?" I rummaged in my belt-pouch for the vial of tahn tincture.

"Then I'll get a light head as well, but if you fancy carrying her, go on." Sorgrad hefted her in his arms. "Any more and we might as well just drop her down a mineshaft anyway. I thought you wanted her to wake up eventually."

"I don't want her getting enough of a grip on her wits to use enchantments," I insisted.

"Hush!" 'Gren halted like a scenting hound, eyes distant. The brazen clamor of horns came up from the lower valley again, clearer this time. "That's a call to arms!"

"Wait here." I ripped off the hampering smock and, tucking my skirts up into my belt, climbed the nearest spoil heap. The broken rock was treacherous and I was soon using hands as well as feet. Reaching a vantage point, I kicked the toes of my boots into the stubborn debris, forcing a footing. Spots of light dotted the slope, the broad orange blooms of cook fires and the smaller sullen red of braziers. Canvas tents glowed like giant horn lanterns, shadows grotesque and distorted on their sides. Black outlines passed in front of fires, hurrying urgently to and fro.

The river was a streak of blackness curving untroubled down to the rocky ridge. Fewer lights, hidden by the curve of the land, pierced the darkness beyond. The frantic scream of the horns came again, floating above hostile roars, bellows of defiance and the unmistakable clash of sword on sword.

"Livak!" Sorgrad's low voice clearly carried his urgency. I started to descend, hands and feet feeling in the dark for any secure hold. I was halfway when a stretch of sun-shattered clay betrayed me and I slid the rest of the way, vicious stones scoring deep into my thigh.

"What is going on?" Sorgrad's question was more important than my stinging gashes.

"There's a fight going on, but I can't say who's attacking who." I ripped off my shredded stockings; skirts really are for women with boring lives.

"Maybe we should have brought Sandy along," quipped 'Gren through the muffling gray wool as he pulled it over his head.

I nodded. "I could stand him dabbling in his water and inks just about now."

"You take the prize package for a stretch." Sorgrad handed Aritane over to 'Gren without ceremony. "It'll hide all that blood."

We moved cautiously on. Our path through the spoil heaps brought us to a close-knit circle of shelters. We took a pace back toward the concealing gloom near the cliff face as a mail-clad runner hurried up, shouting. "Take your valuables and get into the fess! Lowlanders are attacking in the lower valley! Jeirran's going to make a stand at the ridge."

"Good luck to him," I murmured doubtfully.

A drum beat echoed back from the steep rock towering above our heads.

"I've heard that rhythm before," I said slowly. "Winter before last, in the camps along the Caladhria border."

Sorgrad listened. "The Lakeland mobs used a cadence like that."

"So it's men from the Gap?" 'Gren's eyes were bright as

a stag-hound's scenting blood. "They're not so tough. Let's get going."

"Not with her to carry." I nodded at the unconscious Aritane. "What are the other ways out of this valley?"

Sorgrad sucked his teeth. "Precious few, that's the whole point of having the fess here. I don't fancy trying a pass up there with dead weight on my back, never mind the night and lack of any gear." He nodded at the sharp jags black against the star-studded sky.

"Could we keep out of sight until the moons rise?" I suggested.

"Two quarters still isn't enough light." Sorgrad shook his head.

'Gren was kicking at something. "Livak, get this open." It was a small building, roofed with stone slates and thick walls densely mortared but barely chest-high to me. Double doors at the front were securely locked so it wasn't some child's playhouse. I winced as sharp gravel bit into my naked knee and I ran my fingers around the lock plate. "Just what is it with you people and locks?" I muttered crossly as my probing revealed the intricacies of this particular fastening. "Is everyone as dishonest as you pair?"

"You don't steal another man's ore, not yet his ingots." I heard the smile in Sorgrad's voice. "But if he were to lose his tools, so he couldn't go digging till he got them back or traded for new ones, now that would be something else."

I nodded pointlessly, unseen in the shadows, finally snicking the last tumbler free. "So what's worth my trouble?"

Sorgrad reached in blindly. "Rope." He slung a coil over one shoulder. "Sacks; 'Gren, shove a few around the girl. Ah, that's what we want, lanterns."

"Pass one over." I felt for my tinderbox.

"Don't light it," warned Sorgrad. He must have caught the scorch of my glare despite the gloom. "Sorry."

"Let's have a pry-bar." 'Gren looked around with some

difficulty over Aritane's rump. Pushing one into his hand, I took one for myself as well and passed a third to Sorgrad. I didn't fancy my chances trying to explain to anyone that this wasn't actually my fight so this would have to do as a weapon.

People rushing for the fess didn't even look our way as they stumbled over discards in the dark, faces tight with fear. A few figures were forcing their way in the other direction, toward an ever-increasing tumult. Some were mailed with swords in hand, more were trusting to leather, picks, axes and cudgels.

I saw the eagerness in 'Gren's eyes and prodded him meaningfully. "Can't fighting wait until you get back to Lescar? That's why we need to get your lady friend back to the wizards, so they can call off Draximal's hounds, remember?"

"We'll work our way around the far side of the spoil heaps," said Sorgrad decisively. "See if we can slip past down toward the ford." The rounded tops of the spoil heaps faded into the blackness of the mountains above us. I was looking all ways, gripping the comforting weight of the iron bar. My eyes met Sorgrad's and we shared a tight, humorless smile.

Our path brought us to the edge of the battle. Mountain Men were hard pressed, split into separate stands and hemmed in on all sides. The lowlanders had come to exact their revenge and in numbers enough to do the job thoroughly. The noise of battle hammered at our ears and bright light seared our eyes. Fires running out of control ripped away the protection of the shadows.

"Back," ordered Sorgrad. We found ourselves in a dead end of shattered stones, bounded by a conduit full of foul water.

"Arseholes," hissed 'Gren.

"Trouble," I spat. A handful of figures were silhouetted against the glow of the battle. One had already seen us and he alerted his mates with a delighted shout, thick with the accents of Grynth. The other four spread out to block the gaps we might have fled through. These were out to take their recompense wherever they could, slung around with the lumpy outlines of purses and pouches, looted bags and belts. One saw Aritane, bare legs seductive beneath the gaudy blanket. The lowlander licked his lips and showed a gap-toothed smile of eager anticipation.

'Gren dumped the enchantress unceremoniously. "You want a taste of honey, you get past my sting, shit-sucker."

Hearing obscenities from the gutters of Col coming out of a Mountain mouth halted these bravos long enough for me and Sorgrad to take stance either side of 'Gren. All our opponents had swords but held them more with the tight, close grip of the self-taught than the relaxed readiness of the competent.

'Gren took a pace forward and the middle man lifted his blade, but in opening his shoulders he ducked his head forward. 'Gren shoved the beak of his pry-bar up under the lowlander's chin, ripping up into the skull beyond. The man went down like poleaxed beef, blood and spittle spraying.

As 'Gren yanked his pry-bar free, the next man along recovered enough to stab at him. He didn't even look at me in my muddy skirts until my iron bar smashed his arm with a crack audible even above the tumult. He gaped, aghast as I brought the jemmy up under his ear, sending him clean into the Shades. Shoving him hard against his fellow gave me time to slide out of reach. 'Gren filled the gap, a sword sharp in his hand sending the man howling toward a sizable gang of ruffians, clutching a bloody gash to his thigh.

"Leave him!" Sorgrad wiped his own captured sword on a decapitated body.

'Gren halted, expression mutinous.

"You're going to take them all on?" Sorgrad pulled his pry-bar free from the head of another corpse, where it stuck through the temple like a spoon in an egg.

"This way." I followed the conduit up the slope, slabbed rim treacherous and water evil with an oily sheen. It had to be coming from somewhere in the apparently featureless cliff face. I traced the flow to an opening barely perceptible in the inky shadows, 'Gren and Sorgrad hard on my heels, our pursuers shouting their outrage over the bodies we'd left behind.

Once in the mine entrance I flattened myself against the wall, forcing myself to slow my breathing. Sorgrad pushed past and 'Gren came next, Aritane's shift brushing my arm. I laid one hand on 'Gren's shoulder and stretched out the other, running fingertips along the wall to steady myself in the utter darkness. We shuffled slowly forward until shouts behind us made us halt.

I turned and looked at the pale square of starlit sky. At least down here they could only come at us one or two at a time. Sorgrad worked his way to my side, sword ready. The curses and taunts came and went, the only sound the distant clamor of battle.

"Do we risk going out again or do we sit in our hole until they've all killed each other?" My voice sounded heavy in the still air.

"Let's see where this goes first." Cloth rustled as 'Gren shifted Aritane's weight. "Word is you can get right through from the next valley into these seams."

"They say that about any number of sokes." Sorgrad clicked his tongue in thought. "But Teyvafess have been working this valley pretty much since Misaen made it. We could try to get around the fighting through the tunnels."

"What are the odds?" I asked. "There won't be any miners in here?"

"Nothing more than a few surprised rats." Sorgrad led the way. 'Gren slung Aritane over one shoulder like a sack of wheat and I followed close behind, sliding my feet cautiously over the irregular rock, cursing as a cold puddle caught me unawares and splashed my bare legs.

Pry-bar still in one hand, I felt my way along the jagged wall with the other. The stone was slick with moisture and slimy in patches that I didn't want to think about. I looked back over my shoulder to see the square of night sky get smaller and smaller. What had been darkness outside now looked more pale and bright with each step away. The still, cool air smelled of metal and earth, with a faint undercurrent of piss. The faint echoes of the fight outside could have been coming from the Otherworld, they sounded so far removed from us.

We turned a corner and the darkness was absolute, a cocoon of black so total it made no difference whether my eyes were open or closed. Forest blood did me no favors here. I swallowed to get a little spit for the dryness catching my throat and carefully felt for tinder, flint and steel in my belt-pouch. "Sorgrad, can you take the lamp for a moment?"

His hand touched mine and I closed his fingers around the punched-metal cylinder. "Wait till I get the slide open."

I heard a grating noise and struck a spark. The darkness fled at the bright flare of the candle only to come rushing straight back. The boundless black was revealed as a tunnel tapering slightly to its roof and curving gradually in the direction of the valley bottom. The walls were brown and gray, streaked with odd pigments and sparkling faintly, perhaps from moisture, perhaps from some crystal or metal in the rock. My spirits rose at the cheerful flame throwing dapples of light out through the lamp's pierced sides. We were well away from the fighting, we finally had a prize worth holding, and once we found a way out of this warren we could be clear and on our way back to somewhere civilized before sunrise, Halcarion willing.

The Teyvarekin,
18th of Aft-Summer

Jeirran hammered on the gate with the hilt of his sword, bloodied to the pommel and beyond. "Open, do you hear me, open up!"

For all the rage swelling his chest, his bellows made little impression with the clamor on every side. Choking on fury, fear and the treacherous fumes of alcohol, he vomited, the spirits searing his throat. Coughing, he reeled unsteadily, sweat breaking out on his forehead, cold shivers running the length of his body. Without the bulk of the fess wall to support his blindly reaching hand, he would have fallen.

The spasm passed, but little improved. The ground seemed to be rocking beneath his feet and his head was ringing like an anvil. The hollow in his gut had little to do with spewing up the golden liquor, looted bread and meat.

Where was Eresken? Where were the foreigner's promises of lofty enchantments and secret wisdom? Jeirran groaned with confusion; this was no time for wavering, when they were hemmed against the walls of the fess. But why hadn't Eresken warned them of this, asked a treacherous hint of doubt as the press of bodies grew ever thicker, struggling for the gate blind and deaf to their entreaties. The yells of the encroaching lowlanders grew ever more threatening.

"Aritane!" roared Jeirran in frenzy. Some echo of his desperation, some sympathy of blood must surely stir her Sheltya skills. He stood, panting, mouth dry and foul, but felt no gentle touch of her mind on his. Two men shoved him aside, raising bloodied hammers more used to honest toil than warfare. They hit the gate together with three ringing blows. A pause for breath, the same again, and a slide in the arch above the lintel wrenched open.

"Maewelin's mercy, let us in!" screamed someone.

There was a moment of frantic debate, voices raised in argument and fear. "Get ready to run. We can only do this once."

Jeirran fought his way to the front, pulling lesser men aside. He set his shoulder to the gate, heedless of armor digging into his shoulder. The massive gates creaked but did not open.

"Back off a pace," yelled someone in frustration. "The bar can't lift with you all pressing inward."

Hands dragged Jeirran back and the gates swung apart. With a howl of triumph, savage as hunting wolves, the lowlanders redoubled their efforts, desperate to gain the gates before they could be closed.

Jeirran stumbled through the huge doors, fighting the surge of frantic men threatening to carry him past. He grabbed for an iron tethering ring, snatching at those passing him with the other hand. "We have to close the gates!" In that moment he felt sober and certain; the next he longed for the oblivion of drunkenness.

"But ours are still out there! We can't shut them out!"

Jeirran backhanded the man with a mailed glove. "If the lowlanders get in we'll all be deader than winter-killed birds!"

The yelling bloodlust of the lowlanders rang through the confines of the tunnel, unreasoning as a maddened dog. Jeirran pushed against the gate's inner face, digging his heels in the dust. Others joined him, black with gore, arms hanging uselessly by their sides, some even blinded with their own blood, guided by friends and groping for a handhold. As the hinges creaked, others hovered at the narrowing aperture, dragging comrades bodily through, seizing a hand, a belt, a jerkin. Men were passed bodily along, feet barely touching ground littered with weapons, boots, bandages, pitiful fragments of once prized possessions.

New faces appeared in the gap, dark lowland eyes beneath steel-rimmed caps, burning with hot desire for slaughter and revenge. Two got through the gap, then three, then a handful. In some distant corner of his mind Jeirran realized he must surely be killed, a thought bringing not so much horror as resignation, even relief.

"Let us through!" Men from the rekin, old and young, injured and sick, rushed forward, falling on the foe with the tools of ore mill and furnacehouse. Picks and axes bit deep to crack bone and rip flesh. The lowlanders fell back and the gates were forced shut. A knot of lowland men were cut off; assailed on all sides, they soon fell. Shouts of abuse screamed frantic outside, blows hammering in vain on the ancient timbers. The great beams were rammed home in their brackets, bracing the gate against the bulk of the wall, unmoved by the furious assaults.

Jeirran slid down to the ground, gripping his hair in frustrated fists, wits in turmoil. He raised his head to find a ring of questioning faces. Some were hopeful, others doleful, some were expectant, others accusing. All were looking for answers and all were looking to him.

Jeirran scrambled to his feet, feeling a numbness in his legs. His senses seemed awry; silent anticipation on all sides was loud in his ears, drowning out the riot beyond the walls. He stumbled toward the rekin, forcing a ghastly smile, unable to frame answers to the urgent questions thrown at him. Panic threatened to overwhelm him. All this pain, all this carnage, he had started it—and for what? How could he hope to take on even a fraction of the lowlanders? Why had he urged these good and trusting people into such folly? Screams beyond the gates tore holes in the comforting delusions woven by liquor and self-deceit.

Where was Eresken? Cudgeling his bewildered wits, Jeirran headed for the side door of the rekin, heedless of the curious crowd following him. He turned to yell at them, "Let me alone, can't you? Go 'way!" The alcohol he'd drunk in heedless celebration betrayed him with slurred and broken words. Jeirran's courage failed him and he stumbled blindly up the stairs.

The door to Aritane's room stood ajar, a keening coming from it to run around the rekin like a lost shade. The insane sound raised the hairs on Jeirran's neck and the skin on his arms crimped into gooseflesh. A trickle of clotted blood pooled on the threshold like a visible curse. The nerve-rending wailing didn't waver. Jeirran kicked wide the door but backed away from the ghastly sight within, one hand convulsively wiping his mouth and beard. Krelia hugged the lifeless Ceris to her breast, gore and filth covering them both. Her uncomprehending face was that of an animal knowing only its agony.

"What happened? What happened?" raged Jeirran. He dug vicious fingers into Krelia's shoulder, in a vain attempt to halt her noise. All he did was jar her to an even more ear-shredding screech punctuated with noisy sobs. Her eyes remained locked on some unseen vision of horror.

Jeirran gaped at the body of Ceris' father, baffled, retching at the butchered thing beside it. Wrenching aside an overturned table, he halted, shock stifling the breath in his throat. Blood hammered through his head so hard he thought his skull would split clean in two. Eresken was dead, face ghastly pale and head half severed.

Who was this stranger, this thin-faced man with his mixed-blood hair and distant features? Aritane had brought him, told Jeirran to take his unsupported word. Lifelong habits of self-justification and excuse reared up within Jeirran but quailed beneath the cruel lash of inescapable truths. He had urged her to summon this mountebank. He'd turned a blind eye to their unseemly fumblings, telling himself his reclaimed sister deserved to know love, scorning the strictures of Sheltya vows. But that code was necessarily harsh, treacherous memory reminded him, to ensure strict neutrality gave no one grounds to dismiss Sheltya judgment.

"Where is Aritane?" Jeirran yelled at Krelia, his useless hands jerking in impotent confusion, desperate to beat some answers from the howling bitch.

"What has happened here?" Remet stood in the doorway.

"I don't know!" Jeirran exploded with sudden fury. "You tell me; you're Sheltya, all knowing, all wise. Tell me what has happened! Tell me what to do! Tell me why Eresken is dead and why did I ever listen to him! Tell me where to find Aritane!"

Jeirran stormed forward, grabbing the boy's robe and forcing him backward, fistful of gray cloth twisted at his chest, other hand lifted in a threatening fist.

Remet's eyes were huge in his pallid face. "I have no idea where she is. I cannot find her mind," the boy said with a tremor in his voice. "All I know is the soke is under foreign feet, the fess is surrounded and we have no way out."

"I don't know what to do," screamed Jeirran, "I don't know how we came to this. Why has it all gone so wrong?"

"I can't answer you," quavered Remet.

Jeirran smashed his fist into the boy's mouth, shocking a cry of pain from the lad. As he drew back his arm for an even harder blow, Remet wrenched himself free with the unexpected strength of terror. Pausing in his flight at the top of the stairs, he wiped blood from lips gashed on broken teeth. "You'll answer for this, for all of this. Somehow, someday, you'll answer."

As Jeirran took an enraged step forward, Remet's nerve broke and the boy scrambled down the stairs. Lifting his head, Jeirran took a deep breath, straightened his back, beard jutting as he set his jaw. Walking slowly, he took the stairs at a measured pace, closing his eyes for a moment before he pushed open the door and stood on the threshold.

"Give me that." He took an axe helve from a nearby hand, thumping it on the planks at his feet. Three times, three more and three again, the ringing blows echoed above the heads of the milling crowd and the terrified motion slowed, faces upturned, bewildered.

"Everyone who can fight must find a weapon. Those who cannot must take to the upper levels of the rekin." Jeirran struck the wooden balustrade at his side. "Cut this away and pack the lower level with turf and timber, ready to set slow fire in case we lose the walls. Ropes will get the defenders inside if we have to hold the rekin alone."

The crowd exchanged uncertain glances.

"We can hold this place against thrice this number of lowlanders," Jeirran declared with bravado. "Or does Misaen no longer make Anyatimm strong, Maewelin make them wise?" A few faint smiles greeted this sally. "To work!" Jeirran urged them and slowly the people began to move, a sense of purpose soon replacing the earlier aimless fear.

Jeirran jumped down from the wooden stair and, taking up an axe, began reducing it to ragged ruins. Slow fire in the ground level, the barriers of smoke and heat had saved more than one rekin in the past when walls and all seemed lost. It could do so again. If not, well, then he would find oil, spirits, whatever it took to raise fast fire and set the whole rekin alight as a beacon to kindle hatred of the lowlanders in every Mountain heart.

Teyvasoke,
19th of Aft-Summer

There are no chimes to sound inside mountains but by the time I judged we were Poldrion's side of midnight I was feeling far less cheerful. I leaned forward to peer at Aritane; her breath was coming in harsh jolts jerked by 'Gren's increasing pace, but I couldn't believe anyone could lie that limply, so uncomfortably, and be faking. Lifting my lantern to check the color of her skin, I nearly burned her pale wrist on the hot metal as 'Gren halted.

Sorgrad had reached a junction in the workings. "The main seam should be straight ahead. This way." Water dripped on my head and I felt a cold downdraft, suggesting some kind of ventilation shaft. The tunnel roof grew lower and more irregular, ragged diggings branching off, broken rock underfoot, stretches shored up with timber.

"Shouldn't there be more of these props?" I wondered uneasily how much mountainside was hanging over my head.

"No need in this rock. That's one reason Teyvafess has always been so rich," 'Gren said over his shoulder. "Until their copper lode ran out, that is."

I felt our direction changing from time to time but with no reference points beyond the ever-changing yet monotonous patterns of the walls, I soon lost my bearings. When a larger space finally opened out, I lifted my lantern to reveal a lofty cavern, though I couldn't have said if it were natural or dug by hand. Sorgrad was looking for exits, the yellow candlelight throwing his features into sharp relief, the walls behind him melting into darkness.

"Which way?" 'Gren moved Aritane to his other shoulder. "This one's not getting any lighter."

Sorgrad looked at me. "All these seem to lead deeper into the mountain, not down the valley."

I shrugged. "We won't find out standing here. Better keep moving and hope to pick up some kind of crosswise tunnel."

We opted for the widest digging and I walked beside 'Gren as Sorgrad scouted ahead. "I went down to the lowlands because I never fancied being a mole," 'Gren muttered.

"Not because you were scared of the wyrms coming out of the deeps to eat you?" I teased.

"I'd throw them this one." He hefted Aritane to a more secure hold. "She'd choke a litter of wyrms and leave something over for their dam."

"She's not that big," I objected.

"Do you want to try carrying her?" 'Gren threatened to hand over the unconscious enchantress and he wasn't joking.

"I've got the lantern." I waved it hurriedly. "Anyway, I bet she's lighter than a sack of ore."

Sorgrad cursed something in the Mountain tongue that had 'Gren miss a step.

"What's the matter?" I called out to him.

"This is just an adit to get to a series of seams." He came toward us, shaking his head in disgust. A sudden radiance

flared on the metal side of his lantern and Sorgrad dropped
it with an oath.

A familiar voice sounded above the clatter of dented tin.
"Just look into the spell, Sorgrad!"

He picked up the lantern. The candle was dead and gut-
tered but the warm amber light of magic shone in its stead.
Usara's face smiled at us from a swirl of sorcery.

"Hello," I said stupidly before Sorgrad turned the spell
toward himself.

"You're using the tunnels to get past the fighting?" Usara
didn't waste time on pleasantries.

"Have you been scrying us?" Sorgrad asked suspiciously.

"Snatching the odd glimpse. You'll have to work right
down to the bridge; the whole of the lower valley is a bat-
tleground."

"How do you know that?"

"Who's attacked?"

"There's no way these diggings go that close to the ford."
Sorgrad's firm statement overruled questions from me and
'Gren.

"Don't worry about that," Usara said. "You take the second off-hand tunnel."

"What about the enchanters?" I ran a hand over my face
and grimaced at the feel of encrusted muck.

Usara's face was reflected in the blackened tin of the
lantern, overlaid with a yellow sheen, curious faces of Forest warriors indistinct behind him. "I've got the boys keeping up a concealment charm. Anyway, given the present
chaos, I don't see the Sheltya checking for unexpected wizardry."

We hurried to the digging Usara had indicated. The spell
cast a hard-edged light compared to the softer fluttering of
my candle, calling lumpy, distorted shadows to chase us
down the tunnel. The roof sank lower and lower until we
found ourselves dead-ended in a litter of shattered rock and
broken wood.

"Come on, wizard, impress us," demanded 'Gren.

The glow on the lantern faded to leave only the feeble light of my candle.

"Let me take her." Sorgrad lifted Aritane off his brother's shoulder. As he cradled her in his arms, I held a hand in front of her nose, feeling for the reassurance of her breath, when a sudden gust snuffed my candle and left us in utter darkness.

"Saedrin's stones." I groped awkwardly for flint and steel but a new light was already breaking the blackness. It came from deep within the rocks in front of us, dim at first as if unimaginably distant. A faint crazing like the crackle on a pot's glaze grew brighter and brighter, light pulsing steadily, glowing ever more intense with each beat. Soon it was as bright as a festival fire, magic interlaced across the surface of the rock and riven deep into it, rippling and moving like a living thing. We felt warmth coming from it, the pattern extending from the face of the rock, weaving itself into the empty air. Rapid vibration ran through the floor, up through the soles of my boots, to set the nerves in my belly fluttering in sympathy. Sudden cracking sounds sent us a pace backward in one accord. The smell reminded me of an empty cook pot set over a fire, forgotten till someone burns a hand on it.

The rock began to splinter, shards flaking away at first, larger chunks falling free as the stresses of the magic split stone like a child hammering a pan of toffee. 'Gren began to drag rubble aside with his pry-bar, looking up warily to make sure nothing was about to fall on his head. I raked the debris further back down the tunnel, trying to avoid the razor-sharp fragments snapping into the walls.

"That wizard could make himself a fortune if he found a soke willing to mine with magic." Sweat glistened on 'Gren's forehead. "He could do ten men's work in a day."

"Can we get through?" asked Sorgrad, arms full of Aritane.

I paused to ease my back. "Is she stirring?"

Sorgrad shook his head in the uncertain light of the spell.

"Not yet, but I'd rather be out of these tunnels when she does."

"The thassin should keep her sweet even if she does come through the tahn." People chew it to forget grief, poverty, love and hatred, so with Arimelin's grace it should tangle her wits for a while.

"There's a space through here," 'Gren called over his shoulder. I followed him down the glowing tunnel, keeping well away from fading walls now melted and molded like tallow for candles. The light of magic was still bright at the end where 'Gren was prying at the edges of a hole opening into nothingness. A jagged slab of rock dropped into the blackness and slid down some unseen gradient. I relit my lamp and held it out cautiously into the void.

"Where are we going now, Usara?" I demanded of the empty air. I was looking into a cleft heaped with jagged boulders, a rustle of water somewhere unseen below. I squinted up and wondered where the roof might be and if any rocks intended falling on our heads.

A golden tracery shone on the far wall, the pattern spreading like ripples in a pond. The light revealed the full extent of the broken stone we'd have to cover and I grimaced. "Better tie her ladyship to your back, 'Gren. You're going to need both hands and it's not a climb for Sorgrad with a load as well as his armor to unbalance him."

I looked in frustration at my lamp, blew out the candle and clipped it on my belt. I needed hands more than light for this climb. Sorgrad unslung the coil of rope from his shoulder and I knotted the creaking hemp securely around my waist. Sorgrad looped his end around arms and back. I grinned at him and moved out cautiously onto the irregular stones. Getting a footing, I tested my weight before moving my other boot, taking a hold, then another, both hands secure before I moved a foot, both feet solid before lifting a hand to feel for the next grip. I concentrated on the familiar skills that have taken me up more walls and houses than I care to recall and firmly refused to think of unseen, bottomless pits that might lie beneath any one of the tumbled boulders I was trusting myself to. A sibilance of water in the depths or maybe something worse came from between two cracked slabs. Ignoring unwelcome recollection of the wyrms in 'Gren's songs, I moved slowly on. Fingers and toes were cramping with effort by the time I reached the far side of the cleft and I sat on the ledge polished by Usara's magic to get my breath.

"It's awkward, but you just need to keep going straight." I unknotted the rope and looked for some way to secure it. If 'Gren slipped with Aritane on his back, the weight could drag me off my ledge. A little amber light flared beside me as I pulled fruitlessly at a chunk of gray and yellow stone, a spinning circle of magic boring into the mountain. The sorcery faded to muted gold with a hot smell of hearthstones, leaving a hole as thick as my wrist clean through the ledge. Smiling, I threaded the rope through and had it secure in moments. Usara most assuredly had his uses.

By the time 'Gren reached me, I had my lamp relit and the homely flicker shone on the sweat slicking his hair to his forehead. "Get her off me."

Sorgrad's knots were the usual fiendish puzzle but I laid Aritane motionless on the hard floor eventually. 'Gren bent this way and that to ease his back and when Sorgrad arrived he took up the burden of the unconscious enchantress without comment.

I looked down the tunnel where Usara's magic had been crumbling the rock while we'd amused ourselves in the cleft. The bright glow of the busy magic was some distance away now, the walls fading to orange and red and a final muted ocher as the sorcery moved on.

"Watch your footing," I warned unnecessarily. "This is no time to break an ankle." 'Gren and I pushed treacherous shards aside with our pry-bars to clear a path for Sorgrad, whose view of his own feet was obscured by Aritane. She'd better be worth all this trouble, I thought grimly.

"Wait." I went ahead to a gold-rimmed opening and lifted a cautious lantern into a tunnel with walls unmistakably scarred by toolwork. "We're back to a digging proper," I told the others with relief.

"Which way?" demanded 'Gren. "Usara?"

A tinny echo of the mage's voice came from Sorgrad's lantern. "The working goes down a fair distance and then joins a bigger gallery. Turn to the off-hand when you reach it."

We moved faster now; the floor couldn't have been cleaner if my mother had swept it. The bigger gallery came as a welcome relief from the oppressive narrowness of the smaller workings and shafts unseen above gave fresher air. Finally we turned a corner and I squinted uncertainly at a smudge on the edge of my vision. Sliding the shutter across my lantern proved it was no illusion but the way out of the cursed maze. I heaved a sigh of relief.

"You two wait here." I handed Sorgrad my lantern and moved forward slowly, tread silent on the bare rock. I couldn't hear fighting, but that didn't mean much. Back flat to the wall, jemmy ready in my hand, I edged up to the sharp corner and paused, letting my eyes get used to the night. As the featureless gray resolved itself into slope and turf and mountains beyond, I took three stealthy steps outside. We were well down the valley, I saw with relief. The fighting had moved up past the ridge and, although stragglers were looting the lower valley, we should get out of the mine unnoticed.

But the lowlanders held the bridge; torches lined it with men outlined against their smoky glow. Men with helms and pikes, militia from somewhere, not opportunist peasants we might rush past with a couple of swords and a jemmy. I skirted a bulge of grass-covered debris to try and see where the ford might be.

A step behind me clicked two loose stones together. I turned to tease whichever brother had been so careless but the words died on my lips. A gray-robed figure regarded me, face impassive in the light of the quarter moons, lesser waxing, greater waning.

"Where are your companions?" it demanded from the shadow of its cowl. I saw two other shadowy figures emerge from the darkness behind it.

I fixed my gaze on the Sheltya, determined not to look at the mine entrances and began to recite the charm I'd learned against the Elietimm under my breath. "Tror mir'al, es nar'an, tror mir'al, es nar'an."

"You need not fear I will search your mind without cause!" The Sheltya sounded positively insulted.

"It's happened to me before," I retorted before considering the wisdom of my words. "The Elietimm don't waste any time."

"Alyatimm—" The Sheltya's contempt was cut short by a word from one of the others who came down the slope, putting back his hood. His head was shaking slightly and I recognized the old man we'd met at the Hachalfess.

"You're Cullam, aren't you?" I wasn't sure how knowing his name might help, but I didn't see how it could hurt.

The old man nodded. "There are no persons inside either of those workings," he told the first Sheltya, deference in his tone.

"And that one is blocked." The third Sheltya to arrive was the one from the fess, the younger man. He gave me a hard stare. "Where is Aritane? I cannot find her mind!"

I silently repeated the charm over and over to myself, telling myself to believe in it.

"What happened in the fess?" demanded the younger one. "Is Aritane dead as well?"

"Bryn!" Old Cullam rebuked him sharply.

I steeled myself as the Sheltya in charge pushed back his hood. I saw a bald man in his middle years, with a cleft in his chin and fierce brows jutting in a frown. For a heart-stopping moment, I thought his eyes had slid into the blackness of Elietimm possession but then realized he had only blinked. His eyelids were painted black and, while relief weakened my knees, I wondered uneasily what that might signify.

"I'd have every justification in searching your mind for the answers I seek," he said silkily.

I gritted my teeth, trying to summon up whatever bloody-mindedness it was 'Gren had so unexpectedly turned to his advantage in defying Artifice.

"But that would be to forswear my calling and make me no better than the Alyatimm," he continued. "It was to save our people from their abuses that they were driven into the Ice in the first place!"

This meant nothing to me, but I nodded willingly. As long as he was talking, he couldn't be messing around inside my head. Time to try to win some goodwill. "I came here to warn the people of the mountains about these Elietimm," I said hopefully. "We have seen their evil enchantments and—"

"You came here for your own purposes." The Sheltya cut me off disdainfully. "That much I can read without effort. Do not pretend to nobility of purpose."

I felt insulted; turning a profitable rune for myself doesn't preclude doing someone else a good turn. "We came here to warn you," I repeated stubbornly, "and to look for guidance as to how we might recover true magic in the lowlands," I added, sudden inspiration suggesting a way to change the subject. "We were looking to cooperate, to learn from you, to join forces against a common enemy."

"But you brought a mage to do it," the old man Cullam said regretfully. "There can be no meeting between those who govern the four realms of the mind and those who twist the four realms of substance to their command."

I filed that obscure pronouncement away for later examination and decided Sorgrad and 'Gren would have to look after themselves. All I wanted to do now was leave, so I curtsied to Black Eyes with all the grace I could muster in the tattered remnants of my skirts. "If you'll excuse me, I would like to get away from the battle."

"You will depart when I give you leave," the Sheltya stated calmly.

The one called Bryn smirked and I made the mistake of glancing at him. "What did you do to Eresken?" he demanded. "You were outside the room where he lay dead; don't think I don't remember you. Is that how your wizardry is used to murder?"

"The Elietimm enchanter? The one who'd got into your mountains and your counsels and roused half an army to attack the lowlands? He was called Eresken?" I kept my eyes on Black Eyes. "No wizardry was used to kill him, you have my word on it."

"Where is Aritane?" Bryn's voice was thick with a turmoil of anger and fear.

"Don't you know?" Surprise faked for the squirrel game had never been so sincere. "Weren't you one of those helping, what was his name, Eresken?"

Black Eyes pinned me with his stare once more. "Who has done what among Anyatimm is no concern of yours. It is no concern of the charlatan Planir and his covey of greedy conjurors. We will determine the truth and punish the guilty. None have authority over Anyatimm but Sheltya."

"No one seeks to challenge your authority. It's the menace of the Elietimm that we are concerned with. Look at the trouble just one of them has caused." I spared a desperate prayer to Saedrin that there had only been one of the bastards. "The Elietimm are a threat to everyone, Hadrumal, Tormalin and the lands to Solura and beyond. We should all be working together to defeat them. Since you alone seem to have retained true magic, you could do so much to help." And if I could deliver that help, I could name my own price, an optimistic voice commented in some hidden corner of my mind.

Black Eyes looked at me with a contempt that sparked a

rebellious flame of defiance to scorch my paper-thin pretense of humility. This enchanter had scant right to sneer at me when he couldn't even keep his own people in check, arrogant as any wizard.

Cullam muttered something under his breath and frowned for a moment. "The lowlanders have reached the walls of the fess," he said sadly.

Serves the Teyvakin right, I thought uncharitably.

Black Eyes folded his arms, eyes hard in the starlight. "We will remove the lowlanders from our lands. We will find those who conspired with Alyatimm and punish them as we see fit. Should Alyatimm attempt to suborn our people again, they will find us ready and waiting to defend ourselves."

From the certainty in his voice, I wouldn't be taking any bets against him.

"Tell Planir that we do not want his magic in the uplands, we do not need it nor will we tolerate it. We do not want Tormalin weapons or troops or any other lowland incursion under the pretense of sending us aid. We look to our own as we have always done."

I dropped another quick curtsey. "Very good. I'll take your message at once. The sooner Planir knows, the better after all." As I spoke, I glanced around to see if I could spot any hint of the ford. Looking to the front again, I jumped like a startled rabbit. The Sheltya had vanished, all three of them, gone like smoke as gray as their robes.

"Drianon save me from magic in all its forms," I muttered crossly. Since no one from the bridge was showing any interest in this direction, I climbed up to the mine entrance. The opening was indeed choked with stones and rubble, so either the roof had come in on them or Usara had managed some cleverness. I prodded at a rock with a dubious finger but it was solid, cold and very real beneath my touch. No illusion this. I raised my pry-bar but lowered it again. There was no way I was going to clear this on my own, not without getting a double handful of curious soldiery coming to see what was going on. I couldn't see them offering to help, even if I did tell them there was an unconscious maiden wearing nothing but her shift on the far side.

Heaving a sigh, I laid the jemmy across my shoulder and turned for the river. All I could do was trust Usara was getting Sorgrad and 'Gren out of their predicament. If he wasn't, I'd use the pry-bar to persuade him. I knelt to cup a mouthful of water from the river. Now I wasn't so worried about being killed, crushed or captured by the Sheltya; other cares were asserting themselves. I was cold, tired, hungry and had enough scrapes and bruises to keep an apothecary amused for days. I scratched my head again; with my current run of luck, I'd picked up lice.

I finally found the nubby remnants of a post marking the ford. With the river so low, it was an easy enough crossing, but water still left my skirts clinging wetly around my legs and seeped into my boots. I was breaking my nails on my sodden laces when the world whirled madly around me in a flurry of azure and diamond sparks.

"It's all right, it's all right." Sorgrad's voice saying that was probably the only one I'd have believed. Screwing my eyes tight shut against the dizzying sensations and praying I wouldn't be sick, I gritted my teeth until the sensations of being caught in a whirlwind subsided.

"Here you are, all safe with the rest of us," said Usara cheerfully.

I wrapped my arms around myself and counted to five before opening mistrustful eyes. What I saw was the gloomy hollow where we'd left the wizard and Bera's men. As far as I was concerned, we were still a long way from safe, but Sorgrad and 'Gren were there. "So you got them out first."

"As you see," smiled Usara with relief.

I tugged at the wet cloth hampering my legs. "You couldn't have picked me up before I went wading through the river? Where's my bag? I want some dry breeches!"

"We wanted to be sure the Sheltya had left you," said Us-

ara. "I was scrying the whole time. I'd have risked it if anyone had come near you," he assured me, and now that his
smile was gone I could see the lines of effort carved deep
on either side of his mouth.

"She's waking up," said 'Gren suddenly. I saw Aritane
feebly wave a hand in the gray light I was startled to realize
was the first faint promise of dawn.

"The Sheltya have been looking for her." Realization
sounded hollow in my voice. "If she gets her wits together,
they'll find her."

"What do we do now?" asked one of the Forest archers,
gripping an arrow, knuckles white.

The thought of that black-eyed bastard stepping out of
the shadows made me shiver even more than the cold. "We
see which way she's going to jump and if need be we kill
her."

I knelt beside Aritane and rapidly uncovered her ears.
"Don't even think about any enchantments. Try any kind of
escape or magic and we'll kill you, do you understand?"
This wasn't faking sincerity; I meant every word and I
gripped her throat to prove it.

Sorgrad laid the naked blade of a dagger across her palm,
pressing the edge into the soft angle of finger and thumb.
"As Sheltya who forsook her vows, your life is forfeit."

"Nod if you can hear me," I commanded. After a moment, the blind head tilted slowly forward.

"Good." I thought fast. The thassin would be making her
very suggestible, so now was the time to show her any al-
ternatives but mine were worthless. "I have spoken to Bryn
and Cullam," I told her. "They introduced me to another
Sheltya, one with black-painted eyelids." Aritane stiffened
in involuntary panic, fingers nearly cutting themselves on
Sorgrad's knife.

"So the Elders know exactly what you have done," said
Sorgrad sorrowfully. "Betrayal as well as forswearing,
leading those you had vowed to protect into a pointless battle."

"The Elietimm have no love for the Mountain Men," I told her. "All they are doing is stirring up trouble to draw off Tormalin forces that might oppose an invasion in Dalasor. They did the same last year, trying to start a war among the Aldabreshin in the far south, setting family against family. The woman who was gulled into helping them there was pressed to death," I said slowly. "What should we do with you?"

"I can think of a few things," offered 'Gren with relish. Aritane visibly flinched at the sound of his voice. "A woman who betrays her blood to an ancient enemy deserves a slow and painful death."

"Won't the Sheltya give her that?" I asked innocently.

"I imagine so," said Sorgrad pleasantly. "Given the trouble they'll be put to untangling this mess, I'd expect examples made of any ringleaders. We'd have done you more mercy by killing you outright."

"So what shall we do with you? Have you anything to offer us, any talent or knowledge that might make it worth our while to save you?" I was pleased to see a faint tremor in Aritane's hands.

"We have wizards to defeat the Elietimm," said Sorgrad, indifferent.

"But we are curious to learn more about Artifice, aetheric magic, true magic I think you call it," Usara chipped in, finally catching up with the game. "That's what brought us to the mountains, after all."

Aritane's jaw worked helplessly under constricting bandages damp with thassin-stained spit.

"It's your choice, woman," I said harshly. "Do we kill you here, do we leave you for the Sheltya to punish, or do we take you somewhere no Sheltya will ever find you?"

"All the powers of Hadrumal will protect you if you share your knowledge and enable us to defeat the Elietimm," Usara told her earnestly. "They so nearly led your people into a war that would have been the death of them all."

"It's starve or eat your seed corn, my girl," said 'Gren with happy menace.

Aritane held herself tense and stiff beneath the bandages masking her head and the inadequate drape of her shift. A bird whistled a blithe greeting to the sun and the first blush of pink warmed the sky.

This was taking too long. Even with the thassin clogging her wits, it was too much to expect of her. I shivered in the chill breeze and laid a heavy hand on Aritane's breastbone. "Let's just kill her. Forsworn once, she can't be trusted."

The enchantress twisted in vain beneath the pressure and gripped at the blade of Sorgrad's dagger. Blood welled up between her long white fingers. He held her grasp tight around the vicious edge. "Would you make a blood vow? Is that what you want?"

The blind head nodded urgently. Sorgrad winked at me and released her hand. He took the dagger and ran the tip lightly across his own palm, just scoring deeply enough to raise a scarlet line beaded with blood. Clasping Aritane's hand, he nodded at me. "Unwrap her mouth."

I hesitated but 'Gren knelt to do it, cutting through the linen with his own dagger. "As long as she says the words, she's bound for life. If she forswears, 'Grad gets to kill her."

"Sikkar als Misaen, terest Maewelin verath, dolcae en ro-car alsoken."

Aritane echoed Sorgrad's intense words with difficulty, wits still reeling from the tahn, tongue numbed and lips stained brown as old blood by the thassin.

"Will this hold her? Will she remember it?" I demanded of Sorgrad.

He looked at me, eyes mysterious in the pale light. "It's a vow to break all vows. If you make it falling down drunk at your coming of age, you still remember it on your deathbed. She has betrayed everything else and all that's left to her is death at the hands of Sheltya if they find her."

I shrugged and turned to Usara, who was watching wide-eyed, Bera's men behind him even more so. "So what's our best route out of here? We don't want to run into anyone coming up to join the siege and be mistaken for some half-witted raiding party."

"And we have to get her away before any Sheltya come looking." Sorgrad nodded at Aritane.

Usara smiled. "I'll contact Planir and get him to work a nexus. He'll get us back to Hadrumal even if it means rousting half the Council out of bed."

Ten

As a girl, I seldom heard Forest songs in Toremal itself.
These days my grandchildren hum them as they go about
their daily amusements. This is one of my particular
favorites with its hopeful notions for young and old alike.

Three travelers sheltered from sudden hail,
Minstrel and maiden and graybeard frail.
Minstrel to maiden said, "I have seen
The great Tree of Years clad in broad leaves green."
Graybeard said sagely, "I once went there.
I saw it in winter, bough stark and bare."
Maiden she nodded, said, "I once found
Its wondrous fruit fallen to the ground."
Unchanging rock wondered how all three
Seeing such difference could yet agree.
Rain falling formless, new every day,
Paid little heed, rushing on its way.
Trees of the wildwood laughed, "Don't you know?
To live you must bide and yet change and grow.
Baby lies mewling, so helpless, small,
Boy moves to youth and to manhood tall,
Girl becomes maiden and mother wise
Aged still see with the selfsame eyes."

The Chamber of Planir the Black,
Archmage of Hadrumal,
23rd of Aft-Summer

"Once I'd clarified matters with the Sheltya Elders, I realized it was far better that they deal with their own criminals," I explained. "Given the tension between upland and lowland, any demand that we exact justice would just risk worsening the situation. We agreed that they would punish their guilty and make sure word of the Elietimm plot was spread throughout the Ranges. We won't face a repetition of this." I took a sip of the Archmage's excellent wine.

Planir studied me over the rim of his own goblet. I wasn't sure, but I thought that sprinkling of gray at his temples hadn't been there the last time we'd met. What hadn't changed was the charming manner and subtle desirability that cloaked him like insidious scent and tempted a girl to confide all manner of things in him. I smiled again and thought of Ryshad's open honesty, his strong arms and the way his hair curled softly behind his ears.

"Thanks to you," Planir inclined his head with a sardonic smile.

"Thanks to me, to 'Gren and Sorgrad, to the Forest Folk and obviously in no small part to Usara." My expression was as open and honest as the late-morning sun pouring in through the unshuttered windows. "I do hope you are going to reward him."

"Usara will reap all the benefits of his experiences, I assure you," said Planir calmly. Hidden amusement lurked in his eyes but I didn't go looking to uncover it. The Archmage could play whatever other games he liked as long as I came out ahead in mine.

"So, we have left the mountains secure against Elietimm influence," I ticked off points on my fingers, tallying like a merchant, "Gilmarten has gone back to Solura to tell his patron to spread the word of their menace among the nobility there. He is confident Lord Astrad will alert King Soltriss as a matter of the utmost urgency. All of which is a bonus really, something we achieved over and above our original intention of finding aetheric knowledge for Messire D'Olbriot. As far as that goes, we have identified the songs of the Forest Folk as a major source for enchantments and charms—"

"A source perhaps, but one that will have every scholar this side of the ocean scratching his head for years to come," objected Planir mildly. "Your theory may be sound but finding the truth of it will be like hunting pips among peppercorns."

I smiled as I shook my head at him. "I went looking for knowledge; I never made any promises about the form it might take. Anyway, I'll bet Guinalle could unravel a few of the mysteries for you. Why don't you bring her back from Kellarin for the winter? That would be one way of rewarding Usara," I added slyly.

"Yes, I think he would love an opportunity to exchange theories with her." Planir's mischievous grin lifted years from him. "I've already bespoken Naldeth and requested she consider traveling back on the next ship for Bremilayne."

So the Archmage thought he was one move ahead; I reminded myself to play this hand with care. "Then Guinalle will be able to work with Aritane." I nodded my approval. Rather her than me. As Sorgrad had promised, the vow had been enough to hold the Sheltya woman even when the drugs had left her blood, and after that, Usara's scrying had been able to show her the destruction visited on her people as a result of the enchanter Eresken seducing them into a hopeless war. She had listened to the wizard's patient explanations of Elietimm treachery and deceit stony-faced and the bitter knowledge had left her set on a quest for vengeance so implacable I was glad I hadn't realized just what kind of person we'd been kidnapping. I only hoped the soft-spoken Guinalle would be able to guide this remorseless determination into profitable paths for Kellarin and Hadrumal. But that was Planir's problem, not mine.

"Aritane must have increased your knowledge of Artifice five times over by now. And of course her learning is not only entirely comprehensible, but also proven and tested. The discovery of aetheric lore among the Forest Folk would have been enough to make the journey a success but establishing the Sheltya as holders of such knowledge and bringing a practitioner to help you—that was beyond all expectations. I know Messire D'Olbriot will be delighted."

"And duly grateful," agreed Planir solemnly.

"And duly grateful," I nodded. "Given I have spent a season and a half in his service, risked life and sanity five times over and achieved more than even the most optimistic might have hoped."

"I wonder if Messire has been able to work out how the tale of your Ryshad's journey to the Ice Islands got out," mused Planir idly. "Did you hear that Aritane said her brother got the notion of contacting the Elietimm from a ballad, of all things?"

"Shiv was telling me it was being sung the length and breadth of the Old Empire by Summer Solstice." I shook my head. "There really is no way of keeping such things secret, when so many people are involved. There'll be a double handful of versions circulating by now and nothing to be gained by trying to follow them back to their various sources."

"Oh, I think we can be reasonably certain it came from a Forest minstrel," said Planir earnestly. "I've been looking into it for quite some time. Not that I have found anything certain to tell Messire, of course."

"There's no point in wasting his time with rumor, is there?" I smiled. "Not when he has so many concerns over Kellarin, keeping the colony safe."

"There might be a way of finding out." Planir wasn't about to let this mouse get out from under his paw. "I wonder what the runes might be able to tell us. The more I think about it, the more accurate that foretelling you had seems to have been."

I didn't let my gaze waver or my expression change. "Indeed. But rather than raking over dead embers, I think you should see if the runes can shed any light on the future. Some notion of what might happen in Kellarin would be most valuable." I helped myself to more wine. "There's another thing we brought back from our travels that you didn't have before. There's a lot more to the runes than just games of chance."

Planir spread a dubious hand. "I'm not sure how much use that might be. There are so many variables when it comes to interpreting that kind of thing, and any view is bound to be highly subjective."

I shrugged. Whether or not the Archmage made use of the Folk's foretelling was up to him. I'd certainly be finding someone who could pull hints out of a set of runes for me. I had friends in Kellarin, Halice first and foremost, and if the Elietimm were going to come winging in on the northern winds again I wanted her warned. For the present, I wasn't about to let the Archmage escape his obligations. "So obviously Messire D'Olbriot has much to reward us for. Feel free to agree your own contribution with him. I'm sure you'll be able to reach a mutually satisfactory arrangement."

Planir's expression turned serious and he studied the dregs of his wine. "I have rather a lot of calls on my time just at present. I'll grant you Hadrumal has benefited from some of the incidental results of your activities but events have also led to considerable demands on me and the Council. It's all very well you saying the Sheltya undertake to deal with their own culprits but stopping the men of the Gap simply wading into a season of indiscriminate murder and land-grabbing, that's proving quite some task!"

"Yes, another debt to lay at the feet of the Elietimm," I agreed regretfully. "They bear a heavy responsibility for starting all this bloodshed. It's fortunate we were in the right place at the right time to stiffen Forest resistance and stop the whole of Ensaimin catching light."

"Darni will be suitably honored," Planir assured me.

"Oh, I have no doubt that you honor every such debt, Archmage." Curiosity prodded me and I yielded to temptation. "So how exactly did you haul the men of the Gap back from the brink?"

Planir's mask slipped a little and honest merriment widened his smile. "The main contention in the Gap is over mining, isn't it? I don't know if you've ever realized, but one way or another there are a sizable number of wizards working up there. Alchemists too, and many of them have links with Hadrumal. They've studied here or worked with mages visiting the universities at Vanam or Col. I bespoke some wizards in Grynth and had them contact the heads of the guilds on my authority. Once I had pointed out that I could remove all that most vital assistance inside a couple of days, they were inclined to listen when I insisted they withdraw their support from the fighting."

"They agreed just like that?" My question hovered just on the polite side of skepticism.

"No." Planir's smile turned wolfish. "Not until I also pointed out that seizing land or mines would do them little good if that angered an Archmage who could easily render every bucket of ore worthless. My element is the earth after all, and being born and brought up in the Gidestan coal country I probably know more about mining than any guild master."

I couldn't help laughing. One day, when there was absolutely no chance of anything riding on the outcome beyond ill-minted copper, I could see myself playing a hand or two of runes with this man, just to see if he was as good as he thought he was.

Planir's smile faded. "Though having to use the power of the Archmage with such a heavy hand is something that could cause problems in the longer term. Fear and ignorance still colors people's notions of wizardry and making threats like this stirs old prejudice. That's another thing to weigh in the balance."

"Look at the other side of the coin," I urged him. "It has been an opportunity to remind the powers of Ensaimin and elsewhere of the value of magecraft. Isn't that something the Council has been discussing? I'm sure your colleague Kalion must be delighted."

Planir burst out laughing. "That's not quite how I would put it." He rose and crossed to the sideboard standing with unobtrusive elegance against the wall. If Messire paid me half what that piece might fetch on a good day in a Col auction house, I'd have spent my spring and summer profitably. The Archmage took two bottles from the array resting in carved cradles. "You said you were lunching with Shiv? Take this with my compliments."

I stood to take the gift. "That's very good of you." If he thought he was going to pay me off with a couple of bottles of even this finest vintage, the wizard was a few sticks short of a bundle. "You'll be able to bespeak, what's his name, Casuel by tonight? You and Messire should be able to agree a sum between you soon enough. I'll call back for your contribution tomorrow?" I was tempted to ask if he could get me news of Ryshad but decided against putting myself in his debt.

"Make it the day after," Planir suggested. "Rest assured, Livak, you won't find me ungenerous. I know what we owe you and your friends."

There were two edges to that, so I replied in kind. "Assisting you has proved the experience of a lifetime, Archmage."

A thought halted me on the threshold. "I was very sorry to hear about Otrick." I had no need to pretend sincerity. "I didn't know him well, but I liked what I saw of the old pirate. I really did hope that Aritane would know how to bring him back to himself."

Planir ducked his head against a sudden grimace, lifting his face a moment later, mask fully restored. "At least we can bid him a proper farewell now, him and the others so afflicted." He coughed. "Let's hope these are the last deaths we add to the reckoning. Just as I pay my debts, Livak, I collect what's due. The Elietimm will pay in full." He smiled with all the warmth of frostbite.

I managed a fleeting quirk of my lips and closed the door behind me, tucking the wine in the crook of my arm.

Othilsoke,
23rd of Aft-Summer

Keisyl took a long draft of cold water and closed his eyes, savoring the kiss of wind and sun on his brow. If only he could stay here like this, forever, never having to look on his problems again.

"Keis? Lad?" Chance breeze lifted the wary hail over the edge of the hollow.

Keisyl walked out onto the track to see two figures toiling up from the lower reaches of the valley, faces muffled against the dust, clothes stained with sweat. He walked down to meet them, leather jug in one hand and horn cups in the other.

"Mother, Fithian." He handed each a drink and refilled the proffered cups wordlessly.

"So what's it all about, Keisy?" Ismenia demanded once she had regained her breath.

"Fith?" Keisyl turned to his uncle in some surprise.

The old man shook his tousled silver head, mouth downturned. "Not for me to say, lad." He mopped his forehead with a sleeve, the faded yellow of the cuff newly mended with brighter thread. "It's for you two alone. I'll go on up and look to the workings."

Ismenia watched him go with a mixture of resignation, irritation and affection. "He's been itching to get back to the diggings, the old fool. Goats is boys' work, as far as he's concerned. All right, Keisy, what is so important I have to leave the girls and come hiking all the way up here? I'm not as young as I was, you know."

Keisyl managed a faint smile at her determined cheerfulness. It died in the next breath. "Come and see."

Walking into the dell, he skirted the long-dead ashes of the fire and went to the sturdy tool cache. The door was secured by a simple wooden wedge, which Keisyl kicked aside with the split toe of his boot. Reaching into the gloom, he dragged a cowering figure out into the sunlight.

Ismenia's hands leaped to her face to stifle a startled cry. "Jeirran?"

Keisyl looked down at the naked figure hunched on the ground, hair and beard matted with dirt where they hadn't been scorched away by fire, body smeared with heedless filth, feet foul with sores, hands bleeding from raw blisters, one finger missing its nail and swollen into a suppurating mass. "I think so," he said finally.

The sound of voices lifted the wretch's head, face blank, mouth slack and drool glistening on chapped and crusted lips. The eyes were the worst, blue as ever but as mindless as those newly opened in a mewling pup.

"I thought he was dead," whispered Ismenia. "I thought Maewelin had claimed her due, rot his heart!"

"Looks like Misaen wanted him after all." Keisyl chewed on a thumbnail. "Now what do we do with him?"

"Where did you find him?" Ismenia shook her head in wonderment.

"He was scuttling around the diggings." Keisyl couldn't restrain a shudder. "I thought it was some gwelgar knitted out of grass and mud, come to look for naughty children."

His laugh had no humor in it but the miserable thing looked up and mimicked him, the sound hoarse and horrible.

Keisyl raised a hand but could not land the blow. He turned away, shivering despite the hot sun. Ismenia looked down at the hollow shell of a man, just staring vacantly at nothing again. "What are we to do with him?"

Keisyl heaved a reluctant sigh. "I suppose we can keep him up here for a while, clean him up, feed him up." He looked with distaste at the sores where a few maggots still clung. "If it were only me involved, as Misaen made me, I'd do nothing, Mother, I'd drive him off and bless the day, but Eirys—"

"You think Eirys needs this?" Ismenia turned sharply. "You think Eirys, after Sheltya scared her half witless before declaring her guilt-free, do you think she needs this wreck of a man to drain her of hope and life when she should be looking to her child? Eirys must never know of this. You must never speak of it, never breathe a word, not even on your deathbed, not even when Solstice sun stirs your bones." She fell silent, trembling, narrow shoulders hunched as she clasped her hands in a vain effort to still them.

Keisyl drew his mother inside strong arms, her faded hair fluttering against the frayed collar of his shirt. Gradually her trembling eased. "So what do we do?"

Ismenia gently eased herself free, patting Keisyl's shoulder in meaningless reassurance and smoothing the laces of his shirt. "He owes the soke a life, doesn't he?"

Keisyl drew a long breath before answering. "There's Eirys' baby?"

Ismenia shook her head. "That's not the same. That child is her gift to the blood, and as long as she still mopes for Jeirran I can't see her bringing another to bed. Why didn't he die at the Teyvafess?" she raged suddenly. "Then we could have shown her the body and had done."

"And if she'd had his bones to lay in the cavern, that grief could have killed the babe in her belly." Keisyl shook his head. "It was only the hope that he might somehow still live that saved her. You said so yourself."

"So do we take that hope from her? If she's brought to bed before the turn of the season, I wouldn't give much for the chances of the child coming through the winter." Ismenia pulled the embroidered kerchief from her head and twisted the cloth around her hands. "He owes the soke a life," she repeated softly. "If it weren't for him, I'd still have my Teiro, my baby boy." Her face crumpled as if she was about to weep and she hid her face in the meadow flowers dotting the white linen.

Keisyl scrubbed away his own sudden, angry tears and reached for his mother's hands, but when she lifted her eyes they were dry and resolved. "He owes the soke a life and we will claim it."

"We have that right, don't we?" said Keisyl cautiously. "Kinder than letting him wander and starve or die of a fever."

"I don't want to be kind," said Ismenia bitterly. "I'd like to stake him out for the ravens, Maewelin be my witness! No, his life is forfeit and better that we know he is dead than wonder when he's going to come scraping at the gatepost like a lost hound come home."

"He found his way here, Misaen only knows how," agreed Keisyl with distaste.

Ismenia reached for the sun-scorched shoulder draped with foul hair, but drew her hand back. "I'm not touching it," she muttered. "Keisy, get me a stick and fetch yourself a hammer or something. I know where to go."

Keisyl frowned. "Do we want Fithian?"

Ismenia shook her head. "Our choice, our burden."

It didn't take much prodding to get the wretch to its feet, following the old woman biddably enough as she led the way up beyond the workings. They crossed the ridge, the rustling grasses of a sheltered plateau, going beyond to skirt a spread of tangled bushes and finally climbing over a stony speckled bank to find a marshy stretch of broken ground dotted with thick green tussocks.

"The old ways were hard, but so were the times, and given all we've been through this year, I think old ways are called for." Ismenia looked sharply at Keisyl. "You know what to do?"

Keisyl stepped behind the blankly staring figure and hefted the rock hammer in practiced hands. The blow came in hard and sure; the pitiable thing fell face forward and Ismenia pressed her narrow boot down on the back of its neck, pressing hard into the thick brown water of the bog. Keisyl waited silently until she withdrew her foot and then used the hammer to push the corpse farther into the mire.

"I'd have been within my rights to drown him unstunned," Ismenia said, but with little passion. "If the bog takes him and tans him, then that's Misaen's judgment. Still, you can come up here next spring. If there are any bones, you can take them to the cavern in the Lidrasoke. Let him rest with his people and whisper a warning to any who might think to follow his example."

"Come on, my lovely, let's get home." She clapped her hands briskly together and turned to begin walking so fast Keisyl had to hurry to keep up. "We must look forward now," she continued. "We have Eirys and the baby to care for. Maewelin has finally blessed Theilyn, so there'll be no come-by-chance to spoil her prospects. In a year or so we can think about taking her out and about. There are a few likely lads I have my eye on, so if I invite their mothers and sisters to coo over the baby, Theilyn will have a chance to meet them with no one making anything of it. Perhaps she'll make a sensible choice if she's allowed to take her time. One daughter falling in love at first sight, all overcome by Solstice jollities, is quite enough. And there's nothing like a babe in arms to get a maiden feeling broody." She tucked her arm through Keisyl's and smiled up at him.

"There'll be some pretty girl, last in a long family, willing to take her rights in coin and leave her fess to bring children and laughter to ours again, for the sake of a husband as handsome as you."

"Perhaps, one day," allowed Keisyl dryly, but his eyes were wistful.

"We must look forward now," repeated Ismenia firmly. They left the bog without a backward glance.

The Boar and Elder Tavern, Hadrumal, 23rd of Aft-Summer

I had to look around the crowded tap room two or three times before I finally spotted Pered laughing in a corner with a friend. Pushing my way through a gaggle of prentice wizards, I waved to him. He stood up, taking the bottles of wine to free my hands. I snapped my fingers at a serving maid who barely spared me a look and smiled at her when her head spun back for a startled second glance. "Wine please, Ferl River if you have it."

Pered gave me a hug and then held me at arm's length, shaking his head. "You are going to have to do something about that hair."

"Does it really look that bad?" I asked quizzically.

"You look like that striped butter toffee my sister makes for her children," he said frankly. "Ryshad will hate it."

I shrugged. "I've seen him in a beard. I'm not about to risk dying it after bleach; it'll go green or all fall out."

Pered's ready laugh narrowed his hazel eyes. "Oh, I've finished the copy of that song book. Don't let me forget to give it to you."

"Many thanks. You don't think anyone will be wondering why Shiv's been so keen to study it, do you?" I didn't particularly want attention drawn his way, especially not when someone might remember the mage's lover was one of Hadrumal's most accomplished scriveners.

Pered shook his head. "Not when he's spending every day closeted with Usara and that Mountain woman, hammering out some new theory on this Artifice."

"Has he had a chance to bespeak anyone in Toremal yet?" I tried to sound offhand but had to answer Pered's knowing grin with a sheepish smile of my own.

"He bespoke Casuel last night. Cas was being his usual petty-minded self but he did tell Shiv that your Ryshad has 'performed signal service to the Emperor, even if with somewhat unexpected consequences.' Apparently Ryshad wants you to take a ship for Toremal or Zyoutessela as soon as you can. You'd better book passage and make haste to reclaim your beloved from the delights of the Empire."

"As soon as Planir pays up," I said firmly, quelling my own desire to head straight down to the docks and jump on the nearest ship. "Signal service to the Emperor" had to mean Ryshad would have winnings to equal mine, didn't it?

Pered nodded at the bottles. "Our esteemed Archmage probably thinks that fair payment."

"Something on account, perhaps. He doesn't buy me off so easily." I tapped my goblet of Ferl River white against the green glass of the vintage Califerian flagons. "They can wash down lunch."

Pered took a long swallow of his ale. "As soon as the others arrive, we can go home. Shiv's been busy all morning and I must have made ten trips to the market for things he's been wanting."

I ran a finger around a puddle on the tabletop. "How's he taken the news about Otrick?"

The good humor faded from Pered's blunt-featured face. "Badly. He's spent the last few nights just staring at the ceiling, muttering how if he'd been allowed to go then something would have been found to save the old pirate."

"I don't see how he figures that," I retorted. "Even Usara's had to admit there was no hope. Aritane said his mind had been killed outright."

"You know wizards," Pered shrugged his stocky shoulders. "Always think everything's down to them and never take no for an answer."

"Saedrin bless them." I raised my glass in a sarcastic salute.

"I'll give him a few more days and then start asking him who he thinks will be made the new Cloud-Master or -Mistress. That should get him out of the mopes." Pered gestured with his tankard. "He should be a good one to ask for a tip, if you fancy hanging around long enough to make a wager on it."

I turned to see who he meant and saw Darni entering the tavern with an angular woman on his arm. Her face was nothing remarkable, long black hair plaited down her back. Her clothes were everyday honey-colored wool, but she carried herself with considerable grace. "Who's that with him?"

"Strell, his wife." Pered looked surprised. "Haven't you met?"

"I think Darni prefers to keep me and mine out of his home life," I laughed.

"Oh, I got to dance with her last Equinox," said Pered, mock proud. "Darni may not know what to make of me and Shiv, but he does allow we're safe to be let near his wife."

"She looks as if she can take care of herself," I observed.

"She can," Pered assured me. "She's an alchemist. Mess with her and your house will probably burn down."

"Who's burning down houses?" asked 'Gren with interest. Sorgrad was close behind him as they pushed their way to our corner.

"No one," I said repressively. "Pered was saying there'd be money to be made if we can bet on the right candidate for Cloud-Master."

"Mages lay wagers on things like that?" Sorgrad was surprised.

Pered grinned at him. "Mages don't, but the rest of us do."

"Must be the only game in town, somewhere this small," commented 'Gren a trifle sourly.

I tried to gauge his degree of restlessness and looked at Sorgrad. "So, how much longer are you going to be kicking your heels here? I thought Shiv said that Kalion was going to intercede for you with Draximal? Wasn't that what Planir told him to do?"

Sorgrad nodded. "Draximal's all squared away. We're taking a boat for Col in four days' time."

That was a relief; 'Gren should be able to contain himself for that long before looking for mischief. Hadrumal didn't strike me as a good place for him to be bored. I frowned. "That's going to be a long hike to Lescar. Wouldn't you be better off waiting for passage to Peorle?"

"We're not going to Lescar." Sorgrad drained his tankard. "We thought we'd visit Solura."

Pered looked at him with some surprise. "Shiv told me you were mage-born. You're not going to stay here and study?"

"Why should I?" demanded Sorgrad, but not aggressively. "Magebirth's no more than a minor inconvenience to me."

"You know, half the Council are banging their heads against that." Pered heaved a contented sigh. "I do like seeing wizards nonplussed."

"Solura?" I pursed my lips. "Going to look up Gilmarten by any chance?"

"You never know who we might run into," admitted Sorgrad with a dangerous smile. I had his measure; magebirth might have been no more than an unwelcome aberration to be ruthlessly suppressed until now, but having seen its uses in action he wasn't about to pass up a chance of turning it into a useful tool for the future. I wasn't going to criticize; Messire might have agreed the wizards could keep the song book but I'd be looking out for useful tricks in my copy, now that I'd seen Aritane's abilities were as much to be envied as feared.

" 'Gren?" I looked a question at him.

He shrugged. "Just going back to Lescar seemed a bit boring. We've missed the best of the fighting season anyway. I fancy seeing what trouble's brewing on the Mandarkin border."

"And while we're there, we can make sure Anyatimm up that way have the truth of this summer's goings-on in the Gap," added Sorgrad ominously.

"So we're all off on our travels again." I meant to sound bright and optimistic, but somehow my words came out tinged with gloom.

"Speak for yourself, darling," said Pered with a touch of bitterness. "I'm going nowhere far from my copy table, not unless Shiv finally gets sick of dancing to Planir's tune."

"Why not see if Shiv can get a commission to go and look for more mage-born among the Forest Folk or up in Gidesta?" I suggested.

"We'll be back for the Winter Solstice," promised Sorgrad. "Relshaz or Col?"

My spirits lifted. "Relshaz? Charoleia will be there, and she's bound to have news from Halice."

"You bring this sworn man of yours along for us to meet," 'Gren ordered. "What's he been doing with himself all summer anyway, while we've been off having fun?"

"I think he'll have been having a harder time of it than you think," said Pered, all solemn pretense. "After all, he's been working with Casuel."

"And most men would prefer an honest fight with a horde of howling Mountain Men to that," I agreed.

"Then he'll be good and ready to make a Winter Solstice to remember," Sograd nodded. "Make sure you bring him with you."

"Are you going to ask him his intentions?" I wasn't about to have that happen if I could avoid it.

"We might just do that," said Sorgrad. "Anyway, what's

he going to make of you coming back like a bad debt, full
of your adventures and rattling the Archmage's coin?"

"A man could get jealous," observed 'Gren.

"It sounds as if he's done well enough for himself," I
countered. "What I've got to decide is just what to tell him
about our little expedition."

"You want to tell him just enough to make him feel guilty
about spending his summer safe and secure, dancing attendance on that prince of his," advised Pered with the faintest
hint of malice. I knew that was really directed at Planir; if
anything ever drove a wedge between him and Shiv, it was
the Archmage's demands on his lover's time.

"Ryshad will have been working just as hard as me," I assured them all. "Just doing different things."

He'd better have been, I added silently to myself, or all
this year's winnings would be for nothing. The game still
wasn't over until I saw how Ryshad had played his hand.

"I'll tell you something for free," 'Gren said critically.
"You really should do something about your hair before he
sees it."

SF/Fantasy—an escape for people who can't cope with reality?

I often wonder why people condemn SF/Fantasy as "escapism." All fiction is escapist in some sense, taking the reader into an imagined world even if only to one set in Manchester. So what sets SF/Fantasy apart from other writing? Given it ranges from space opera to alternative history to heroic fantasy to cyberpunk, the common link I see is the basic question "what if . . . ?"

So what questions does Fantasy ask? Quests certainly feature; think of Frodo's journey to destroy the One Ring, exploring moral responsibility along the way. That aspect of the genre is as old as Arthurian legend. Tolkien was the Merton Professor of English at Oxford University, and much fantasy is based on eminent scholarship and detailed research. Alternate histories rely on the reader's basic knowledge of past events, otherwise they are pointless. Fantasy readers are encouraged to look outside their own culture, taken to a spectacular array of different realms, where societies defy easy assumptions, often to be challenged by the same questions on race, sex, and tolerance that perplex the world we live in. Writers such as Melanie Rawn and Robin Hobb ask what if magic really existed, how would societies and governments function? What if there really are dragons? Anne McCaffrey has woven an intricate and intriguing world around that idea. What if people from our world find themselves caught up in the stuff of legend? Alan Garner's *Weirdstone of Brisingamen* rests on that notion, so does *Buffy the Vampire Slayer*.

What if all the gray compromises of modern living could be cut through, with a broadsword for preference? Heroic fantasy, often with a hard edge all its own in writers like David Gemmell, pursues those ideas and their unforeseen consequences. Much of heroic fantasy is highly virtuous; simple tales where evil is punished and right triumphs. This may well be a welcome escape from the grim reality of news bulletins, but unconsciously absorbing the teachings of Aslan as a child makes aggression and injustice all the more intolerable for the adult.

At its best, SF/Fantasy offers answers to all of these questions, but more than that, the genre gives us superb stories. Characters leap off the page and grab you by the throat, vivid description transports you with no need for twenty-fourth-century technology, plots keep you turning the pages long past lights out. Celebrated modern writers such as Iain Banks find their talents equally at home in the best of mainstream fiction and of SF/Fantasy.

And then there is the nonsense. We have the surreal imaginations of Tom Holt and Robert Rankin, the inspired comedy of Terry Pratchett. Laughter is certainly an escape, but aren't we all refreshed by that release? For satire and parody to work, the reader also has to share the author's piercing eye for the absurd in the everyday world. While mainstream fiction can be inclined to take itself rather too seriously, SF/Fantasy gleefully sends up the ridiculous within the genre with titles such as *The Tough Guide to Fantasyland*.

So is SF/Fantasy an escape for people who can't cope with reality? Not as far as I'm concerned. Reality is a refuge for those who can't handle the challenge of SF/Fantasy!